THE DEAD DETECTIVE

ALAN RUSSELL

BLOODHOUND BOOKS

PROLOGUE

Witching hour, and the onset of my nightmare.

As water pours into the small boat, the human cargo wave their arms in terror. Desperate eyes lock onto mine as their prison begins to sink. Horrified mouths open wide to scream, but not for long, as their faces begin to slip from view.

And they disappear from this world into the next.

Their terror pulls at me, an undertow that feels as if it's dragging me down with them.

With a shuddering gasp, I take in air, and awaken saying, "Shit, shit, shit."

I wonder if that's what the caged humans cried as the sea swallowed them.

My 911 call from the dead has left me cold, and I wrap my arms around myself for warmth. I'm drained and empty but don't know if my nightmare is to blame. An accusatory clock shows me the sins of my ways; its red numerals tell me it's 3:14.

Why can't demons work banking hours? In six hours, I have a long-overdue appointment with a doctor. Months of feeling like shit have forced me to finally seek help.

I want to blame stress. I'm hoping there's a pill for what I have. Groaning, I rise. My exhaustion is bone deep.

Coffee won't help, but it's all I have.

CHAPTER ONE

I hadn't met my primary physician before, which spoke to how long it had been since I'd seen a doctor.

Dr. Nguyen looked as if he was just out of medical school. His white coat was big on him, like a kid dressing up for career day. They say you can't be a good doctor until you've killed a few patients. I hoped he wasn't planning to start with me.

He asked me questions about my health while doing his poking and prodding. It was a good thing he'd gone into medicine and not professional poker. Having been a cop for almost twenty years, I'm good at reading people, and the more time he spent conducting my physical, the more I didn't like what I was reading.

"Tenderness here?" he asked, touching my abdomen.

"Yes."

"Have you been experiencing nausea?"

"On occasion," I said.

"For how long?"

I thought about it. "Months, I guess."

"You came in with an elevated temperature. Have you been experiencing fevers?"

"Some days I run hot," I admitted.

"What are your symptoms?"

"I'm warm and flushed, and my pulse is racing."

"Does this happen during the day or night?"

"It's an equal-opportunity offender," I said.

He didn't smile. "Day sweats? Night sweats?"

"Both," I confirmed.

I detected a slight wince, and his eyes shifted away from me. Two bad signs. Then he retreated back a step and crossed his arms. Two more bad signs. I see that body language when suspects are wary of looking or sounding guilty.

Dr. Nguyen began scratching his nose. Not good. I don't know what it is about itchy noses, but whenever people feel like they're on the hot seat, they suddenly start with the beak scratching.

My doctor was uncomfortable, and that made me doubly so. So much for my finding out what condition my condition was in.

He said, "After we're done here, I'd like you to go to radiology for some imaging."

"Today? I've got a lot of things going on at work."

"This isn't something you should put off."

I could hear the seriousness in his voice, which cracked slightly. Either my doctor was going through puberty, or offering up another nervous tell.

"Okay," I said.

"I'll need to see you tomorrow afternoon at two o'clock," he said.

He was scratching his nose again. Really digging at it. I was pretty sure he wasn't experiencing eczema.

I left the office feeling worse than when I'd come in, and that was saying something.

CHAPTER TWO

Because of construction going on at the hospital, MRI scanning had been set up in the temporary quarters of a converted trailer. While I was changing into a hospital gown in a makeshift dressing room, I overheard the nurse and MRI tech carrying out a conversation in Tagalog.

When I emerged, I said, "*Kumasta na*," which means "How's it going?"

Judging by their expressions, they weren't expecting those words out of the mouth of a forty-something white guy. I guess it was like what Samuel Johnson said about a dog walking around on its hind legs; the surprise wasn't that the dog didn't do it well, but that he did it at all.

Both started speaking to me in Tagalog, but I raised a paw and said, "I'm afraid I'm not fluent."

Before becoming a detective, I'd done a stint on patrol in Northeastern Division, which included Mira Mesa, a city that was home to many Filipino Americans. That's where I'd picked up my smattering of conversational Tagalog, although that wasn't something I volunteered. Like most cops, I don't like advertising my vocation to strangers, and let the two of them assume I was just another San Diegan who had visited the Philippines via a cruise with the US Navy.

The nurse placed a reassuring hand on my shoulder. She was small in stature, but like most nurses, made it clear who was running the show. Her complexion was smooth and wrinkle-free, although she was probably north of fifty.

In an accent that bespoke her origins, she asked, "Have you ever had an MRI before?"

"First time," I said.

She explained what I was going to experience, and then said, "Before we begin, I need to administer contrast agent."

"Which means what?"

"By injecting dye into you, we see image better."

"Will I glow in the dark?" I asked.

She ignored my comment. "Most people don't react to agent, but there's chance you feel sick, or get itchy skin, or become dizzy."

"Understood."

"You relax arm now," the nurse said, searching out a vein.

I averted my gaze from her needle work.

"Little sting," she warned.

As I was being stuck, I resisted saying "*Pakshet*," one of the favored curse words of Filipinos.

But I sure thought it.

The tech guy, a twenty-something kid with styled hair and shiny white teeth, told me what I was about to experience.

"Good to go?" he asked. "Any questions?"

"Sounds pretty much like what they tell me at the car wash. So, let's skip the wax job today."

He laughed. "Okay, no wax. Keep your arms at your sides, and stay still. Okay?"

I nodded.

"I'll be monitoring you throughout your imaging," he said. "There's an intercom that allows us to talk to one another. Every ten minutes or so, you'll hear me checking in with you. If you decide you want to stop the MRI, just squeeze this ball I'm placing in your hand. Okay?"

"Got it."

"Try and do your best to stay as still as possible. Cool?"

"Chill as a dill."

He made sure my headphones were snugly in place, flashed me a smile, and then gestured like a blackjack dealer.

"Ready for your ride?" he asked.

"Aye, aye, captain," I said, and then was sent into the tunnel of love.

Before I worked what most people call the chain-gang homicides, I'd never experienced claustrophobia. That case had changed me. Twelve people chained together in leg cuffs had been confined in a mini shipping container and transported by small boat. Or, as it turned out, their coffin.

Pakshet, pakshet, pakshet.

I tried to regulate my breathing and fight off my panic. Loud, bizarre banging and clicking sounds filled my too-small chamber. Banshees were keeping me company.

It was almost mid-afternoon before I made it into work. I was the new kid on the block, having transferred into the Cold Case Team six months before. Prior to that, I'd spent a decade working on Homicide Team II. It was considered a lateral transfer, but my peers thought I was batshit crazy to do it. Among cops, there's a cachet that comes from working homicide, whereas cold case is viewed as a last stop before retirement. Everyone thought I was too young to end up at the old elephant's graveyard, but I was good with my decision.

The Cold Case Team was made up of not only SDPD detectives, but also investigators from a wide variety of backgrounds, including the DEA, NCIS, and U.S. Customs and Border Protection. It was possible that the chain-gang homicides crossed all of those jurisdictions, giving me ready resources to continue my mostly off-the-books investigation. My expectation was that the change of scenery would afford me more time and opportunity to work the case. That had proved true up to a point, but it wasn't as if I'd been able to concentrate solely on that case to the exclusion of others.

Usually, I drape my blazer over my back, but today I kept it on to keep the vampire handiwork under wraps. What I could hide from others, though, I couldn't hide from myself. As much as I didn't want to admit it, I was worried that something was seriously wrong with me. Maybe I had just misread Dr. Nguyen's body language and my paranoia had colored my impressions. That's what I tried to tell myself.

As I approached my cubicle, Mark "Aloha" Adkins nodded at me. Aloha is infamous for the loud Hawaiian shirts he wears when away from the job. He had come to the Cold Case Team from U.S. Customs and Border Protection. His plan was to retire in two years at the age of fifty and move to Hawaii.

"The cómo se llama mamá was looking for you," Aloha said.

That was one of Sergeant Lopez's nicknames. Everyone on the Cold Case Team had a nickname, except for me. Nothing had stuck yet, even though Aloha was trying to pin me with Frank Ocean. He thought the singer's name worked because my surname's Lake, but the others hadn't bought into it.

Nancy "Boots" Parker leaned back in her chair and said, "You just missed out, Wyatt."

Like me, Boots had transferred from homicide. She'd had her nickname before coming to cold case. Boots was the mother of three, all by different fathers. She had left all her husbands, and was known for her take-no-prisoners attitude. As the story went, a coworker had spotted her in public wearing oversize boots. That, and Nancy Sinatra's song "These Boots Are Made for Walkin'," cemented her moniker.

She pointed an accusatory finger at Pat "Bear" Waller. "If you'd come in five minutes ago, there would have been some cookies for you, but someone didn't even leave you any crumbs."

"They were delicious," Bear said.

Bear was big and hairy and had been christened with his nickname in high school. Prior to working the Cold Case Team, he'd been a Special Agent with the DEA.

"You've got no shame," Boots said.

"How was I to know there was a limit on cookies?"

"Ever hear of common etiquette?" she asked.

"Bear's getting ready for hibernation," Aloha said.

Bear nodded. "What he said."

"It's June, morons," Boots said.

"Wouldn't know it," Bear said. "We've barely seen the sun all month."

Spring had only intermittently sprung in San Diego. A months-long persistent marine layer had resulted in "Graypril," Gray May, and now June Gloom.

"I don't know why you're singling me out anyway," Bear said. "Before I got to those cookies, Aloha finished most of them."

"I'll bet Frank Ocean doesn't even care about the cookies," Aloha said. "Right?"

"It was nice of Boots to bring them in," I said.

"Bear and I got something Frank would like more than cookies anyway," Aloha said. "Information."

I'd enlisted the other detectives to assist me in my off-the-books chain-gang investigation.

"The boat that went down wasn't a panga, but something custom," Aloha said.

A panga boat is essentially a skiff with a raised bow that's popular with Mexican fishermen. They were also popular with those smuggling human cargo out of Mexico to the States.

"But it wasn't exactly a drug-sub either," Bear said. "Or at least not a drug-sub known to any of my DEA contacts. The boat doesn't quite fit the profile of other semi-submersible boats used in drug trafficking, but it was riding low in the water, probably to avoid Coast Guard and Customs sonar."

"Which cartel runs the most drug subs?" I asked.

"These days, Sinaloa. The cartels are always trying to find a better way to transport their product."

It didn't matter if that product was drugs or people.

The phone on my desk buzzed. I picked it up, and Sergeant Lopez said, "Got a minute?"

"On my way."

I walked over to her office, stopped at the entrance. "What's up, Sarge?"

"Come on in and have a seat," she said.

No quick exit, I thought, sitting down. Earlier that morning I'd left a message with her saying I wouldn't be in until the afternoon, but hadn't provided details. We exchanged nods, and I found myself having my usual stare down with a wolf. Behind the sarge's desk is a heraldry plaque that explains the name Lopez is derived from the Latin *lupus.* In the middle of her coat of arms is the wolf. *La Loba.*

"How are things?" she asked.

I felt like hell and looked like hell, but said, "Great."

She waited for me to elaborate. When animals are sick or hurt, they try to hide their condition, not wanting to reveal their weakness to others. Maybe that's why I'd kept my doctor's visit to myself, and felt no inclination to reveal it. Especially to La Loba.

"You come from the zoo?" she asked.

The San Diego Zoo is only two miles from SDPD's downtown headquarters. It's no secret I often spend my lunch hour there.

"Not today," I said.

The sarge must have decided we'd had enough workplace camaraderie. "There's a case I'd like your eyes on, a homicide from twenty-five years ago."

Shit. When a case is that old, it's almost impossible to get any traction on it.

La Loba must have picked up on my vibe. "It was a big case at the time," she said. "Really big."

Which meant a lot of homicide detectives had already put in long hours trying to solve it, and none had succeeded.

"No one from this department ever reworked it?" I asked.

"You replaced the detective most recently assigned the case. I'm afraid he never got anywhere with it."

This was sounding more and more like a waste of time. The she-wolf pretended not to notice my lack of enthusiasm.

"As I said, it was a big case. Because of that, it wouldn't surprise me if the media picks up on the fact that next month will mark twenty-five years since the homicide. That's why I'd like you to start working it ASAP."

The timing for my being handed the case suddenly made sense. The department would be able to tell the media that the homicide was still being actively investigated.

La Loba was watching me with her large, probing brown

eyes. What was it Little Red Riding Hood had said to the wolf? "My, but what big eyes you have."

Lopez smiled. Showed me her teeth. But I didn't comment on how big they were.

She said, "I want your fresh eyes. It's a big file. Let's talk in a few days after you've gone through it and are up to speed."

It wouldn't do to cry wolf, so I said, "Will do."

When I returned to my desk, Bear and Aloha were nowhere to be seen. As much as I wanted to continue our conversation, it would have to wait. Besides, the latest Pandora's box needed to be opened. As La Loba had warned, it was a big file. What I wasn't expecting was my familiarity with the case. The homicide had occurred when I was in high school. In fact, the girl who'd died had been the same age as me.

"Dana Silva," I whispered, recalling the name.

Or, as my parents had referred to her, "That poor girl."

She had been murdered in a spot not ten miles away from where we lived. The story of Dana, and her friend Chloe Landers, had been played up locally and nationally. For parents, it was a cautionary tale to impart to their children.

Dana and Chloe had both been sophomores in high school. They had concocted a plan to attend a rock concert at what was then called the San Diego Sports Arena. Both girls told their parents they were staying at the other's house, after which, the two fifteen-year-olds hitchhiked from their homes in La Mesa to the sports arena, a distance of approximately fourteen miles. At the conclusion of the concert, they'd stood on Sports Arena Boulevard holding a sign that said La Mesa. Almost immediately, a car stopped to pick them up.

Old memories surfaced, and I heard my mother's voice once more admonish me: "Never hitchhike. Never."

It had been a frequent lecture of hers. Only when I got a beater car had she put it to rest, and gone on to other warnings.

I went back to reading the file. When the two girls got into the car, they were impaired. During the concert they'd smoked weed and taken "X," the drug MDMA, now known as "Molly."

The driver who picked them up was an approximately twenty-five-year-old white male with long brown hair who identified himself as "Stu" or "Stewie." According to Chloe, Stu also offered his surname, what she said was a one-syllable last name that started with the letter B. Whenever interviewed by police, and that was a lot of times, Chloe seemed to recall he had identified himself as Barnes, Bourn, Burns, or Burr.

Killer B.

Judging by what was in the file, Homicide Team I and its four detectives had tirelessly beat the bushes looking for Stu B. Years had been spent on the case, but their hard work had gotten them nowhere.

A dozen years passed before Cold Case took up the investigation. I was the third detective from the team to be handed the torch. That meant at least seven had worked the case, not to mention the army of officers and support personnel who assist with investigations.

I went over Chloe's account of what had happened. She said that when they set out on the drive, Stewie told the girls he would have to take a back route because he didn't want the cops pulling him over for being above the blood-alcohol limit. The girls offered no objections, also wanting to avoid the scrutiny of the police. Since neither Chloe nor Dana drove, and were far from home, they were unfamiliar with the route Stu traveled.

According to Chloe, at the start of the drive, all seemed well. Stewie acted friendly and joined in with the good-humored conversation. Gradually, though, both girls began feeling uncomfortable with the way he scrutinized them through the rearview mirror.

Stu's route took them to the Mission Trails Regional Park, a nearly 7,000-acre preserve just ten miles from downtown San Diego. That's where he pulled over to ostensibly smoke dope. When Stewie told the girls he didn't want to smoke out in the open, they reluctantly followed him along a park trail that was officially closed after sundown, but rarely monitored by authorities.

As they walked behind him, the girls had a whispered discussion, where each tried to convince the other that Stewie was harmless. The remoteness of the location deterred them from fleeing, as they had no idea where they were, or how they could get home. At the time, cell phones were just becoming popular, but neither girl had one. This meant that even if they ran off, they would have to find a phone in the urban wilderness. And while they might be able to manage that, they were worried about the parental fallout they would face after confessing all their deceptions in getting to the concert. Their default decision was to hope things worked out for the best, even as Stu's behavior became increasingly erratic.

After taking them to a spot far from any potential prying eyes, Stu started smoking a joint. The young women declined his offer to take a hit. Their hope was the pot would make him relaxed and mellow, but it seemed to do the opposite. As he took more hits, his conversation became more frenetic, and Chloe grew alarmed when she heard Stu babbling about his having applied a "dusting of angels" on his weed. Back then, phencyclidine (PCP) was known as angel dust, a hallucinogen with a reputation for causing violent episodes.

As the drug took its hold on him, he became increasingly frenzied, and Chloe grew alarmed.

"We're going to have to run," she whispered to Dana.

Stu must have sensed their intentions. Without warning, he suddenly attacked the girls, first striking Chloe on the head with a large rock and knocking her out. For Chloe, that proved to be a blessing, as it spared her from having to witness Dana being brutalized and murdered.

When Chloe regained consciousness, she struggled to see. It was dark, and her vision was blurred from a concussion, but what she saw was so horrific that she had difficulty making sense of it. An unmoving and mostly naked Dana was spread out on the ground next to her. Blood covered her friend's body.

"Dana!" she cried out. "Dana!"

Her friend was beyond hearing. But not so the murderer. Nearby, Chloe heard something move. As she turned her head, Chloe was struck from behind, and once more blacked out.

Later, when she began to come to, Chloe awakened in fits and starts to excruciating pain. She became aware of being sticky all over. As much as her head throbbed, what hurt most were her legs; her jeans were heavy with blood, and Chloe began to get some idea of the severity of her injuries.

Stu was nowhere to be seen. He had left her, presumably thinking she was dead or dying. It was up to her to prove him wrong, to somehow find a way to survive. She had to live—for herself, and for Dana. Because of the severe wounds to her legs, Chloe was unable to stand, and had no recourse but to drag herself along the trail. Inch by torturous inch, she worked her way toward the road. How many times Chloe lost consciousness, she couldn't be sure, but each time she fought through the pain. Finally, as dawn broke, she reached the side of the road. From her position on the ground, she tried to wave down passing cars. Several drivers drove by; Chloe wasn't sure if they didn't notice her or were just too frightened to stop. At last, one car pulled over.

At the hospital, ER doctors treated multiple life-threatening wounds. Her most serious injuries were the deep cuts to her legs, delivered by what appeared to be an axe. Because the damage was so severe, doctors had no choice but to perform above-the-knee amputations of both her legs.

I skimmed through a *San Diego Union-Tribune* story that had been placed in the police file. In it, Chloe was described as "the lucky one" because she survived. I wondered if she concurred with that assessment.

Over the years, Chloe had been interviewed by the police numerous times. It had been four years since a detective had sat down with her, an interview conducted at her office on 5th Avenue in Hillcrest, a neighborhood near downtown San Diego. She was now Dr. Chloe Landers, a psychologist specializing in grief and trauma counseling.

La Loba had made it clear I was supposed to prioritize the case, and that the sooner I talked with Chloe, the happier she would be. Her file included a work number, as well as a cell phone number, and I hoped both were still current.

I went with calling her cell phone. After three rings, a woman answered with a terse "Yes?" Since I was calling from an SDPD landline, I assumed caller ID had clued her into who was on the other line. Chloe had been dealing with prying cops for a long time, so it didn't surprise me that she wasn't thrilled to be talking to another one.

"Dr. Landers, my name is Wyatt Lake, and I'm a detective with the San Diego Police Department. I work with the Cold Case Team and have been assigned your case. I'm calling in the hope that we can schedule a time to talk."

She didn't hide her sigh. The bloom was definitely off the law enforcement rose. "What purpose would that serve, Detective? Albert Einstein once said that the definition of insanity was doing the same thing over and over again and expecting different results. Your department hasn't made any headway in my case. Why should I expect that to change?"

"Every detective looks at a case differently," I said. "It's possible I might see something that others have missed."

"That's a claim I've heard before," she said.

"You have every right to be frustrated," I said. "But if I'm to work the case properly, I'll need a little bit of your time."

"No, Detective, you'll need far more than that. You'll want me to dredge up the past and think about matters I've been trying to put behind me for twenty-five years."

"And how's that working for you?"

She didn't respond for a long moment, and I was afraid my irreverence had sunk my chances of getting a face to face with her, but then she offered up a small laugh.

"That's a question I've been known to pose to clients locked into habitual and unhealthy patterns," she said.

I managed to keep my mouth shut, which I hoped showed that I wasn't locked into habitual and unhealthy patterns.

"Okay," she said. "As much as I'd like to put off our meeting, I know that procrastination will only make matters worse. Does tomorrow at four o'clock in my office work for you?"

I had a 2:30 appointment with Dr. Nguyen, which would leave me enough time to meet with Chloe at four. It would mean a long night spent acquainting myself with her file, and preparing my questions, but that was probably a good thing. The busier I was, the less time I had to worry about my own health.

"Four is good," I said.

I confirmed her work address, and thanked her for speaking with me.

"Namaste," she said, and clicked off.

I didn't exactly know what namaste meant, but it was enough for me that it didn't translate to fuck off.

CHAPTER THREE

It usually takes me no more than fifteen minutes to drive from my workplace to the South Park neighborhood where I live. When I bought my modest home, I paid a quarter of a million dollars for it, which seemed like a hell of a lot of money at the time. My home is still modest, but I'm told it's now worth north of a million dollars. On paper, I'm a millionaire. When I was a kid, we used to speak of millionaires as if they were unicorns. The price of San Diego real estate has made many of its citizens millionaires, but that doesn't mean most of us aren't still just scraping by.

I parked in my one-car garage and was glad I didn't have to fight for street parking, as did so many in my neighborhood. My arrival didn't go unnoticed. Even from inside my car, I could hear the clacking of nails on the cement floor of the garage. Lola jumped up on the driver's door. In the darkness, her one bright-blue eye glowed. That was courtesy of her being half husky. She also had a brown eye that came from her shepherd half. Her mom, Janis, calls her a shepsky.

"Down," I said.

She responded by licking my window. When I slowly

pushed open the door, Lola backed off for a moment before taking that as an invitation to jump back up and settle in my lap.

"Yes, I love you," I said. "But not as much as my dry cleaner does."

Any Lola encounter means lots of hair. Huskies and shepherds are great shedders, and Lola was true to both breeds.

"I need to invest in a lint roller company," I told her, but mine was a feeble protest, and Lola knew it. She lifted her muzzle to give me yet another kiss.

"Yes, it's good to see you, but it's time you got down."

If anything, Lola settled into my lap a little more.

From outside the garage, a raspy voice called out, "Park it elsewhere, Lola."

With great reluctance, Lola departed my lap.

"What a hussy you are," Janis said. "In my day, the old ladies would have called you a shameless saucy minx. I should know. That's what they called me."

Janis combined a cough with a laugh. Her phlegmy voice spoke of more than half a century of smoking, although she had replaced tobacco with weed decades ago. I'd been a neighbor of hers since before marijuana was legalized in California, and remembered how Janis had tried to conceal her habit after learning I was a cop. When I told her I didn't care what she smoked, and that she didn't have to worry about me hassling her, she had thanked me from the bottom of her "old hippie heart."

My generation had missed the Age of Aquarius. I think we could have used one.

"Long day?" Janis asked.

Her hoarse voice made it likely she had already smoked a bowl full of weed, but that hadn't prevented her from noticing I was dragging.

"Long day," I agreed.

"We better leave the detective in peace, Lola."

The shepsky pretended not to hear, staying close to me.

"She's welcome to visit for a few hours," I said. "Work's going to keep me up for a while."

"You sure?"

"What Lola wants, Lola gets," I said.

Our shepsky was all but dancing, as if privy to every word being said.

"I'll send her home when I hit the sack," I promised.

To simplify Lola's comings and goings, Janis had installed a doggie door at her home. I was happy with the arrangement. My odd work hours conspired against me having a dog, but I was happy that Lola visited most days.

"Don't let her talk you into another dinner. She's already eaten."

"Will do."

"And, Wyatt?"

"Yeah?"

"Don't stay up too late. You look like shit."

When your geriatric pothead neighbor tells you you're looking like shit, you can be pretty sure that you are.

Even though I wasn't hungry, I forced myself to make a quick, healthy meal. I nuked a sweet potato and topped it with black beans, shredded cheese, taco seasoning, scallions, and salsa. It was a hell of a lot healthier than a frozen pizza, and about as fast and easy to make.

Lola and I took over the sofa while I ate. She cadged a few bites of my sweet potato, which was just as well, as I could only finish half of it. Just then, my phone began pinging, and I saw that my health care provider had sent my test results.

I was curious, but also afraid, like a little kid scared to peer under his bed for fear of seeing a monster lurking there. In the end, it was easier to convince myself that looking at the Landers/Silva papers took precedence over whatever my blood work said, and I returned to reading the file.

In the case notes, Chloe had been consistent in saying she'd never seen Stu B before, or, as the murder book referred to him, the unsub—which was law enforcement lingo for unknown subject. For my own notes, though, I decided to follow Chloe's lead and use the name Stu B. Unsub made the killer anonymous; calling him Stu gave me a target to aim for.

Almost 14,000 people had attended the concert, but Stu wasn't believed to have been among that number. What had brought him to the Midway District all those years ago? Was he some transient, or a local? Then, as now, there were plenty of fast-food restaurants in the area, but no employees remembered serving anyone who looked like Stu that night, and Landers didn't see any sign of to-go packages in his sedan.

Despite a massive search for the killer's car, nothing credible had turned up. Investigators had gone through local and state DMV records, looking for hits on a dark Ford Taurus or Toyota Camry, what Landers believed were the most likely makes of the vehicle Stu was driving. Unfortunately, back then, those were the two most popular sedan models on the road.

The sports arena is situated on forty-eight acres, something that has remained constant throughout the years. That's almost an anomaly in Southern California, with lots of redevelopment having gone on in and around the Midway District in the last quarter of a century. Plans were in the offing for the area to be revamped, but details were still being worked out. Although the area is more built up now, back then it was still a massive enterprise for investigators to visit all businesses within a three-mile radius of the arena.

At the time, there were two popular strip clubs, The Body

Shop and Les Girls, located less than a mile away from where Dana and Chloe had been picked up. The dancers at the clubs had been questioned. When they were shown an artist's sketch of Stu, a few of the dancers said he looked familiar, but none remembered seeing him on the night in question. It hadn't helped that Stu was of medium height and weight, with nothing about him standing out.

I studied a copy of that artist's sketch. By appearance, Stu looked like an average Joe. He had long, almost shoulder-length, brown hair. At the time, that wasn't uncommon.

Chloe Landers was certain she had never seen Stu before that night. His sketch had been circulated to the friends and family of Dana Silva, and one of her acquaintances thought there was a resemblance between the sketch and a local Point Loma fisherman. As the crow flies, the coastal city of Point Loma is about five miles from the arena. For a time, the SDPD hoped they'd caught a break, especially after learning that Silva came from a Portuguese family that had been part of the formerly sizable tuna fleet based in the San Diego/Point Loma area, but it was another lead that ultimately never panned out.

Every business in the area had been looked at in the hope of determining if Stu was an employee, or known customer. At that time, the biggest employer within the search area was the Naval Training Center, even though the base was in the finishing phase of being shut down. In the nineties, San Diego was home to almost twenty percent of the worldwide U.S. Naval fleet, but the training center was formally closed in 1997. Today, it's home to Liberty Station, one of San Diego's largest commercial developments.

Lola curled up a little closer, demanding an ear scratch, and impeding my view of the laptop screen. Her subject complied, which gave me a little time to think about what I'd read.

The SDPD investigation had been thorough, especially

given the massive undertaking required of the job. The extended Midway District was a busy commercial area, with heavy car traffic.

So, assuming Stu hadn't gone to the concert, what had brought him to the area at that time of night? It was possible he'd been driving along Sports Arena Boulevard to get to one of the freeways. Interstates 5 and 8, at the time the two most traveled freeways in San Diego County, were in proximity to where the girls had been picked up.

Most of those who'd worked the case believed Stu was a disorganized offender. His attack on the two young women, and the crime scene itself, didn't evidence premeditation or planning. Usually, disorganized offenders are easier to apprehend than organized offenders, but not Stu. Two witnesses had seen Chloe and Dana entering Stu's sedan, but they could only describe him and his ride in the most generic of terms. Nowadays, CCTV cameras would have provided ample footage to nail Stu, but back then there were no cameras.

The working theory was that Stu hadn't initially planned to harm the two young hitchhikers, but their proximity and his altered state of consciousness had brought his darkness to the fore. That was guesswork, of course, but to me it felt right.

Still, SDPD had flagged any suspicious or criminal activity involving young women, going back two years prior to the attack. They'd pulled files on everything from rape to sexual harassment. The investigation had turned up plenty of suspects, but none had panned out.

In her witness statement, Chloe had said that at first Stu hadn't raised any red flags, but during the ride that had changed. Mr. Hyde began to emerge.

Stu, or Stewie. That's the name he gave to the girls when he first met them. He'd even offered a mumbled last name. How many killers offer their names? But Stu was a fake name, or at least that's what the investigation had concluded. Offering up the bogus name had probably been a ploy to put the young hitchhikers at ease. Still, there had been a thorough investigation into the names of Stu and Stuart. SDPD had pored through records and databases, turning up forty-three males in San Diego County named Stuart. The investigation had also looked at potential suspects with the surnames of Stuart or Stewart.

What had prompted the murderer to give the girls *that* name? The idea he'd offered it as a familiarizing ploy was a plausible theory, but I wasn't convinced. Assuming he wasn't really called Stu or Stuart, how had he happened to choose it? To me, it didn't feel like a random name, but I wasn't sure what it was. And I was too tired to think about it anymore.

"You have to go home to Mama, Lola," I said.

She jumped off the sofa and looked at me hopefully. Sometimes we ended our evenings taking a walk, but that wasn't going to happen tonight.

"No, Lola," I said. "You need to go straight home."

I escorted the reluctant Lola out front. Even in urban San Diego, packs of coyotes are known to run along our streets, and I wanted to make sure she was safe. At the sidewalk, we parted company, and I watched her run over to her doggie door and disappear.

As I retraced my steps up the walkway, I came out of my fog and saw the message that had been left for me on my stoop. The pile of raven poop, I suspected, wasn't haphazard. It was pure luck I hadn't stepped in it on my way out.

Dammit, Lenore.

Lenore was an injured raven who'd taken up residence in the Catalina cherry tree in my front yard. Her wing, if not broken, was damaged. My guess was that a neighborhood kid had shot her with a BB. She'd been around for three weeks. During that time, I'd left out food offerings and observed her condition. Through furious flapping, Lenore could just get airborne enough to reach the low-hanging branches. I had called animal control earlier in the week. It had seemed like the right thing to do, but Lenore apparently didn't think so.

Two days ago, an animal control officer had come to my house, but we'd failed to capture Lenore. From atop her tree perch, she had watched while we did our Keystone Cops best to imprison her. Occasionally, we caught sight of cold ebon eyes looking out from behind foliage, shooting daggers at us.

Lenore had exacted revenge for my narcing on her.

The raven poop looked similar to chicken droppings. Or a Jackson Pollock painting. I was glad I hadn't stepped in it. In the morning, I'd apologize to Lenore and leave her some food. Ravens are scavengers and will eat just about anything, but Lenore was particularly fond of dog kibble and unsalted peanuts. Maybe she'd forgive me if I gave her a double offering as an apology.

CHAPTER FOUR

Before leaving for work in the morning, I hosed down the stoop and scattered peanuts and canned corn in a spot near the tree. Even though I couldn't see Lenore, I suspected she was watching everything I was doing, and judging accordingly.

I arrived at work at a little past eight. My goal was to get through as much of the murder book as possible before leaving for my 2:30 appointment with Dr. Nguyen. Even though I was the first from my team to make it in, there was a visitor waiting for me.

"I almost gave up on you," said Detective Tomás "Tommy Boy" Garcia. "Must be nice working bankers' hours."

Tommy had his feet propped up on my desk. The two of us had worked together for almost a decade on Homicide Team II, where he was still assigned. Tommy had the reputation of being a big kid. He was six feet tall and burly. Still, he was surprisingly agile, and didn't need any prompting to join in soccer games in the park, or take a swing on the dance floor. He had a full head of thick dark hair, and was overfond of running a comb through it.

Pointing to a cup of coffee on my desk, he said, "Caramel

Ribbon Crunch Frappuccino. It always hurts me to have to put in that order. You know how much sugar is in this? I'm surprised you don't have diabetes."

Diabetes. Maybe Tommy Boy was onto something. It wasn't as if I wanted to have diabetes, but that could explain why I was feeling so crappy.

I reached for the cup, took an exaggerated sip, and nodded contentedly. "Almost sweet enough," I said.

"Real cops drink their coffee black."

"You're the one ordering it," I said.

"I only do that because Rosa's always nagging me to be nice to *el padrino*, so I tell her that I've been buying your damn *café dulce* for years."

Rosa was Tommy's long-suffering wife. I was godfather to their six-year-old son, Joe. Since I don't have any kids of my own, I like to dote on my godson, something Rosa appreciates.

Tommy finished up his coffee and then took aim at my wastebasket. His cup hit the rim and then bounced away.

"That's what happens when you're seeing double," he said.

"You work an all-nighter?" I asked.

"You must be a detective, Lago."

In Spanish, *lago* means "lake." I sort of liked having my one-syllable last name transformed into two syllables. Tommy Boy stretched out and yawned.

"Got the call yesterday afternoon," he said. "Two pipe fitters were on the job removing old cast-iron piping and replacing it with copper, when one of them decided to use the old pipe to cave in the other guy's head."

"Bad plumbing can be a real pain."

Tommy ignored me, continuing with his story. "Man meets pipe was a result of a love triangle gone bad. The victim was involved with the wife of his coworker, and hubby decided he'd had enough."

"So, the victim paid the piper?"

This time Tommy couldn't pretend he hadn't heard. He directed a baleful stare my way and then used his middle finger to scratch his nose, before continuing.

"Anyway, hubby decided to do a runner. He headed for the border, but then changed his mind and started hitting a bunch of South Bay bars instead."

He went clubbing, I wanted to say, but decided to spare Tommy. All-nighters tended to make him cranky.

"So, I'm with his wife, and this guy keeps calling her. I'm whispering what to say, and she keeps telling him that he needs to give himself up. He agrees, and says he's going to do just that, but then keeps acting like a prick tease. Every time, he changes his mind and ends up at another bar, where he calls the wife again, and we go through the same thing.

"After, like, two hours of this, we finally catch up with him, but by then he's got seven or eight drinks under his belt. When we pick him up, he's ready to confess, but we keep putting him off, stalling him with coffee and food, and doing everything we can to put a cork in his confession. We tell him before he can talk to us, he needs to be sober, so every half hour we administer the booze kazoo. It keeps ticking downward, but all the while he's getting more and more antsy. With each passing minute it's looking like he might ask for a lawyer, but thank God that doesn't happen. Finally, he's as sober as a judge. That's when I welcomed him into my confessional booth."

"Sounds like he should have gone with a real priest."

Tommy made a disdainful sound. "Let me send you the crime scene photos, and afterward you can tell me if you're still feeling so charitable toward this guy."

"I'll pass."

"You're getting soft in your new job. In the old days you

were always up for breakfast, no matter how gory the crime scene. What do you say for old times' sake we go out for a bite?"

"Can't," I said. "I got stuck with a new old case and need to get through the file this morning."

Tommy coughed up the word *bullshit* into his hand. "You telling me anybody really gives a shit about some oldy-moldy case?"

"La Loba told me to prioritize it. We're coming up on the twenty-fifth anniversary of the homicide, and she expects the media will be taking notice."

"No chance," he said. "No one remembers yesterday's news, let alone something that happened twenty-five years ago."

I shrugged. "You're probably right, but I got an afternoon meeting with a witness who was there at the crime scene."

"Waste of time," he said.

That's what I'd been thinking when I was assigned the case, but it wasn't something I was going to admit to Tommy.

"We'll see," I said. "Funny thing is, I remember the case from when I was a kid, so it's made me curious."

"What case?" he asked.

As I began telling him about it, Tommy started nodding. When I finished, he said, "Even I remember that one, which is damn surprising, because when it went down, the only things that interested me were the *chicas*, and football, in that order."

Tommy was a year older than me, and had also grown up in San Diego County, living in the South Bay, or as he called it, "Chulajuana."

"Killer leave any of his DNA at the scene?"

"Afraid not."

"Then you don't have a snowball's chance in hell of solving it, and we should definitely go to breakfast."

"Rain check," I said.

Sighing, he got to his feet. "Anything new on your other case?" he asked.

Tommy didn't need to specify which case. Both of us had given our all to the chain-gang homicides. Tommy, like everyone else on our team, had finally put it behind him. That's something I hadn't been able to do. Tommy thought my obsession was a fool's errand. Like everyone else, he believed it was a case of human trafficking gone bad, and the Mexican Mafia had decided to cut their losses. Dead men tell no lies, and it was easier for them to simply get rid of the witnesses rather than be incriminated by their human cargo.

"Not a damn thing," I said.

"Same old bad song," he said. "*Adios, amigo.*"

"Thanks for the coffee."

"I'd hardly call it that, but at least it's caffeine. I'm the one who's been up all night, but you look like you haven't slept in days."

"Sleep's overrated."

Tommy suddenly perked up. "You seeing somebody?"

"Could be," I said.

I wasn't, but didn't want to admit that to Tommy. He was a ladies' man, and couldn't understand why as a single man I wasn't juggling multiple women. Being married had never stopped him from doing just that.

"Tell Papa everything," he said.

"Next time. Give my love to Rosa and Joe."

He waved, and walked away.

Before seeing Dr. Nguyen, a nurse took my weight and blood pressure, which I was told was high. That didn't surprise me. My palms were already sweaty and my heart was racing. At the best of times, seeing a doctor or a dentist made me feel anxious. With the way I was feeling, it definitely wasn't the best of times.

After being shown to an examination room, I was told the doctor would be with me shortly. A few minutes passed, and I spent my time doing nonstop worrying. *Be diabetes*, I thought, remembering what Tommy had said. I could live with diabetes. There was one thing wrong with that diagnosis, though. To the best of my knowledge, no one on either side of my family had ever had sugar sickness.

Maybe I had some kind of autoimmune disease. That wouldn't be so bad, as long as it was treatable. Or I could have something like mononucleosis. As a kid, we'd called it the kissing disease.

The door finally opened, and Dr. Nguyen stepped inside. "Good afternoon," he said without meeting my eyes.

Not good. He wasn't going to tell me I had mono. Or even

diabetes. Whatever news he had was causing his shoulders to slump. He crossed the room, managing to not look at me.

"Did you look at your lab results?" he asked.

"No."

"Oh," he said, sounding both surprised and disappointed. It would be up to him to deliver them. "Then I'd better bring them up on the monitor for you to see."

He did some tapping and then directed my attention to his screen. Before getting into the numbers, he addressed the elephant in the room and said, "The results were not what we would have wanted."

It almost felt as if I should offer an apology for that. Dr. Nguyen began elaborating on those disappointing results.

"These are your CBC numbers," he said. "That means a complete blood count. Your last CBC was some years ago, which doesn't give us a recent baseline, but your current numbers are troubling."

My doctor seemed much more comfortable talking about those numbers than he did talking to me. He started referencing my white blood count, red blood count, hemoglobin levels, and platelets, and then began going over my mean corpuscular volume, hematocrits, neutrophils, and lymphocytes. I didn't understand most of what he was saying, but I did understand that what he was telling me wasn't even remotely encouraging. I had a very low hemoglobin, white blood, and platelet count, which he said would account for my headaches, fatigue, and pale skin.

"Initially, I wondered if these numbers suggested you might have lupus," he said.

For a moment, I was hopeful. I knew lupus was bad, but seemed to remember that most people could manage its symptoms.

"But your MRI suggests we're looking at something else."

Something, by the sound of it, that was worse.

"In yesterday morning's examination, I was concerned about your abdominal pain and fever, and when palpating your abdomen, I discovered your gallbladder was swollen. The imaging suggests a likely reason for this."

On the screen, I found myself looking at a bunch of black-and-white shapes.

"This is your liver," he said, pointing to the largest image. "On the upper right of that is your gallbladder, and on the lower right is your left kidney. In the middle of the image is your pancreas, and to the right of that is your spleen."

Dr. Nguyen looked at me for the first time since he'd entered the room, and I nodded to show that I was following his anatomy lesson.

He stretched his hand to the tablet and clicked a key. "What we're looking at here are a series of images showing your pancreas."

Using his index finger, he swiped along the screen, bringing up several images. To my untrained eye, the pancreas sort of looked like a sideways comma, but I wasn't really focusing on it. In my head, a word was playing over and over.

Pancreas.

I didn't know a damn thing about the pancreas, other than it wasn't a word you ever wanted to hear come out of your doctor's mouth.

Dr. Nguyen said, "The pancreas sits behind your stomach, and is in front of your spine. You can see how it lies along the first segment of your small intestine."

I'd delivered plenty of bad news during my time as a homicide detective, but one thing I'd learned was that you don't leave people hanging any longer than was necessary.

"Do you mind cutting to the chase?" I asked.

He pointed to a dark spot. "I did a quick consult with a radiologist, who believes this is a mass on your pancreas."

"A mass?"

"A tumor."

"Which means what?"

"We'll know more after additional tests. I've already forwarded your information to a gastroenterologist, as well as an oncologist. We'll also be bringing in a medical diagnostician because of certain anomalies you're presenting."

"Anomalies?"

"Your organs look"—he paused to consider the right word—"compromised. And your numbers suggest your pancreatic tumor might not be your only medical concern."

"But even by itself, that tumor is more than cause for concern, right?"

Dr. Nguyen took a deep breath. "As I said, more tests need to be conducted. But yes, such a tumor is very concerning."

"Do I have pancreatic cancer?"

"We haven't made a definitive determination."

"But it appears likely?"

The doctor wasn't comfortable being put on the spot, but after a moment he nodded. Suddenly, he didn't look so young anymore. Delivering death sentences tends to age people.

"And if it *is* cancer, how long do I have?"

He looked away. "That's something you need to take up with your gastroenterologist. I hear Dr. Kumar is excellent."

"But he's no miracle worker, right?"

"She," Dr. Nguyen said, and then looked embarrassed by his correction. In a softer voice he said, "No, she's not."

"And isn't pancreatic cancer a death sentence?"

"We still don't know..." Dr. Nguyen's voice trailed off as he became aware how lame his disclaimer sounded.

"Yes," he finally said.

"How long?" I asked again.

"That's not a question that can be answered without more tests," he said.

His hedging was understandable, but I wanted answers, so I consulted another source. I lifted my phone, and asked it, "What's the survival rate for pancreatic cancer?"

The electronic voice replied, "Pancreatic cancer has the highest mortality rate of all major cancers. Only about 8.5 percent of all patients are alive five years after their diagnosis."

Having successfully backed my doctor into a corner, he nodded, reluctantly agreeing with my phone's prognosis.

"Maybe I should get a second opinion with another phone," I said.

Dr. Nguyen didn't look amused by my gallows humor, so I went back to asking him questions.

"You were saying that this mass doesn't look as if it's the only thing wrong with me, is that right?"

"More tests are in order," he said. "The specialists I'm referring you to will be performing those. Because it's important you start your course of treatment as soon as possible, Dr. Kumar has agreed to see you today."

"Today's not good," I said, an understatement if ever there was one. "I have an appointment I need to get to."

"I'm not sure you understand the gravity of your situation," Dr. Nguyen said.

"I wish that was the case, but I understand only too well."

I turned away from the screen and began walking toward the door.

"Please sit down, Mr. Lake," Dr. Nguyen said. "There are many things that we still need to discuss."

I paused at the door. It was my turn to avoid eye contact.

"Why don't you send me that information, along with your

findings, through the medical portal? This time I promise to read everything in my file."

"You're leaving against medical advice," he said.

I didn't feel like apologizing, so I just shrugged and agreed. "Yeah."

"Before you go, will you at least make an appointment with one of our mental health professionals? My staff can help arrange that."

"Send me the number, and I'll look into setting something up."

I'm not sure Dr. Nguyen believed me. I'm not sure I believed what I was saying either.

"Can you please sit down?" he said. "I'd like to discuss potential treatment options with you."

"What do you mean?"

"Some patients want as aggressive a treatment as possible, while others prefer a palliative treatment."

"I'll give the matter some thought," I said.

"Since you are so intent on leaving, Mr. Lake, I need your assurance that you're not considering taking any action that would constitute a harm to yourself, or to others."

"Usually, I don't blame the messenger," I said. "However, in your case, I am thinking about leaving a so-so Yelp review. That's about the extent of any harm I'm considering."

CHAPTER SIX

Palliative care. Those words kept going through my head. That was my short-term future. There was no long-term one.

I wanted an option other than getting my affairs in order, even if there didn't seem to be one.

"Remission, remission," I said aloud—a prayer, a wish, a cadence, a plea for my life.

Speak it into existence. That was a favorite New Age cliché spouted by Sandy, one of my former girlfriends. Sandy was a believer in telling the universe what she wanted. I found it hard to believe the universe was listening to her, but maybe that was projection on my part, because it was hard enough for *me* to listen to her. That's probably why the two of us never even made it to our three-month dating anniversary.

Then again, I never heard her say to the universe, "I'd like to marry Wyatt Lake." That wasn't something she had wanted to speak into existence.

I drove past the Trolley Barn Park in University Heights, and for a fleeting moment considered making a quick stop there to try and clear my mind. The park was named for the streetcars serviced in a huge barn a century ago. *Next time,* I told myself, driving by it.

Next time. Would there be a next time?

Doctors don't know everything, I thought. *They're human. They make mistakes.* As Ben Franklin was fond of observing, "There are more old drunkards than old doctors."

I don't drink much, but suddenly the prospect of being an old drunkard, an old anything, appealed to me.

"Remission, remission," I sang.

I hoped the universe was listening, and I hoped it didn't mind that my singing was off-key.

Chloe Landers's office was in a professional building in what is known as the University Heights district. The area's long-standing name was based on wishful thinking. More than a century ago, developers had thought the University of Southern California was going to build a second campus in San Diego, but Tommy Trojan never came to town.

I parked on Adams Avenue. Prior to conducting an interview, I like to review my case notes and go over any questions I need to ask, but that wasn't happening today. My mind was already on overload. I'd just have to wing it.

It was too bad Tommy wasn't here to see that. When we used to work together, he was always telling me to loosen up. My methodical ways drove him crazy. But it was those differences that had made us an effective team. Tommy was outgoing and intuitive; I was introspective and orderly. He flew by the seat of his pants; I liked to be in control of the situation.

But what's a control freak to do when confronted by something over which there is no control?

At five minutes to four, I stood on the sidewalk studying the listings on a name board of a small professional building that housed mostly mental health professionals. I found Chloe Landers's name and pressed the intercom. By way of introduction, I held up my wallet badge to a CCTV camera overlooking the building's entrance. A moment later, I was buzzed in.

Dr. Landers's office was on the first floor. I cut across a small interior courtyard, walked down a corridor, and found myself facing another locked door and security camera. This time I didn't hold up my badge, but just pressed the intercom doorbell. A moment later, the door unlocked.

As I stepped inside, a voice called out, "Back here." I walked down a short hallway to an office and came to a sudden stop at the open doorway. Across the room, a woman in a wheelchair was sitting behind a desk.

Surprised, I said, "I know you."

She nodded and said, "When I saw your face on the security camera, I recognized you as well. We've probably nodded to each other dozens of times."

"You're the—" I stopped in mid-sentence, biting off my words.

She smiled, finishing what I'd been about to say. "Wheelchair Lady."

"I'm sorry that I never learned your name," I said.

"Don't be. I never learned yours either. To me, and I think most of the staff, you're the Zoo Detective."

"Wyatt Lake," I said, walking across the room. As we shook hands over her desk, she said, "Chloe Landers."

"Small world," I said.

"Please have a seat, Detective."

"Call me Wyatt," I said, surprising myself. In my

professional life, I never offered my first name. Then again, the two of us had a history, albeit an unspoken one.

"I'm Chloe," she said.

In offering her first name to me, I got the feeling she was breaking one of her professional rules as well.

I sat down and took out my notepad and pen. Chloe began to do the same, before reconsidering. "Guess I won't be the one asking questions today," she said.

"And how does that make you feel?"

She laughed, showing her teeth and a dimple. I wondered why I hadn't taken more notice of her during our encounters at the zoo. Maybe I didn't want her to think I was gawking at her disability. She was an attractive woman. Her sandy blonde hair with red highlights was cut short and showed off her fair complexion. I liked her full, unapologetic eyebrows, which set off her dark, intelligent eyes.

Usually, I'm not one for small talk during an interview. I like to ask questions and get the subject talking. But this time I was slow to get down to business. It had been a hell of an afternoon.

"How long have you been part of the Zoo Retinue?" I asked.

"About ten years," she said. "What about you?"

"Pretty much the same. You ever see any of the other regulars outside of the zoo?"

"The Wolfman had a holiday party last year, but I begged off. And three or four years ago, the Leopard Lady arranged a picnic for the Zoo Retinue."

Most of the zoo regulars had a preferred enclosure, or animal, and spent most of the time around that exhibit. Their visiting preferences earned them their nicknames.

"How did that go?"

"Everyone seemed to be getting along until the two Gorilla Girls became territorial."

Each of the women claimed they were the "original" Gorilla

Girl; one could typically be found at the zoo on Monday and Wednesday, and the other on Tuesday and Thursday.

"Hate it when humans go ape," I said.

"You really didn't say that? If the word got out that the Zoo Detective made bad puns, it would ruin your reputation."

"What reputation?"

"Everyone thinks you're the cool and aloof mystery man. Especially after what happened." Chloe locked eyes with me and said, "I was there that day, you know."

I didn't need to ask her what day that was. For weeks after the Big Shake, everyone in San Diego was asking each other, "Where were you when it happened?"

It's not every day you experience a 7.3 magnitude earthquake. Thank God.

"So, how did you know an earthquake was about to happen?" she asked. "One of the keepers said you must be psychic."

"Far from it. I acted on an educated guess."

"Which was?"

"The lemurs began making strange cries unlike anything I'd ever heard out of them. And then I became aware of this growing refrain of howls and roars and calls coming from all corners of the zoo. I know the usual animal choruses, and this wasn't like that. Then I noticed something else: animals were moving to the high ground of their enclosures. They knew something was going down. As it happened, just the night before I had read an article about how animals often appear to be prescient when it comes to natural disasters such as tsunamis or earthquakes. That was enough for me to act."

"How did you get the tram shut down?"

The Skyfari Aerial Tram travels above the treetops around much of the zoo's hundred acres.

"I convinced the manager on duty that an earthquake was

about to happen. Luckily, the zoo's staff is trained to respond to emergency situations."

"But didn't the manager question your claim?"

"She knew I was a cop," I said. "And when I said the words *large earthquake*, she listened. Of course, it's possible she thought I was privy to inside information provided by one of the Southern California earthquake agencies."

"And why would she think that?"

"I might have made an allusion or two."

"What if she'd called your bluff?"

"When seconds matter, you have to make a call and act. She made the right call, closing down the Skyfari, and getting people to safe spots."

"What if you'd been wrong?"

"I would have apologized. The worst outcome would have been inconvenienced visitors, and some egg on my face. I was okay with that possibility."

"I was in the Herpetology and Ichthyology Building when the order came through to evacuate the building. At the time, I kept asking, 'Why?' Not long after, all the shaking started."

"Good timing," I said. "No one wants an encounter with an agitated snake."

"It's a miracle no one was hurt that day. But I think it's even more of a miracle that the staff listened to you."

"The zoo's been my second office for a long time," I said. "I walk its grounds like I'm a beat cop on patrol. That's made me a familiar face to most of the keepers and crew."

"And yet you always managed to keep a low profile. If I hadn't kept asking around, I never would have found out what happened. When I heard you sounded the alarm, I wanted to ask you about it, but never did."

"Why not?"

"You usually seem preoccupied, which doesn't make you very approachable."

"And here I thought it was the 'Do not disturb' sign I carry."

"If you want people to look the other way, just get a wheelchair," she said.

The mood in the room changed. Now that we'd finished with our pleasantries, we both withdrew into our roles. I was the cop, and she was the reluctant victim who was tired of having law enforcement pull at her scabs.

"For the past two days I've been reviewing your file," I said. "If it's all right with you, I'd like to go over what happened on the night of the attack."

She sighed. "And what if it isn't all right with me? What good will it do to rehash what happened to me and Dana? That's ancient history now. Over the years, the police have asked every question imaginable but have never gotten anywhere. I've now reached the point in my life where all I want to do is put what happened behind me."

"I can understand that, but this case isn't only about you. Your best friend was murdered. I want her murderer to pay."

"What makes you think he's still alive?"

"In your first interview with the police, you gauged your attacker's age as somewhere around twenty-five. Assuming you're right, that would mean he's now around fifty. Given that age, the odds are good he's still alive."

"But what makes you think you can find him when so many other detectives couldn't?"

"I can't promise you I'll succeed in doing that, but I can promise you that I'll be tenacious. It's been my experience if you keep digging, things turn up."

"I don't share your optimism, Detective."

"You don't need to, but will you at least answer a few questions?"

"The definition of a few is a small number. If that's the case, go ahead."

"Thank you," I said. "Your attacker identified himself as Stu or Stewie. At what point in the drive did this occur?"

"At the onset," she said. "He asked us our names, and then volunteered his. One of the first things he said was, 'I'm Stewie B.'"

"And when he said this, you thought he was just being friendly?"

She nodded.

"Do you think his plan all along was to attack you and Dana?"

"I really don't know."

Her answer surprised me. "And yet in previous interviews, you stated that you didn't initially think there was anything threatening about him, and it was only later in the drive that you became concerned."

"Haven't you heard by now that I'm an unreliable witness?"

"What do you mean?"

"That's the message SDPD and the media told the world. In the morality play that was presented, Dana and I got our just deserts. We were what happens when you lie to your parents, take drugs, and accept rides with a stranger."

"I'm sorry if that was your experience, but that doesn't answer my question."

"I don't know when he decided he wanted to kill us. Okay?"

"Okay," I said. "Although in previous interviews, you said Stu's behavior changed during the course of the ride."

"Maybe that's what I wanted to believe. Or it could be that as a teenager I was a terrible judge of character. Do you know that old song 'Smiling Faces'?"

I nodded.

She half-sang/half-spoke the line about evil being hidden behind smiles.

"So, now you believe Stu always intended to kill the two of you?"

"I think he was a good actor who was initially able to mask his true intentions with a false smile."

"In a number of your previous interviews, you reiterated that Stu seemed to undergo a Jekyll/Hyde transformation during the time you spent with him."

"I was a I young woman who experienced hell firsthand. My best friend was murdered, and my life was turned upside down. In the years since, I've been trying to move beyond what occurred. As a therapist, I've seen up close how physical trauma can affect memory. Victims often have difficulties processing and storing information because of their trauma. That puts into question what the victim does, or does not, recall—including my own account of what happened."

"Are you saying I should be skeptical of your account? Then, and now, is that right?"

Instead of answering, she said, "I think we've exceeded your quota of a *few* questions. Are we done here?"

"No, we're not," I said. "I feel like this has been a waste of time."

"On that, we both agree."

"I don't have time to waste. Not anymore."

Chloe must have heard something in my response. She met my eyes and asked, "What do you mean?"

I shook my head, but she wasn't so easily dismissed. "This case has been ongoing for twenty-five years," Chloe said. "Why your urgency?"

"It's the way I am."

We were taking turns dissembling, and I was pretty sure each of us knew that.

I said, "If you're willing to answer my questions without hedging, I'll do likewise."

She allowed herself a cautious nod.

"Do you think Stu B. intended on harming you and Dana from the first?" I asked.

"I'm not certain," she said, not meeting my eyes.

"Okay. Do you think that when he offered up the name of Stu or Stewie, he knew what he was going to do?"

"That's unclear. I know most of the detectives who worked the case think he just offered up some randomly assumed name."

"You said he also introduced himself with a one-syllable last name."

"Take that memory with a grain of salt."

"You thought Barnes, Bourn, and Burns were the three likeliest."

"I suppose so."

"And now you believe the name he offered up was a false one?"

"That's what the investigation concluded, correct?"

I opened my mouth to ask another question, but she raised a finger. "My turn," she said.

"Go ahead," I said reluctantly.

"You told me that you don't have time to waste, at least not anymore. Explain that."

Just lie, I thought. But as I opened my mouth to do that, something else came out.

"I'm dying," I said.

Chloe sat there, still, statue-like. She didn't blink or react, just waited for me to say more.

"About an hour ago, my doctor told there's a mass on my pancreas."

"I'm sorry," she said.

"I'm hoping there's some miracle cure in the pipeline, or that things aren't as dire as they sounded."

"I'm sure you discussed that with your doctor."

"Not really. What he had to tell me didn't sound like anything I wanted to hear. So, I told him I had an appointment, and pretty much ran out of his office."

"Why didn't you cancel our appointment? Given the circumstances, I'm amazed you didn't."

"And do what instead? I've spent the last two days familiarizing myself with your file. I started something, and I'm not one to walk away."

"My situation can wait. Yours can't. Is there someone in your life with whom you can talk things out?"

"No wife, no family, no girlfriend," I said.

"Let me make some calls for you. I know some excellent palliative care therapists who work with clients facing circumstances like yours."

"You're talking end of life?"

"I'm talking therapists that deal with life-threatening situations."

"The business of dying," I said. "I was a homicide detective for a decade, so I guess that's something I should be familiar with. I suppose that's a bit ironic."

She offered a sympathetic nod, and then reached down to a pocket in her wheelchair and pulled out a cell phone. "With your permission, I'd like to make an appointment for you with a colleague who is exceptional."

"I appreciate that, but I'm not ready."

Chloe reluctantly put her phone away. "Please don't put it off for long. You'll need to make plans for the coming months."

"Make a bucket list?" I asked.

"Figure out what's important to you."

"I already know."

She didn't ask, probably out of respect for my privacy, so I volunteered my thoughts. "There are two cases I want to close. That's how I'd like to go out."

"I'm surprised," she said. "Most people facing their mortality don't prioritize their work."

"Dying doesn't change my obsessions. One of the cases I've been working for years."

"And the other?"

"I was assigned it the day before yesterday, but it's already got me by the short hairs."

"I don't want you spending your precious time on something that's not really important to me."

"I find that hard to believe."

Chloe didn't respond, didn't tell me I was wrong, but chose to look away. Finally, she asked, "Are we done here?"

I nodded and said, "For now, but I'd like to talk more. What time are you going to the zoo tomorrow?"

CHAPTER SEVEN

Chloe lingered in her office, replaying in her mind the conversation that had just taken place. The detective had surprised her. He had actually made her feel off-balance the way he'd looked at her with his dark, probing eyes. Skeptical eyes. Disarming eyes.

Two hours ago, he'd learned he was dying. Most individuals would have been incapacitated by that kind of news. Wyatt Lake hadn't cancelled his appointment with her. Neither had he seemed distracted or sidetracked. The only reason he'd even confided his condition was to try and get her to open up.

The detective was intriguing. And dangerous. He might be dying, but that didn't mean he wasn't totally engaged in the present.

There was something about him that made Chloe think he was a kindred spirit. It wasn't just their zoo connection, although in the past she had wondered about the enigmatic cop when she'd seen him taking his solitary strolls.

He's an outsider, Chloe thought. *As am I.*

It was easy for the world to see that she was disabled. What about him? Was he encumbered in ways not so readily apparent? He admitted to being without wife or family. How long had he been alone? And why had he chosen to travel such a path? Had he chosen his fate, or had it been thrust upon him?

A chance encounter had changed Chloe's life, and even now, the past kept her in its grip. For a quarter of a century, she had been experiencing survivor's guilt, feeling the need to live a life not only for herself, but for Dana. In many ways, her *raison d'être* had centered around expiating that guilt.

It was in her best interests to stay clear of the detective. He wanted answers from her that she didn't want to give. The past was painful. It was a black hole, and made her remember all the ways she'd failed Dana. And herself. Chloe had already accommodated the detective's questioning. That should have been enough.

So why was it that she had agreed to meet with the cop again?

CHAPTER EIGHT

As I approached the Queenslander House landing, I saw Chloe observing a mother koala and her joey perched in a tree. I came over and joined in the watching.

"Hope you haven't been waiting too long," I said.

"I wouldn't know," she said. "I'm on koala time. When I'm in their presence, everything slows down."

"Care to venture further into the Australian Outback? Look at the wombats, or spiny anteaters, or Tasmanian devils?"

"I'm a little wary of them," she said. "They always seem to start screaming when I'm around. It's easy to believe the story about English settlers hearing their cries and being convinced it was the shrieking of devils."

"The Australian aborigines probably thought the same thing about the English newcomers," I said.

That got a little smile.

We started on a leisurely pace down the path. Her wheelchair was a vivid yellow, and she noticed me observing it.

"Like my ride?" she asked.

"Very colorful," I said.

"I call it Tweety Bird because of its canary color."

"When we get to the big cats, I'm probably going to feel compelled to say, 'I thought I saw a puddy cat.'"

That got another small smile.

"Is it hard navigating the zoo in a wheelchair?" I asked.

"Not if you have racing gloves."

She lifted a hand, showing off a colorful glove with a large blue butterfly design. "Blue morpho," she said.

"Stylish."

"I'm one chic cripple."

"I'd be glad to push you, if you want."

"Thank you, but this isn't a transport wheelchair. Besides, how do you think I got these guns?" She offered a pose that exaggerated her biceps.

"Remind me not to arm-wrestle you."

"Smart man."

We slowly made our way through Australia, and entered Asia.

"Is this pace too leisurely for you?" she asked. "Yesterday, you said that you walk the grounds like a beat cop."

"Today I'm just a cop who's beat," I said.

She nodded, taking a moment to study me. I hoped I didn't look as tired as I felt.

"Last night I called my colleague who specializes in hospice care," Chloe said. "He's not taking on any new clients at this time, but said that he would make an exception in your case. I can either text or email you his contact information."

"I appreciate you going out of your way for me."

"But?"

"But what?"

"I sense you have no intention of following through."

I shifted my head from side to side, as if weighing my answer. "At the moment, I just don't think I'm ready to discuss my situation with anyone."

"DABDA," she said.

"What?"

"It's an acronym for the five stages of grief people experience that was developed by a psychiatrist named Elisabeth Kübler-Ross. The D in DABDA is for denial."

"So, what comes after?"

"Anger."

"And then?"

"Bargaining."

"Door number four?"

"Depression."

"And the grand finale?"

"Acceptance."

"Okay," I said.

"That's it?"

I shrugged.

"I have trouble believing you're that impassive about your situation."

"I have the same doubts about you."

"How so?" she asked.

"You want me to think you've come to accept what happened to you, and just want to move on. That feels like bullshit to me."

She stopped her wheeling. "I am beginning to think our meeting today wasn't a good idea."

"Why? Because I touched on a sore subject?"

"I'm sorry you're sick, but I don't think that obligates me to talk to you."

"It doesn't. And the truth is, I wish I hadn't said anything. It just sort of came out while I was in shock. Last night when I was trying to fall asleep, I was kicking myself for having said anything to you."

"Why's that?"

"Because I don't want your sympathy. And I hate it that I resorted to offering up some poor pitiful version of me."

"You didn't come across as pitiful. If anything, you were remarkably composed."

"Smoke and mirrors," I whispered.

"We all have our veneers," she said.

Chloe resumed her wheeling of Tweety, and we entered the Mother Continent. We didn't comment on the animals as we passed klipspringers, dwarf mongooses, and rock hyraxes. She just kept wheeling, and by the looks of it, thinking.

"What is it you want from me?" she finally asked.

"The truth."

"And what will you do with that truth?"

"I'll try and track down a very evil man."

"But it won't be just you, will it? In the past, I never dealt with only one detective. It always felt like I was dealing with a bureaucracy."

"No cop is a one-man band," I said. "But I should point out that as a cold-case detective, the initial part of my job is reviewing the work that's already been done by others. That's why it's important I question you, so if something in the record is wrong, or needs to be pursued, I can do that at the onset of my investigation."

"But given your personal situation, why is my case so important to you? Like the saying goes, 'No one on their deathbed ever wished they'd spent more time working.'"

"Maybe I'll be the first. What should I do instead? Travel around the world? Dine at some Michelin-starred restaurant? Go on a real safari, and not just the zoo version?"

"Why not? Are those things you've always wanted to do?"

"To be honest, no. As wonderful as they sound, I can live without them. And die without them."

"There must be something you regret never having experienced in your lifetime?"

Instead of immediately answering, I pretended interest in a Nubian ibex. Having already told her I was dying seemed like confession enough.

"Nothing that strikes me at the moment," I said.

We continued down the path. There are six wildlife venues in Africa Rocks spread over eight acres. The zoo advertises it as taking a journey from the savannah to the sea. As we approached the Madagascar forest exhibit, Chloe's attention went to a distraught-looking red-haired woman, and she said, "Please excuse me."

She wheeled ahead, and although I kept my distance from them, I was able to hear some of their conversation.

"Lisa, I was so sorry to hear about Masoandro," Chloe said.

The keeper leaned down, and the two women hugged. Clearly struggling to keep her emotions in check, Lisa said, "She was so, so sweet. Just like her name, she was sunshine."

"You can talk about it with me if you'd like," Chloe said. "We could either do it in person, or do a video call."

"I'd appreciate that," the keeper said, wiping her eyes. "I've barely been able to keep it together today. In fact, I've got to get back to work. All of the lemur troop is upset at Masoandro's death, and I don't want to be weepy around them. That would only make them more upset."

An encouraging Chloe said, "Call me."

The keeper managed a smile, nodded a few times, and then walked away. When I rejoined Chloe, she didn't seem to be in any rush to start moving.

"I don't think people realize how difficult the life of a zookeeper is," she said. "They have this notion that the keepers are so lucky being able to work with animals, without realizing that most of them live their jobs 365 days a year, and are always worrying about their charges."

"Masoandro was a lemur?"

Chloe nodded. "A red-ruffed lemur. They're endangered, and have all but disappeared in the wild. So many of the animals in this zoo are endangered, and every keeper feels the weight of that. They're trying to fight a terrible tide, and feel guilty that they can't do the impossible."

"I don't think I could do their job."

"Nor I. It seems the more committed keepers are, the more they suffer compassion fatigue. As a group, they are among the most committed individuals I've ever known."

From what I'd seen, it didn't matter if the zookeepers worked with animals that slithered, crawled, burrowed, swam, or flew. They were all-in, regardless.

Chloe spun Tweety around. "If you don't mind, I think I'll cut my visit short."

"Is it all right if I walk out with you?"

She nodded, and we set out in silence. Chloe spoke first. "Why are you so sure that I haven't achieved acceptance?"

"Your friend was murdered, and you were left for dead. The wounds you sustained were life-changing. I've read your police interviews over the years, and don't believe you have forgiven or forgotten."

"But I *have* managed to build a successful practice, and I'm a well-regarded therapist."

"I'm not saying you don't have a successful professional life."

Her face flushed in anger. "I also have a life outside of work that includes friends and activities and hobbies."

"But it's not the life you once envisioned, is it?"

"It's a fulfilling life, regardless."

She picked up the pace, forcing me into maintaining a brisk walk just to keep up.

As we neared the exit, I said, "I'm going to continue working your case whether you co-operate with me or not, but I'd like your help."

"I'll think about it," she said.

"I'm the perfect individual to share with," I said. "What better confessor is there than someone who's dying?"

"Perhaps *you're* the one who needs to confess. Yesterday, you said there was another case you wanted to clear. Why is it so important to you?"

"I worked the chain-gang homicides," I said.

Chloe winced at its mention. I was glad she hadn't forgotten, as so many had.

I said, "Someone made a decision that those lives were expendable. Someone rigged that boat so it could easily be scuttled, and those chained inside it would die."

"Wasn't the Mexican Mafia responsible?"

"That's the consensus, and it's true they're behind most of the human trafficking coming out of Mexico, but there's no definitive proof they committed these homicides. God knows, they've done lots of terrible things, but it seems almost too easy to throw all the blame their way."

We reached the exit, and a gate attendant familiar with Chloe gestured for her to go through. She turned to say her goodbyes, but I spoke before she could and asked, "May I walk you to your car?"

"I don't want to intrude on your zoo time."

"You're not. I like my visits short and sweet."

"Suit yourself," she said.

Both of us exited through the gate, and I followed Chloe as she navigated Tweety.

I asked, "Do you have a busy workday ahead of you?"

"Not too bad," she said. "Two teleconference calls, and one in person. What about you?"

"I'll be doing more reviewing of your file."

"How much longer do you plan on working your job?"

"As long as I can."

"Have you told your colleagues about your condition?"

"No," I said. "And I don't intend to."

"Why?"

"I can do without the sympathetic bullshit from my coworkers. And I don't want the brass to force me into taking a mandatory medical retirement."

"What will you do when your illness begins to show itself?"

"I'll say I'm dealing with some kind of annoying autoimmune disorder."

"Word to the wise, there's always a cost to keeping secrets," she said. "It's been my experience that sharing with others is therapeutic."

"Is that something you practice?"

Chloe didn't answer, coming to a stop at a white Tesla Y.

"No canary yellow?" I asked.

"That wasn't a color option."

The passenger door opened, and she backed her wheelchair toward the car seat. Using one arm to steady herself, she shimmied her backside into the vehicle, and then reached down, folded up the chair, and hoisted it into the passenger seat.

Chloe met my gaze and answered the question I didn't ask. "Hand controls," she said.

"Nice. So, can we continue our conversation at the same time and same place tomorrow?"

"No," she said.

Disappointing, but not surprising.

But then she added, "Let's meet up at the river hippos."

Chloe closed the door behind her, backed out of the space, and silently drove off.

CHAPTER NINE

At my work cubicle, I pored through the case notes, trying to reconcile fifteen-year-old Chloe Landers with the now forty-year-old therapist. In her file were graphic pictures showing her wounds; most people would have died from shock and blood loss, but Chloe had proved herself a fighter.

Closing my eyes, I pictured Chloe in her blue morpho racing gloves furiously rolling her canary-yellow wheelchair. Our zoo visit had shown she cared about people—and animals—and had a soft spot for all underdogs. At the same time, she wasn't an open book. Over the years I'd interviewed hundreds of people, and knew when they were being cautious and holding information back. I was certain she was doing that.

If I was right about Chloe possessing information that wasn't in the case files, why was she reluctant to pass that on to me? It was one thing to not be forthcoming, but another to offer up misdirection, and that's what I suspected her of doing. When people change their story, or clam up, they're worried about potential consequences.

"Good afternoon, Detective Lake."

I knew the voice, but didn't respond other than to turn my head and acknowledge my visitor with a nod.

"Okay if I sit down?"

Detective Luca "Loco" Calderon didn't wait for my response, taking a seat in one of my cubicle's empty chairs. Calderon worked for SDPD's Internal Affairs Unit. I wasn't surprised to see him. Every few months he turned up unexpectedly, reminding me that he was still out there, still interested in a case I'd worked. And still interested in me.

Calderon was an ambitious cop. He'd gotten his detective shield while still in his twenties, and had hooked on with Internal Affairs. That wasn't the chosen career path for most cops, but Calderon was ambitious, and out to fast-track his way to the top.

"Working on a new case?" he asked.

"What can I do for you, Detective Calderon?"

"The last time we talked, I asked if you might have crossed paths with a man named Daniel Hernández, and you told me you'd think on that. In the two months since that conversation, I wondered if you'd recalled any interaction that you might have had with Hernández."

"Afraid not," I said.

"Why don't you look at another picture of Mr. Hernández before committing yourself to that answer."

He held up a picture I hadn't seen before. Hernández was deferentially standing next to a table where two other men were seated.

"Looking any more familiar?" he asked.

"Which one is he?" I asked, pretending not to know.

Calderon tapped his finger on the young man in the picture.

"Does he look familiar?" I asked. "Of course he does. I imagine there must be a quarter of a million men in a twenty-five-mile radius that fit his same ballpark description."

"But you never met or talked with this particular individual?"

"To the best of my knowledge, no."

"What about the two other men in the picture?"

I took a good look at them and finally shook my head. "No and no," I said. "Who are they?"

"The muscle on the left is Luis Garcia, street name Aguijón; and the other man is Matías Vasquez, better known as El Tipo."

El Tipo translated to "the Guy," which is what Vasquez was. He ran the Sinaloa Cartel throughout Baja California.

Calderon said, "In case you're wondering, this picture was taken about a month before Hernández was shot in Tijuana."

I wondered how Luca Loco had gotten the picture, but didn't ask, not wanting to appear overly curious.

"In that case, it sounds like you should be talking with El Tipo and—what's that name?—Aguijón. What's that mean, anyway?"

"Stinger. Aguijón has a reputation for getting people to talk. He stirs up bagged yellow-jacket nests right before he starts asking questions. If he doesn't like the answers he's getting, Aguijón tosses rocks at the bag until it breaks. When his *chaquetas amarillas* fly free, they're not happy. When bodies are found with hundreds of wasp stings, everyone knows Aguijón was there."

"Never met him," I said. "Never even had the opportunity to tell him to buzz off."

Calderon's eyes narrowed, and his scowl turned his handsome features ugly. "You never used Hernández as your snitch while trying to get information on the chain-gang homicides?"

"If I don't recognize the man in the picture, how could he have been a CI of mine?"

My non-denial denial drew an eye roll from Calderon, but then he shrugged it off and leaned in closer to me.

"I've been told that at your behest, Hernández was asking about what happened out at sea."

There wasn't anyone else within hearing range. Calderon invariably arranged his visits so that our conversations were always private.

"Who told you that?"

"I have my sources."

"Better get a more reliable snitch."

He said, "Unlike you, I follow the rules for informant handling. When those rules aren't strictly adhered to, people like Daniel Hernández die."

Any SDPD detective working with a confidential informant is supposed to follow clearly defined procedures. To protect the CI's identity, SDPD's Criminal Intelligence Unit oversees and controls all pertinent information. No one else is supposed to have access to those files, but I had my doubts.

I said, "Since time immemorial, people have been posing the question, 'Who guards the guards?'"

"My unit guards the guards," Calderon said. "I'm here to remind you of that. Do you know how Daniel Hernández died?"

"I heard he was shot."

"With a 3D-printed ghost gun."

"I thought ghost guns were untraceable."

"The bullet might not show any barrel striations, but 3DP polymers have their own unique signatures, like fingerprints."

I considered that piece of news. "What are you saying?"

"I find Hernández's death curious, don't you? He was taken out with a very particular and anonymous type of firearm."

"What's your point?"

"That this case isn't going away, and if you had any dealings with Hernández, it's in your best interest to talk."

"I'm afraid I can't help you."

"Do you know what an S-Visa is?"

"S for snitch, right?"

He nodded. "An S-Visa is something the government can offer to noncitizen informants and co-operating witnesses, especially those with verifiable safety concerns. S-Visas are often dangled in front of informants. They're told that by co-operating, they can get one, but in reality, it doesn't work that way. It can take up to a decade before the Justice Department and other governmental agencies sign off on the paperwork and the visa gets issued. For a snitch living on the razor's edge, that's an eternity."

"And why are you telling me about S-Visas?"

"I've heard the reason Hernández co-operated with you is that he thought he was going to get an S-Visa. What he didn't know was that only Justice or DHS could initiate that paperwork. Since your snitch was off-the-books, you could promise him the moon, and then do a bait and switch."

"We're done here."

"I'm not the enemy, Detective."

"Are you sure?"

"I know you're still consumed by the chain-gang case. That's a good thing. But there's a right way of working it and a wrong way."

Calderon stood up. Loco Luca wasn't a large man. Maybe that's why he so enjoyed throwing his weight around.

"Thanks for your time, Detective," he said.

Another Calderon fishing expedition, I thought. Still, I didn't like having to lie to him, and hoped it wouldn't bite me in the ass. Hernández wasn't a stranger to me. Tommy and I had grown frustrated with our team's stalled chain-gang investigation, and had used Hernández to see if he could provide answers. At the time he started working for us, he was a peripheral player, a low-level gofer for the Sinaloa operations in Tijuana and Ensenada. He'd initially agreed to co-operate with us as payment for not being charged as a bagman working the border city of San Ysidro. That had been the quid pro quo. We had never talked about getting him a snitch visa.

Tommy and I had opted for secrecy and bypassed the usual CI channels. It was easy to be paranoid about the influence of the Sinaloa Cartel, and where it extended. Keeping the identity of our snitch off the books had seemed like the smart way to go.

I wanted to believe that Hernández's death had nothing to do with his being our snitch. According to one of Tommy's sources, the cartel had caught Hernández skimming on his collections. It wasn't something we could investigate without raising the attention of Calderon and his ilk, not to mention *La Eme,* Spanish for *M,* and shorthand for the Mexican Mafia. During the six months Hernández had been our snitch, he hadn't given us much, even though he'd said he was getting close to something. Since his death, we'd concluded that his story had likely been a ploy to cadge more spending money.

Hernández's death by a 3D ghost gun offered up an interesting wrinkle, though. Sinaloa hits aren't subtle. And it wasn't as if they didn't have plenty of throwaway weapons in their arsenal. Of course, Calderon could be making up his ghost gun story just to stir the pot. Anyone who was as ambitious as he was didn't care about stepping on toes, or playing people off each other. For the past year, he'd leaned on me much more than he had Tommy. Did he think I was the weak link? Is that why he targeted me when no one else was around, hoping I would talk? Or was he worried about someone overhearing what was being said?

It was easy to be paranoid, especially now. My illness was making me increasingly jumpy, which was a little strange given that I was already looking at a worst-case scenario. Still, it was no longer as easy to push away dark thoughts, not after they'd come home to roost.

CHAPTER TEN

For once, I arrived home while it was still light outside, so I went on a Lenore search. The food I'd put out for her was gone. Maybe that's why there wasn't a new pile of raven crap on the stoop.

Even experienced ornithologists have difficulty determining if a raven is male or female, but even without anything to justify my beliefs, I was still convinced that Lenore was a female.

I lingered out front, doing some much-needed gardening while monitoring the cherry tree. The milkweed plants looked as if most of their leaves had been clear-cut by a mini buzz saw. Bending down, I spotted the familiar coloring of a handful of black, yellow, and white monarch caterpillars. As a kid, I could remember watching the stream of monarchs floating by our yard during their migration. On some days it seemed as if their numbers were limitless. It was hard to believe that the species was now endangered. Monarch caterpillars only eat milkweed. At one time there were fields of milkweed all around the country, but with development, that food source dried up. Because thousands of people like me don't want the species to starve to death on our watch, we've taken to providing monarchs with milkweed way stations. It seemed like an unlikely Band-Aid, but I hoped it would be enough to stave off their extinction.

Awk awk awk.

The unmistakable call of a raven got me looking around. Lenore, or one of her ilk? There were no birds to be seen, so I assumed the calls had come from Lenore. She liked playing mind games, which isn't surprising. In Native American lore, ravens are often thought of as tricksters. Lenore certainly was. One of her favorite sounds mimicked a dog barking.

I filled the birdbath with water. During the hot months, the birdbath gets lots of winged visitors, most coming to drink rather than bathe. Ravens typically choose to nest near to a water source. Because of her bad wing, I was now placing water bowls near the base of the Catalina cherry tree.

My presence in the front yard hadn't gone unnoticed. From next door, Lola came sprinting at me. I leaned down to greet her, and she got up on her back legs to shower me with kisses.

"Get off him, you hussy!" Janis yelled.

Lola reluctantly complied, and then went over to the water bowls I'd just filled and lapped them dry.

Janis joined us and said, "Don't make me look like a bad mom, Lola. You've got a full bowl of water in the house."

"It's no problem," I said.

"You leaving the water out for that crow?" Janis asked.

I nodded.

Janis looked up at the cherry tree. "Where is it?"

"I'm not sure. She's mostly stayed silent."

"Have you heard that thing bark? Sounds just like Lola."

"Ravens are good at mimicking sounds."

"Something's not right about a bird that barks. And coughs. Whenever it does that, I get the creeps."

I tried to hide my smile. Lenore was talented at duplicating Janis's phlegmy cough.

"Ravens are smart," I said. "Some studies have shown they're smarter than dogs. They're tool users, and problem solvers. Supposedly, they've even held funerals for ravens that died."

"You're shitting me."

I shook my head. "The researcher who published that study said she believed some ravens used the funeral gatherings as a way of teaching other ravens about potential dangers."

"That's damn creepy."

"If it's true, that speaks to their ability to plan ahead."

"You really think they hold funerals?"

"I'm not sure."

"I'll bet that thing's spying on us right now."

"You're probably right. With her bum wing, there's not much else for her to do."

I didn't want to anthropomorphize, but couldn't help but believe Lenore was leading a lonely life. On a few occasions, I'd heard her calling to ravens winging by. No bird had yet stopped.

"I'm surprised he's still alive."

"I can't help but admire her pluck."

"What do you think happened to his wing?"

"Probably hit by a BB or pellet," I said.

"It was probably those juvenile delinquents from down the street," she said.

Janis didn't think much of Jonny and Colin Greenwood. The parents had named their boys after the Greenwood brothers who played guitar in the band Radiohead. Janis's dislike stemmed from the theft of four of her marijuana plants the year before—she believed the brothers were the culprits. Janis had asked me to talk to them, which I had. I think she was disappointed that I hadn't put them under bright lights and beaten them with rubber hoses. The brothers said they had nothing to do with ripping off the "old stoner's weed." When I told Janis I believed them, she'd said, "Et tu, Brute?"

Lola began pawing my leg, her signal for me to pay attention to her. I got down on one knee and began scratching her nape. She responded by licking my nose.

"No tongue, Lola," Janis said. "Be a lady."

"Good girl," I said, rubbing the base of her ears. Soft grunts of pleasure accompanied my scratching.

"Why don't you have your own dog, Wyatt?"

"Guilt," I said. "I wouldn't want to subject a dog to my erratic work hours. I always thought one day I'd have a wife, kids, and a dog, but I guess that wasn't in the cards."

"You're young. It could still happen."

Not in this lifetime, I thought.

"C'mon, you hussy," Janis said. "We need to go shopping."

"If you want, I could look after Lola."

"Sure?"

"It's no problem."

"Need anything at the store?"

"I could use a few bananas, if that's not too much trouble."

"What trouble? You want 'em ripe, or green?"

"Either way is fine."

"I'll get you two ripe and two green."

"Sounds good."

"When my mother was in her eighties, she told me to only buy her ripe bananas. 'I'm too old for green bananas,' she'd tell me. 'I might die before they ripen.' So, for ten years, I always got her ripe bananas."

I wondered if I should change my banana order and have Janis bring me only ripe bananas, but decided to be an optimist. For now, I could still wait on green bananas to ripen.

When Janis went off, I played fetch with Lola, using a fallen orange for the ball. It was nice engaging in a mindless activity, but after about a dozen throws, the orange began to disintegrate. I thought about grabbing another orange from the tree, but by then it was getting dark.

"Come on, Lola."

The shepsky ran to my side. As we started for the house, I heard barking. There was something a little off in the sound. Maybe it had to do with the fact the barking was coming from up in a tree.

Lola had also heard the barking, and stood there with a cocked head.

Trickster, I thought. But that wasn't the only take on ravens. Other cultures believed them to be messengers of the gods, and harbingers of the afterlife. That's not to say ravens are universally beloved. Folklore said that seeing a solitary raven was bad luck, as it signified the news of someone's death.

I spoke to the shadows, whispering Poe's words: "'Deep into that darkness peering, long I stood there wondering, fearing.'"

The abyss didn't speak back, for which I was thankful.

Lola turned her attention to me, restless to get moving.

"Good night, Lenore," I called out.

The enigmatic raven chose not to respond.

I pulled out a bag of ravioli from the freezer. According to the instructions, I could boil, bake, or microwave it. I went with the latter, and added a can of diced tomatoes so I could pretend I was eating something other than processed food. But changing my diet at this stage of my life, I thought, was like closing the barn door after all the animals had escaped.

Lola joined me on the sofa. She carefully avoided eating any tomatoes but was happy to take any ravioli handouts.

When we finished eating, I decided to catch up on the phone messages I'd been ignoring all day. My doctor's office had called twice. Instead of responding to the messages, I decided to call up an article I'd put aside a few days before.

I turned to Lola and asked, "Did you know there's a full-time Ravenmaster working at the Tower of London?"

Lola batted her eyes of blue and brown at me, pretending great interest, hoping for another ravioli.

"Folklore says that should those ravens ever abandon the Tower, that the Crown will fall, and Great Britain with it. Because of that, a Ravenmaster makes sure there are at least six ravens living in the Tower at all times. Silly superstition, right? But even Winston Churchill knew better than to ignore it. When the Tower of London was bombed by the Germans, only one raven survived, so Winston immediately ordered five more replacements."

With no prospect of more ravioli, Lola's eyes had closed. I continued reading the article, but silently. The Tower ravens are officially enlisted as soldiers of the Kingdom. Because of that, they are subject to being discharged for unacceptable conduct, something that has happened on several occasions. Raven George was said to have destroyed five TV antennas in just one week, and for his crimes was posted to the Welsh Mountain Zoo. And ravens Hugine and Jackie, who loved to squabble, were also sent off for "conduct unbecoming to Tower residents."

Despite the perks of their work, which included receiving daily room service from the Ravenmaster, all the Tower ravens have one wing clipped to keep them from flying away. They can still flutter about, but not far. *Like Lenore*, I thought, and wondered how she would fare as a soldier of the Kingdom.

And whether her crapping on my stoop would have gotten her removed from that service for conduct unbecoming.

At half past eight, I heard knocking at the front door. Poe and ravens were still on my mind, so I said to Lola, "'Tis some visitor, tapping at my door, only this and nothing more.'"

Lola knew better, of course, and ran to the door to greet her mom. Janis greeted me by extending a bag. "Two ripe and two green."

"Maybe I should eat one before going to bed. I hear bananas help you sleep."

"If you want to sleep, I've got a strain of indica that will knock you on your ass," Janis said.

"Rain check."

"Yeah, sure."

I tried to hand Janis a few dollars for the bananas, but she waved me off. "I'm sure Lola ate half your dinner."

"She might have snacked a little."

"If she's gassy, I'm going to send her back to you."

We said our goodnights, and I watched Lola and Janis disappear from sight. With dog-sitting duties done, I finally decided to check the phone messages I'd been putting off, including the latest from Dr. Nguyen's office.

"Mr. Lake, this is Amber Hogan, Dr. Nguyen's nurse. The doctor would like you to call his office at your earliest convenience so that we can discuss your treatment options."

Amber paused before starting to speak again, where she sounded more human and less like an automaton.

"We know what a difficult time this must be for you, Mr. Lake, but it's not in your best interests to put off treatment. Dr. Nguyen wants to make sure that you're seen by those specialists as soon as possible. It's our hope you might qualify for a clinical trial, which is why time is of the essence. Please respond to this message through your medical portal, or call me at our office, so we know you're up to date with all of our communications."

Nurse Hogan repeated her name, and gave a number where she could be reached. At least she didn't conclude by telling me to have a good day.

Don't blame the messenger, I reminded myself.

There are some messages that can't be sugarcoated, nor should they be. Because I'd worked as a homicide detective, I knew that better than most. I'd witnessed dozens of families weeping just outside the crime scene tape, and too often it had been my job to intrude on that grief and anger, and ask questions. Most of the bereaved had tolerated my imposing. I could be as tolerant as they had been, and more.

Using my phone, I went online and opened my medical portal. After reading the email sent from Dr. Nguyen's office, I briefly replied to it, and promised I would soon be following up.

CHAPTER ELEVEN

Maybe it was the banana, or just exhaustion, but I slept for more than six hours. Not quite Rip Van Winkle, but good.

Breakfast was peanut butter toast, washed down with tea and lots of honey. Lenore's breakfast offerings were a little more elaborate. I cut up some banana and sprinkled unsalted peanuts over it. The ravens in the Tower might have turned their beaks up at my bird breakfast, but it looked pretty good to me. I took the bowl outside and considered where to leave it. If the food was placed in a clearing, Lenore would have a clear line of sight to any approaching cats or dogs, or a kid with a BB gun.

Her disability would probably require a running start to get airborne. I picked a spot that I thought would be safe, and then retrieved one of the water bowls and placed it next to her banana parfait. That would allow her to eat, drink, and dash.

"Room service," I called out.

I took a few steps back and started scanning the cherry tree. It's around forty feet high and twenty-five feet wide, offering plenty of room for Lenore to hide, especially with its thick foliage. In the midst of all the leaves, I finally picked her out. Lenore's dark eyes were carefully regarding me.

"There you are," I said. "Breakfast is served."

She didn't seem inclined to talk to the help, so I turned around and walked back to the house.

I had been at work for an hour before other detectives from the Cold Case Team began to trickle in. My peers do most of their work off-site. We don't have the ticking clock that most detectives do. By definition, our race is not to the swift.

The intercom rang, and I picked up. "Got a minute for a face to face?" Sergeant Lopez asked.

"On my way," I said.

When I sat down in her office, the wolf on her wall seemed to be staring at me, its expression hungrier than ever.

"Let's talk Silva/Landers," she said. "What's new?"

"I've talked in person with Chloe Landers two times, and will be meeting her for a third time today at noon."

"That sounds promising."

"Maybe," I said.

"But maybe not?"

"Outwardly, she's co-operating, but when I press her for details, I'm hitting a wall. Not only that, her story seems to have changed over the years."

"In what way?"

"Her recounting of how the killer initially presented himself has become increasingly vague, and less certain."

La Loba said, "Couldn't that be just a function of memory? If you asked me what I ate for dinner last night, I'd have to think about it. You're pressing her for memories from twenty-five years ago. Details get fuzzy over time."

"It's more than details getting fuzzy. Her new narrative has this kumbaya vibe. Nowadays, she says it's all about putting the past behind her."

"Is that surprising? I wouldn't want to dwell on being carved up and left for dead."

"Her best friend was murdered. She was maimed. For years, Dr. Landers wanted an eye for an eye. But now it's time to turn the other cheek?"

"Perspectives change. Maybe she decided by not focusing on payback, she could get on with her life more easily."

"Anything's possible," I said, knowing La Loba was playing devil's advocate.

"Your case is about to get some media exposure," she said. "Sonia in media relations called to say that she heard from a *U-T* reporter who's doing a piece on Dr. Landers. The reporter wanted to know if her case was still being actively investigated, and if so, which detective was working it."

"What's the reporter's name?"

La Loba tapped at her computer, and then said, "Audrey Campbell. Know her?"

I shook my head. In the aftermath of the chain-gang homicides, I'd gotten to know several of the *Union-Tribune* reporters, but she hadn't been among them.

"I'm surprised Dr. Landers is co-operating with the reporter," I said.

"Why?"

"If she's really trying to move on with her life, why is she consenting to be interviewed? All she needed to do was say 'No comment' and that would have killed the story."

"Maybe she thinks doing the interview is a public service. I know I'm going to make my kid read the story when it comes out. She's fourteen, and thinks she's immortal."

"Once upon a time, I thought that as well."

As I approached the overlook of the hippo habitat, I didn't see Chloe or the hippos. Since the best hippo watching takes place in the viewing area below, I made my way down to the giant terrarium exhibit.

The zoo's two hippos, a mother and daughter, were pressed up against the glass. A captivated crowd was loving their underwater performance, watching behind the oversized glass pane. The submerged movements almost appeared synchronized, and reminded me of the underwater ballet of dancing hippos in the movie *Fantasia*.

Another film memory came to mind, the Cowardly Lion posturing about after singing, "If I Were King of the Forest." When Dorothy asked him what he'd do if he came face to face with a hippopotamus, the lion responded, "Why I'd trash him from top-to-bottom-us."

I could feel my lips curl into a surprise smile. That memory prompted another, taking me down an unexpected rabbit hole. When I was young, my father liked reciting Ogden Nash poems to me. I think it was his way of trying to find a bridge between the usual father–son disconnect. One of his favorite Nash poems, I recalled, was about the hippopotamus. That much I could remember, but not the words.

As I retraced my steps back upstairs, I tried to channel my father's distant voice, and Nash's prose. Other animals, and their rhymes, came to me, but I couldn't draw the hippo poem out of my hippocampus. A heart attack had claimed my dad when I was a junior in college. I missed him, and his funny poems.

The upper viewing area was still deserted, with no sign of Chloe. I took my place along the rail and waited. The hippo habitat is deep within what the zoo calls The Lost Enclosure. Three trails lead into it, but all require a circuitous route, especially for someone in a wheelchair.

I started going through rhymes for hippo and hippopotamus, first in my head, and then under my breath. Zip-po, flip-po, lip-po, and tip-po didn't cut it.

"Muss, cuss, fuss, discuss," I whispered, hoping to stumble on the right rhyme, but knowing Nash's poems could go in all sorts of unexpected directions.

"I hope I'm not the cause of all that muttering."

Somehow, Chloe had wheeled up undetected.

I turned to her and said, "No," and wondered if I should explain. *What the hell,* I thought. "I was trying to remember Ogden Nash's poem about hippos."

"Since I don't know who Ogden Nash is, I'm afraid I can't be of much help."

"He was a poet best known for his playful rhymes. I guess the only reason I'm familiar with him is that my dad memorized a lot of his poems and liked reciting them to me. He was especially enamored of the silly ones. I was, too."

"Were you and your father close?"

"Yes, but we were both stubborn, which means there were times we spent weeks not talking to one another. He died unexpectedly when I was twenty. When I see certain animals on exhibit, I'm reminded of those Nash poems."

"He must have really loved the poems to memorize them."

"He did, but it helped that they were all quite short. I suppose they were perfect for my poor attention span."

"It says something that he wanted to include you in his fun."

I nodded. "It was like we had our own little club. Over time, I heard the poems often enough that I memorized some of them, even if for the life of me I can't remember that hippo poem. If you'd come along a minute from now, I probably would have resorted to using my phone's search engine to call it up."

"These days that's the default, isn't it? But I wonder what we're missing by taking that shortcut. Sometimes I purposely opt out of immediate gratification and let my mind take me on its own journey when I'm trying to access my memory vault. It's a way of reminding myself that it's the journey, and not the destination."

"Spoken like a philosopher. Or shrink," I said.

"I'd like to think the two aren't mutually exclusive."

For whatever reason, the lock in my head suddenly clicked open, and I triumphantly began my reciting, starting with the words "Behold the hippopotamus!" And then managed to get the next line as well.

"Bravo," she said.

"I think there's another line or two, but they escape me."

"For the moment. And when they do come to you, who knows what else might accompany them?" Chloe removed her racing gloves, wiped her glistening forehead, and said, "I worked up a sweat on the way over."

The June Gloom had lifted, and it was a sunny day.

"Maybe you ought to get some racing goggles along with your racing gloves. All you'd need is something with yellow lenses and frame to complete your Tweety ensemble."

"I could rock that look."

"I have no doubt that you could."

From below, we heard the shrieking and laughter of excited children.

"One of the hippos is probably pooping," I said.

"Better below water than above," Chloe said. "On land, you'd swear a sprinkler head was sending out a brown shower."

"I'm glad I've missed seeing that."

"It's not to be forgotten. Alas."

Trying to remember, trying to forget. We'd gone full circle.

"I understand you've agreed to be interviewed by a reporter from the *U-T*," I said.

"Where did you hear that?"

"A reporter called SDPD's media relations department asking about your case. She also wanted to know who was working it. I was surprised you chose to talk to her."

"Why?"

"You said that you preferred not to dwell on the past."

"That's because I don't want what happened in the past to dictate my future. But to your point, I've already told the reporter that certain topics are off-limits, and that I'll only talk about the present, and not the past. She said the article will recap what happened to me and Dana, but the emphasis of her piece will be on my choosing a career where I'm helping others surmount the difficult circumstances in their own lives."

"Do you talk to your clients with grief and trauma issues about the ordeal you experienced?"

"Not as a rule. It's their issues that need to be discussed. But most are aware of my story."

"The one where the phoenix rises from its ashes?"

My words caused her cheeks to flush. "What gives you the right to judge me?"

"I'm not judging you, but if I hope to make headway in this case, I need to hear the truth."

"And shouldn't I expect the same from you? Shouldn't trust go both ways?"

"I've been up front with you."

"Really? That's hard to believe when you're not even being honest with yourself. You're running away from your own issues, and yet you expect me to trust you with mine?"

I hadn't expected Chloe to call me out. There was more to her story—she had all but admitted that—but it was clear I wasn't going to hear it without earning her trust.

The hippos suddenly appeared in the water below. From our rail, we had the perfect view. In short order, we were joined by a crowd, which put an end to our talking.

Mother and daughter hippo moved around the water, but after a few minutes they disappeared again. Some of the viewers started for the lower observation area, while others moved on to other exhibits. Chloe and I stayed where we were.

Finally, I broke our silence. "I guess I'm still in denial. It seems easier that way."

"It's not, but I think you already know that."

"I'll try and make an appointment with your colleague from the hospice."

She didn't say anything, but waited me out.

"I suppose it wouldn't hurt for me to call today," I said.

That got a somewhat distant nod.

"I'll call now," I said.

"Do you have David's number?"

Chloe had sent me his contact information, but I'd deleted it. That wasn't something I was willing to admit to her, but was pretty sure she was already aware of it.

"Not on me," I said.

She checked her phone contacts and gave me the number. I made the call in her presence. It was a short conversation. When it was over, both of us returned to our viewing. There were a few birds floating about the water's surface, but no hippos.

"You want to go see if the okapis are out?" I asked.

"Lead on," she said.

"I'm afraid I can't stay long."

"Oh?"

"Your guy had a cancellation today, and said he'd be available to see me at two."

"Good timing."

I wondered if that was a coincidence, especially as Chloe didn't look surprised.

"Guess so."

CHAPTER TWELVE

David Chasen's office was located on Second Avenue in an area known as Banker's Hill, so-called because it was once home to San Diego's wealthiest residents. It's still a well-to-do neighborhood, although nowadays those with the deepest pockets have settled in the northern parts of San Diego County.

I was able to find street parking, and walked over to a three-story medical building—5th Avenue was only a few blocks away, an area called Pill Hill by the locals because of its many medical buildings. The practices associated with Pill Hill health care has expanded over the years, but I assumed the main reason for Chasen choosing his office's location was its proximity to San Diego Hospice on 3rd Avenue. I took the stairs rather than an elevator, trudging up to the second floor, and followed a sign directing me to the Behavioral Clinic visitor manager, who handled traffic for all the mental health practitioners in the building. A well-groomed man about my age was sitting behind a desk and smiled as I approached.

"I'll be seeing Dr. Chasen for the first time today and was told I needed to fill out some paperwork."

Maybe it was my imagination, but it appeared the

receptionist's smile faltered for a moment. I was clearly there to see Dr. Death.

"Your name, please?"

"Wyatt Lake."

"I'm Marcus, Mr. Lake. If you have any questions, I'll be glad to help."

He handed me paperwork and a pen, and I got to work on the forms. When I finished, I handed everything back to him. He looked through the pages, seemed satisfied with what I'd done, and paper-clipped them together.

"I'll just need to make a copy of your medical insurance card," Marcus said.

I passed it over, and Marcus scanned the card before handing it back.

"David is in Suite 2C," he said, pointing in the direction of where the office was. "If you'll wait in the sitting room there, it shouldn't be too long before he sees you."

"Thank you."

"Is there a preferred day or time that you'd like for future sessions?" Marcus asked. "David has a very full schedule, but we do our best to accommodate all requests."

"I imagine his clientele turnover leaves lots of gaps in the scheduling."

I regretted the words as soon as I said them. Marcus's smile faltered, and I could see he was at a loss as to how to respond. So much for my vow to not be an asshole.

"If you don't mind, I'll get back to you with the best days and times for me."

Marcus looked fine with cutting short our conversation.

The reception area furniture was sparse, and consisted of two chairs, a love seat, and a coffee table with this month's issues of *Sunset, San Diego* magazine, and *Architectural Digest*. I sat down and gauged the area. It was around twice the size of the container that had held its human cargo of a dozen people. Seeing the space in those terms would have been a strange observation for anyone else, but since working the case, I often saw the world in the dimensions of the mini container, and the boat transporting it.

An average-size shipping container would have been too large and too heavy to be hauled in the panga-like boat carrying the human cargo, whereas the mini container could have been hoisted into the vessel with a standard forklift. And it easily fit in the bed of a half-ton truck.

I was the first detective from Homicide Team II to appear at what had been reported as the crime scene. When I arrived, there was no body, but there was a body part. A Good Samaritan had gone out early that morning to pick up trash on the beach and had come across a woman's size 6 red sneaker wedged in the stones. As the Samaritan pulled it free, she realized there was something odd about her find. The shoe was heavy and waterlogged, but not only from the sand inside it. She was holding the mostly skeletal remains of a decomposed foot.

It's common for trash to wash up on shore; Sunset Cliffs even has the unfortunate nickname of Garbage Beach. There are those who will tell you the name stems from the strong-smelling kelp that washes up on its rocky shore, but most say the term goes back in time to when people used to dump their garbage over the cliffs into the ocean waters.

Traversing those cliffs to the shore has never been easy. Nowadays, there's a rope to help with the climb down the rocks. Luckily for me, the callout to the homicide team occurred while it was low tide. Still, when I arrived on the scene, the clock was ticking. Time and tide wait for no man. I had to act before the area became unworkable.

I took some pictures of the red sneaker, and the Good Samaritan showed me exactly where she found it. We've all heard stories about people finding a message in a bottle. When I first saw the foot in the shoe, I couldn't shake the thought that the universe had delivered a message to me. Years later, I was still trying to decipher the note.

The other shoe dropped, so to speak, four days later. A size 9 man's sneaker washed ashore not far from where the first had landed; inside was another decomposed foot.

There was some initial speculation that the disembodied feet could be the handiwork of a fetish murderer who had dumped the body parts at sea, but the real explanation turned out to be much more pedestrian. San Diego wasn't the first beach to experience the phenomenon of athletic shoes containing severed feet washing ashore. In recent history, dozens of skeletal-filled sneakers have washed ashore in the Pacific Northwest, mostly as a result of deaths at sea. While many of those bodies were never recovered, the footwear still managed to make the journey to land.

These days, athletic shoes are much more buoyant than they used to be. The severed feet that showed up on Garbage Beach weren't the result of a murderer with a butcher's knife, but sea scavengers. Small foragers like to dine on the softer parts of the human body, especially the ligaments and tendons around the ankles. Over time, the feet detach from the body, and coastal currents carry the athletic shoes and their remains to shore.

When the case came to us, "Saint Bill" Brennan was the sergeant at Homicide Team II. Sarge got his nickname because he frequently quoted the Bible. Because of Saint Bill, everyone on our team came to know Revelation 20:13: *And the sea gave up the dead which were in it; and death and hell delivered up the dead which were in them.*

Amen, I thought.

It was up to our team to try to find the location of where death and hell had occurred, and deliver up the bodies of the dead. Scientists from Scripps Institution of Oceanography in La Jolla, and the National Oceanic and Atmospheric Administration, plotted the likely location from where the sneakers had traveled by analyzing tides, currents, and ocean conditions. We sought out our needle—not in a haystack, but a huge sea. The original working theory was that there had to have been some kind of boating accident, or maritime disaster.

That was before we stumbled upon the decomposing bodies of the chain gang inside of their shipping container. It was Davy Jones's locker times twelve.

A door opened, and lost in the horrific memory, I threw up my hands in fright.

A bald fortyish man softly said, "I'm sorry to have startled you."

"Not your fault," I said.

"David Chasen," he said, and walked toward me with an extended hand.

I got to my feet, and we shook hands. "Wyatt Lake."

The two of us sat across from one another, each of us in an easy chair. Apparently, my shrink didn't like a desk between himself and his patients. There was no sofa to lie down on, which was good by me.

He asked, "Before we begin, do you have any questions?"

I shrugged and said, "Being new to therapy, I really don't even know what questions to ask, Dr. Chasen."

"Please call me David," he said. "I'm a licensed clinical social worker, but even if I had a PhD, I'd still go by David. Is it all right if I call you Wyatt?"

"Works for me."

"Have you ever been to a therapist before?"

"Not unless you count a bartender," I said.

That got a smile, but not much of one. "In that case, you should know that it's not uncommon to be apprehensive about the process. Did you experience that?"

I nodded and said, "I find the idea of therapy a bit unsettling."

"What, in particular?"

"I know some Greek philosopher once said, 'Know thyself,' but to me that sounds kind of presumptuous."

"Why's that?"

"I don't know. It just does. I seem to recall that there was some wiseass like me who once said, 'Know thyself? If I knew myself, I'd run away.'"

David said, "Since we're on the subject of Greek philosophers, Socrates said, 'The unexamined life is not worth living.'"

"But what good does it do to be overly introspective?"

"Introspection and awareness aren't the same things. But since it sounds as if you're suspicious of therapy, that begs the question of why you're here."

"There's a part of me that knows therapy could be beneficial for me, but I doubt we'd be having this tête-à-tête if not for Chloe Landers. I've been assigned to her cold case, and I'm trying to gain her co-operation."

David's thick eyebrows, at odds with his bald head, furrowed. "Let me see if I understand this: you're here because you think it will put you in good with Dr. Landers."

"I'm here because Chloe thinks I'm unwilling to confront my medical issues. For her, that raises a trust problem."

"So, you're here reluctantly?"

"I'm not opposed to being here, but it wouldn't my first choice for spending my free time."

"That presents a problem for me, Wyatt. It's been my experience that clients only get out of therapy what they put into it."

"I'll do my best to be open to the process."

"That sounds half-hearted."

"Call it a short-timer's attitude. I'm assuming all your patients are operating under an expiration date."

"Everyone on this planet is, as you characterize it, operating under an expiration date."

"But most people don't buy a carton of milk about to expire."

"You're right in that no one willingly chooses a terminal illness, but that's where we are. If you don't want to be here, and you're not open to therapy, this process won't work."

I backed off a little and said, "I'm sure there will be some benefits to my having a sounding board."

With a sternness that surprised me, he said, "That's not good enough for me. If we're to continue down this path together, you'll need to make a commitment. These sessions can't be some means to another end. Therapy won't succeed if you're doing it for someone else, or for an ulterior motive. That would be a waste of your precious time."

I wasn't expecting tough love, but then again, I wasn't sure what to expect.

"Okay," I said. "Count me in."

"Lip service won't work for me. Just because you're sick, that won't let you off the hook. Abraham Lincoln said the definition of a hypocrite was the boy who murdered his parents, and when he appeared before a judge, pleaded for mercy on account that he was an orphan."

"I've arrested people who've tried using that ploy," I said.

"Then you can understand why it won't fly in this courtroom."

"I'll do my best to comply with your ground rules," I promised.

David nodded.

"I'm wondering if you'll satisfy my curiosity, though," I said. "What made you want to work with dying patients?"

"I believe working with the sick and the dying is my life's calling," he said. "Counseling is actually my second career. For almost ten years, I was an attorney specializing in mediation. I enjoyed the work but found it limiting. It's possible I'd still be practicing law today if not for my mother getting sick. At the time, I felt helpless to do anything to relieve her distress. She needed counseling, and someone other than me to hear her out, but we found that her therapy options were extremely limited.

"As her illness progressed, I came to learn that some discussions are better suited to an outsider than to a family member. There were things my mother needed to say, but was reluctant to discuss with me or my siblings. While looking for a professional to assist her, I realized I could translate many of my mediation skills into becoming a therapist, and assist those who are sick and/or dying."

I found myself nodding, and feeling a little more comfortable.

"That's my long answer," he said. "My short answer is that I was a momma's boy, and I wanted to help people like my mother who needed to talk to someone at life's end."

"Do you like your work?"

"Very much. It's taught me to live in the moment. My husband is much more of a planner than I am, so he probably wishes I wasn't quite so blithe. He says we're at our limit for adopting old rescue cats, but the truth is that neither one of us can say no to a geriatric feline in need."

I told him, "When I worked homicide, I tried to help the pets that were left behind before calling in animal control. It always seemed a small mercy if one of the relatives took the animals in. I know of this one detective in the department who over the years adopted several cats from crime scenes that otherwise would have gone to the shelter. He calls himself the CAT-cher in the die."

David's smile was more polite than amused. "Do you have a pet?"

"Not really, but sometimes it feels like I'm co-parenting the neighbor's dog."

"Dr. Landers mentioned that you aren't married and don't have children."

"True."

"And your parents are no longer alive?"

I nodded. "My father died of a heart attack when I was twenty. I consider him the lucky parent, because his end was quick and pain free, unlike my mother. She lived with osteoarthritis for a decade and died when I was in my early thirties."

"OA killed her?"

"One way or another, it did."

"Explain that."

"She was in chronic pain for a long time. The OA was in her hands, knees, hips and spine. She called her joints the Rice Krispies chorus, you know, snap, crackle, and pop. Over time, she essentially became bedridden. I took care of her as best I could, but she couldn't stand all the limitations the disease forced upon her. One day she decided enough was enough, and took an overdose of pain medication."

"She ended her life?"

"Officially, it was called an accidental overdose. But it wasn't."

"And you were her main caregiver for ten years?"

"There were also home health aides."

"That doesn't sound like an easy situation for a young man."

"I wasn't the one who was sick."

"Still, I imagine that made it difficult for you to have a social life."

I shrugged.

"Do you have any relatives?"

"An uncle and a few aunts. They're out of state, but I usually get Christmas cards from them."

"Any other family in your life?"

"Not blood," I said. "But I do have a godson."

"Are the two of you close?"

I nodded. "And I'm best friends with the boy's father, who's also a detective."

"When I walked out to the waiting room, I startled you. Do you mind telling me what you were thinking about?"

I took a deep breath and said, "A dozen dead people."

His thoughtful brown eyes asked me to continue.

"I worked what the media called the chain-gang homicides."

David nodded, clearly familiar with the case. "You said that's what the media called them. Did you have your own name?"

"I usually think of them as The Twelve, or The Jury."

"Why's that?"

"Twelve victims, twelve on a jury."

"They're judging you?"

"That's how it feels."

"You said you're working the case unofficially?"

"Ever since the Feds took it over."

"You've been unable to put it aside?"

I nodded. "When I do sleep, which seems rarer and rarer these days, I'm haunted by the dozen people who died. I want to give them peace. And me."

"And you can only do that by solving the case?"

"It's the only way I can think of."

"It sounds as if you're setting yourself up for disaster if you're solely basing your self-worth on that."

"Maybe so, but for a long time the case has felt like my reason for existence."

"Obsessions and fixations can feel that way. But why do you think this particular case is so important to you?"

"Twelve people died unnecessarily."

"And I don't mean to downplay the horrific nature of those deaths, but I'm sure in your line of work you saw many terrible things."

"I'm sure it sounds silly given my current circumstances, but drowning has always seemed an awful way to die."

"And what makes you think that?"

"I almost drowned once," I said.

"What happened?"

"I was a freshman in high school, and my best friend, Pete, talked me into going to Black's Beach supposedly to body surf. The truth of the matter is that we both hoped to see some naked women."

Black's Beach is San Diego's only clothing optional beach.

"Anyway, neither one of us was familiar with the surf conditions. There's what's called a submarine canyon offshore that's like a steep-sided valley, and it can play havoc with the swells and currents. That day I got an education in rip currents. As I was being swept out to sea, Pete stayed with me, telling me what to do. If not for him, I would have panicked even more, and not made it back. On the day I saw my first naked woman, I almost died. Afterwards, Pete and I used to laugh about that."

I smiled at the memory, but only momentarily. David must have noticed the abrupt change in my features.

"What is it?" he asked.

"I was thinking about Pete," I said. "He died his senior year of high school. Skateboarding accident. I'm sure he was doing some trick he'd done hundreds of times before, but this time he lost control, and hit his head on a curb."

"You weren't there?"

I shook my head. "I've never been sure if that was a good thing, or a bad thing. But I wish I'd been there for him, like he was for me."

"He saved your life, and you should have saved his?"

"Something like that."

"Do you think your own near-drowning plays into why it's so important for you to solve this particular case?"

I thought about it, and finally ended up shaking my head. "I don't know. When it comes to my having worked that case, it feels like I ran a marathon but couldn't make it to the finish line. Maybe my own baggage kept me from getting there."

"What do you mean?"

"I'm not sure." But I was, and after a few seconds of silence, offered it up.

"This is privileged information, right? The DA can't subpoena your records down the road?"

"It's a confessional vault. What you tell me stays between us. Unless you're planning on harming someone."

"And this confessional vault stays locked after I die?"

"Even then."

"As a cop, I've always played by the rules. But on this case, in the pursuit of trying to get answers, I cut some corners."

"And that bothers you?"

"I was hoping the ends would justify the means."

"Do you want to talk about what you did?"

"Not today," I said. "Maybe down the road."

"Does that mean you'll be committing to future sessions? Because I got the sense you were thinking this session would be a one and done."

No smiles from him. No bonhomie. His bullshit detector was in great working order.

"That did cross my mind, but I'll do my best to make this work. What kind of a commitment are we talking about?"

"Two fifty-minute sessions a week to start with, and we'll see where it goes from there."

"You make it sound as if I'm on probation."

David nodded and said, "That's because you are."

CHAPTER THIRTEEN

David didn't let me leave without assigning homework. I had to make appointments with all my specialists ASAP.

"I'd also like you to read this before our next session," he said, passing me a thin dog-eared paperback titled *Tuesdays with Morrie*. "I'm always looking for copies in used bookstores," he said. "Are you familiar with the book?"

I shook my head.

"It won't take you long to read," he promised. "And there's one last assignment. I'd like you to create a haiku."

"Haiku?" I asked, skeptical.

"Seventeen syllables," David said. "First line five syllables, second line seven, third line five."

"I know what a haiku is. What does it have to do with therapy?"

"I guess you'll find out," he said.

David offered me parting words as I stood to leave. "Know that I will be here for your journey," he said. "I want you to consider me, and this office, your safe haven."

I didn't know it, but that was what I needed to hear. Through a tight throat, I managed to say, "Thanks," and then with a backward wave made a quick exit from his office. Before leaving the building, I stopped to see Marcus, and arranged times to see David.

Once I reached the street, I took my phone off of silent mode and looked at my missed texts and calls. I began listening to my messages, including one from Tommy Boy.

"I got my marching orders, Lago," he said. "Rosa expects you for dinner tonight at six. She's making your favorite: chile rellenos. And if you need a guilt trip for an additional incentive, this morning Joey said he was missing his uncle Y."

When he'd first started talking, Joey had trouble saying "Wyatt." That's how I became Uncle Y.

"See you at six. Come hungry."

Of late, I'd had little interest in food, but the thought of Rosa's cooking reawakened my stomach.

During my drive back to work, I made good on part of my homework: scheduling my medical appointments with the specialists. Until recently, I had never even met my primary physician. Now I had four doctors.

My godson threw the front door open and yelled, "Uncle Y!"

I looked over his head, seemingly in search of something. "Where's little Joey?" I asked. "I got him something."

"I'm Joey," he said.

"Nah, the Joe I know is only this tall." I placed my hand at the height of the boy's neck.

"I grew, Uncle Y."

I put my head down to his level and shook my head. "You can't be my Joe. The Joey I know is a little kid."

"I'm in kindergarten now."

"You're a kindergartner? Wow."

Tommy came up behind his son. "El Padrino is impressed because he flunked kindergarten."

"Really?" asked Joey.

"What your father is saying is called projection, Joey. I'm afraid he was the one who repeated kindergarten. Three times, wasn't it?"

Joe decided to ignore us and direct his attention instead to the wrapped package I was holding. "What did you bring me, Uncle Y?"

"An umbrella," I said, handing him a rectangular package.

"Thank you," he said, trying not to look disappointed.

"Open it," I said.

Without much enthusiasm, Joey tore at the packaging, and then suddenly brightened.

"It's a kite!"

"Since people are always telling your dad to go fly a kite, I thought the two of you could have fun with it."

"You shouldn't have," Tommy said, sounding like he meant it.

Joe began jumping up and down. "Dad, can we fly it now?"

I said, "Yeah, can we, Dad?"

Under his breath, Tommy whispered so that only I could hear, "*Pinche madre.*" Then, he placed a hand on his son's shoulder and said, "It's almost dark, Joey. We don't want to lose the kite on its first flight, so let's wait until the weekend to send her up."

"Aw."

"He's right, buddy," I said. "You'll need to fly it earlier in the day, and find a spot away from trees and power lines."

"All right," Joey said.

Rosa emerged from the kitchen, and the two of us hugged. At just over five feet, she was a foot shorter than her husband. I had always thought her smile looked beatific, and somehow cast its own sublime light.

"I'm glad you could make it, Wyatt," she said. "Since you transferred departments, we don't see enough of you."

I handed her a sunflower bouquet. "I thought about getting roses for a beautiful woman named Rosa, but since you're always a ray of sunshine, I couldn't resist these."

"They're lovely," she said. "I'll go put them in a vase."

Tommy and I adjourned to his backyard for beers. He flipped the cap off a Modelo Negra, handed it to me, and then did the same for himself.

"*Salud*," he said, a toast that meant "health" in Spanish.

"*Salud*," I said.

"And to my tía Consuelo," Tommy added.

When his aunt Consuelo had died, her bequest allowed Tommy to buy his beautiful four-bedroom house in Otay Ranch, an upscale development within the city of Chula Vista.

"Were you surprised that your aunt remembered you?" I asked.

"Not completely," Tommy said. "She was family, and Tía Consuelo and Tío Diego were never able to have kids, thank God. But my sister and I weren't expecting that kind of windfall. When we were kids, my mother used to drop us off at their ranch. We kind of dreaded that, because it was a lot more work than play. They had cornfields and a big garden and a few dozen head of cattle. I remember them not having a TV, and the ranch feeling so remote. Just getting to it meant traveling along a bunch of rutted dirt roads. At the time, no one could imagine Valle de Guadalupe taking off like it did."

Valle de Guadalupe is called Mexico's Napa Valley. The

area isn't far from Tecate, another San Diego County border city. Nowadays, there are more than 200 wineries in the valley.

"I need an Aunt Consuelo," I said, looking around and admiring Tommy's villa.

Rosa appeared on the back porch and called out, "Make sure you offer our guest some chips and guacamole, Tomás."

I turned to him and said, "Why, yes, I'd love a plate, Tomás."

She said, "And I'll be bringing some empanadas out in just a minute, Wyatt."

"*Muchas gracias*, Rosa."

Before going to get my plate, Tommy tilted back his bottle and drained the contents. Then he rose with a grunt and went off to get the food. On his way back, he stopped for two fresh beers. He dropped my plate down on a tiled side table and handed me the beer. We lightly tapped bottles.

"Had a visitor the day before yesterday," I said, keeping my voice low.

"Oh?"

"Loco Luca," I said.

"Asshole," he whispered.

"He brought up Hernández again, and showed me a picture of him standing at a table where El Tipo and his guerrero were seated, a soldier known as Aguijón. Ever hear of him?"

Tommy thought for a moment and shook his head.

From inside the house, a small voice called out, "Uncle Y?"

"Let's talk about this after dinner," Tommy said.

"Yes," I said, speaking both to Tommy and Joey.

I leaned back in my chair and patted my stomach. There had been a Caesar salad with pepitas, a seasoned corn on the cob called elote, and Rosa's famous chile rellenos.

"How do you do it?" I asked her.

"My mother taught me you must cook with love," she said.

"I'm sure love is an important ingredient, but what you do is magic."

"It's actually very simple," Rosa said. "You cook the poblano chiles over a flame, remove their skin, and stuff the peppers with Oaxaca cheese. Then you make your egg batter, fry them, and finish up by drizzling crema over them."

"Are you sure you only have brothers, Rosa?"

"Alas, yes. Growing up with four older brothers was not easy. But Tomás tells me there's a woman in your life. I told him she was welcome to join us tonight, but he said she couldn't make it."

For a moment, I was confused about a girlfriend I knew nothing about, but then remembered Tommy's recent speculation about my dating life. Instead of dispelling the rumor about my imaginary girlfriend, I decided to play along. She could be useful in sparing me from commitments.

"No comment," I said.

Tommy and Rosa gave one another a look. "See," he said.

"Come on, Wyatt," Rosa said.

"I don't want to jinx the relationship," I said.

"Jinx?" she asked.

"*Gafe*," Tommy translated.

"Oh, jinx," Rosa said, and began nodding her head. "That's probably wise. But I don't want you to hide her away from me."

"I won't," I said.

Although I suspected that in a few weeks Tommy would be telling his wife that things hadn't worked out between me and my erstwhile girlfriend.

Rosa stood up and extended a hand toward her son. "Joseph, come with me. Let's leave these two to talk."

"Do I have to?" he said.

"I'll soon be taking the flan out of the oven," she said. "Don't you want to be the first to get some?"

That got Joey to his feet, and mother and son started off.

"Given any thought to having another kid?" I asked.

Tommy raised an index finger to his lip and said, "Shh!" He looked in Rosa's direction to see if she'd heard my remark, but she and Joey were busy with their own conversation.

"Rosa's more than ready," he said.

"You're not?"

"Things are complicated. You know, down south."

A few years ago, Tommy had taken up with a woman who lived in Tijuana, and fathered a girl.

"I thought that was over."

"It was supposed to be. But…"

"But what?"

He looked around, made sure no one was in the area to overhear, and said, "She's pregnant again."

"Shit," I said.

"I can't end things with her until after she has the baby. Once that happens, I'll set something up for her and the kids and end it."

I whispered, "Rosa still doesn't know?"

"I've managed to keep it from her, thank God."

"You're nuts. You could lose Rosa, Joey—everything."

"I know," he said. "I love my family. But I love Ana Sofía as well, and my little jewel Isabella."

I raised a hand his way. "No names," I said. "I've told you before, the less I know, the better."

"My bad."

Tommy blamed his absence from home on work. On one occasion, I became unwittingly involved in his deception. A concerned Rosa called me about a wildfire burning in Chula Vista, and wanted to know if there was any way I could get word to Tommy at his "stakeout." After we finished talking, I'd texted Tommy, given him a heads-up, and warned him he better not ever expect me to be his fucking beard again.

He squeezed my shoulder with one of his big hands. Quintessential Tommy. It was impossible to stay mad at him.

"Ready for another beer?" he asked.

"No," I said. "I'm good for the night."

Tommy was at least two beers ahead of me, but got up to get another. I sighed, worried that my best friend's self-destructive streak was going to end up biting him in the ass. Rosa was the best thing to ever happen to him, whether he knew it or not.

I turned my gaze to the south. Tijuana was only about a dozen miles away, and the city's sea of twinkling lights—more than two million people live in TJ—looked close enough to touch.

And out there among those lights was Tommy's other family.

"Quite a view, huh?" Tommy had returned with his beer.

"Beautiful."

"Like most things, TJ's better seen from afar," he said. "My lady's always talking about how bad the gangs are. That's why I moved her and the little one into a gated community."

"TMI," I warned.

"Right, right." Tommy raised his bottle and downed half of it. "You know things are bad when it seems half of Tijuana's wealthy residents have resettled in eastern Chula Vista. When they cross over to do business in TJ, they drive around in a beater, but here they got their BMWs and Porsches."

"Doesn't Rosa drive a Lexus?"

"Just keeping up with the Rodriguezes," Tommy said. "And we bought it used. A new compact would have set us back almost as much."

He tilted his beer and drained what remained. Then he

looked to the right and the left, making sure we were alone. "What else did that bastard want?"

Tommy was not a fan of Loco Luca, or any of the Internal Affairs detectives.

"It was the usual Calderon song and dance," I said. "He tried pressuring me into admitting that we used Hernández as our snitch. I denied, denied, denied, so he tried to lay a guilt trip on me, saying Hernández got killed because of us."

"*Pendejo*," Tommy swore. "Don't let Loco get into your head. We had nothing to do with Hernández getting whacked. He was playing both sides, and got burned. I doubt anyone was surprised when he got caught with his hand in the till, and that includes Calderon. Especially Calderon. But that's not something he'd tell you."

"He said Hernández was shot with a ghost gun."

"Interesting," Tommy said. "The cartel usually makes public examples of anyone skimming money from them. Staying in the shadows isn't their way. And neither is using a ghost gun."

"That's what I was thinking."

"It doesn't sound right," Tommy said. "And how would Loco even know a ghost gun was used?"

"Maybe he heard it through TJ brass."

"No chance. Tijuana's got the highest per capita homicide rate of anywhere in the world. They're overwhelmed. Just this year, they're looking at two thousand homicides."

Shit. That was even worse than I'd imagined. In an average year, San Diego had between fifty and sixty homicides.

Tommy was shaking his head. "There's no way the TJ cops would go the whole nine yards for a small-time crook. Their investigators are working caseloads of more than a hundred homicides, and their clearance rate is under five percent. And their morgue isn't even fit for the dead. How would they know it was a ghost gun? It's rare for them to even do ballistics tests."

"You think Loco was feeding me a story?"

"It wouldn't surprise me. Loco likes making people paranoid. He's shaking a tree and hoping something falls out."

"What about the Silver Badges Hernández told you about?"

Tommy made a disdainful sound. "I don't even think Hernández believed the stories he was telling. And selling. Why would some secret group called the Silver Badges, or Silver Legion, or whatever it was, be involved with the chain-gang homicides? It was a bullshit story concocted by him to get a payday."

"Probably. But Loco brought up the chain-gang case when we talked. He knows I'm still trying to get answers."

Tommy's brows furrowed. "Why would he even care about that? That's way outside IA's purview. They're supposed to look into police misconduct, not old homicide cases, or a shooting in Mexico."

The patio door opened, and we heard Rosa call out, "Careful!"

We turned our heads and saw Joey walking toward us carrying a tray with two bowls.

"I brought you some flan, Uncle Y," he said. "It's really good!"

"Thanks, buddy," I said, pretending enthusiasm.

CHAPTER FOURTEEN

June Gloom's coastal clouds began to descend over San Diego during my drive home. When I pulled into my driveway, I decided it was too dark, and too late, to check on Lenore.

My talk with Tommy had left me feeling unsettled. He'd always been a player, but I thought things would change after he married Rosa. When he asked me to be padrino to Joey, Tommy promised me he was done with his catting around. At the time, I think he believed what he was saying. Hearing the news about his girlfriend's second pregnancy made me feel like crap. I couldn't excuse his behavior as a fling. Tommy actually had another family. That had to weigh on him, because it sure as hell weighed on me.

As good as Rosa's food had been going down, it was now talking back to me. Worry and rich food aren't a good combination, especially when combined with a terminal illness. I grabbed a can of seltzer water, hoping the carbonation would settle my stomach. Gradually, I felt some relief, but I was still too wound up to sleep. My usual default is TV, but I'd heard the screen's blue light impedes nodding off.

There were books on my to-be-read pile, but none of them were the mind-numbing variety I needed. And if I started going through case notes again, it was likely I'd be up all night.

But there was some paperwork I could do.

I grabbed a pad of paper and a pen. Were haikus titled? I didn't know. I held the pen expectantly, waiting for the ideas to flow. When nothing came to me, I blamed my paralysis analysis on David's not assigning a topic. Having a blank canvas felt overwhelming. Finally, tired of staring at the blank page, I began writing my poem. Five, seven, five, I thought. What was so hard about that? It didn't take long to find out. I tried several opening lines, but there was nothing special about them. No magic.

Start and stop. Words written, and then scratched out.

Did David expect a revelatory haiku? A confession meant to reveal my inner thoughts? Quit dancing, and write my truth. With that resolve, the words came.

> *I work homicides*
> *That's all I know how to do*
> *Would that I knew more.*

Close, but not quite there. Back to the drawing board. I did more scribbling, created my seventeen syllables, and the title *Vaquita*.

> *I mourn their passing*
> *Extinction of a species*
> *My tears do no good.*

Most people didn't know about vaquita, the smallest of the cetaceans. Today, the shy, beautiful porpoises might already be extinct. The only hope for species survival can be found in the

San Diego Zoo's Frozen Zoo, where vaquita cell lines were grown and then stored away in a cold vault. Instead of waving a white flag at the inevitable, scientists at the Frozen Zoo dreamed of Lazarus. The biodiversity bank is the largest repository of its kind, and offers the hope of resurrecting extinct species in the future.

My vaquita haiku brought me a sense of relief, and didn't prove to be the only topic I felt the need to explore. Four spirits had come to Scrooge. I thought Ebeneezer got off easy; a dozen apparitions visit me regularly. The Twelve. That's what I needed to write about, and tried to find the words.

> *Twelve souls call to me*
> *Drowned in an uncaring sea*
> *Only I hear them.*

The final haiku felt right, or maybe after a long day, I was willing to settle. I yawned. It was time to try and sleep. As I crawled into bed, I didn't offer up a prayer, or presume to wish for sweet dreams; it would be enough to not see my jury.

Serenely with the giraffes. Seven syllables. From a distance, I studied Chloe. She was off by herself taking in the Masai giraffes that were munching on the acacia branches in their enclosure.

It would have made a good sketch, had I any artistic ability, but all I could manage was an unfinished haiku. Ever since starting David's assignment, I'd found myself capsulizing my thoughts in haiku form.

As I approached Chloe, my pulse quickened, a physical

reaction that surprised me. What had changed that I now looked forward to spending time with her? I opened my mouth to call out a greeting, but suddenly feared intruding. We hadn't made arrangements to meet, and I didn't want to impose. I turned around but didn't get far.

"Wyatt?"

I felt the heat on my face and hoped it didn't appear flushed. Act innocent, and pretend our meeting was happenstance? Or risk looking like a stalker?

"Hey," I said, turning toward her. Confess, I decided. "You looked so serene I didn't want to disturb you."

"Seeing giraffes does that to me. They're good for the soul, and give me vicarious thrills."

"You'll need to explain that," I said.

"Just look at their eyelashes," she explained. "And I'd kill for their long legs."

She smiled, and I smiled back.

"How'd you find me?" she asked.

"I asked the staff if they'd seen you. One keeper remembered you passing her on the way to the Urban Jungle. If I'm intruding now, just say the word, and I'll mosey away."

"No need to *mosey*," Chloe said. "I've always found that such a funny word."

"Not as funny as what you call a group of giraffes."

Without hesitation, she said, "Towers."

"Smarty pants."

Both of us turned our attention to the zoo's towers: the six Masai giraffe in the enclosure.

Aloud, I said, "I lift up my neck."

Chloe turned to me. "And?"

"I decided that should be the first line of my giraffe haiku," I said. "Five syllables. David gave me homework of writing a haiku."

"And you're going to write about giraffes?"

I shook my head and said, "I was just doing it as a mental exercise. Last night I wrote my haiku. Actually, I wrote four of them."

"You must have enjoyed the assignment."

"Not at first, but now I'm finding it hard to look at anything without thinking about a haiku."

"What's the rest of your giraffe haiku?"

"I came up with a second line while watching you observe them: 'serenely with the giraffes.'"

"I like that," she said. "What's the last line?"

"Still to be determined."

"If I was given your assignment, I think I'd start with the last line first to have a good sense of where I was going."

"Do you have your patients do haiku?"

"No," she said. "And it's not something I've heard of other therapists doing, but seeing as how it inspired you, it's something I might consider."

We turned our attention back to the giraffes, and I thought we'd exhausted the topic of haikus when Chloe announced, "Heads reaching for clouds."

"Excuse me?"

"The closing line for your giraffe haiku."

"Heads reaching for clouds," I said.

"Now that I hear it aloud, I'm having doubts," Chloe said. "It doesn't quite capture the sense of awe I get watching them."

"Doesn't 'heads reaching for clouds' say that?"

"Maybe, but I'll probably perseverate all day trying to improve on it."

"Perseverate?"

"It's a word mental health professionals love to use. Basically, it means a repetitive action or thought."

"I don't want you to perseverate," I said, test-driving the word. "Maybe you should just write your own giraffe haiku."

After a moment's thought, she said, "Feeding a giraffe. There's my opening line."

"That was fast."

"Have you ever fed one?" I shook my head and she said, "You're missing out. It's incredible. They have twenty-inch tongues."

"Sounds like you have your second line," I said, and we both laughed.

We went back to watching the giraffes eat, and I couldn't help but focus on their snaking tongues.

"I doubt you sought me out to discuss poetry," she said.

"I didn't, but maybe I should have. I guess I wanted to thank you for helping me get an appointment with David. In addition to having me write a haiku, he also insisted on my making appointments with all my specialists."

"So, what you're telling me is that you made good on your promise, and it's time for me to do the same."

"You did say something about trust, and quid pro quo."

She nodded, and said, "You're right. And you're right, I haven't been able to put what happened in the past behind me."

"It would have been hard for even a saint to do that."

"And I'm far from that," she said. "The truth is, I've had a private investigator working my case for the past two years."

"He's been looking for Stu?"

"She has."

"Has she turned anything up?"

"I think it would be best if you asked her that yourself. I'll call her later today and find out if she'll talk to you. But I should warn you that she's not a fan of local law enforcement."

"Is there a reason for that?"

"A number of reasons, I'm told, but that's something best heard from her."

"What kept you from telling me you have a PI working the case?"

"That's a good question," she said.

"Do you have a good answer?"

"I do, but not one I want to share at this time."

CHAPTER FIFTEEN

Aloha and I were the only ones at our cubicles. He was working a fatal hit-and-run case that had happened eight years ago. He'd been on it for months, cultivating one contact in particular.

"You know you'll feel a lot better doing the right thing, Ana. Imagine if you were the mother, and that was your kid run down in the street. Wouldn't you want justice?"

Aloha waited out her response. "You might be right about him being a nice guy, Ana, but he did drive off and leave that poor kid to die. That's not right, and you know it."

Once again, Aloha heard her out. "We know he did it, but we need your help to finish building our case. Are you a religious woman? Do you believe in God?"

When she concurred, he said, "Then clearly you know right and wrong. Do me a favor. Talk to your priest, and ask him what you should do. I'm thinking he's going to tell you to get right with God."

He listened to her response and said, "Okay, that sounds good. I appreciate you talking with me, Ana. I'll call you again soon. Bye-bye."

Aloha hung up and looked at me. "I've almost got her to the finish line. It's been inch by fucking inch."

"Isn't it always?"

"Her boyfriend was driving her car and claimed he hit a fire hydrant. He promised to get the body work done, but somehow her car ended up in a chop shop. That's when he proposed to Ana, and got her to report the car as stolen. Fast-forward to now. The marriage never happened, and our driver's taken up with an old flame who lives a few blocks from where the hit-and-run happened. Ana's now thinking he was probably at her place the night the accident happened."

"Sometimes justice is a long time coming," I said.

"Sometimes there's justice, and sometimes there's just us."

That was a line cops had been using for a long time.

Aloha said, "In our line of work, crooks, drugs, druggies, and dumbasses equal job security."

My cell phone rang, and an unfamiliar number came up. I picked up anyway. "Lake."

"Dr. Landers says you want to talk to me," a woman said. "I told her that didn't sound like a good idea."

"You're the PI?"

"No shit, Sherlock."

"What's your name?"

"Your colleagues usually referred to me as Bobbit. But my real name is Penelope Hill, formerly Penny Hughes."

Penny Hughes was a name I knew, as did most San Diegans.

"Do you still want to talk to me?" she asked. "Or should I tell Dr. Landers that we both decided not to waste our time?"

"Let's talk now, if that works for you."

"It doesn't," she said. "I'll need to see the whites of your eyes. Let's meet in one hour at Tuna Harbor Park at the statue of the groper and the nurse. Don't be late."

"I'll be there."

The official name of the "groper" statue is *Unconditional Surrender*, but to most it's the Kissing Statue. The twenty-five-foot-high sculpture of a sailor kissing a nurse was based on Alfred Eisenstaedt's iconic photo taken in Times Square on VJ Day.

Tuna Harbor Park was about a mile from my office, but rather than search for an elusive parking space, I decided to take the San Diego Trolley there. Before leaving, though, I decided to acquaint myself with the former Penny Hughes.

Her trial had been a cause célèbre, a he said, she said slugfest that pitted husband against wife, but what went on in the courtroom didn't compare to what had transpired outside of it. Hill's phone ID was an acknowledgment of Lorena Bobbitt. At the time of her arrest for attempted murder, it was reported that Penny had tried to emasculate her husband, as Lorena Bobbitt had once done.

The case provoked a media frenzy, as well as a slew of jokes. During the court proceedings, every call-in radio program in town referenced how Penny's lawyer seemed to enjoy cutting off her husband's testimony. Late-night talk shows also got in on the act, with one comedian saying, "The reason Penny wasn't found guilty is that the evidence wouldn't stand up in court."

Five years had passed since the trial. I was surprised it had been that long, and thought of Dr. Seuss's line about time passing so quickly, and how "it's night before it's afternoon." Time seemed that way now. Seuss, aka Theodor Geisel, had lived most of his adult life in nearby La Jolla.

Inside and outside the courtroom, both husband and wife had tried to portray themselves as the wronged victim. Bradley Hughes claimed his wife had become unhinged and histrionic and had attacked him with a kitchen knife, an encounter that left him with severed genitals.

Penny told a very different story. She alleged Bradley had

raped her, something she said he'd done many times before. She insisted the sex on the night in question was nonconsensual; he said it was. Penny also claimed that for years she'd been a frequent victim of her husband's physical, sexual, and psychological abuse, which had left her depressed and suicidal.

According to Penny, she was so traumatized after her husband's sexual assault that it was a struggle for her to even get out of bed. Penny went to the kitchen, pulled a chef's knife from its block, and then took a seat at the breakfast table. While she claimed to be deep in thought, she said her husband crept up from behind and attacked her. Penny said he slammed her head on the table and then threw her to the ground where he began kicking her viciously in the ribs. According to her testimony, she screamed for him to stop, but instead of deterring him, he grew aroused by the beating. Naked, he stood over her and demanded that they "do it." As he lowered himself toward her, Penny claimed she acted without thinking, grabbing the knife on the floor and swinging it upward. The blade cut his testicles.

Bradley Hughes had a different version of events. He claimed he was asleep in the bedroom when his wife came at him cursing, and waving a knife. After managing to throw her aside, he ran to the living room and said he was trying to escape when he stumbled over a pile of laundry and fell to the ground. As he tried getting up, he said his wife brandished the knife and screamed, "I'm going to make you a gelding!"

That was the most repeated line from the trial. Depending on the teller, it was often accompanied by horse sound effects.

I continued to scroll through the stories. None of them were recent, and my search for what happened to Penny Hughes after she received a not-guilty verdict didn't yield any results. Penelope Hill's name did come up when I conducted a private investigator license search with the California Department of

Consumer Affairs. State records indicated Penelope had been a practicing PI for the past two years.

As the doors to my trolley opened at the Santa Fe Depot, I took off at a trot. Normally, it's a five-minute leisurely walk to Tuna Harbor Park and the Kissing Statue, but since I was running late, I did it in half that time. I was breathing hard when I reached my destination.

There were maybe a dozen people milling about, but I didn't see Penelope among them. My mistake was that I was looking for someone who resembled the notorious Penny Hughes. I scanned the faces a second time and saw a woman frowning at me.

I approached her and said, "Penny?"

Her frown deepened. "Penelope."

"Sorry."

At the time of her arrest, Penny Hughes had been a plus-sized woman with long blonde hair. Penelope Hill had short brown hair, and the figure of someone who was serious about her physical training. She was wearing the kind of athletic garb that wasn't for show, but for go.

"Can you talk and chew gum?" she asked. "Or do we need to sit for you to input notes into your electronic notebook?"

"Walking and talking works for me, seeing as I don't even have an electronic notebook."

She said, "Just so you know, I'm taping our conversation. I don't trust cops."

"Record away."

She started walking without looking back; I hurried to catch up.

"For the record, I'm here voluntarily," she said. "That means I won't respond to questions I don't feel like answering."

"Fine," I said. "How should I address you?"

"Anything but Penny, bitch, or cunt works."

"How do you know Dr. Landers?"

"She was my therapist."

"For how long?"

"I first started seeing her before the trial."

"And when did you stop seeing her?"

"Around a year after the trial," she said, and then asked, "Were you late because you were reading up on me?"

"I thought I made it on time."

"You were five minutes late. Admittedly, for a cop, that's good. The detectives who worked my case were chronically late, or prone to cancelling interviews at the last minute. That was their way of screwing with me."

I had a passing familiarity with the detectives she was speaking about. They were not SDPD's best.

"I'm sorry I was late. And yes, I was reading up on you."

"Find anything interesting?"

"I think what interested me most was how you managed to drop off the radar after your trial. And going from being an insurance customer service representative to a private investigator was also surprising."

"After my arrest, I was fired from my insurance job. That was probably the best thing that ever happened to me. The only reason I was working that job is that my former rapist husband used my employment as his personal ATM."

"How did you select Dr. Landers as your therapist?"

"Her specialty is trauma therapy, and I was in desperate need of her services."

"But now you work for her as a PI?"

"Only in an unofficial capacity."

"But you *have* been working her case?"

"I've made some inquiries."

"What am I missing here?"

"Sounds like lots," she said.

"Then why don't you bring me up to speed?"

"What you didn't read in the media accounts was just how debilitated I was after years of abuse. I could barely function after my arrest, and since what little money I had was going to my lawyers, Dr. Landers took me on as a pro bono patient. When we started our sessions, I was basically catatonic. With patience and kindness, she helped me find my way. That made all the difference during my trial. She helped me find my voice, and come to the realization that for too long I'd been a victim. I was fortunate the jury believed me."

I nodded, but said nothing. My silence seemed to amuse her.

"In the court of public opinion, I know most men will always think I'm guilty," she said. "SDPD, and the opposing lawyers, assassinated my character, and spun the story that I was a witch with a knife. The truth is that after being raped that night, I went and got a knife to kill myself. The only reason I didn't succeed is that I was so completely drained I couldn't even move. As I sat trying to work up the energy to commit suicide, it already felt as if I was dead. If my rapist husband had come along five or ten minutes later than he did, he would have discovered me bleeding out."

"But you found the will to live when he attacked you?"

"No," she said. "It was only after working with Dr. Landers that I found the will to live. That night, I reacted out of instinct. Something in me refused to get raped for a second time in one evening. I swung the knife blindly."

"You didn't scream, 'I'm going to make you a gelding'?"

She offered up a derisive laugh. "I wish I had. To my thinking, it's better to be a femme fatale than a victim. As I tried to tell the police, my husband wouldn't have sustained his injuries if he hadn't tried to violate me again. And despite what the media reported, his wounds were mostly superficial. His penis remained intact, which I think is a shame. In my mind, castration is an appropriate response to rape."

"I've often thought the same thing," I said.

She pulled up short, coming to a stop to stare at me. "Are you just saying that?"

I shook my head.

Neither one of us said anything for a minute. Each of us retreated into the scenery around us. June Gloom had taken a day off, and it was a postcard-perfect day in San Diego. I found myself looking across the water to the USS Midway Museum. The converted naval aircraft carrier is a popular tourist spot. During the almost half century it was commissioned, 200,000 sailors called the ship home, but for the past twenty years it's been a floating museum.

Penelope followed my gaze. "Did you serve in the military?"

I shook my head.

"For a long time, the Navy was a sacred cow in this town," she said. "It was untouchable, and had an outsized influence on our community."

"Do you think Dr. Landers's attacker was associated with the military?" I asked.

"I wouldn't be surprised if that was the case," she said.

"Based on what?"

"For one, the numbers would suggest that likelihood. The Naval Training Center was a huge complex back in the day, with more than 130,000 uniformed personnel assigned to it.

And Dr. Landers gauged the age of her attacker as being in his mid-twenties, which also lends credence to that theory. There was also the proximity of NTC to the sports arena."

"Dr. Landers said her attacker had long hair."

"There were 30,000 civilians working on base who weren't subject to the Navy's grooming standards. But that's not to say the attack couldn't have been carried out by someone who was active duty. A high and tight haircut could be disguised by someone wearing a wig. Off-base, lots of sailors had long hair, courtesy of wigs purchased right at the base PX."

"Did you run this theory by Dr. Landers?"

"That's not something I feel inclined to answer. If you want to know what she thinks, you'll have to ask her."

"Has the Navy assisted you in your inquiries?"

"I don't have the kind of badge that you do, so that's limited what I've been able to find out. And the sheer numbers of all the active-duty personnel assigned to NTC have made it all but impossible for me to get much traction."

"If you think SDPD dropped the ball, it didn't," I said. "Nor did the Navy put any kind of kibosh on our investigation. Detectives spent countless hours at NTC conducting interviews, and checking base records. It wasn't for lack of effort that no arrests were made."

"If you say so," she said, clearly doubting that.

"Is that why Dr. Landers hired you? Does she really think SDPD sandbagged the investigation?"

"As I've already told you, I am not employed by Dr. Landers. I owe her a debt for the years of therapy that she provided me at no charge."

"But she asked you to look into her case?"

"That's another question you'll need to take up with her. She practices patient–client confidentiality. So do I."

"You don't advertise," I said. "How do clients find you?"

"Word of mouth, mostly," she said. "Almost all of my clients are women who have been abused in one form or another by men. I advocate for them. When I go up against their abusers, I make sure those assholes know about my history. Normally, that's not something I advertise, but for them, I find it useful to be known as a castrating bitch."

"Have you come up with any suspects in the Silva/Landers investigation?"

"I continue to look at persons of interest."

"Any thoughts as to why Dr. Landers initially engaged in misdirection when I interviewed her?"

"What misdirection are you referring to?"

"She tried to tell me she was no longer interested in finding the identity of her attacker, and the man who murdered her best friend. Your ongoing investigation proves otherwise."

Penelope stared at me without answering.

"No comment?" I asked.

"I can't speak for Dr. Landers, but as for me, I sure as hell got sick of dealing with incompetent and corrupt cops. And I only had to put up with your kind for a year or two, not a quarter of a century."

"Since both of you distrust the police, what would you do if you discovered who the killer is?"

"If that happens, we'll just have to see," she said. "Anyway, I gotta run. I need to get to another appointment."

"I'd like to look through your case notes," I said.

"Unless Dr. Landers compels me, that's not going to happen."

"Why not?"

"I've learned less is more when it comes to your department."

Penelope pointedly inserted earbuds into her ears, forestalling any more questions. Then she lifted up one knee to her chest, and then the other, tapped a few times on her Fitbit, and took off at a run.

I watched her strong, confident strides until she passed out of sight, and decided to walk the mile and a half back to headquarters.

CHAPTER SIXTEEN

Aloha was gone by the time I returned, and Sergeant Lopez's office was dark. With no one around, I could make phone calls without anyone overhearing.

It had been some time since I'd talked to Marvin "Bad News" Barry, but I wasn't surprised to hear him begin our conversation by saying, "I hope you're not calling to whine after all this time. Like I explained to you and your compadres at the time, my job title was district attorney investigator."

"But didn't your badge say SDPD?"

"I was still reporting to the DA's Bureau of Investigation office."

"You should have played for our team, and not been a ringer."

"The Legal Eagles made me a much better offer."

Every year, SDPD and the DA's office square off in a basketball game for hoops bragging rights. A decade ago, I'd been just good enough to play for the cops. Our hopes for winning the game were dashed when Bad News decided to throw in his lot with the lawyers.

At the time, Marvin could still slam, and he was faster and

more skilled than anyone on our side. The lawyers had played a zone, putting Bad News in the middle of the key. After being on the wrong end of a few of his monster blocks, our guards stopped taking it to the hole. By halftime we were down by a dozen, and it went downhill after that.

"I heard karma got you for playing against us," I said.

Just a week after our game, Marvin had ruptured his Achilles.

"You want some cheese with that whine?" he asked. "And speaking of wine, you guys showed real class sending me that half-empty bottle of Two Buck Chuck along with that get well card displaying a horse's ass."

"It was the least we could do."

"Yeah, it really was."

"We all contributed to your wine," I said. "I hope you didn't drink any of it."

"I had the HAZMAT team remove it."

"I hear you haven't been plaguing our team of late."

"A few years after the Achilles tear, I blew out my ACL," he said. "That's when I hung up my sneakers. What about you?"

"I retired from the game as well, but I can't blame injuries. Age and ineptitude did me in."

"No one beats Father Time."

"He's undefeated," I agreed. "Anyway, I didn't only call to bust your balls. There was a situation that happened down in Mexico that I'm trying to get some information on, and I remembered that the DA's office has an investigator who works full-time as a liaison with Mexican law enforcement."

"Ricky Cortez," Marvin said without hesitation. "Enrique is essentially our office's ambassador to Mexico. He interfaces with liaisons from CHP, DEA, and the FBI."

"Interfaces?" I said, pretending to be impressed. "Maybe you played for the right team, after all."

"I'll try and use one-syllable words so you can follow."

"Appreciate it," I said. "So, Cortez knows all the players in TJ?"

"He's your guy. Our office is always going after scumbags who've fled south to avoid prosecution, and since we're dependent on Mexico's co-operation to get them back, Ricky's always traveling to TJ and Ensenada for meetings. Word is that he's got the biggest expense account in our office. Every month he takes the gringo hunters out to dinner."

"Gringo hunters?"

"It's what we call the Mexican police squad that tracks down and arrests American criminals in Mexico."

Since American law enforcement can't operate in Mexico, we're reliant on a little help from our friends. Extradition has never been an automatic thing, though. In the past, the Mexican authorities were known to turn a blind eye to American fugitives, especially those with the means to bribe them.

"How does the extradition process work?" I asked. "Do the gringo hunters serve arrest warrants?"

"It's simpler than that," Bad News said. "They just deport them for violating Mexican immigration law, and once they cross the border, they're all ours."

Fifteen minutes later, Enrique Cortez called. "Thanks for getting back to me so quickly," I said.

"Not a problem," he said. "I would have called sooner if Bad News hadn't spent ten minutes telling me how he single-handedly took down your team in the Copper tournament."

"I wish I could say he was a liar. Anyway, Marvin says you're the Tijuana brahma, and could direct me to someone who'd know about a homicide that took place in Tijuana about eighteen months ago."

"High profile?"

"Just the opposite. He was a low-level player who was gunned down."

Over the phone, I heard Cortez sigh. "That might be tough just because of the numbers. With TJ being a war zone between vying gangs, some days their turf wars are so bad the authorities have to deal with ten, twelve bodies. Very few of those deaths get investigated."

"You'd think those body counts would make the local news."

"That would impact the tourist trade, which is not what Mexican officials want. Stories of violence are suppressed. They don't want to let that cat out of the bag."

I said, "It wasn't a cat in a bag that was left for Tijuana's police chief."

"It sure wasn't."

A few years ago, Tijuana's new police chief was greeted on his first day of the job with a sealed bag and a note. Inside the bag was a decapitated head, along with greetings from one of the cartels.

"So, what can you tell me about your homicide?" he asked.

"Very little, I'm afraid. The shooting interests me because it might tie in to a bigger case I'm working. From what I know, the vic was associated with the Sinaloa Cartel, and did some running for El Tipo."

"What's your vic's name?"

"Daniel Hernández," I said.

I heard faint sounds of a pen being applied to paper. "Any idea how old he was?"

"Early twenties."

"When was he shot?"

"The December before last."

I was reluctant to mention that Hernández had been shot with a ghost gun for fear of the information getting back to Calderon. If possible, I wanted my investigation to stay in the shadows.

"Do you know where in TJ the homicide occurred?"

"Afraid not."

"If there was an investigation, it would have been conducted by the *judiciales*," Cortez said. "The judiciales are their detectives, and work for the prosecutor's office. But since this sounds like a low-level killing, it was likely handled by Tijuana's Policia Municipal. I regularly have lunch with one of their *jefes*, an assistant police chief named Domingo Sanchez. If you want, I can text him with your contact information and tell him you're looking for any information they have on Hernández."

"How's his English?"

"He speaks it just fine when it suits him."

"Is he trustworthy?"

"Off the record, I'd say Sanchez is probably more honest than most in a corrupt police force, but I'm doing my grading on a sliding, slippery scale. A few months ago, four of his officers were caught on film hanging a man upside down by his feet. The cops claimed he was a criminal. That might be true, but it doesn't explain the same guy turning up dead a few days later."

"What happened to the cops?"

"A month's suspension, but they're now back on the job."

At home, I made a tuna sandwich and took a preemptive sleeping pill. Normally, I hate how sleeping pills make me feel the next day, but I was desperate to be spared from my nightmare jury of the drowned.

My alarm awakened me at seven. I'd avoided being judged

by the dead, but the sleeping pill made me feel like a zombie. I microwaved some instant coffee and poured in a lot of sugar to make it drinkable. There was no pleasure in drinking my brew, just the hope of caffeine giving me a boost. Breakfast was half a banana, but it was a struggle getting it down.

After mashing up the rest of the banana and adding it to some dry food I keep for Lola, I took the food out front.

An unkindness of ravens.

That's how humans describe gatherings of ravens, along with treachery of ravens, conspiracy of ravens, and rave of ravens.

I looked for Lenore in the Catalina cherry tree, studying the small openings in the foliage, but she wasn't to be seen. The tree was native to Southern California, but anyone hoping to use the cherries in a pie would be sorely disappointed, seeing as they consist of big stones and little else. Birds aren't as picky as humans, though, eating the cherries and then dispersing the pits in their droppings.

The food I'd previously left Lenore was gone. Whether she had gotten it, or another critter had dined, I couldn't be sure. To improve the chances of her getting the food, I decided to leave the banana bowl in a crook of a branch.

"Lola! Lola!"

Janis's voice alerted me to the shepsky streaking my way. As I bent down and collected dog kisses, a wiggling Lola carried on an excited conversation with me. Huskies like to talk.

A coughing Janis, wearing a bathrobe and slippers, joined us. She said, "Excuse the outfit, but this one conned me that she had to go so she could throw herself at you. Hussy," she added, and began coughing again.

"Maybe you should have that cough looked at," I said.

"I hate going to the doctor."

I found myself nodding, thinking of my own doctors' appointments scheduled later that day.

Lola tried getting to the bowl I was holding. "Not for you, Lola," I said.

"You feeding that crow again?" Janis asked.

"That was the plan."

"He gives me the willies," she said. "I took Lola out yesterday afternoon and heard this muttering. I'm looking for where the sound's coming from when I heard this evil laugh. I'm talking *muwhahaha*, but worse. It scared me shitless, when I suddenly realized it had to be the crow. I would have thrown a rock at that bastard, but he stayed out of sight."

I did my best not to smile. "I'm sure that was scary, but it's not unheard of for ravens to talk. Believe it or not, they're in the songbird family. Just go to YouTube and you can find videos of them speaking. They're quite the mimics."

"I'll bet that snoop's listening now."

"I'm sure you're right. With her bad wing, she's a captive, and to survive, she needs to be aware of what's going on around her."

"Peeping Tom," Janis muttered.

"Ravens are observant," I agreed. "In Norse mythology, Odin had two ravens that flew around the world, and returned to tell him stories of what they'd seen."

"And they probably shat on people everywhere they flew."

Laughing, I said, "I don't remember reading that account."

Janis caught sight of the contents of the banana bowl. "You're feeding him one of your bananas?"

"Just a little bit of what I couldn't finish this morning."

She offered up a disapproving "Hmm," then seemed to think better of it. "I guess it's not right to let him starve, but I've never been a big fan of birds. Word of advice: don't ever watch Hitchcock's *The Birds* if you're stoned."

"I'll try to remember that."

"Say goodbye to your boyfriend, Lola. Time to go home."

Instead of complying, Lola stayed with me. When Janis reached her yard, she looked back, placed four fingers in her mouth, and whistled. As Lola went running to her, another noise filled the air—the sound of a loud wet cough.

Janis made a hand gesture of horns to ward off the evil eye.

"Damn bird," she said, coughing.

Another cough came from on high, a perfect duplication of Janis's hack.

Without turning around from her retreat, Janis raised her arm and gave the bird to the bird.

CHAPTER SEVENTEEN

I spent the morning working from my cubicle while hoping to hear from the TJ Comandante, but that didn't happen before I had to leave for the first of my medical appointments.

Although Daniel Hernández had been Tommy's and my unofficial CI, I'd had little contact with him. Hernández's English was just a bit better than my Spanish, so it had only made sense for him to communicate through Tommy.

Neither Tommy nor I had ever looked into Hernández's death. It was easy to believe if you live by the sword, you die by it, but Calderon's saying he'd been shot with a ghost gun made me want to take a closer look into his death. Hernández's talk of the "silver badges" also needed further investigation. Was it possible that Hernández's asking about the chain-gang homicides *had* gotten him killed?

My phone alarm went off, telling me it was time to leave for my first doctor's appointment of the day.

The Grim Reaper, I learned, doesn't only wear a black robe. Instead of wearing a cowl, Dr. Levin had on a white lab coat, and he wasn't holding a scythe but a tablet. He had short gray hair, was about sixty, and must have learned in his years as an oncologist that it was better to not sugarcoat his message.

"You have stage IV cancer," he said. "What that means is your cancer has metastasized to other parts of your body."

There was no stage V. There was only the exit stage.

"I'm afraid your tests rule out any possibility of our attempting a pancreaticoduodenectomy," he said.

"English," I said.

"A pancreaticoduodenectomy is often referred to as a Whipple procedure, which is a fairly complex operation that involves removing the head of the pancreas, part of the small intestine, the gallbladder, and portions of the bile duct and lymph nodes. Sometimes it's also necessary to remove parts of the stomach and intestines."

"But you're not recommending this Whipple thing?"

"It's not a viable option."

"Thank heaven for small mercies," I said.

"I don't think you're following."

"I get it," I said. "My cancer is too far gone for you to slice and dice me."

"That's right."

"So, what's next?"

"I'd like to start you on a round of chemotherapy, and then afterward consider combining that with radiation therapy."

"What's the point, given that we know the ultimate outcome?"

"The treatment could buy you time."

"Could? If I'm going to lose my hair, and feel even more shitty than I already do, I'll need more of a guarantee than I *could* live longer."

"Studies have shown that patients have an extended mortality when they pursue such a course of treatment."

"How much longer?"

"Perhaps a year."

"I'll need to think about it. Any other options?"

"There's immunotherapy, but the response rate is low. I'd also like to start you on several drugs."

"Give me a list of those drugs and I'll see if I'm interested in taking them. I don't want to look and feel like a zombie in the time I've got left."

"I understand your reluctance, but there aren't any great solutions or alternatives," he said. "Since your gastroenterologist will be in charge of your day-to-day case management, she'll also have input into the drugs we'll be prescribing. You'll be seeing Dr. Kumar later today, right?"

I nodded.

"She'll probably suggest an endoscopic ultrasound."

"Which is what?"

"She'll put a tube down your esophagus and take pictures of your pancreas to give us a better look at the mass, and a baseline of where we're working from."

I shook my head and said, "Pass. If you need a picture of my mass, just use my license photo. It looks just like a tumor."

"Um," he said, having trouble responding.

"Like they say, dying is easy. Comedy is hard."

My oncologist's posture suddenly relaxed. I wasn't a threat, and probably wasn't crazy. Just a little warped. He offered a small smile and said, "Don't quit your day job."

I nodded and said, "Tough room."

"None tougher," Dr. Levin agreed.

My cell phone began ringing as I approached my car in the hospital parking lot. The display said the call was originating from Mexico.

"This is Wyatt Lake."

A formal, accented voice said, "This is Domingo Sanchez of the Tijuana Policia Municipal. Enrique Cortez texted me saying you wished to discuss the homicide of Daniel Hernández."

"That's right, Commander. Thank you so much for calling me. Please hold for a moment."

Luckily, I wasn't far from my car. I ran to it, jumped into the driver's seat, and pulled out a pad and pen.

"Thank you," I said, doing my best to not sound breathless. "Hernández's name recently surfaced in a case I'm working, and I wondered if you had a file on him, or could tell me anything about his death."

"And what case is it that you're working?" Sanchez asked.

I had hoped to finesse the conversation without revealing anything of import. That wasn't going to happen.

"The chain-gang homicides," I said.

"Hmm," he said, sounding skeptical. "I thought your federal government was in charge of that investigation."

"They are, but I was on the homicide team originally assigned to that case and continue to work it unofficially."

"Hmm." The sound came across as even more mistrustful. "And what connection have you found between Daniel Hernández's death and the chain-gang homicides?"

"Nothing specific, but I was told his death might not have been as straightforward as originally thought."

"Hmm."

This time I didn't react to his skeptical note. After a few moments, he spoke.

"And what about his death was suspicious?" he asked.

I responded with a question of my own. "Do you know if an autopsy was performed on Hernández?"

"There was no autopsy. The report I have says he was buried in a *fosa común*, which means…"

He paused, trying to come up with the translation.

"Pauper's grave?" I suggested.

"We call it a common grave," he said. "He was buried in the Municipal Pantheon 13 Cemetery along with several others."

"Does that mean no one claimed his body?"

"Correct."

"Where was the body found?"

"In eastern Tijuana on a dirt road."

"I was told that El Tipo had him killed for skimming."

"There was that speculation, but who knows? As we like to say, *cristal* takes no prisoners."

Cristal was the Spanish word for "methamphetamines." Most of Tijuana's homicides resulted from drug-trade turf wars.

"So, there wouldn't have been any ballistics tests done on the bullets that killed him?"

"None. Why do you ask?"

"I was told Hernández was shot with a 3D-printed ghost gun."

"That is news to me. Who told you this?"

"An SDPD detective," I said.

"I would like to know how he obtained that information."

So would I, but I didn't tell him that. "I can ask, but he might not tell me for fear of losing a source. This detective also showed me a picture of Hernández standing at an outdoor table where El Tipo and Aguijón were seated."

"And you're curious as to who took this picture?"

"Yes. Was someone on your force monitoring El Tipo and taking pictures of his associates?"

"I am not aware of any surveillance having taken place. As

for Hernández, he was not—what's the expression?—on our radar."

Judging by the voices I could hear in the background, the commander was busy, and I decided not to tie him up any longer.

"I appreciate your taking the time to talk with me, Comandante."

"*Pero por supuesto,*" he said.

At a drive-through, I ordered a shredded-chicken burrito, and while waiting for it, sent Tommy a text with the message: *It's about time we caught a Padres game.*

Ten minutes later, Tommy responded to our long-standing prearranged signal.

"Hey," I said, "remember that ghost story I told you the other day?"

"Sure do," he said.

Tommy knew I was talking about the ghost gun. Our speaking in code was probably silly, but while working the chain-gang case, we'd gotten into the habit of communicating cryptically.

"I'm still not sure if there's a good explanation for the ghost. In fact, I talked to an expert down south who seemed skeptical of the picture evidence. A *jefe.*"

"How did that conversation come about?"

"I got a referral from a friend. The *jefe* said he knew of no surveillance of our guy, or his better-known associates. And there was no autopsy on their end."

"Maybe the ghost story was made up."

"Ghost stories usually are."

"Word to the wise," Tommy said. "I wouldn't go around

talking about ghosts. It sometimes brings out other evil spirits. Watch your back, amigo."

"You too."

———

Five hours later, the sun was going down as I drove home after my second medical appointment of the day. Usually, I unwind by listening to music, but today I rode in silence, thinking dark thoughts.

This is as good as I'll feel for the rest of my life, I thought. It didn't seem like a cause for celebration.

Dr. Kumar had unwittingly made me feel particularly vulnerable. Her large brown eyes and gentle manner had disarmed me. In her presence, I hadn't resorted to my usual defense mechanism of gallows humor. We discussed options for my treatment; none were good. At least Dr. Kumar believed in an aggressive approach to palliative care. Pain meds weren't going to be a problem.

"I will do everything in my power to not let you suffer," she told me.

Remembering that started my waterworks. As tears rolled down my cheeks, I angrily wiped them away. I was mad at the world, mad at the hand dealt me. What was coming down the pike scared me. For the first time in my life, I began contemplating the possibility of suicide. It's a family tradition, I thought, thinking of my mother. By ending my own life, I could avoid the pain, and the wasting away. I didn't have to be a victim, but could go out on my own terms. It wasn't as if my death would even be noticed. Some friends would be bummed, but they wouldn't fault my choice. Tommy would be more upset than anyone, but at least he'd have the support of his family.

That is, his two families.

Dr. Kumar had gently asked me a few questions about my life. I sensed she felt sorry for me, not so much because of my impending death sentence but the fact that there really was no one special in my life. Judging by the handful of personal pictures on display in her office, she had a large and loving family.

I took a deep breath, then asked myself the Hamlet question: To be, or not to be? My inner jury was still out. But what about the other jury, The Twelve? Maybe it was time they haunted someone else.

It wasn't only the dead who needed justice, though. I thought of Chloe Landers, with her canary-yellow wheelchair, and blue morpho racing gloves. Thinking about her gave me a momentary respite from the darkness. During Chloe's encounter with evil, her best friend had been murdered, and she'd been mutilated, but that hadn't killed her spirit. I needed some of her never-give-up moxie.

It was semi-dark when I arrived home and parked in my garage. As I exited my car, I heard the sound of a door being slammed shut, and looked up to see a figure in a black hoodie standing outside the passenger door of a dark SUV parked across the street. He stood there, motionless. Sitting in the driver's seat, I could make out the silhouette of a second individual.

On-duty detectives are supposed to carry their firearms, a rule some cops like me choose to ignore when it doesn't suit them. Today, I'd stored my Glock in the trunk's car safe to avoid the hassle of carrying it into my appointment with Dr. Kumar. It was still there.

The SUV was parked in the darkest spot on the street. I was pretty sure the vehicle didn't belong to any of my neighbors. The figure in the hoodie continued to linger outside the SUV.

I thought about retrieving my gun from the trunk but

decided not to bother. Still, I wasn't ready to close the garage door and retire inside my house. A few months back, cars on my street had been hit by thieves going after catalytic converters. Maybe that's what these two wanted.

Time to stroll to my mailbox, I thought. Take a little look-see. I was halfway up my driveway when the SUV's engine turned on. Instead of getting back into the vehicle, the passenger in the hoodie came out from behind it and began walking toward me. His hand reached under his sweatshirt and pulled something out.

An accented male voice called out, "I got a message for you."

I saw a glint of metal and decided it was a message I could do without. The man was holding a gun.

As he raised his arm, I swerved to the side, trying to put the cherry tree between me and the line of fire. He continued his advance, but suddenly stopped at the sound of a loud hacking cough. Hoodie man swung his head from side to side, looking for the source of the noise. I took the opportunity to sprint for refuge, but my attempted escape didn't go unnoticed. I heard a muffled percussion, and then the sound of a bullet shattering glass.

Behind me, a dog began to furiously bark. I swung my head back for just an instant and saw the shooter spinning around, trying to level his gun at the source of the barking.

As I ran into the garage, I heard a car door open and a voice calling out, "*Vamos!*"

Moments later, the SUV raced away.

My heart was pounding, but at that moment, I knew one thing for certain.

To be.

CHAPTER EIGHTEEN

Tommy sat in an easy chair across from me. He'd been my first and only call since the gunshot.

He said, "When I warned you to watch your back, I wasn't expecting something like this."

"I'm not sure if the shooter meant to kill me or warn me," I said.

"Splitting hairs, aren't you? That's like those pendejo wife-beaters saying, 'I didn't really hit her all that hard.' If someone's shooting at you, they're shooting at you."

"Before the shot was fired, the shooter said, 'I've got a message for you.'"

"I'd say a bullet is a pretty unmistakable message."

"I'm still wondering what he might have said if he hadn't been interrupted."

"I'm betting on, 'You're dead.'"

"So, should I call in the shooting?"

"That's the same thing you asked when you called me. Something made you hesitate then, and now. What is it?"

"It would probably be a waste of time. Odds are the SUV was stolen, and the license plates were switched."

"You're going to have to do better than that," he said.

"I guess I'm feeling reluctant at the thought of answering a bunch of questions, even from our own."

"Sounds like you're having trust issues," he said.

There it was, even if I didn't like it.

"You got a take on what happened tonight?" I asked.

Tommy sighed. "I think you lit a fuse, but I'm not sure when it was lit, or who it was lit under. You clearly made someone, or some group, very unhappy. What was it Saint Bill used to like to say? There was a *precipitating* event. He loved using that word, didn't he? Someone, or something, wasn't happy having their toes stepped on. Earlier today, you told me you made some calls, including one down south. Who'd you talk to?"

"Comandante Domingo Sanchez. Know him?"

"Only by reputation. I hear he's a hard-ass."

"Is he dirty?"

"I'd be surprised if he wasn't."

"He called a little before one, and we talked for ten, fifteen minutes."

"About what?"

"The death of Daniel Hernández."

"Shit. You got a death wish?"

"Why would Sanchez order a hit on me?"

"I'm not saying he did. But maybe he passed on the details of your call to someone with a vested interest in letting sleeping dogs lie."

"The timing seems off," I said. "Everything would have needed to be arranged damn quickly."

"With the cartels, all it takes is one call. They've got plenty of people working both sides of the border."

Too true, I thought.

Tommy asked, "How'd you get Sanchez's name in the first place?"

"I went through a co-worker of Marvin Barry's," I said.

I could see Tommy trying to place Marvin's name, so I said, "Bad News Barry."

That got a nod of recognition.

"Bad News referred me to Enrique Cortez, who's the border liaison for the DA's office. He was the one who reached out to Sanchez for me."

"What story did you tell Cortez?"

"I didn't give him any specifics. The comandante was another matter. He refused to give without getting, so I had to tell him about my involvement with the chain-gang homicides, and how I'd heard a rumor that Hernández's death could have had some connection to it."

Tommy shook his head. "I really wish you hadn't made that call. In fact, I wish you hadn't talked to anyone. We can't even be sure you weren't played from the get-go by Loco Luca. For all we know, his ghost gun story might have been designed to flush you out."

"Sanchez said Hernández was buried in a pauper's grave, and that there was no autopsy on their end."

"You believe him?"

"It sounded right."

"Well, assuming Luca's story isn't another one of his lies, it means he's got people down south willing to do things like fish bullets from a body. Or, maybe he knew about the ghost gun, because he was the one who ordered the hit on Hernández in the first place."

"That sounds like a conspiracy theory."

"Just because I'm paranoid doesn't mean they're not out to get me. In fact, weren't you the one who suggested there might be some kind of SDPD departmental intrigue when it came to our investigation?"

"The chain-gang homicides got everyone on our team imagining things."

"Said by the man who tonight ended up being on the wrong side of a silencer."

I didn't respond.

Tommy said, "That's the real reason you didn't call in the shooting, right? You weren't sure what you should reveal, or who you could trust?"

It was crazy for a cop to be thinking like that, and yet I found myself nodding.

Before leaving for work the next morning, I tried to make good on my debt to Lenore, gathering together a bounty of raven offerings.

I approached her cherry tree bearing gifts. Since I couldn't spot Lenore, I spoke to the tree. "I caught some slugs and snails for you. They tried making a break for it, but they couldn't outrun me. For now, they're corralled. Better get to them before they escape."

Reaching into a bag, I pulled out my gastropod bowls and distributed them along some low-hanging branches. Then I listened for any sounds from Lenore, but she remained silent.

I continued speaking to her tree. "I also dug out some big white grubs for you. I know they're juicy, because I gathered some small sticks and made kebabs."

Stepping back from the tree, I held up my impaling handiwork, hoping Lenore would take notice of my efforts. Whether she did or not wasn't clear, but I suspected she was watching and listening.

"Anyway, I'm placing your kebab skewers among the bark. It ought to be a hell of a scavenger hunt for you."

I began distributing the kebabs with the verve of a raven Santa Claus. As I worked, I didn't hear any hacking cough, or barking. Lenore was keeping to herself.

When I finished, I called out, "Bon appétit."

Then I walked back toward the house, pausing just long enough to use the hose to wash my hands of grub guts.

Although Chloe and I hadn't made plans to meet up, she came wheeling up to me at the Galapagos Tortoise Exhibit.

"Lunching with the tortoises?" she asked.

"It's a quiet spot," I said. "I think it's not as popular as other exhibits because most people equate watching tortoises with watching paint dry."

"I hope you don't mind my intruding on you," she said. "Since I haven't seen you lately, I wanted to check up on you."

"I'm here for inspiration," I said. "I needed to see that slow and steady can win the race. I would have asked you to join me, but I got the sense you needed a break from me."

"I needed a break from my past. Maybe I should practice what I preach. I tell my clients to not escape their past by avoiding it, but by accepting it."

"I imagine that's easier said than done."

"I can testify to that, even though I should know better. Consider the phrase 'carry a grudge.' When you hold on to anger, you have to carry a great weight."

"You don't believe in an eye for an eye?"

"Gandhi said, 'An eye for an eye leaves the whole world blind.'"

I didn't have an answer for Gandhi, but I wasn't alone in that. The British Empire never found an answer for him either.

We went back to our giant-tortoise viewing. Some of the

males tip the scales at close to 600 pounds; the females are half that. One of the bigger males awakened from his sunbathing and began moving along in tank-like fashion.

"How'd you find me?" I asked.

"I asked around, and one of the tour guides said he noticed you walking in this direction."

"If you'd called me, I'd have told you where I was."

"I wanted to impress you with my sleuthing," she said.

"Consider me impressed. You hungry? I have half an uneaten sandwich."

"Thanks, but there's a salad waiting for me back at the office."

We continued watching the tortoises. Our conversation was unhurried, just like the animals we were observing.

"Any favorites in this lot?" she asked.

"The venerable ones," I said. "I always check out the oldies first."

Several of the tortoises had been brought to the zoo in 1928. The oldest of them, a female known as "Grandma," was believed to be 140 years old.

"Guess I'm feeling a little jealous of their longevity today," I added.

"I'm sorry."

I shrugged. There wasn't much going on in the enclosure, with most of the tortoises basking in the sun. We were following their good example.

"I talked to Penelope about the meeting you two had," Chloe said.

"I hope you got more out of her than I did."

"Penelope is protective of me, as I am of her."

"I get that, even if I'm not sure why the two of you preemptively circled your wagons when I came on the scene."

"Penelope's not a fan of SDPD."

"Join the club," I said. "But that still doesn't explain why both of you seem so reluctant to discuss anything that might help with my case."

"What about you? Don't pretend you're an open book."

"The first time we met, I told you I was dying. That sounds pretty up front to me."

"And then you said you regretted telling me that."

Even though there were no spectators near us, we had begun whispering to one another, which made our conversation feel that much more intense. So did Chloe's flushed cheeks.

"I don't have a hidden agenda," I said. "Can you say the same?"

"Don't pretend you're always forthcoming."

"What do you mean by that?"

"The other day when we were talking at the koala exhibit, I asked you if there was something you regretted not having experienced in your life. And you pretended there wasn't."

"What makes you so sure?"

"It's my job to hear the unsaid."

"You must have great hearing."

"I do."

"Then what was it I didn't say?"

Her voice softened. "I don't want to upset you."

"Don't worry about that. I want to see the great psychic in action."

We stared at one another, my eyes challenging her to speak. She shook her head and said, "Forget it."

"No. Don't stop now. I'm a big boy."

"All right," she said. "Your biggest regret is that you've never loved, or been loved."

To my ears, my sudden intake of breath sounded like a gasp. Maybe it was. How could she have known? I managed a lungful of air, and hoped I didn't appear as unsteady as I felt.

"How?" I asked.

"Your body language showed how uncomfortable you were with my question. Love is a topic that makes people, and men in particular, feel vulnerable."

"I always thought there would be time," I said. "I always thought the right woman would come along."

Chloe nodded.

"You must be a hell of a therapist," I said.

"I'd like to think so," she said. "But it wasn't only mind reading on my part." Her cheeks reddened as she confessed. "It's easy to know what someone else is thinking, if you're thinking the same thing. When I watched you struggle with my question, I knew why it was difficult for you, as your discomfort mirrored my own. We share the same regret."

"Thanks for telling me that. I know you didn't have to."

We managed a small intimate smile for one another. Chloe's cheeks returned to their normal color.

"How about joining me for dinner tonight?" I asked.

I'm not sure which of us was more surprised. The words had just come out.

"Dinner?" she said, not immediately answering. "I'd like that, but I have some misgivings."

"Such as?"

"Whenever we're together, it always feels as if you're on the job. Being constantly put on the defensive makes me uncomfortable."

"So, you need me to not be a cop for an evening?"

Chloe nodded.

"Done," I said. "If you join me for dinner, I promise to be a civilian, and not a cop. That means no questions relating to your case."

"Thank you."

"Anything else?"

"Would it be all right if I pick our restaurant? Sometimes dining out can be a nightmare for the disabled."

"I'm happy to let you choose the place. Anything else?"

"We split the check."

"Okay by me."

We went back to looking at the tortoises, watching in companionable silence. Finally, I asked, "Have you ever come here late in the day?"

Chloe thought about that and shook her head. "I don't think so. I rarely visit at any time other than midday."

"Same. But for whatever reason, I found myself here one day just before closing time. And it was the damnedest thing. One of the keepers came out and used a cowbell to call the tortoises into their barn."

"A cowbell?"

"You really need to be here to see it. And hear it. He took this cowbell and started whacking it with a stick, and with the clanging sounds, these plodding tortoises suddenly came to life, making a break for their barn."

"The charge of the tortoises?"

"That might be overstating it, but they did amble with purpose."

"To the call of a cowbell?"

"I'm assuming what the tortoises were hearing was the dinner bell."

"More cowbell," she said.

That got a big smile out of me. "You know that skit?"

"It's a classic," she said.

Will Ferrell and Christopher Walken had performed the skit on *Saturday Night Live*. Ferrell and his bandmates were playing the song "Don't Fear the Reaper," and Walken kept insisting "It needs more cowbell!"

"Life could always use more cowbell," I said.

CHAPTER NINETEEN

We didn't linger at the tortoise exhibit, with work demands claiming each of us. Our conversation was light as we made our way out, with no mention of our dinner plans, and I wondered if Chloe was having second thoughts about it.

As we passed through the zoo's exit, I said, "Should we talk about tonight?"

"Let's find a spot where we don't have to shout," Chloe said.

We moved away from the crowds. I was half expecting Chloe to say she had reconsidered dinner, but instead she said, "Are you good with Italian food?"

"More than good."

"And do you mind eating on the early side?"

"I actually prefer it."

"Give me a sec and I'll get us a reservation."

Chloe began tapping into her phone, then looked at me with a satisfied nod.

"All done," she said. "We have a six o'clock reservation at the Old Piedmont Restaurant in Point Loma. Know it?"

"I know of it, but I've never dined there."

"You're in for a treat, then. It's street parking, but since we'll be eating early, there shouldn't be any problem finding a space. You should wear a coat, because we'll be dining outdoors on the back patio, but they do have heat lamps."

"Thanks for doing the organizing," I said.

"See you at six," she said.

Chloe managed a small wheelie, and I watched Tweety Bird fly away.

I arrived at the restaurant fifteen minutes early, and regretted not having had the opportunity to change my clothes. Most of the male diners were wearing the casual attire of jeans and polo shirts. I removed my tie, slipping it into the pocket of my blazer, doing my best to not look like a cop. The longer I'd been on the force, the tougher that was.

It's not even a date, I told myself. Or at least I didn't think it was.

I decided to wait out front. At a little past six, a scowling Chloe came wheeling along the sidewalk. I hoped her frown had nothing to do with me.

When she saw me, she said, "Sorry, I'm late. I didn't expect the disabled-parking spots to be taken."

She gestured toward the two spaces in question. In one of them was a Jeep Grand Cherokee, and in the other a Toyota Tacoma.

"Just a second," I said, walking over to the vehicles.

The Jeep had a California disabled placard hanging from its rearview mirror, but not the Tacoma. With Chloe watching me, I did a full circle around the truck, making sure I wasn't missing anything. Then I checked the signage. The disabled-parking spaces were well marked, as were the penalties for those parking there illegally.

"The truck doesn't have a disabled sticker."

"Shocking," Chloe said. "Gambling in Casablanca."

I smiled at her reference, and to show it hadn't gone over my head, hummed a few bars from "La Marseillaise."

"Excuse me a moment," I said, moving a few steps away to make a brief whispered call.

Rejoining Chloe, I said, "If you want to re-park, I have a feeling a spot will be opening up before too long."

"And how do you know that?"

"It's probably better I don't say, but I'm assuming you've had to deal with situations like this before."

"Too many times," she said.

"And on each occasion, you probably asked, 'Where's a cop when you need one?'"

"I might have said that one—or possibly 200—times."

"Tonight, there's no need for you to say it."

We were seated on the back patio. While Chloe was removing her blue morpho racing gloves, water glasses and menus were delivered to our table.

I picked up my menu and began looking through it. Chloe's menu remained on the table.

"Know it by heart?" I asked.

"By stomach."

"Any suggestions?"

"I'm not sure if I'm a good source, as I usually go with the vegetarian selections."

"I'm good with my veggies. Suggest away."

"My favorite appetizers are the Brussels sprouts, baked artichoke, and garlic bulb and brie."

"Keep going," I said.

"When I have a salad, I go with the walnut gorgonzola."

"Entrées?"

"If I'm in a pasta mood, I like the ravioli stuffed with ricotta and topped with marinara sauce. And if I'm leaning toward having pizza, my favorite is the fig and pear."

"Fig and pear pizza?"

"Don't knock it until you try it. But if you're not that daring, the margarita is also good."

"No dessert?"

"That's no contest. I love their giant chocolate and oatmeal cookie topped with pecans and vanilla bean gelato."

"You had me at cookie," I said, and put my menu down.

"Decided already?"

"I've decided to let you order for both of us."

"Even if I go with the fig and pear pizza?"

"Even that."

We'd been seated for fifteen minutes when we became aware of loud cursing. Neither of us even tried to hide our smiles.

I said, "I'm guessing he just learned that not only is he on the hook for a $250 parking fine, but also has to pay towing and impound fees."

"I shouldn't be enjoying my *schadenfreude* as much as I am," Chloe said.

"I don't know what that means, but I assume it has something to do with getting payback."

"*Schadenfreude* means deriving pleasure from the misfortune of others."

"Derive away. He deserves your *schadenfreude*, and then some. A little birdie told me he also has some unpaid parking tickets."

We heard more shouted curses. Our smiles became wider.

"Thank you," she said.

"For what? Officially, I didn't do anything. I was off-duty, and just happened to call a friend on the force, where I might have mentioned the illegally parked vehicle."

"Could you get in trouble for what you did?"

"For having a conversation with a friend? No. As for his sending out an officer and a tow truck on my bequest, that's a bit of a gray area. But let's just say I'm not worried about any repercussions. My medical prognosis allows me the ultimate short-timer's attitude."

Our server reappeared, a smiling young woman whose red-and-black Aztec dangle earrings were clues she'd attended my alma mater, San Diego State.

"Here's your Chianti Classico," she said, placing the glasses on the table.

Chloe had ordered the wine for us, which was a good thing. My knowledge of wines doesn't extend much beyond their colors.

The server looked at me and asked, "Have you decided yet?"

"We have," Chloe said, and our waitress redirected her gaze.

Chloe offered up our choices, giving me a side glance while ordering the fig and pear pizza, as if expecting to hear an objection. My mouth moved, but only to smile.

When our server left, I lifted my glass and said, "To fig and pear pizza."

"And making you a believer."

We clinked glasses and drank. "Like the wine?" Chloe asked.

"I do."

"The only time I drink Chianti is when I'm eating Italian food," she said.

"Can you really call our fig and pear pizza Italian food?"

"*Certo,*" she said in accented Italian.

"Have you ever visited Italy?"

"Not yet, but now there are a lot more options for wheelchair-accessible vacations. I hope to get there in the near future."

"Don't put it off."

She heard the note of regret in my voice, and nodded. Then we both took another sip of the wine.

"How did your parents decide on the name Wyatt?" Chloe asked. "Is it a family name?"

I shook my head. "My father actually named me after Wyatt Earp."

"Who's that?"

"The Gunfight at the O.K. Corral? Tombstone, Arizona? Doc Holliday?"

Three shakes of her head.

"Earp was a famous Old West lawman. In film, he's been portrayed by such actors as Kevin Costner, Henry Fonda, Kurt Russell, and James Stewart."

"I'm afraid I've never been very fond of Westerns. I imagine your father was."

"Not particularly. He actually chose the name Wyatt because of his being a local history buff. Back in the late 1800s, Earp and his wife lived on Third Avenue for almost a decade."

"Where he was a lawman?"

"Not quite. He opened four gambling halls during his time in San Diego."

"That's quite a career change."

"Yes and no. Even though his renown came from being a lawman, Earp worked as everything from a gold miner to a boxing referee."

"Do you think being named after him might be why you ended up in law enforcement?"

I shook my head. "Pure coincidence."

"What did your family think of you going into police work?"

"My father died before that happened, and my mother was always a bit bewildered by my career choice. As far as I know, no one from either side of my family was ever a cop, which isn't the norm. Most cops I know have family members who served on the force."

"People do tend to gravitate toward the familiar."

"What about you? Do you come from a long line of mental health professionals?"

"Hardly," she said. "My father was an electrician, and my mother worked as a homemaker and substitute teacher."

"Siblings?"

"I have an older brother and a younger sister. He's a builder, and she's a physical therapist."

"Do you have a good relationship with them?"

"We get along now. That wasn't always the case. I think I spoil my nieces and nephews to make up for how I acted to my sibs when I was a teenager. After I lost my legs, I was angry at the world, and took it out on my family."

I resisted the urge to follow up with a question. For this evening, at least, I would keep to my promise and not ask anything that might have to do with her case.

"How's your haiku doing?" she asked.

"I guess I'll find out tomorrow when I see David. I'm debating between two haiku finalists."

"Need my help in choosing one of them?"

"I wouldn't want to depress you with the subject matter. One is about vaquitas, and the other the chain-gang homicides."

"Deep topics, but I'd still like to hear them."

"I don't remember them exactly."

"Seventeen syllables?"

"Thirty-four. There were two of them."

"Dare I say that sounds like convenient amnesia?"

"I'd call it more of a cop-out."

"Good choice of words," she said.

"All right, all right," I said. "But don't say you weren't warned."

I took a deep breath and began my recitation. "I mourn their passing, extinction of a species, my tears do no good."

Chloe nodded. "That's exactly how I feel about the vaquita situation," she said. "I hate not being able to do anything for them."

She gets it, I thought. The passion in her voice made me want to reach for her hand, but I was afraid of the moment, so I tried reaching out with my words instead.

"Haiku number two," I said. "Twelve souls call to me, drowned in an uncaring sea, only I hear them."

Chloe did what I hadn't dared, and extended a hand my way. Like a drowning man, I reached for her safety line.

Two hours later, I lifted up my white napkin and waved it.

"I surrender. Not another bite."

"I'd call your restraint admirable, if we even had a bite left between the two of us to eat."

I studied the remains of our dessert. "There are enough cookie crumbs to qualify for a bite."

"Maybe for a mouse."

"Thank you for a truly enjoyable evening."

"I was about to say the same," she said.

"I can't even remember the last time I went out to dinner."

"I'm lucky to have a few persistent girlfriends who force me to go out," she said.

"There's no one special in your life?"

It was a question I'd been wanting to ask, but now wondered at its appropriateness.

"Not now," Chloe said. "Not for years. In fact, I've pretty much given up on men."

"Why? If that's not too personal."

"It's my Catch-22," she said. "I want to be liked by a man, but I immediately distrust any who show an interest in me. That pretty much assures a dysfunctional relationship."

"Since you already know that, can't you do something about it?"

"Physician heal thyself, right? It's not that easy."

"Sorry. I shouldn't have said anything."

"It's not your fault, or your issue. Let's blame old scars. Literally. Losing my legs at the age of fifteen crippled me as much emotionally as it did physically. After I was maimed, it seemed the only men who took notice of me were real creeps, and I pretty much became convinced that no man could be interested in me who wasn't a pervert."

"I'm sorry."

"Having that lack of trust in the opposite sex basically sabotaged my being able to enter into a long-term relationship. I've been working on my issues, even if that sounds like a cliché."

"At least you're trying," I said. "I wish I could say the same."

"Sometimes I dream that I'm whole and undamaged. My psyche must not see me as the Wheelchair Lady."

"I regret saying that."

"Don't. That's how you saw me. And that's what made it easy for you to look past me. As odd as it sounds, I found that reassuring. You didn't have a savior complex, and you weren't a deviant who had a thing for scars, or a maimed woman."

"I'm looking at you now," I said.

She met my gaze and said, "I'm glad."

CHAPTER TWENTY

Despite my jogging, I couldn't keep up with Chloe as she wheeled toward her car. "Not fair," I called. "I don't have wheels."

"Pick up the pace," she said. "I'm in training. Next year I'm entered in the San Diego Rock and Roll Marathon."

"For real?"

"Cross my heart."

"In that case, I'll be eating popcorn on the sidelines cheering you on."

She slowed down, letting me catch up with her. "I'm shooting for two hours and forty-five minutes."

"For twenty-six miles?"

"Twenty-six-point-two miles."

"That's fast."

"The best wheelchair marathoners—and I'm certainly not one of them—beat the times of world-class runners by half an hour or more." Chloe came to a sudden stop. "Dammit!"

"What?"

"My car's left front tire is flat."

We drew closer to survey the damage. I bent down and ran my finger along the tire, locating a gash. "Do you have a spare?"

"The car didn't come with one."

"It's a deep cut. I doubt if roadside assistance will be able to patch it."

"In that case, I'll have the car towed to a tire center."

"Why don't I just give you a ride home? The tire shops are closed, so forget about getting a replacement at this hour. And by letting me help you, I won't feel so guilty."

"What do you have to feel guilty about?"

"I suspect our scofflaw decided to get revenge on the person he thought had him towed, and targeted your car because of its disabled placard."

"That still doesn't make it your fault."

"Tomorrow, I'll see if security footage in the area shows who did this, but for tonight I'd like to take you home. I don't want this evening to end on a bad note."

"I'm not about to let a First World problem ruin my night."

"Then take me up on my First World solution."

She thought about it for a moment. "Okay, I will. Thank you."

We followed the coastline of San Diego Bay, taking North Harbor Drive toward Chloe's 5th Avenue condominium in Bankers Hill. The body of water was mostly hidden in darkness, a presence felt more than seen. Chloe lowered her window partway down and inhaled deeply.

"I love that smell," she said.

I lowered my window as well, taking in the scent, but after a few moments closed it.

"Too cold for you?" Chloe asked.

"No," I said. "Too many memories. I spent a lot of hours around here working the chain-gang homicides."

Chloe raised her window up.

"That's really not necessary," I said.

"I've already had my fill," she said.

"Good. I'd rather smell your perfume anyway. Is it jasmine?"

"Gardenia," she said. "I have a client who makes an extract of gardenia by steeping its flowers in alcohol."

I did a little not-so-subtle sniffing.

"You're making me self-conscious," Chloe said.

"I'm just stopping to smell the gardenias."

As we drew near to Chloe's condominium, I said, "Your place is even closer to the zoo than mine."

"That was a big selling point for me, along with my building's subterranean garage."

"Is that where I should park?"

"It's okay if you just drop me out front."

"I'd like to walk you to your door."

"There's really no need for that. I live in a security building, with a lobby attendant."

"That's good, but I'm still not going to leave you at the curb."

"It's best if you park in the garage, then," she said.

To me, she sounded pleased.

The elevator door opened, and I announced, with a bad British accent, "The lift awaits, madam."

"This is really far enough, Jeeves."

"I shan't retire, madam, before seeing you to your door."

"Very well, then."

Chloe wheeled inside, and we took the elevator to the fourth floor. We traveled down a hallway, until she stopped in front of a doorway.

"Home sweet home," she said.

"I had a great time tonight," I said. "And tomorrow morning, I'd like to drive you to your car."

"Thank you, but there's no need."

I ignored her words. "Does 7:30 work for you?"

"I don't want to put you out."

"You're not."

"Okay, I'll call a towing service and see if they can meet us at eight. But just to be sure, let's confirm in the morning."

That was my signal to leave, but I wasn't quite ready. I wondered if leaning down and kissing Chloe on the cheek would be too familiar; I wondered if throwing her a wave goodbye would seem too informal.

"Are you okay with a goodnight hug?" I asked.

She answered by opening her arms. I leaned down, and we squeezed one another for a long moment, before breaking off our embrace.

I said, "Now that you've introduced me to fig and pear pizza, I wonder if my world will ever be the same."

"Let's hope not. 'A foolish consistency is the hobgoblin of little minds.'"

"I was just about to say the same thing."

"Since you're here, would you like to see my place? The offer comes with a beverage of your choice."

"You're probably tired."

"I'm not."

"That sounds great, then."

Chloe unlocked the dead bolt, wheeled inside, and called out to Alexa to turn on the lights. A moment later, her condominium was illuminated throughout.

I looked around and whistled. "Nice digs," I said. "It's a real grown-up space."

"Grown-up?"

"As in everything looks nice and has its place."

"It's still a work in progress," she said. "My priority was to have the best wheelchair accessibility possible."

"My home decor comes from the catch-as-catch-can school."

"Are you saying your design evolved organically?"

"If by organically you mean chaos theory, yes."

Chloe smiled, which made me smile. "Feel free to look around while I get us drinks. What would you like?"

"Whatever you're having," I said.

"'Eye of newt and toe of frog, wool of bat and tongue of dog?'"

"Double, double, toil and trouble."

"You know your Macbeth."

"False pretenses," I said. "The only reason I knew your rhyme is that last year the Old Globe Theater provided some complimentary play tickets to SDPD, and I got one to a production of *Macbeth*. Seeing those three witches huddled around a boiling cauldron actually sent shivers down my spine."

"In that case, I won't bring out my cauldron tonight," she said. "And our beverage won't have any amphibian parts."

She wheeled off, leaving me to start my self-tour. Most of the living-room wall space was taken up with watercolor and oil landscape paintings.

I called out, "You have quite the gallery."

"I'm a sucker for paintings from the California impressionists' school," she said. "And I'm especially fond of those artists who painted around San Diego."

"How old are these paintings?"

"1920s, 30s, and 40s."

"Is that the California Tower I'm seeing?"

"Good spot," she said.

The Spanish colonial-style 200-foot-tall California Tower is the largest structure in Balboa Park.

She returned to the living room and parked her wheelchair next to a coffee table. There was a carrying case in her lap that she unzipped, and then she removed a bottle of red wine and two glasses.

"Would you like to do the honors?" she asked, extending a corkscrew.

"I'll give it a try, but I need to warn you that I've been bested by a cork more than once."

Luckily, this wasn't one of those occasions. The cork came out easily, and I filled the glasses. Then I handed Chloe her glass and raised my own.

"I'm afraid I only know two toasts, and one of them is 'Cheers.'"

"What's the other?" she asked.

"Down the hatch."

"Let's go with that one," she said, and we clinked glasses.

I took a sip of the wine, and felt its warmth going down my throat.

"I think you're the first person I've ever known with an art collection. That's impressive. And intimidating."

"There's no need to be impressed or intimidated. My next-door neighbor gave me two of those paintings—the Maurice Braun oils—when I was just a teenager. She remembered I liked them when I was a little girl, and gifted them to me when I came home to recuperate after the attack. During my convalescence, I looked at them for hours at a time. That's how I learned about the California impressionists, and began collecting."

"The closest I came to that was collecting comic books," I said. "Do you have any early artwork of the zoo?"

She shook her head. "I don't, but in my study are reprints of very old photographs that were taken there. My favorite picture shows the first three lion cubs born at the zoo: Faith, Hope, and Charity."

"I've always liked virtue names," I said.

"Me too," she said. "Will you be zoo-bound tomorrow?"

"I'm not sure if I can carve out the time. I have an appointment with David, and need to finish some homework beforehand."

"I hope I'm not contributing to your delinquency."

"I wouldn't even have a therapist if not for you. Besides, I'm mostly done with the reading."

"Good. I was afraid you were going to ask me to write a note saying the dog ate your homework."

"Next time," I said.

Beyond the living room was the balcony. Floodlights illuminated a space filled with greenery and planters.

"It looks like you're growing a jungle out there," I said.

"It's my urban garden," she said. "If you're interested, I can give you the nickel tour."

"Lead on," I said. "Can I hold your wine glass for you?"

"Tweety's got a cup holder," she said, "but thanks for asking."

She wheeled along the hardwood floors to the sliding door that led out to the balcony and I followed her out to the deck.

"Surprisingly spacious," I said.

"I got one of the coveted double-balconies," Chloe said.

"Am I seeing milkweed in that planter?"

"You are. When I first started my garden, I wasn't sure what to expect. I was hoping some pollinators might stop by, but never expected the variety that comes to visit. There are birds, bees, butterflies, and moths. Occasionally, there's even a red-tailed hawk that perches on the balcony."

Tweety came to a stop between me and one of the large planters, and my hip ended up pressed next to Chloe's shoulder. Even through our clothing, I could feel her warmth.

Both of us sipped our wine and took in the view. Neither one of us was in a hurry to disengage and go back inside.

"Tomorrow morning I'll have to fill the hummingbird feeders with sugar water," she said.

"I'm also on bird duty," I said, and then told Chloe about Lenore, and her ability to mimic sounds, but stopped short of mentioning how she might have saved my life the night before.

"And here I thought Poe made up a talking raven," Chloe said.

"Nevermore will you think that."

She bumped me with her shoulder.

"That will only encourage me," I said.

When each of us finished our wine, we returned inside for more. I reached for the bottle just as Chloe was doing the same, and our fingers touched. Neither one of us pulled away, but instead, squeezed each other's digits. That emboldened me to lean over and lightly kiss her. She pressed back with her lips. As our mouths began to grind against each other, our breathing became a series of gasps.

Chloe came up for air and asked, "Are you sure?"

"Same thing I was going to ask you," I said. "And yes, I'm sure, unless..."

"Unless what?"

In a strained whisper, I said, "Unless you're doing this as some kind of mercy thing on your part."

Chloe's laugh came with a tear. As she wiped it away, she said, "I was just about to say that to you."

CHAPTER TWENTY-ONE

No words, not at first, but sounds of discovery, and longing. We were riding the storm, unafraid of where we were being carried, each of us holding on to the other and not letting go.

And then, a descent into stillness, and a slow return to where we had started, but somehow a new and different place.

I put my hand on Chloe's chest and felt her breathing, felt her heart.

"You're not a dream," I whispered.

"No."

"You made me feel as if I'm still alive."

"You are."

"With you, I am."

"That was most unexpected," she said.

"In a good way, I hope."

"Yes."

"No regrets?"

"None," she said. "You?"

"None."

I said the word assertively, without ambiguity. It made her smile. Then I drew Chloe to me, enclosing her in my arms. We kissed until both of us were taking in air in gasps, not wanting the sensations we were feeling to stop.

Later, we cuddled with whispers and giggles and wonderful sweet nothings. And probably, most of all, relief. Somehow, despite our fears, and the scars we both carried, we had found a way to come together.

"Talk to me," I said.

"I'm usually more comfortable listening."

"I want to hear what you're thinking."

"I don't want to think. I don't want to be in my head. I loved the amnesia of us, of escaping my second-guessing. Intimacy has always been scary for me."

Then, in a small voice, she confessed, "I have trouble accepting my body."

"Why? You're beautiful."

"I wish I could believe you."

"One day you will."

This time, she drew me toward her, squeezing me tight, and we both fell asleep in one another's arms.

I woke to the sounds of suppressed sobbing. It took me a moment to gather my thoughts and remember where I was. Chloe had her back to me, her face pressing into her pillow in an attempt to muffle her crying.

"What's wrong?"

She shook her head.

"If I made you feel this way, I'm sorry."

"Not you," she managed to say, her chest still heaving with every breath. "Me."

"It's all right," I said.

"No, it's not."

Chloe turned to face me. Her eyes were puffy. She was trying to still her sobbing, but the spasms in her chest weren't co-operating. I reached for her and held her until the tremors stilled.

"I'm sorry," she said.

"I'm sorry you're in pain."

She took a deep breath, and then said, "I think you'd better go."

"If that's what you want. But I need to know if I said or did something wrong."

"Just the opposite," Chloe said.

"I don't understand."

"It's better that way."

"No, it's not."

Chloe averted her gaze, and refused to look back at me. I watched as she opened her mouth to speak, only to bite back the words. She tried a second time, but once more defaulted to silence.

Finally, she said, "I can't have a relationship with a dying man."

"Oh."

It made sense but still hurt like hell. There was no future for us. Never had been. Chloe recognized that. Cutting me loose was the right thing to do. It was better to end it now, before the two of us grew closer.

Intellectually, I understood that, but it was still a punch to the gut.

I moved the bedcover aside and started gathering my clothes. For just a little while, I had been able to forget that I was a dead man walking. Now, the dark shroud began to once more drape itself over me.

In my own despair, I almost didn't hear her sobbing, or her words.

"Please forgive my lie," she whispered. "My lies. I only said that to drive you off, and to spare me from having to tell you the truth."

I looked at her, and waited for her to continue.

"You've been right all this time. I've never forgiven the creature who attacked me, and murdered my best friend. He destroyed the life I was meant to have. Time never healed my wounds. Far from it."

She took a few angry breaths, trying to stave off sobs.

I said, "Of course you're angry. How could you not be after what happened to you and Dana?"

"I am far past anger," she said. "Only retribution will satisfy me. That's why we can't have a relationship."

"I'm not following."

"We're working at cross-purposes. You want to arrest the bastard, but that's not enough for me. I want to kill him."

Hearing her say that, I almost felt relief. Chloe hadn't rejected me because I was dying. But there was still the not-inconsequential matter that she wanted to murder someone.

Was plotting to murder someone.

"That's why you hired Penny Hughes to find the man who attacked you twenty-five years ago."

"Her name is Penelope Hill," Chloe said. "And even though she is no longer my client, I'm ethically bound to not discuss her situation."

"If you're truly concerned about her situation, then you should consider what would happen to her if she successfully locates him and you follow through with your intent to inflict bodily harm upon him."

"I can't see how she would be liable for any actions that I might commit."

"If you hurt the man who attacked you, Penelope would likely be charged as an accessory to the crime you committed if it could be shown that she had a reasonable expectation of what you might do. Has Penelope developed any leads on the suspect?"

"No comment," she said.

"Do you honestly think you're even capable of taking a human life?"

"What he did to Dana and me makes him inhuman."

"Not in the eyes of the law. Killing him isn't worth screwing up your own life. You know that, don't you?"

She refused to answer.

"And even if you got away with murder, do you think that would be the end of it? I know you wouldn't be able to murder without a lifetime of suffering afterward. You don't want that."

"I've been waiting most of my life for any semblance of justice," she said.

"You realize that if you were convicted of premeditated murder, you'd likely get a life sentence?"

"When I was mutilated, I already got that life sentence."

"Tell me this entire discussion is theoretical," I said. "Please."

Chloe didn't answer.

I said, "Okay, let's say you've got a lead on this guy. If you go after him, if you kill him, this piece of shit could destroy everything you've built in your life. Do you want him to cripple you a second time?"

"Whatever I do won't be a rash decision."

"But will it be the right decision?" I asked.

Chloe had seen how hurt I was when she'd lied about the

reason for not wanting to see me, but by coming clean, by sparing my feelings, her admission had made her vulnerable.

Still, I couldn't unhear her words. Couldn't pretend I didn't know what she was plotting. There was only one thing I could do.

"I'm leaving now, but when I come back tomorrow morning, I'd like to talk further."

"I've changed my mind," she said. "I won't be needing your help. Tomorrow, I'll contact roadside assistance."

"Don't shut me out," I said.

"I'm not the one making the ultimatums," she said.

"I'm looking out for you, even if you can't see that. I'll do anything I can to stop you from hurting yourself."

"Too late," she whispered.

CHAPTER TWENTY-TWO

As I turned down the street to my house, I looked around for anything that might be amiss. All appeared to be quiet, which wasn't surprising given it was half past three. There was a bit of déjà vu in my getting home so late. When I'd worked homicide, we often didn't sleep for days at a time at the onset of a case, and I recalled all the occasions when I had arrived home in darkness. Back then, it had felt as if I were returning from combat, and it was hard not feeling aggrieved at my oblivious neighbors safely tucked away in their beds.

Tonight, I didn't see any obvious threats to my life, but still proceeded cautiously. This time, my firearm was on my person. Given how little I'd slept the past two nights, I should have been exhausted, but for some reason I didn't feel tired. My night with Chloe had brought me out of a long hibernation. Somehow, my awakened libido hadn't been hindered by my cancer, but now I had to deal with a lover who had all but confessed she was planning a murder.

So much for a storybook romance.

Gun drawn, I entered my house, going from room to room until I was satisfied there was no danger. Because I was sure the sandman wasn't going to be visiting anytime soon, I decided to forgo tossing and turning in bed, and do some reading.

I opened the book that David had given me and brought out a highlighter. *Tuesdays with Morrie* is a small book, but not short on substance. I decided to read it from the beginning. It only took me an hour to finish, all the while marking it up in neon green.

After I put the book aside, I slept like the dead.

Before going into work, I put some food out for Lenore, leaving it in spots I hoped would minimize the danger to her. As I went around distributing it, I did some whistling, calling, and barking, trying to get Lenore to respond, but she didn't answer.

Because Lenore was still able to lift her wings a little, my hope was that she had suffered a strain rather than a break. After animal control had failed to corral her, I'd searched out other potential alternatives. There were some wildlife rehab centers willing to look at Lenore, but only if I brought her to them secured in a cage. Maybe that wasn't quite as daunting a prospect as mice trying to figure out how to bell the cat, but it didn't promise to be easy.

Still, I wanted to do something before more time passed. By not using her wings, Lenore was in danger of losing the muscle definition needed to fly. Her condition also made her a target for predation. Not seeing or hearing from her made me fear the worst, and I walked around the cherry tree searching for ebon feathers.

I was glad not to see any, but something else caught my eye.

Along the front walkway, several objects had been laid out in a pattern that roughly formed an isosceles triangle. I bent down to get a better look. How had a bottle cap, a washer, and a pink glass bead ended up on my path?

The items hadn't been there before. My first thought was that I was looking at some kind of cryptic message. As it turned out, that was more right than wrong.

There was a bald patch of ground next to the walkway that was still slightly muddy from the sprinklers. In the muck, there were broken lines about three inches in length.

Raven tracks.

Lenore had been playing Santa Claus. I had heard stories of ravens and crows offering "payment" in return for food, or even kindnesses, but had believed those to be old wives' tales. Lenore had left the objects for me.

"Thank you," I called out, carefully gathering her offerings.

At I stared at my swag, I found myself blinking away tears. I was probably being anthropomorphic, and assigning a human meaning to Lenore's presents, but I was still touched. Clearly, I couldn't interpret the mindset of a raven, but I believed Lenore had left me the items as gifts.

When I got to work, I took another deep dive into the Dana Silva murder book, and sifted through all the case notes. I thought of all the detectives who had preceded me, perusing the same pictures and reading the same reports. Normally, that's daunting, but this time my prospects didn't feel quite so hopeless. If, as I suspected, Chloe Landers and her PI had managed to get a lead on the suspect, then I could too.

I reread Chloe's earliest witness statements, where she referenced her assailant as a monster, murderer, and butcher, but most of the time she had just called him Stu.

That seemed at odds with her two most recent witness

statements. In them, Chloe had referred to her assailant as "my attacker." The only time the name Stu surfaced was when I specifically questioned her about how he had first identified himself when she and Dana had hopped into his car. During our interviews, Stu was not a name she volunteered aloud, as she had in the past.

Was that just a consequence of time, or was Chloe trying to hide something?

My alarm went off, and I reluctantly closed the file. Before leaving, though, I decided I could learn a lesson from Lenore, and arranged for a gift of my own to be delivered.

After I'd settled in my seat, David looked at me and smiled. There were well-worn laugh lines in his face.

"I'm glad you came back, Wyatt."

"Did you have doubts?"

"I did. I wasn't sure if you were ready to commit to therapy."

"The jury might still be out on that one," I admitted.

"Understood," David said. "But you're here now, so I consider that a good sign. My usual procedure is to inquire at the onset of a session if there's anything on your mind, or if there's something in particular that you'd like to discuss."

I kept a blank face. The subject I most wanted to talk about was Chloe, and her desire to murder the man who'd crippled her, but that was off-limits.

"Nothing stands out," I said.

David tentatively nodded. "If something does come to mind, I hope you'll share it with me."

I suspected that was his way of telling me he knew I wasn't being completely forthright.

"In our last session, I assigned you homework," he said. "Did you get to it?"

I nodded.

"Would you prefer starting with your haiku, or should we discuss *Tuesdays with Morrie?*"

"The book, I guess."

"Did you like it?"

"*Like* might not be the right word, but I did find it a worthwhile, and even moving, read. If I wasn't dying, though, I'm not sure I would have been drawn into the story as much as I was."

"Where did the book fall short for you?"

"The ending wasn't exactly a surprise," I said.

"You can do better than that."

"Don't be so sure. I've been making bad one-liners for a long time."

David waited me out for a better response.

"It felt like Morrie was too saintlike."

"What do you mean?"

"He's dying, and he's confined to his room, but he still manages to be at peace. I find that a stretch, especially given his situation."

"And yet Morrie admitted there were times he cried, and felt low, and hated that his body was wasting away. But despite all that, he refused to wallow in grief. He didn't want the end of his life to be about feeling sorry for himself, and somehow even found hidden blessings in his condition. Can you remember some of them?"

After a few moments of thought, I said, "His disease allowed him the time to say his goodbyes, and he said most people weren't that fortunate."

David nodded. "Anything else?"

"He said by learning how to die, you learn how to live."

"I believe that's one of the central points of the book. What do you think about that?"

"It feels intimidating."

"In what way?"

"The eleventh hour is pretty late to be trying to find purpose and meaning in life. And speaking for myself, I'm skeptical about the prospect of death being liberating."

"That's understandable. But as he faced the inevitable, Morrie didn't try to avoid it. Instead, he embraced it. It was Morrie's contention that half-measures wouldn't take you where you needed to go, and that you had to learn to give out love in order to receive it."

"That's easier said than done."

"Yes, it is. But Morrie said what made him feel most alive was giving whatever he could to other people—be it an ear, or a smile, or a caring presence."

"Lennon, McCartney, and Morrie: all you need is love."

"Yes," David said. "One of my favorite biblical passages is about casting your bread upon the waters, and the notion that in doing so those blessings that are sent out have a way of multiplying and coming back. By giving, we receive."

"Then how come it always seems that no good deed goes unpunished?"

"Has that been your experience?"

I shrugged. "When you're a cop, you get daily lessons in cynicism."

He nodded and said, "Is there anything Morrie said that particularly resonated with you?"

"Yes, and I'm not saying this to be a wise guy. Early in the book, Morrie confessed it bothered him to think that one day he'd be dependent on someone wiping his ass."

"And that worries you as well?"

"I don't have ALS, like Morrie did, so I'm hoping wiping my

ass will be something I can do to the end, no pun intended, but I have his same fear of being dependent on others. I don't want to end up like my mother."

"Are you angry at your mother for taking her life?"

"Of course not. I understand how the pain got to be too much for her."

"You had no idea what she was planning?"

"None. But at the same time, I wasn't surprised."

"Explain."

"Unlike Morrie, she wasn't at peace with her situation, or at least that was my perception."

"How often did you see her?"

"For the last five years of her life I saw her every day. I moved into her house to help tend to her."

"That must have played havoc on your social life."

I shrugged.

"Are you afraid of being a burden to others like your mother was to you?"

"She wasn't a burden. She just needed assistance."

"Like Morrie, but to a lesser degree?"

"I suppose."

"When Morrie couldn't wipe his ass, as you phrased it, he was able to let go and let others take care of his bodily functions."

"He didn't have a choice."

"There's always a choice when it comes to how you respond to your circumstances. The psychologist Erik Erikson formulated a theory on psychosocial development, and believed the key to psychological well-being for those facing the twilight of their lives was knowing whether they had led a meaningful life. Those who were satisfied they had were able to face their end with few regrets, whereas those who were dissatisfied had a much more difficult time."

"What about the in-betweeners? I don't feel like my life has been wasted, but I'd be lying if I said I was completely at peace with how it's gone."

"I'm sure Morrie would have said that in your time left, you should be doing what comes from the heart. And forgiving yourself. There's no one who's perfect."

"I'm still hoping God is an easy grader," I said.

I was hoping we'd finish the session without there being time for my haiku, but that didn't happen.

"Before we conclude today, I'd like to hear your haiku," David said. "Would you mind reading it?"

"Okay," I said, reaching for my homework.

Before reading it, I asked, "Do you know what a vaquita is?"

David's brow furrowed as he considered the word. "It sounds familiar, but I can't place it."

"Think of a small shy porpoise," I said. "It's believed there are just a handful in existence, if that. Vaquita have these expressive eyes, and what looks like a Mona Lisa smile on their faces. That is, if they're not already extinct. Their home isn't far from here, in the Gulf of California. It's a case of being so close, and yet so far, because it seems as if there isn't a damn thing that can be done to help them survive.

"Anyway, the title of my haiku is *Vaquita*."

I cleared my throat. Public speaking has never been a favorite activity of mine, and the intimacy of David's office made me unexpectedly nervous. *Only seventeen syllables*, I thought, and started reading.

> "I mourn their passing,
> Extinction of a species,

My tears do no good."

While I silently let out a pent-up breath, David nodded and said, "Thank you."

I nodded back.

"How did you settle on your subject matter?" he asked.

"It just came to me. The plight of the vaquita has bothered me for years. None of the attempts to help them have met with any success. If anything, they just sped up their demise. The Frozen Zoo now seems to be their only hope."

"That's a repository for frozen genetic materials?"

"Yeah. They're cryopreserved in liquid nitrogen."

"Have you ever considered cryonics for your own situation?"

"No," I said. "In the scheme of things, I'm nothing. It's possible that one day the Frozen Zoo will be able to reverse the extinction of a species, or de-extinction, as it's referred to. Why would I expect medical science to have the will, or desire, to thaw me out when our species has already overrun the planet? To paraphrase Rick in *Casablanca*, 'My problems don't amount to a hill of beans in this crazy world.'"

"What made you think of that quote?"

"It's a favorite of mine and puts matters in perspective."

"I'm curious, do you think Rick does the noble thing by letting Ilsa get on the plane to leave with Victor? Isn't that at odds with the notion of love conquering all?"

"Love does conquer all. Rick sacrifices for the greater good."

"Has there ever been an Ilsa in your life?"

"Afraid not."

"Before we finish, Wyatt, do you mind if I ask you a few questions about your haiku?"

"Shoot."

"Was your poem just about vaquita, or was the subject of vaquita a metaphor for something else?"

"Such as?"

"Your own death."

I shook my head and said, "I'm pretty sure that didn't factor into it."

"What can you tell me about your closing line?"

"It consists of five syllables."

"Other than that."

"I'm afraid I'm not clever enough that you need to read between the lines. My point was that tears aren't enough, even if there's nothing else you can give."

"Thank you for your creation," David said. "I was moved by your words. They taught me something, and made me think, and feel."

His praise was unexpected, and made me feel a bit uncomfortable. Still, I managed something resembling a half-bow, and David nodded in return.

CHAPTER TWENTY-THREE

I was on the way to my cubicle when Sergeant Lopez motioned for me to join her. I detoured to her office, and found my eyes drifting to the wolf on her wall. It was looking hungrier than ever.

"Any updates for me?" she asked.

"The *U-T* reporter just left a message saying she'd like to talk to me about the Silva/Landers case."

"Good timing, then," La Loba said. "You can pass on some breaking news to her. The department gave us the green light to film a *Cold Case File* on the Silva homicide."

"That can't hurt," I said, even though it hardly seemed like breaking news that a twenty-five-year-old homicide was going to be featured in a video.

SDPD *Cold Case Files* were relatively new developments in the department. The mini documentaries recapped the crimes we were investigating. The hope was to jog the memories of viewers, and get new eyes looking at old crimes. Normally, the passage of time works against the police, but on occasion, witnesses who'd been too intimidated to come forward when the crime occurred weren't as reluctant to speak with us years later.

She said, "You haven't had any of your cases featured in a *Cold Case File*, have you?"

"This will be a first."

"Media relations will co-ordinate with you. Have you watched the other productions?"

"A few of them."

"Then you know the film opens with a summary of the case. Our hope is that by appealing to their better instincts, someone out there might be prodded to come forward."

"Guilty consciences work for me."

Sarge nodded.

"When will we start putting the video together?" I asked.

"Next week," she said. "You and media relations will design a storyboard, and figure out your talking points. The idea is to personalize the video by talking about the victim, and the crime. I know production is hoping your psychologist will participate in the filming."

I did my best to keep my features impassive.

"Yesterday, I talked with Dr. Landers at length," I said. "Since she's already agreed to do the *U-T* story, I'll try and talk her into participating in our *Cold Case File*."

"Do whatever you can to make that happen," La Loba said. "And tell me how things go with that reporter."

I offered her an upraised thumb and exited her office.

***

I had almost reached my cubicle for a second time when my phone began vibrating. Chloe was calling. I veered away from my desk, and any prying ears, and took the call in the hallway.

"How are you?" I asked.

"Much better after getting your delivery," she said. "I've

been with clients all afternoon, so this is the first chance I've had to call. The flowers you sent are beautiful."

"I'm glad you like them."

I had consulted an internet flower guide before sending her a bouquet of mixed roses. According to what I'd read, the color of the roses you send is meant to convey a particular meeting. I'd opted for an assortment of colors to better hedge my bet.

"They're like a gorgeous rainbow," she said. "And they have a divine scent that's better than any perfume. I wish I could share their aroma with you over the phone."

"I'll have to live vicariously," I said. "By the way, how did things go with your car? That's been on my mind all day."

"Everything went smoothly. It now has a brand-new tire."

"I haven't yet had a chance to look at CCTV footage in the area to see if it shows who vandalized your vehicle, but I hope to get to that before day's end."

"Please don't bother. My insurance covered everything."

"Maybe so, but if our disabled-parking desperado slashed your tire, I don't want him to get away with it."

"Didn't you say something about a $250 parking fine, along with towing and impound fees? That sounds like a $500 lesson."

"I'm not sure that's enough."

"I am. The way I see it, I came out way ahead with these flowers. So, do nothing. Please."

"As you wish," I said.

Over the phone, I heard an intake of breath, and then Chloe laughed and said, "That's not fair."

"What's not?"

"Using Westley's line from *The Princess Bride*. Did I tell you that's a favorite film of mine?"

"You didn't."

"But you know it?"

"Know it? I can even tell you Westley directed those words to Princess Buttercup. Maybe I should have included some buttercups in your bouquet."

"The roses are perfect as is. In fact, they make me feel like a princess."

"That was the idea."

"They also make me feel guilty for sending you home the way I did."

"Why? You could have left me devastated, but you put my situation ahead of yours. That couldn't have been easy."

"I was merely righting a wrong of my own creation. It's tough to walk a tightrope when you're in a wheelchair."

"Some situations call for a safety net," I said.

Both of us were talking obliquely. I wanted her to rethink her desire to find, and murder, Stu B, but she wasn't of the same mind.

"And sometimes you have to proceed even when you know actions have potential consequences," Chloe said.

"You know my feelings. I hope you understand that I just want to help."

"And I appreciate that."

We'd both said our piece, so I decided to back off. It wouldn't do to push her any further. I could only hope her decision wasn't set in stone. Failing that, I needed to make sure I found Stu B. first.

"So, all day I've been trying to figure out some clever line to convince you to see me again, and I finally settled on my hope that ours wasn't a one-and-done date, and that you'll consider going out with me again."

After a moment, she said, "I'd like that."

"Did I detect some hesitation?"

"You did, but I can assure you it wasn't for any lack of enthusiasm on my part. I do want to see you, but what gives me pause is that when I'm in your company, I don't want to feel like a suspect. My hope is that when we're together, you can turn off the cop."

"I'm not sure I can do that completely, but I'll try to keep my work life from intruding on our private lives."

"That's good enough for me."

"When can I see you again?"

"When's it good for you?"

"What are you doing later today?"

We agreed to meet for drinks. It was about as much as either of us could manage, as we were both operating on fumes, and in need of a good night's sleep. Luckily for me, it seemed as if Chloe wanted to see me as much as I did her.

The Pure Project Brewery was located on 5th Avenue, just down the street from Chloe's condominium. I arrived fifteen minutes early and secured an outdoor table for us. Just prior to our six o'clock meetup time, I caught sight of Chloe wheeling along the sidewalk. I stood up and flagged her down. She lifted a hand off of Tweety, waved, and wheeled my way.

After navigating through the restaurant, Chloe braked to a stop just short of our table.

"Training for that marathon of yours?" I asked.

"I'd better. I don't want to be the last to cross the finish line."

She removed her morpho gloves, dropped them on the table, and looked around. "For years, I've been meaning to stop by this spot."

"If you like beer, you won't be disappointed."

I handed her a menu, and Chloe looked over it. She made several surprised noises as she studied the choices.

"I don't usually drink beer," she admitted. "Do you know what you're having?"

I met her eyes and said, "I'm going with Dark Romance."

That made her laugh. She studied the description of my beer selection then asked, "Is that your usual choice?"

"To be honest, I don't remember seeing it on the menu before tonight. But it felt like the right choice."

"Stout with vanilla, cacao, and strawberry," she read. "As much as I want to say let's get two of those, I'm not feeling it."

"A dark romance is not for the faint of heart."

"Agreed. Which is why I'm going to gravitate to the light, and go with Everything Gold May Stay."

"Did you make that choice based on the beer, or on the name?"

"The name, of course. I couldn't even tell you what a Golden Flanders is. Do you know?"

"It's a Belgian beer, but the only reason I know that is because it references Flanders. I'm sure our server would be glad to tell you everything about it, and then some."

"No need. The name's enough for me. I suspect the brewmaster was an English major before turning to mixology."

"And why that conclusion?"

"One of my favorite poems is Robert Frost's *Nothing Gold May Stay.*"

"The clue was right there in front of me, but I had no idea."

"I always knew my minoring in English would come in handy one day," she said.

"What's the poem about?"

"The impermanence of nature, and how everything fades, but it's because of that we need to appreciate ephemeral beauty all the more. At least that's how I remember it, but it's been many years since I last read it. Or heard it."

Chloe raised a finger and then spoke into her phone. A moment later, a raspy male voice began to speak, and I listened to Frost's recitation of his verse. It was a short poem, which didn't diminish from the impact of its words. When the poet finished speaking, neither of us said anything for a time.

"There's something so poignant about it, and especially hearing it in Frost's voice," Chloe said. "While listening to him recite the words, it took me back to my long convalescence. After losing my legs, my world became small, and I only went out when I had to. Back then, I spent a lot of time reading everything and anything."

"I'll bet you're the first person to ever know how that beer got its name."

"I'm also probably the first to order it without knowing what a Belgian beer is."

A smile came to my face. I didn't have to think about it. It just appeared.

Our server approached the table, a man in his late-twenties with tattooed arms and a handlebar mustache. After offering us a greeting, he asked, "See anything you like?"

"I'm going with a ten-ounce glass of Everything Gold May Stay," she said.

"Very good."

He turned his attention to me. "And I'm ready for a Dark Romance."

"Aren't we all?" the server said. "Any appetizers?"

I consulted Chloe with my eyes, and caught a small shake of her head. "Just the beer," I said.

"I'll bring your selections right out," he promised.

Two minutes later he returned with our drinks. As he placed the glasses on the table, he said, "For the lady, an offering of gold. And for the gent, the Dark Romance he wanted. By the way, sir, your timing is impeccable. I've been told this is the last week we'll be offering Dark Romance."

"Is it being replaced by Bad Breakup?" I asked.

"Or better yet, Happily Ever After?" Chloe said.

The server said, "I like both those names, but you'll have to wait until next week for the new beer unveiling. We like to do our launches with a bit of pomp and circumstance."

"It would be ironic if Pomp and Circumstance was the name of the beer," I said.

"A beer with that name should be served with a mortarboard cap and golden tassels," Chloe added.

"Do both of you work in marketing or advertising?" the server asked.

"Nothing so exciting," I said. "I'm an insurance adjuster."

Both of us turned our gazes to Chloe. "And I'm a feng shui consultant," she said.

"Feng shui," our server said. "That's very cool." Then he took his leave, saying, "Enjoy."

When he was out of earshot, I said, "Feng shui?"

"Excuse me," Chloe said, responding to my note of skepticism, "I thought that was pretty good, especially on the spur of the moment. It's not as if I'm in the habit of offering up some made-up occupation to others."

"I do it all the time," I said. "Too much baggage comes from telling strangers I'm a cop, so I usually go with insurance adjuster. In all the years I've used it, no one has ever asked a follow-up question about my work. But feng shui? What would you have done if our waiter started asking you about your work?"

"I'm not sure. Blame yourself for putting me on that slippery slope. Since I'm not very good at telling tales, I might have just confessed. Then again, after chanting an om or two, I might have tried to fake it."

I raised my glass and said, "To your career in feng shui."

"And yours in insurance."

We lightly tapped glasses and then did our sipping.

Turning off the cop in me was harder than I would have thought, even in the company of Chloe. Or, perhaps that's what made it all the harder to turn off. My romantic interest was contemplating murder, or maybe even planning it. I wanted to ask her questions, but not enough to jeopardize our promising romance.

I was warmed by the company, and as my glass emptied, the beer took the edge off of the day. My senses seemed heightened, and everything felt new to me. It was almost easy to forget that I was dying, but that sudden realization reined in my feelings of joy.

Chloe must have noticed the pall that came over me. "What's wrong?" she asked.

"Nothing," I said. "That's the problem. Being with you makes everything feel right, until I realize I'm embracing a fool's paradise. I finally make a connection with someone I care about, and the universe decides the joke's on me."

"I feel the same way, so let's enjoy the here and now," she said. "No relationship is all sunshine and roses. In fact, my favorite part in traditional wedding vows is when each partner declares to the other that they will be there in sickness and in health, until death do them part."

"Those are vows usually made by young people who think they're immortal. Spending time with me isn't fair to you. It's not a relationship with a future."

"I'm here, aren't I? Willingly. Happily. In my practice, I often treat clients who have trouble living in the moment. Let's neither of us do that. Tomorrow will bring what it brings. We have *now*, though."

I let out some air, and felt a little less weighted down.

"I also know that you must be exhausted," Chloe said. "The world always seems bleaker when you're sleep deprived."

"I hate crying in my beer," I said. "It makes it too salty."

Chloe extended a hand my way, and I took it, holding on for dear life.

For dear life.

We ordered another small draft Belgian beer that went by the name of Sacred Space. Once again, our choice was based on the name of the beer. Huddled together, we had our own sacred space, sharing sips of the same glass. Neither one of us was particularly thirsty, but it gave us an excuse to linger together a little longer.

When we took our leave of the brewery, I said to Chloe, "Are you sure I can't walk you home?"

"Not tonight," she said. "I want to get in a workout, so I'll probably take an extra swing around the block before calling it a night."

I made a tsk-tsk sound and said, "Drinking and driving is a serious crime, you know. Before you set out, I'm afraid I'll need to administer a breathalyzer."

"But I only had one and a half small beers, officer."

"We'll see what the breathalyzer says."

I leaned down and kissed her, and it felt as if an electrical charge coursed through my body, leaving me tingling from my mouth to my toes. As our lips disengaged, both of us made the contented sound of "Mmmm."

Then, Chloe asked, "Did I pass?"

"With flying colors."

"See you tomorrow?"

"Count on it," I said.

She gave me a small wave before taking off, and it wasn't long before she and Tweety disappeared from sight.

CHAPTER TWENTY-FOUR

I drove home without thinking about the route, or having any awareness of the landmarks along the way. There was turbulence during the ride, but not from atmospheric pressure or winds. The unrest was in my thoughts, and in my head.

My relationship with Chloe made no sense. I knew that, and Chloe had to as well, but neither of us was choosing to acknowledge it. Our being together was crazy, and yet wonderful. What was going on between us felt like a word I dared not think, let alone say.

But I whispered it anyway: "Love."

To the best of my memory, it wasn't a word I'd ever said to another human being, even my parents. In my case, I'd always been unsure of the concept of romantic love, and had wondered if it was truly a thing, or just some societal construct. Because I'd never experienced it, I had doubted its existence.

As a teen, I'd felt puppy love a few times, before becoming a love skeptic as an adult. Desire I could understand. Lust. But what I was now experiencing went beyond that. I wanted to be with Chloe. When we were together, it felt right. For the first time in my life, seeing to someone else's welfare felt more important than tending to my own.

I was dying, but at the same time I was falling in love. Weren't those things contradictory? Wasn't I supposed to be relegated to a hospice somewhere? I had always heard that love conquers all, but how was that possible? Death was the undefeated champion. It took no prisoners, vanquishing all.

But now I had someone, and something, to live for. At the same time, I wondered if I was getting ahead of myself. It was possible Chloe wasn't feeling what I was. When we'd kissed, though, it had felt as if she was falling as hard as I was.

Once more, I tried out the word. "Love," I said.

It seemed to fit. And it made me smile. Dead man smiling, but even that thought didn't rein in my joy. I began happily humming, although I was initially oblivious of the song. Then I added some words to the tune, and realized I was singing "The Shoop Shoop Song." It was an oldie, first recorded before I was even born. Female and male recording artists had been singing it for more than half a century, asking the question of how to tell if something was true love. In the song's refrain was the answer.

It's in her/his kiss.

Maybe there were more accurate ways to gauge feelings—and love—but I was good with the song's metrics, and hummed to my earworm all the way home.

I pulled into the garage at dusk, with just enough light for me to check on Lenore. Most of the food that I'd left out earlier had been eaten. As ravens are diurnal, I decided it would be best to wait until morning to leave more. It was possible Lenore was already snoozing, as most birds sleep for at least ten hours.

"Incoming," a woman called, and a familiar black-and-white

dog bounded over to me. As I bent down and ran a hand through Lola's fur, she raised herself up, putting her front paws on my chest to better deliver some doggie kisses.

"It's good to see you too," I said.

"No tongue!" Janis yelled.

Lola ignored the directive of her mistress, and I wiped away her kisses with my hand. As Janis came closer, she said, "You need to do a better job of discouraging that hussy, Wyatt."

"Why would I do that? Lola makes me feel like a VIP."

"Her kisses come with a price, and I'm not talking about her breath. Next time I go to Costco, I'll get you one of those monster packs of lint rollers that they sell. These days, she's shedding like crazy."

I looked down at my blazer, saw all of Lola's hair, and shrugged. "Shed happens," I said.

Janis laughed. "You must have been working late last night. Lola got me up at some ungodly hour and tried to get me to let her out to see you."

"I didn't know she was keeping tabs on me."

"She's almost a stalker, the way she monitors you. Her name should be Mutt-a Hari."

"Are you a spy?" I asked, rubbing Lola under a chin.

She offered a preoccupied tail wag, while carefully sniffing the legs of my pants.

"Looks like she's onto the scent of something," Janis said. "Or someone."

It was clear Janis had noticed the strange hours I'd been keeping over the past few days. Or maybe she'd seen a newfound bounce in my step.

"I probably spilled some food."

"Uh-huh." She didn't sound convinced. "Let's go, Lola. Wyatt needs to eat."

Instead of obeying, Lola looked at me, hoping for a reprieve.

"How about I throw a ball for her for five or ten minutes, and then bring her over?"

"I know she'd love it, but I'm sure you must be tired."

"I'm fine. It will take me two shakes of a lamb's tail to get a tennis ball."

It might have taken me three shakes, but not much more. When I came back out, Lola saw the ball in my hand, and started trembling with excitement. The motion sensors had tripped on, allowing enough illumination for our game of fetch.

With her eyes fixated upon the toy, Lola took no notice of Janis's departure. I tossed the ball, and Lola tore away in pursuit, tracking it down while it was still rolling. Then, in triumph, she raced back to me. Again and again, our game of fetch continued, until darkness shut us down. When I walked Lola to her house, she carried the ball proudly in her mouth, chewing nonstop on the sodden mess.

At the door, Janis said, "Give Wyatt his ball back."

"No need," I said. "I have others."

"I was afraid you'd say that," Janis said.

I kept expecting to drop over with exhaustion, but my time with Chloe, and play with Lola, must have released an abundance of endorphins. Someone as sick as I was shouldn't have been feeling so good, but there it was.

My plan for the evening had been to finally get some much-needed sleep, but my mind apparently hadn't gotten that memo. Most evenings, it's my habit to ruminate on the events of the day. I had always imagined that when I got married, I'd have a wife to share stories with, but my solitary musings had become a way of life for me.

Tonight, I had pleasant thoughts to occupy me, and spent

time dwelling on the words and looks that had passed between Chloe and me. I had this sense, though, of some unfinished business, of something needing reexamining.

The poem, I thought. But it wasn't Robert Frost's words, or not exactly. It was Chloe's knowing how one of the brewery's beer offerings had gotten its name. I had been unaware of a clue that was right out in the open. It wasn't an obvious clue, especially since I knew next to nothing about poetry, but if I'd used a search engine to ask a few questions, the origin of the beer's name would have been apparent.

My nagging voice began talking to me again. I started thinking about Stu B., and how he had left Chloe for dead. There were clues, but no answers. But what questions did I need to ask to get those answers?

When the homicide occurred, search engines weren't the commonplace tool they are now. It was time to play some word games, I thought.

I asked my phone, "Words that start with *S-T-U*."

On the screen, a list of words appeared, including *stub, stud, stupor, student,* and *stupid*.

"Words that start with *S-T-E-W*," I said.

Up came a handful of words including *steward, stewbum,* and *stewpan*.

I asked my phone, "What is a stewbum?" It told me it was a drunkard, or a drunken tramp.

For many years, Chloe had referred to her assailant as Stu B., until he suddenly became her Voldemort, as in He-who-must-not-be-named. In the world of wizards, it was considered dangerous to say Voldemort's name aloud. I wondered if in Chloe's world the same rule now applied.

Aloud, I said, "Stu B."

Nothing magical happened, other than my phone offered up the surnames of Stubee and Stubbe. I wondered if the killer could have offered up the name Stu B. as a play on words, in much the way singer and songwriter Cardi B had come up with her name as a play on Bacardi Rum.

When first questioned, Chloe said Stu had offered up a one-syllable last name that started with the letter *B*. She had thought the most likely possibilities were Barnes, Bourn, Burns, or Burr.

"Stu-born," I said. Stubborn.

It sounded like a made-up name. That could have been the killer's little joke. He announced himself not as Stu Bourn, or Stu Burns, but stubborn. As kids, all of us had fake names ready to give out if questioned by adults, or some authority figure. To the best of my memory, no one in my peer group ever had occasion to use those names, but among ourselves we employed such pseudonyms as Ben Dover, Neil Down, Lon Moore, and Hugo First.

At the time, we had thought we were clever.

Is that what Stu had thought? Had he gone around with a ready pseudonym?

"Stu Burns," I said.

That sounded like a made-up name. I repeated the name to my phone's search engine, and then began flipping through screens that showed pictures of men named Stu Burns. After reading through half a dozen bios, other contexts showed themselves, including an explanation of how to get the burnt taste out of stew (add sugar or honey). That didn't interest me, but something else grabbed my attention.

A stewburner, I read, was slang for someone who worked in a naval commissary. It wasn't an obscure reference, but had long been used in the U.S. military, especially the Navy. What seemed to have started as a disparaging description of a mess-hall cook was now a nickname that was affectionately self-owned, with many naval culinary specialists proudly referring to themselves as stewburners. In fact, there were stewburner conventions, stewburner websites, a stewburner clothing line, and even a Stewburner Way in Port Orchard, Washington.

I sat up straight, suddenly finding myself wide awake. In my line of work, eureka moments are few and far between. Had I actually stumbled upon the occupation of Dana Silva's murderer? An electrical charge surged through me, leaving my nerve endings tingling.

The Naval Training Center had always been the elephant in the room. The Office of Naval Intelligence had looked at naval and base personnel under the age of thirty who had previously been brought up on such charges as violence, bodily harm, use of force, abuse of authority, and unwanted sexual conduct. Those flagged under various articles of the Uniform Code of Military Justice had been interviewed by both the military police and the SDPD. The sheer numbers of potential suspects had made the joint investigation a logistical nightmare.

When I'd questioned Penelope Hill, she'd suggested the Navy's sacred cow status might have spared them from the kind of scrutiny that should have been directed their way. I had told her that wasn't my take, and said that judging by everything I'd seen in the murder book, it didn't appear there had been any preferential treatment.

Now, I suspected Chloe's private investigator of playing me. By casting doubt on the investigation, Penelope had gotten me to comment on what I'd seen. She'd also said the Navy hadn't fully co-operated with her own inquiries, implying that then, as now, they had preferred to leave matters well enough alone.

Penelope had done more than tell me to ignore the man behind the curtain; she'd suggested that if Chloe's attacker was in the Navy, the powers that be had all but assured he would stay invisible.

That's the kind of thing you do to misdirect.

I looked at the time and saw it was almost ten o'clock. The

late hour kept me from calling Chloe, but it was more than that. Only after I'd promised Chloe to "not be a cop" had she decided to give our relationship a second chance. Trying to question her now could potentially jeopardize whatever was going on between us.

"Shit," I said.

The adrenaline rush abandoned me, and I actually began to shiver. It was sixty-six degrees outside, and I was trembling. I needed to do my job, as much as I didn't want to.

There was no way to finesse the questioning. In fact, the best way to get answers from Chloe would be to ambush-interview her when she least expected it.

Could she forgive me for doing that? Probably not. She would see it as a betrayal of my promise.

Earlier, I had been thinking about the meetup we had planned for tomorrow at the zoo, and wondered if I would find the courage to tell Chloe what I was feeling.

Love wasn't going to be on tomorrow's docket.

I wondered if it ever would be.

CHAPTER TWENTY-FIVE

It wasn't until after midnight that I dropped off in a fitful sleep. At a little after six, my cell phone alerted me to a text. From Chloe: *Where should we meet at the zoo? And what time is good for you? XOXO*

Hugs and kisses. If I'd received the same text the day before, it would have made my heart go pitter-patter. Now, it made me feel like Benedict Arnold. Last night, I'd sung about true love being revealed in a kiss.

Now, I was thinking about a Judas kiss.

I texted back, *Does high noon work for you?* Three times I typed XOXO, and three times I deleted my hugs and kisses. *Hypocrite,* I thought. I was plotting an ambush, but wanted to respond with something that didn't feel so underhanded. *Let a picture do my talking,* I thought, and typed in the words *funny kiss,* searching through the GIFs that popped up. When I saw footage of a chimpanzee applying an open-mouth kiss onto the camera lens, I attached it to my message.

Within seconds, Chloe responded. *LOL! That is so perfect. It's almost like you were reading my thoughts. I was going to suggest we either meet up at the polar bear exhibit, or the bonobos. But now I say we should definitely go with the bonobos!*

I wrote, *The fates have spoken*, and closed with *LFTSY*, shorthand for looking forward to seeing you. That didn't feel as dishonest as XOXO, but it still felt shitty.

Me2, Chloe wrote back.

Many consider bonobos the most intelligent of nonhuman primates. Of course, seeing that humans have always done those rankings, they need to be taken with a grain of salt. *Homo sapiens* in Latin means "a wise man." It's a presumptuous title to give ourselves, but humans have always been the unquestioned masters of anthropocentrism. As a species, we have long believed that nature can, and should be, exploited by humans.

Because bonobos resemble chimpanzees, they were formerly called pygmy chimpanzees. Unlike other primates, bonobos have never been observed killing one of their own. Maybe that's a result of their complex social structure being ruled by females. Hippies used to chant, "Make love, not war." Bonobos can't vocalize those words, but they can live them. Females seem to defuse aggressive behaviors through sex, which likely explains why bonobos get along with each other better than any other primates do.

I arrived fifteen minutes early at the enclosure with sandwiches from my favorite market on 5th Avenue. By eating, I hoped to avoid having to do much talking.

Chloe showed up a few minutes later, waving and smiling. I did the same, and then leaned down and kissed her. Being in Chloe's presence made me reconsider confronting her. Maybe I could get answers without rocking the boat. Or sinking it.

"Hungry?" I asked.

"Famished," she said.

"What's your sandwich preference? There's the vegetarian option of tomato, Swiss cheese, avocado, and coleslaw with Russian dressing on a French roll, or curry chicken with brie and mango chutney in a pita."

"You are the yummy in my tummy," she said. "Let's go halfies with each."

"Sandwiches first, or bonobos?"

"We can do both at the same time," she said. "Tweety provides me a platform wherever I go."

"As long as you don't wheel away with the food," I said.

"No guarantees."

Chloe used the bag and some of the napkins as a liner, and spread out the sandwiches on her lap. We both took a section of the coleslaw and Swiss cheese. After biting into it, her head began bobbing up and down in approval.

"Delicious," she said. "It's like having a Reuben without the pastrami, but better."

She smiled at me; it was easy to smile back.

As usual, the bonobos were being chill in going about their day. Their enclosure had ropes and hammocks, along with bamboo sway poles, but while we watched, the troop remained earthbound, seemingly content to loll about.

"It wasn't long ago when people were insulted by the notion we descended from apes," Chloe said. "Now, science has shown that humans and bonobos share ninety-nine percent of the same DNA."

"Don't tell that to the bonobos," I said. "They'd be insulted."

The two of us continued chewing our sandwiches and watching the primates.

Chloe suddenly pointed and said, "You see that one bonobo

taking leave of the other? She reached out and touched her as she left. They do that both coming and going."

I wasn't surprised. Even *Homo sapiens* communicate much more nonverbally than verbally. On the job, I learned the real message was expressed through body language, tone of voice, and facial expressions, more than words.

Chloe asked, "Did you ever see the musical *Come From Away?*"

I shook my head.

"If you get a chance, I highly recommend it," Chloe said. "It's a play based on the true story of what happened in the aftermath of 9/11 when all sorts of planes were diverted to an airport in Newfoundland, Canada. Thousands of passengers were stranded in the small town of Gander. In fact, there were almost as many passengers as townspeople. The residents of Gander opened their homes and hearts—not only to humans, but to the animals being transported in the planes. An SPCA worker put in charge of them said stress wasn't only specific to humans, and talked about her having to comfort a grieving bonobo who had miscarried and lost her baby."

"That sounds like a hell of a play."

"It comes to town every few years," Chloe said. "Let's see it together the next time it does."

The words were out of her mouth before she could take stock of their implication. There was a good chance I'd be dead the next time the production was showing.

"Actually, there's no need for us to wait," Chloe added. "I can get us a taped version of it."

"I'll bring the popcorn and Milk Duds."

"It's a date," she said.

"How about this weekend?"

Chloe turned away from me, suddenly interested in the

bonobos. "I can't," she said. "Didn't I mention to you I'll be out of town on business?"

Something was off. Her voice sounded strained and had risen in pitch. And she was still looking away.

Trying to sound casual, I asked, "Going anywhere nice?"

"Not really. Just a convention hotel. Therapists love to gather and talk. Comes with the job, I guess."

I suspected Chloe was making up her story on the fly. She hadn't identified her destination, or where she was staying. Why?

Her hand was now covering her mouth. That was something I often saw when questioning suspects who were reluctant to provide answers.

She commented on the goings-on in the enclosure. "Not much activity today, but that's a good thing."

"Oh?"

"To my thinking, the less drama, the better. There's always some ruckus going on in the chimp enclosure. With bonobos, you see far fewer acts of aggression."

"Long live the matriarchy," I said.

"It seems to work for the bonobos."

Chloe appeared to relax. She returned to eating, taking a bite of the curried chicken pita with mango chutney.

"Yay or nay?" I asked.

"Definite yay as well. Both sandwiches have great sweet-and-sour combinations."

Part of me didn't want to turn over the stone to see what she was hiding. But what had compelled her to tell a story about her plans for the weekend? What was she afraid of me finding out?

Leave it be. *Don't throw a monkey wrench into the works*, I thought, especially at the monkey enclosure. By my saying nothing, we could continue on as we were.

Chloe made contented sounds as she chewed. "You're going to have to tell me where you got these sandwiches."

She was expecting me to offer up the name of a market, or deli. But what I said was, "Stewburner."

Her face drained of color. Of expression. Of life.

"You don't want to go through with your plan," I said. "You can't. It will destroy you, and murdering him will only ruin your life."

She swiveled her wheelchair, ready to get away from me, and my words.

"I love you," I said.

The words were offered too late. I should have led with them. Chloe began wheeling away.

"Stay," I said. "We need to talk."

She gained speed, and the remains of our sandwiches flew out of her lap and onto the walkway.

"Come back!" I called. "Please."

Tweety flew even faster. There wasn't any way I could catch up to her.

I followed behind, picking up the ruins of our lunch, and then tossed them into the trash.

CHAPTER TWENTY-SIX

Once more, I called Chloe's number. As with previous calls, it went unanswered. This time I didn't leave a message. Instead, I tried a different number. If I was lucky, Chloe hadn't yet communicated with her partner in crime.

On the third ring, it was picked up and a voice growled, "Hill."

Since the private detective had answered, it probably meant she hadn't talked to Chloe.

"This is Detective Lake, Ms. Hill. I just finished meeting in person with Chloe. I'm afraid she left quite upset."

"What did you do?"

"I told her not to go through with her plan this weekend."

"What plan is that?"

"She intends to commit a murder, but you already know that."

After a moment's silence, Penelope said, "I guess nothing has changed at SDPD in the last five years. Is there a handbook given out to detectives that teaches them how to browbeat and intimidate?"

"Not that I'm aware."

"What you're doing feels like déjà vu, Detective. It's SDPD intimidation tactics 101. You insinuate you know things you really don't in the hope of scaring suspects into talking. That type of coercion won't work with me."

"If Chloe goes through with her plan, your false indignation won't spare you being an accessory to murder."

"I have no idea what Dr. Landers has planned for this weekend."

"We both know that's bullshit. For years you've been working to find the name of the man who butchered Chloe, and murdered Dana Silva. When you succeeded in that, instead of bringing the information to the police, you passed it on to Dr. Landers. That's the same thing as giving her a weapon you knew would be used in the commission of a crime."

"You sound like someone who's bluffing, and really doesn't know jack shit."

"I don't know the suspect's name yet, but I will, given a little more time. That's what I need. You have to stop Chloe before she makes the biggest mistake of her life."

"I've heard enough of your guesswork."

"Stewburner," I said.

I let the word hang there. Penelope considered her response, and finally said, "What's that?"

"It's the vocational alias that our suspect came up with when he gave a ride to Chloe and Dana," I said. "In the Navy, the official title for a stewburner is a culinary specialist, but I'm not telling you anything you don't already know. I am sure it took a lot of work for you to track down the right Stewie Burns. So, how many culinary specialists were working the NTC mess twenty-five years ago? Fifty? A hundred?

"I'm sure you kept your stewburner investigation on the down low, but you'll have left a trail of your movements. There will be phone calls, emails, and texts. I'm sure you used a series of cover stories and did a lot of your questioning in person. Did you use the Good Samaritan ruse and go around Stu's neighborhood pretending a package addressed to him was delivered to you by mistake? The problem with that is people tend to remember those kinds of encounters."

Penelope didn't say anything, but neither did she hang up on me.

"We have to intervene, Penelope. For Chloe. For yourself. If you think your first go-around with the criminal justice system was bad, you'll find that was a cakewalk compared to what will happen to you if Chloe tries carrying out her plan."

I could hear her breathing. I could almost hear her thinking. Finally, she spoke. "What do you want from me?"

I told her.

At half past five, Penelope knocked on the door while I waited out of sight. Only after the door swung open did I move into view.

"You!"

Chloe's pronouncement was wrapped in hurt and betrayal, and I tried not to wither under her gaze. She turned from me to Penelope.

"I'm sorry," Penelope said. "He said you weren't taking his calls and convinced me that it would be best if you talked to him in person."

Chloe lowered her head, not wanting to look at either of us. After a few moments of not responding, she swiveled around and started wheeling toward the living room.

I said to Penelope, "Can you wait outside and give us five minutes alone?"

"Only if Dr. Landers is all right with that," she said.

"Chloe?" I called out.

Keeping her back to both of us, Chloe said, "Five minutes."

"I'll wait in the hallway," Penelope said.

I joined Chloe in the living room. She didn't turn around, or look my way.

"I'm sorry about today at the zoo," I said. "It wasn't my intention to entrap you like I did, but I began to panic after you said you were going out of town this weekend. You're not a good liar, Chloe. I imagined the worst reason behind you telling that lie, which scared the hell out of me. I couldn't stand the thought of losing you."

"You'd better get used to it."

"No. That's not something I can do. That's why I had to intervene, even if it drove you away. Love is for the brave, they say. I had to be brave, even at my own expense. I had to save you."

"I didn't ask to be saved. Or to be controlled."

"That's not what I'm doing. I'm trying to spare you from the fallout that will come from committing a murder."

"I've lived with that fallout for twenty-five years. You've seen my scars and my maimed body. But it's the scars you can't see that take the biggest toll. As the years passed, I healed as best I could, but I could neither forgive nor forget what he'd done to me, and to Dana. For all the pain and misery that monster inflicted, he needs to pay."

"Yes, he does."

She whipped her wheelchair around and stared at me accusingly. "I wasn't talking about you arresting him."

"I wasn't either."

"Then what?"

"I need you and Penelope to tell me everything you know. If I'm satisfied with the conclusions of your investigation, then I'll act."

"Act how?"

"I'll be the judge, jury, and executioner."

Her eyes widened, and her mouth opened. She struggled to find the words.

"I can't ask you..."

"You didn't."

"This is my responsibility."

"I'm dying, Chloe. But somehow, I was granted a miracle. I found you. And the only good thing about my death sentence is that I don't have to worry about what will happen to me. I can act with impunity. That can be my gift to you."

"My wanting to see him dead shouldn't fall to you. That's not right."

"It might not be right, but neither is you going to prison, or suffering for the rest of your life. You wouldn't be able to walk away from murder unscathed, Chloe."

"And what about you?"

"It won't be easy, nor should it be, but I have always believed offenders should pay for their crimes. The man who attacked you and Dana brought this death penalty down on himself, and it only makes sense I should be his executioner. If you can have a good life after I'm gone, then I can die knowing I did the right thing."

Tears started dropping from Chloe's eyes, and her breathing became shaky.

"Want a shoulder?" I asked.

"Tissue," she said. "I don't want to ruin your shirt with my snot and mascara."

I retrieved a box of tissues from an end table and took a knee next to her, giving her Kleenex and my shoulder. We held one another as the used tissues began to grow.

Finally, her tears abated, and Chloe said, "Last night I wrote in my journal, 'It's crazy, but I think I'm falling in love.' The journal is on my bedstand, if you'd like to see the entry."

"No need. I hoped you felt as I did. But even if that wasn't the case, it wouldn't have changed matters. I've got to be the person to do this."

She reached for me, and we kissed, until she pulled her head back.

"God, I'm a mess," she said, using the back of her hand to wipe away her tears and blow runny nose.

Undeterred, I went in for a second kiss, but we were interrupted by the sound of knocking.

"I guess we've exceeded our five minutes," I said.

The three of us sat in the living room, each casting glances at the other, but none of us knowing what to say. To me, it felt like the standoff scene in *The Good, the Bad, and the Ugly*.

Finally, Chloe turned to Penelope and said, "Wyatt has proposed an alternate arrangement to what was to take place this weekend."

Penelope directed her glower my way.

"Before considering the best way to proceed, I'll need to know everything the two of you have uncovered," I said.

Penelope shook her head and said, "You'd like that, wouldn't you? If we admit that we were plotting to kill someone, you could implicate us on the felony charge of conspiracy to commit murder. There's no fucking way you're getting anything from me."

"I'm not looking to charge you with anything. What I'm asking is to join you. That's why I need to see everything you've gathered. I have to be convinced you've targeted the right person. That means my going through your case notes, and asking questions."

Penelope turned to Chloe and said, "We agreed from the start that we'd keep all our findings just between us."

"I think you'll feel differently when you hear what Wyatt's proposing," she said.

"I doubt it," Penelope said.

"I can't murder someone without being absolutely convinced he's the guilty party," I said.

Penelope did a double take, and looked from Chloe to me. "What?"

"If the evidence is there, I'll act."

"And you're not talking about just arresting him?" Penelope asked.

"I'm not."

Penelope said, "Why the hell would you agree to this?"

"Because I'm dying," I said. "And I'm in love with Chloe."

Penelope's jaw dropped. "Are you fucking with me?"

"I've been blessed and cursed," I said.

"Let's start with the dying part."

"The specialists are giving me about a year, give or take a few months."

"Shit," Penelope said. "And what about falling in love?"

"That's a recent development," I said.

"For both of us," Chloe added.

"I need a drink," Penelope said.

"I think we all do," I said.

CHAPTER TWENTY-SEVEN

Most conspiracies to commit murder don't start with glasses of chardonnay and appetizers of Costco mini-quiche, but ours did. Still, as the three of us began comparing notes and hatching our plan, I thought of what Ben Franklin had said about secrets: "Three may keep a secret if two are dead."

I wasn't sure if my being half-dead fit into Ben's equation.

Penelope took the lead, talking about what her investigation had uncovered.

"Our suspect is Abel Lynch," she said. "He is forty-eight years old and served twenty-five years as a Naval Culinary Specialist, retiring just last year as an E-6."

"Lynch?" I said, trying to remember if his name rang any bells. "I'm pretty sure he was never on SDPD's suspect list."

"Were other naval personnel identified as potential suspects?" Penelope asked.

I nodded. "There were at least a dozen persons of interest that investigators talked to. Most were active duty, but some were civilians employed by the Navy. All of them were ruled out fairly early in the investigation."

"But you don't believe Lynch was ever interviewed?"

"I'll check to make sure, but I don't think he was."

"There's a reason he might have slipped through the cracks," Penelope said. "Within days of when the attack occurred, Lynch shipped out."

"Good timing for him," I said.

"I think it's safe to assume Lynch knew he was going on sea duty, as it's usually scheduled months in advance," she said. "Essentially, it was the perfect moment for him to commit a crime. With the Naval Training Center closing shop, and its personnel being transferred all over the globe, his trail was muddied from the start.

"Three days after the attack, he sailed off on the aircraft carrier the USS *Kitty Hawk* and spent time at sea traveling around Asia. More than six months passed before Lynch and the ship returned to port in San Diego, but that wasn't even a way station for him. After a month's leave, Lynch was transferred to Naval Station Norfolk and worked at their shore station for three months. Then it was off to sea again."

"Great way to stay clear of a homicide investigation," I said. "Were you able to access Lynch's service evaluation reports?"

Penelope shook her head. "I never even made the attempt. There's no way the Navy would have released that information to someone without official standing. Besides, it was my goal from the start to keep the investigation covert, and not leave a trail with my name on it."

"How were you able to key in on Lynch?"

"About a year ago, I created a cover story that I was working on a cookbook called *Navy Gravy*," Penelope said. "I contacted the stewburner community through social media and told them I was looking for recipes, as well as personal stories offering insights into the lives of naval culinary specialists. Over time, I talked to dozens of mostly retired stewburners, and one connection led to another. That's how I made contact with individuals who worked at NTC during the time period in question."

Chloe said, "Because I was concerned about what Penelope's investigation might stir up, she worked under the alias of Sarah Williams."

"How did you choose that name?" I asked.

"We looked up the most popular first and last names from thirty years ago," Chloe said. "Sarah was the third most common girl's name in the county, and Williams was the third most common surname. Since there are thousands of Sarah Williams out there, we thought the name would provide her with camouflage if anyone tried to look into her background."

"I created a bio for Sarah, as well as an email account," Penelope said. "She has her own social media platform where she's active. And to make sure our identities were kept separate, I disguised my features in all the Sarah pictures. Whenever I'm in Sarah mode, I wear a long platinum-blonde wig, and glam up with heavy eyeliner and fire-engine red lipstick. I doubt if even my friends could look at Sarah's pictures and have any idea that it's me in dress-up."

"What personal information about Sarah did you release on social media?"

"She's a self-described 'Navy brat,' a rolling stone with little in the way of roots. In Sarah's profile, I wrote that she attended Texas A&M. We chose that university because it has one of the largest undergraduate student populations in the country. Sarah identifies as a freelance writer and editor, as well as a social influencer. She is a self-described foodie and wine connoisseur, and frequently posts on where she eats."

Penelope raised her glass of chardonnay, and offered up the kind of fake happy smile seen too often on social media pages.

I asked, "Does that mean anyone looking at Sarah's social media will know she lives in San Diego?"

Penelope shook her head and said, "We thought it better to give her some distance from here, so Sarah's profile says she lives in Carlsbad. I even set up a PO box there for her to receive mail, and got Sarah her own cell phone with the North County area code of 760."

Carlsbad was a good choice. Not only was it thirty-five miles north of San Diego, but the city had well over a hundred thousand residents.

"That all sounds good," I said. "But were you able to keep Sarah away from any face-to-face meetings?"

"That wasn't a possibility because of Sarah's supposed work on *Navy Gravy*," Penelope admitted. "In fact, to better establish Sarah's identity, I met with a number of stewburners. Those meetups invariably involved cooking, and was documented in photos."

I turned to Chloe. "Did you accompany Penelope to any of those meetings?"

She shook her head.

"And as far as you know, there's nothing to connect you with Sarah?"

"Not a thing," Chloe said.

Penelope said, "Most of Sarah's social media promotes *Navy Gravy*, which is supposed to be published early next year. On her site, you'll find recipes, pictures of food, profiles of stewburners, and stories of their lives in the service. *Navy Gravy* gave me a good reason to meet lots of people, and ask lots of questions."

"You should go look at the website," Chloe said. "There's even a display with the book's front cover that we had made up."

I entered the book's name in my phone's search engine. The website that came up looked legit. There was a quote from

Napoleon saying, 'An army marches on its stomach,' and links to movie clips showing naval galleys portrayed in such films as *Top Gun*, *The Hunt for Red October*, and *Crimson Tide*.

"Click on the link to *At War with the Army*," Chloe said.

It wasn't a movie with which I was familiar. When I hit the link, it showed Jerry Lewis slopping beans in an army galley and singing about how the Navy gets gravy whereas the Army gets beans.

"I was steered to that one by an old stewburner who said the title of my book must have been inspired by the Dean Martin/Jerry Lewis film," Penelope said.

The importance of stewburners in the military was played up throughout the website. On one page were pictures taken from the galley of the USS *Midway*, where stewburners had served up to 13,500 meals daily.

"You did a lot of work on this," I said.

"It allowed me access into what otherwise would have been a closed community," Penelope said.

"Is that how you got Lynch to surface?"

"In a roundabout way, yes," Penelope said. "Because of my involvement in the stewburner community, I began following the social media accounts of hundreds of current and retired culinary specialists. Five months ago, one of the stewburners posted a Throwback Thursday photo that showed him working the line at NTC along with two other cooks. Abel Lynch was one of the cooks identified in the shot. When I showed Dr. Landers the picture, she reacted strongly."

"To be honest, when I saw the picture of Lynch, I pretty much had a full-blown panic attack," Chloe said. "It's one thing to advise clients on the best ways to deal with their panic disorders, but another to experience it. I had heart palpitations, nausea, and alternating sweats and chills."

"From the picture, you recognized your attacker?"

Chloe nodded.

"We knew the time frame fit," Penelope said. "The picture was taken just a month prior to when Dana and Dr. Landers were attacked. Still, we knew her identifying the suspect wasn't proof enough to establish his guilt, and that we'd need more evidence to show Lynch was our man. That's what I've been compiling ever since."

"What'd you find?"

"During his time in service, Lynch had two wives. Both were foreign born: one seven years younger, one ten years. Neither of the marriages lasted very long. In both court proceedings, the women cited 'ongoing domestic disputes' as reasons for divorce, and stated they'd been victims of domestic violence."

"Were you able to communicate with these women? Get statements?"

"Unfortunately, no. One wife returned to Mexico, and the other went back to the Philippines. There were no children in either marriage."

"Where's Lynch living now?"

"Six months ago, he settled in Lompoc, where he has a one-bedroom apartment."

Lompoc was about a four-hour drive north. If memory served me, there was a military base there, as well as a federal penitentiary.

"Is Lynch currently working?"

Penelope nodded. "A few months ago, he started working as a cook at the Royal Meridian in Goleta."

"Have you met with Lynch in person?" I asked.

The two women exchanged glances. "That was a topic of debate between us," Chloe admitted.

"And?"

Chloe said, "Through her Sarah Williams persona, Penelope reached out to him."

"Lynch has virtually no presence on social media, but I was able to get his current email address through a stewburner he used to work with," Penelope said. "I wrote to Lynch about the project, and asked if he would consider contributing some recipes and/or stories to *Navy Gravy*, but he never responded to my email."

"Are you sure he received it?"

Penelope nodded. "My website was designed for me to be able to monitor all the traffic coming into it. After I wrote to him, Lynch visited the site on two occasions, and spent a good deal of time looking around it, but unfortunately, he never rose to the bait."

"It's probably good that he didn't," I said. "Not having contact with him leaves you in the clear in the event of an investigation."

Penelope said, "I suppose I should add that although the two of us never met face to face, in the past few months I have been in Lynch's proximity."

"Doing what?"

"I conducted stakeouts in Lompoc and Goleta, where I recorded footage of him to show to Dr. Landers."

I turned my gaze to Chloe.

"And I'm convinced he's our man," she said.

"Based on what?"

"Based on the obvious. You heard how I picked Abel Lynch from an old picture. Nothing I saw in Penelope's footage changed that belief. In some of her recordings, she even managed to capture his voice. It matches up with my memories of the man who tried to kill me."

"What memories? Did your attacker have some kind of an

accent? Was there some verbal giveaway, or perhaps a memorable expression, that linked the past with the present?"

"None of those things," Chloe said. "But the recordings Penelope made sound eerily similar to the voice I've been hearing in my nightmares for the last twenty-five years."

"I don't have to tell you that people's memories are unreliable," I said. "I'm sure you've seen it in your work, as have I."

"We know the mind can play tricks," Penelope said. "To corroborate Dr. Landers's memories, we did a series of reverse age-progression imagery."

"Reverse age progression? I'm familiar with age-progression imagery. We did that with a missing child's case to see how she'd look as an adult. But I didn't know the process could be reversed."

"It's not something age-progression software was specifically designed for," Penelope admitted. "But that said, if you look at our results from the picture of Lynch while he was working the line at NTC, and compare that to the identikit images made at the time of the crime, you'll see how closely they resemble one another."

"That's not good enough," I said. "If we're going to sentence Lynch to death, I need more than some passing resemblance. If I'd brought your so-called evidence to the DA, she'd point out how circumstantial everything was, and refuse to bring charges without me getting her more."

"What if there isn't more?" Chloe asked.

"Then you turn over more rocks until there is."

"Figures," Penelope said. "It sounds like you're looking for an excuse to not act."

"I'm not going to apologize for needing to be sure of Lynch's guilt," I said. "That's my price for committing murder."

"We have more," Chloe said. "Penelope has compiled evidence and put it in a file."

"I'll need to see everything," I said.

The two women exchanged glances, and both nodded.

"When do you want to review the file?" Penelope asked.

"No time like the present," I said.

CHAPTER TWENTY-EIGHT

Chloe and I had a hurried conversation, while Penelope waited out of earshot.

"I've changed my mind," she said. "I don't want you to do this. In my job, I'm always advising my clients to not make impulsive decisions."

"I'm not your client."

"The point is, you're not thinking clearly. I don't want you acting on my behalf because you're trying to shield me from doing something terrible. It's enough that we love one another. Can't we just do that?"

I bent down, and we kissed.

"Oh," she said, a happy note, with just a touch of surprise and disbelief.

Like it couldn't be happening. It was the same sensation I was feeling: wonder and amazement that was somehow surfacing even under these crazy circumstances. Finding love in such a situation should have been impossible, but there it was.

"We'll talk tomorrow," I said.

"I really don't want you acting out of some misguided need to show that you love me," Chloe said. "I've reconsidered. Go make your case against Lynch, and then arrest him. That will be enough for me."

"You almost sound convinced of that," I said. "And maybe in this moment you are. But seeing as you've had years to process your decision, and decide on what you'd do if you ever found your attacker, I know it's not something you came to lightly. This weekend, you were planning on taking a life. In your mind, there was no backing out, was there?"

"There wasn't, but maybe there should have been."

"When I intervened, you were beyond furious."

"I wasn't looking forward to murdering Lynch, but I felt it was something I had to do. For me. For Dana. But as livid as I was when you interfered, I knew your heart was in the right place."

"Right here on my sleeve," I said.

"I know it's barbaric, but I still want him to pay with his life."

"In your work, I'm sure you've had to deal with patients who were unable to get over some trauma from the past."

"Many."

"And how did you help them do that?"

"It depends on the client. There's no one size fits all. Some respond to trauma-focused cognitive behavioral therapy. There are antidepressants and anti-anxiety medication. But usually what works better than anything is talking it out. I like to tell stories to my clients with take away messages. I know that might sound banal, but it works."

"Give me an example," I said.

"One of my favorites is the story about the two wolves who live inside each of us. Supposedly, it's a Native American tale, but I think its message is universal. As the story goes, an elder is talking to a boy and tells him, 'There are two wolves locked in combat who live inside each of us, the one wolf unfeeling, harsh, and vengeful, and the other wolf caring, compassionate, and loving. Each of these wolves vies for control of our soul.' After hearing this, the boy asks, 'Which of these wolves will win?' And the elder replies, 'Whichever wolf you feed.'"

"Good story," I said.

"Telling it to you now makes me feel like a hypocrite, seeing as I've been feeding the wrong wolf for a very long time. And yet I still want Lynch to die."

My GPS guided me to Penelope's apartment on Essex Street in Hillcrest. What it didn't guide me to was an open parking space, but I finally found one on the street just off of University Avenue, two blocks from her complex.

After being buzzed in, I made my way up to her unit on the second floor. I rang her doorbell. When Penelope opened her door, my way was blocked by a security screen.

"Don't even think about it," Penelope said, words directed at the figures lurking behind her. To me, she said, "Be careful not to let the boys out. They pride themselves on being escape artists."

She unlatched the dead bolt, and I cautiously made my way inside. Eyeing me warily were two similar-looking shorthair gray cats with black tabby stripes.

"These characters usually go by the names of Heckle and Jeckle," she said. "But sometimes I call them Jekyll and Hyde. They're brothers."

I looked around her minimalistic apartment. There wasn't much to see in the small space other than a couch and a folding chair.

"I can offer you beer or tap water," she said.

"I'm good, thanks."

"These are my ground rules," she said. "You can take notes, but nothing leaves the apartment. My Abel Lynch files are encrypted, and they're going to stay that way." In a prickly tone, she added, "I had planned to delete the files after the events of this weekend."

"Were you going to accompany Chloe to Lompoc?"

"I wanted to, but Dr. Landers insisted that whatever happened this weekend was going to be on her, and I needed to establish an airtight alibi while she was away."

"Didn't it concern you that a woman in a wheelchair was going to stand out to potential witnesses?"

"It wasn't our plan to have Dr. Landers wheeling up and down the main drag of Lompoc waving sparklers. The idea was for her to be as close to invisible as possible."

"And how were you going to achieve that?"

"There's an Irish bar in town that's open until two in the morning most nights. Lynch is a regular there. His apartment is located about a mile from the bar, and Lynch makes a point to cycle there and back. I suspect he does that to avoid the possibility of his getting a DUI. He usually leaves the bar between midnight and one. In the times I've observed him, Lynch always takes the same residential route home that avoids the main streets. Along that route, we identified several good spots for an ambush."

"And you expected Chloe to be able to hit a moving target at Zero Dark Thirty?"

"There's a full moon this weekend. And we had a plan in place to slow, or stop the target, by setting up an obstacle in the path of the bicycle. Dr. Landers was going to take the shot from inside her car. I wasn't worried about her marksmanship. The two of us have been taking target practice in remote spots around the Anza-Borrego desert. She has become quite proficient in her shooting. In fact, she's a much better shot than I am."

"What kind of gun was she going to use?"

"A bolt action rifle. And to answer your next question, I purchased it at an out of state gun show, and paid cash. No paperwork was filled out."

"A rifle's a lot more conspicuous than a handgun."

"That's why Dr. Landers was going to set up for her shoot in a spot well away from the main road and businesses. As far as I could determine, the area is clear of any surveillance cameras, and none are in the nearby vicinity. As for the doctor's coming and going, I plotted her arrival and departure routes along quiet residential roads, and boosted a spare set of license plates that she was going to install once she got outside Santa Barbara. Finally, the white Tesla Y she drives is one of the most common vehicles on the road in California."

Penelope explained all this in a flat tone of voice, which didn't quite hide her annoyance.

"I know you wish I hadn't intervened, but I acted in what I believe are Chloe's best interests."

"You don't think I had her best interests in mind?"

"I'm sure you believed you did."

"I've known Dr. Landers for years. You barely even know her."

Penelope sounded more than defensive; she sounded jealous.

"And yet, we fell for one another. I don't think either of us expected to fall in love."

"The timing seems very convenient for you."

"Why do you say that?"

"Because I have my doubts that you'll even try to take out Abel Lynch. I think all you'll be doing is running out the clock."

"You're wrong. If I can determine Lynch is guilty, I'll go after him."

"And if you die before carrying out your verdict, it will be our tough luck, right?"

"I have no intention of leaving it for Chloe to murder Lynch, if that's what you're implying."

"We'll see," she said, not hiding her skepticism. "What's that saying about justice delayed being justice denied?"

"If we're hanging our hats on legal sayings, maybe we should be talking about the one that says it's better for a guilty man to go free than an innocent man to hang."

"And you're all about fairness, right?"

"When it comes to the dispensation of Abel Lynch, yes, but I have a feeling that's not what you're talking about."

"Do you think encouraging Dr. Landers to love you, a dying man, is fair?"

"Probably not. But neither Chloe nor I have control over that emotion, or feeling, or whatever the hell love is."

"How sick are you? Really?"

"Dead man walking sick."

"In that case, you are the right person for the job," she said. "Let's hope it's not just talk, though."

For the better part of two hours, I studied Penelope's Abel Lynch file. Heckle and Jeckle curled up and slept on either side of me while I worked. Finally, I closed the laptop, afraid I was going to nod off with the cats.

"I have to call it a night before I doze off," I said.

"I'm right there with you," Penelope said, looking as tired as I felt.

I handed her the laptop, and stretched.

"Well?" she asked.

"You were very thorough," I said.

"That sounds like you're damning me by faint praise."

"If it did, that's not what I meant. What you've compiled is a long report, and right now I feel as if I've only skimmed the surface of it. I'm going to have to digest what I read."

"Do you think Lynch is our man?"

"I'm not yet prepared to answer that question."

"What's your gut tell you?"

"I'm not listening to my gut. I'm looking at the evidence."

"And you don't think there's a strong case against Lynch?"

"I didn't say that. If you think I'm looking at your report with a jaundiced eye, you're right. But what you need to understand is that I do the same kind of nitpicking with my own cases. I question everything, and look for holes in the evidence."

"And you found some holes?"

"I found areas that need to be looked into further."

"For example?"

It was a conversation I hadn't yet wanted to get into, but clearly Penelope wasn't about to be put off.

"Okay," I said. "In Chloe's witness statement, she talked about the suspect smoking weed, and then his making comments about spiking it with angel dust. Stu's using PCP raised flags with me. The armed services have a zero-tolerance policy, and for the last fifty years they've been testing for drug use. Since that's the case, how did Lynch avoid testing positive?"

"The tests are random, aren't they?" she said.

"As far as I know."

"I've heard that sailors can beat the system by using fast-acting detox kits, as well as synthetic urine."

"That's a possibility," I admitted. "But most lifers don't go around jeopardizing their pension and benefits in the hopes they can beat a drug test."

"Lynch probably wasn't planning on being a lifer way back then."

"It still seems like an unnecessary risk."

"Maybe he'd just had a drug test, and knew his number wasn't going to be called for another year."

I said nothing, which only appeared to annoy her all the more.

"What else?" she asked.

"I had some problems putting Lynch at the crime scene," I said. "At the time of the attack, he'd been in the Navy for around seven years, correct?"

"That sounds about right."

"Then, it only makes sense that as a culinary specialist, he'd have the kind of knife skills necessary to work in a big kitchen. I imagine part of his job was butchering large sides of meat, and breaking down animal carcasses. That would involve using such implements as a boning knife, cleaver, and a handsaw."

"So?"

"Chloe and Dana's attacker knocked them senseless by smashing their heads with a rock. Based on forensics, he then used a hand axe to hack the women's limbs. Because the crime scene looked like a slaughterhouse, law enforcement believed the attacks were the work of a disorganized killer."

"What are you saying?"

"Wouldn't an experienced cook have been able to use that hand axe to more effectively butcher the two women? The crime scene, and the injuries suffered by the women, suggested their limbs were brutally hacked up. In weight and heft, his using the axe wouldn't have been that different from his working with a cleaver. Cooks know about joints and ligaments and the best ways to dismember. If you can cut up a chicken, or a side of beef, you should be able to do the same to a human body."

"But he was out of his mind on PCP," Penelope said.

"Even taking that into account, wouldn't you think that with seven years on the job, he'd have been more adept with his bladework?"

"I'm sorry the women weren't butchered to your satisfaction," she said. "But maybe there was more than just his drug use to explain those botched dismemberments. Wasn't it the SDPD's contention that the murderer was an opportunistic killer?"

I nodded.

"Then isn't it likely he was in some kind of frenzy, and acted on the spur of the moment?"

"It's possible."

"He's zonked on angel dust, and probably on an adrenaline overload when he starts attacking his victims. But you still expect him to carve straight?"

"I'm not here to argue with you," I said, disengaging myself from Heckle and Jeckle and getting to my feet.

"I'm sorry," Penelope said. "Ignore what I said. It's just that I'm frustrated as hell."

"I know the feeling."

She could hear the long history in my words, the cases that were still holding me hostage, and still awaiting some kind of hoped-for resolution.

Speaking softly, in a non-confrontational voice, Penelope asked, "Isn't it also possible that Lynch purposely disguised his knife skills?"

Trying to keep my voice neutral, I said, "It's possible." But she knew I wasn't buying her explanation.

"Where else does my case fall short?" she asked.

"Every investigation falls short," I said. "Sometimes, no matter how hard you look, there are questions that remain unresolved. One area that I want to look at more closely is Lynch's timeline, and how it tracks with his personal life."

"Specifically?"

"You wrote that after one of his failed marriages, his wife Maria filed for divorce and returned to the Philippines. It was your belief that Lynch received the divorce papers during the time he was deployed, but ultimately, he was able to get the marriage annulled."

"That's because Maria never followed up and filed the divorce paperwork."

"She didn't try to exact a settlement or benefits?"

"From what I know, Maria was essentially a mail-order bride. And since she was only in the States for a short period of time, I was told it was unlikely she qualified for citizenship, or even a Green Card. Given that information, I just assumed she was glad to be done with him. What are you suggesting?"

"I'm not suggesting anything. All I'm doing is looking at potential loose ends. I'm not saying Lynch isn't the prime suspect, or that your conclusions are wrong. But I still need more."

"Thank you," she said. Her words sounded deflated, but sincere.

CHAPTER TWENTY-NINE

I slowly emerged from my fog, and became aware of a ringing phone. Sleep had eluded me for much of the night. It's hard to count sheep when you're contemplating murder. I squinted, trying to make out the phone's display, and saw it was Tommy Boy Garcia calling.

"Hello," I said, or tried to say, croaking out the word.

"Were you actually sleeping?" Tommy asked.

"Sort of," I said.

"I thought you were always an early riser. What's that saying? Up with the larks?"

"I've switched teams. Lately, I'm down with the owls."

"Does your being used for target practice the other night have anything to do with you being up late?"

The last time I'd seen or talked to Tommy had been the night of the shooting.

"It didn't exactly help my insomnia," I said.

"So, who doesn't like you?"

"Lots of people, but I still don't know who wanted me shot. I had to put that investigation on the back burner when my other case started heating up."

"Heating up? You look at dinosaur bones. That's not like working an active investigation. Ancient history can wait."

"My favorite criminal justice professor used to quote some philosopher who said: 'History is the study of all the world's crime.'"

"At Southwestern, we had a bunch of retired cops teaching our courses, but the only quote I remember any of them ever reciting was Miranda."

"Maybe you shouldn't have been sleeping through all your classes."

"Someone had to heat up the nights for all those deprived South Bay ladies."

"Was it anyone you know?"

"You need to get over your case of the cranks, Lago. Since you're clearly in need of coffee, or what you think passes for it, how about I get you a cup and we meet up to shoot the shit."

"Our coffee klatch will have to wait for another day. This morning I've got too many things on the docket."

Tommy said, "If someone had taken a potshot at me, my priorities sure as hell wouldn't be some oldie-moldy."

I didn't want to talk about the case, because that would mean talking about Chloe. It was better to say nothing.

Tommy continued to push. "You think it's a coincidence that the shooter came gunning for you right after you started asking questions about our dead informant? That's certainly got me wondering if you're right about a conspiracy in our ranks. Ever since you floated that theory, I've been doing a lot of looking over my shoulder."

"It was probably just my paranoia talking."

"Being paranoid doesn't mean they're not after you. Someone sent a bullet your way. That wasn't some random incident. You upset someone's apple cart, but whose?"

"I'll start looking into that as soon as I find the time."

Even to my own ears, that explanation sounded lame. Tommy was used to being my sounding board, and I didn't want him wondering why I was holding back on him.

I said, "Anyway, the truth of the matter is that it's not only work that's been keeping me up nights. It's something else, or I guess I should say, *someone* else."

"Now we're getting the real story," Tommy said. "I knew there was something you weren't telling me. So, let's hear about this unlucky woman. I'm assuming she is a woman, right?"

"Very much so," I said.

"Rosa's going to want to know all the details," he said. "Spill 'em."

I couldn't use Chloe's name, especially if it might lead back to Lynch.

"She's a doctor," I said.

That was true. Sort of.

"You're kidding? What's she doing with a knuckle dragger like you?"

"I'm smart enough not to ask."

"How'd the two of you meet?"

Shit, I thought, trying to navigate my tale with half-truths. "She had a flat tire, and I helped her."

"The Good Samaritan ruse," he said. "Works every time. In fact, there was a serial killer who used to go around slashing women's tires, and afterward offered to help them. I'm assuming that was your MO as well."

"I assisted a damsel in distress. And that's all you're getting out of me for now. Tell Rosa I'll give her the full rundown the next time I see her."

"You're not going to get rid of me that easily, Lago. Give it up. You've already played doctor with her, right?"

"Yeah, she tickled my funny bone."

"What'd the two of you talk about when you were in the sack? Acute angina?"

"Give my best to Rosa and Joey," I said, hanging up.

With a late start on my workday, I tried to make up time by hurrying through my morning routine. Lenore remained hidden while I placed some food in the cherry tree, and refilled her water. My breakfast was a protein bar that I ate during my commute to work. Luckily for me, I have friends in low places. When I arrived at my desk, I found a still-warm cup of coffee. On it, Tommy had used a Sharpie to leave a message: *Some rocket fuel for lover boy.* Beneath those words, he must have had the barista kiss the cup, because the message came with a lipstick kiss.

Typical Tommy. I looked around to see if anyone was watching for my reaction. Only two of my colleagues were at their desks, and neither appeared to be taking any notice of me. Lifting the cup, I took a sip of my Caramel Ribbon Crunch Frappuccino. It was like having a doughnut and coffee all in one.

I spent my morning reviewing case notes, and trying to find out what I could about Abel Lynch without raising any red flags in the system. It wouldn't do to have his name appearing in any of my searches, so I did my best to work around it.

Over the course of the morning, Chloe and I sent several texts to one another. I told her my schedule wasn't going to allow for a meetup at the zoo, as I had an afternoon session with David. She texted back *I will miss you,* and followed that with several heart emojis. That put a smile on my face, and I sent a GIF of an excited little boy doing a happy dance. For the first time in my life, I was a fan of texting.

My phone rang, and for a moment I hoped Chloe had decided to talk instead of text, but the display told me she wasn't the one calling. As tempted as I was to let the call go to voicemail, I picked up and said, "Lake."

"This is Audrey Campbell from the *Union-Tribune*, Detective," she said. "Is now a good time to talk?"

Earlier in the week, the reporter and I had exchanged emails and agreed on a time and date for a phone interview, something I had conveniently forgotten.

"Now's fine," I said. "Have you talked to Dr. Landers yet?"

"We're meeting tomorrow at her office," she said.

At least that would give me time to clue Chloe into everything the reporter asked me.

She added, "Dr. Landers wants to discuss the here and now of her life, rather than what happened in the past."

"How she emerged on the other side."

"Exactly. Dr. Landers doesn't want to dwell on what happened to her. She said holding on to anger is like drinking poison, and expecting the other person to die."

It would have been a lot easier for me if that's what Chloe really believed. The reason behind Chloe's agreeing to be interviewed by the journalist was making more sense to me now. Saints don't plan a murder.

The reporter said, "However, I can't do my story without referencing the events of twenty-five years ago. Dr. Landers understands I need to write about the attack on her, but since she doesn't want to discuss it, I'm hoping you can provide that background."

"Question away," I said.

The interview only took about fifteen minutes. The reporter had already done her homework, and was aware of the details of the case. She fed me some easy questions, and I responded with the expected answers. Between feeding her the quotes she wanted, I made a strong push for her writing about our department's forthcoming *Cold Case File* program. The more eyes that saw the video, I told her, the better the chance it might bring a witness from out of the woodwork.

"That might make for a good sidebar," she said, sounding moderately interested. Then she thanked me for my time and ended our conversation.

Going into my session with David, I felt nervous. Maybe I was afraid of saying something I shouldn't. That's not a comfortable position to be in, especially when my being honest was supposed to be critical to our process. Still, I couldn't talk about the conspiracy I'd entered into, nor mention the name of Abel Lynch. If I even hinted that I was considering harming someone, David would have to break client confidentiality and report me to the authorities.

After we were both seated, David paused before starting our session, his attention directed toward something on the ground. My jiggling foot. I immediately tried to rein it in by pressing it to the floor.

"How have you been?" he asked.

It was a simple question, but I struggled to answer. There were too many taboo subjects. Like Chloe. Like Penelope. Like Abel Lynch. Like murder.

Finally, I said, "I don't know."

"Why's that?"

"There's been a lot to process. And at the moment, I'm feeling sort of fluish."

That much was true. My stomach was unsettled. David

nodded to acknowledge my words, but his gaze once again took in my foot, which had resumed its bouncing. Once more, I squashed it to the ground.

"When you came in today, what was your main concern, Wyatt?"

"What do you mean?"

"Was something in particular pressing on your mind?"

"Nothing I can think of."

"I know you've been reluctant to open up to others about your prognosis, but by doing so you have to carry that burden by yourself. With each passing day, it will only grow heavier."

Chloe had said much the same thing. I nodded, but didn't comment. Or, more accurately, didn't say anything. As if it had a mind of its own, my foot started jiggling again. Once more, I tried to will it into submission.

David said, "The poet Robert Bly wrote that if a man hides his limp, somebody has to limp it."

"What's that mean?"

"It's not easy to hide something, and when you do, it's likely to manifest itself in all sorts of ways. When all is said and done, it's probably better just to limp."

"I'm not sure if I agree. In fact, I wonder if it's in our DNA to try to hide our wounds and illnesses. In nature, that's what wild animals do. Even in domestic animals, we see that."

"In the wild, a visible infirmity sounds a dinner bell for predators."

"Are things that much different in our so-called civilized world?"

"I would hope so. Do you think seeking help is a sign of weakness?"

"No," I said. "But it's still not something I feel comfortable doing."

"You're going to need to get over that discomfort," David said. "Before long, you'll increasingly be needing the assistance of others. In fact, it's none too early for you to consider working with an end-of-life doula."

"What's that?"

"A death doula will assist you in transitioning through the stages of your illness."

"I thought that's what you were doing."

"Seeing you for only two hours a week limits me as to what I'm able to do," he said. "What you're going through is overwhelming. The doula can help put your affairs in order, and assist you with such matters as filling out advance health care directives, and making sure all your wishes are known."

"Like a will?"

"That, and much more."

"To me, this conversation feels premature. I am not ready to put the cart in front of the horse. Or the hearse."

"I apologize if it seems that way, but there are questions that need to be asked sooner, rather than later."

"Such as?"

"Such as, have you made it clear what kind of funeral arrangements you'd like? Do you want to be buried, cremated, or composted?"

"Composted?"

"Currently, that option's available in several states, and soon will be allowed in California. On the books it's referred to as natural organic reduction, but almost everyone refers to it as human composting. Essentially, your remains return to earth as soil. It's an option for you to consider."

"I'm actually good with the idea. Maybe my composted remains could go into the zoo's botanical garden."

"That's the kind of thing a doula could look into."

"I'll give it some thought, but not today," I said. "Let's wait until I feel shittier."

"Understood," David said, then folded his hands together and looked at me. "Am I right in sensing there's something in particular you'd like to discuss today?"

"How about something other than my own death? In fact, I'd like to talk about the polar opposite of death. Love."

David looked surprised. "When we touched upon that topic in a previous session, you told me you'd never been in love, and said there had never been an Ilsa in your life."

"Well, that's changed. I've found someone. Or, are you going to tell me that's impossible?"

"That's not for me to say. Only you know what you're feeling. But I have a two-word response to your news: *mazel tov!*"

I took a deep breath and said, "Thank you."

"When did you realize you were in love?"

"A few days ago," I said. "This feeling came over me. Washed over me, really. I tried to discount it, but couldn't."

"Does she know about your feelings, and your illness?"

I nodded. "I feel grateful and lucky that she wasn't scared off. And maybe a bit confused."

"Confused?"

"I'm a dead end. Literally. Why would she want to waste her time with me?"

"Have you discussed that with her?"

"In a roundabout way. But the truth is, I'm reluctant to open that can of worms."

"Why?"

"What if she realizes there isn't any real upside in having a relationship with me?"

"If she truly believes that, isn't it better to know it now?"

I shrugged, unconvinced.

He added, "It sounds as if she's entered into this relationship with her eyes wide open. That should tell you something."

"I hope so," I said.

"You don't sound very confident."

"I'm new at this."

"What about her?"

"Another virgin heart," I said.

"How does being in love make you feel?"

"Sort of helpless, to be honest."

"Explain that."

"I just didn't expect love to be so consuming," I said.

"How did you think it would be?"

"I'm not sure. I find myself constantly thinking about her, and worrying about her, and wanting to make sure no harm comes her way."

I caught myself before I said more, stopped myself getting any closer to discussing Abel Lynch.

"That's why I wanted to know if it's possible to find true love even as you're dying. Or, has my illness just deluded me into thinking I'm in love?"

"I have no doubt that someone with a terminal illness can fall in love. And there's nothing you've said that makes me question your sincerity, or resolve."

"It's scary. I didn't expect that."

"You find love scary?"

I wished I could take back those words; I had to keep the discussion far away from Abel Lynch. "By that, I mean it makes me feel as if I'm not in control."

"It sounds as if you'd like to rein love in."

"I think I would. I find myself in this strange twilight world of love and death. That doesn't seem right, somehow."

"Love and death, Eros and Thanatos, might not be the

opposites that you think them," David said. "Freud believed some people have a death drive, while others have a life drive."

"And what do you think?"

"Most things Freudian I take with a grain of salt," he said. "Like the ancient Greeks, I believe love can take many forms, with passion or eros only being one of them. The Greeks thought the highest form of love was *agape*, which essentially is unconditional love. It's even been described as a sacrificial love that heals."

"Agape," I said.

Maybe that was the kind of love I had for Chloe. I was willing to sacrifice for her. Kill for her.

"Has she told you that she loves you?"

I nodded. "But the next time she says it, I'm going to tell her, 'No refunds.'" At David's side-eye, I said, "I finally have an excuse for my gallows humor."

"Is that a way of telling me you've had enough love talk?"

"We can talk about it at our next session, if you want to get on to something else now."

David's eyes shifted for a moment, taking in the clock. "In that case, I was hoping we could revisit something you said during another session. You alluded to having bent the rules of your job, saying you did so in the hope that the ends would justify the means. Did they?"

"No," I whispered.

"Is that something you'd like to discuss with me now?"

My stomach clenched. Was I ready to talk about that slippery slope I'd traveled? Even though there was no direct line leading to Abel Lynch, it would mean putting my shadow side on display.

Without looking at David, I said, "I told you I worked the chain-gang homicides."

"Yes."

"That case got to me like no other."

"What, in particular?"

"Twelve people," I said. "My jury. Someone gave the order to scuttle the boat. The victims were tied not only to one another, but placed inside a cramped shipping container. No life jackets. No flotation devices. They were dragged down to the depths."

"Why were they chained and placed in that cage?"

"The working theory is that whoever was captaining the ship didn't want his expensive cargo running off."

"Is that what you believe?"

"I have my doubts. Pangas smuggling humans have run aground on San Diego beaches on any number of occasions. Sometimes, that beaching was planned, with vehicles waiting to transport the human cargo. Most of the time, though, boats have gone aground because of mechanical failures, or dangerous surf. None of those passengers were ever chained and contained like The Twelve."

"And why do you think that was?" David asked.

"Whoever was in charge didn't want any witnesses to survive. The dead don't talk. Maybe this individual panicked at the prospect of a Coast Guard or Customs interdiction at sea. Maybe he got some signal that trouble was on the way. I don't know what happened, but someone out there does."

"And you said you crossed the line to try and obtain those answers?"

I nodded. "My team was getting more and more desperate. When we got word that the Feds were going to bigfoot the case and take it from us, I kind of lost it. My best friend, Tommy, was on my homicide team working the case with me, and we decided we had to do whatever it took to get answers. Instead of bringing suspects in for questioning, we conducted our interrogations far removed from lawyers, and the rule of law. We questioned people in a spot we called the Badlands, a remote canyon in the back country of Otay Mesa about five miles from the border."

"Somewhere very isolated."

"That was the point. To get to the Badlands, you leave civilization behind and travel inland along a dirt trail. We did our questioning where there were no prying eyes, or ears, or cameras. We held guns on those we interrogated, and they didn't know whether they'd live or die."

"How many people were subjected to this?"

"Half a dozen or so."

"Did you torture them?"

"I like to tell myself that we didn't, but that's not true. There were times we tried beating their secrets out of them. And when we didn't get the answers we wanted, we took turns threatening them. But none of it got us the confessions we wanted, and the coerced leads never really panned out."

"You regret what you did?"

"Every day," I said. "We mainly targeted criminals, men and women associated with the Mexican Mafia. We tried to believe that justified what we were doing."

"What happened to your victims?"

"We let them loose within sight of the paved road, and I always made sure they had water."

"No one was permanently hurt or killed?"

"Many were beaten and bruised, but no one was killed," I said. "Still, that's not saying our hands might not be bloody."

"Explain," David said.

I told him about our off-the-books informant, and how he'd ended up dead.

"We initially blackmailed the kid into doing our bidding," I said. "I can't be sure he died because of what we had him looking into, but that's my fear."

The two of us sat in silence for a minute. Finally, David

said, "Our time's up. I know you would have preferred not to talk to me about this, but I think it's important you did."

"Then why do I feel so shitty?" I asked, getting to my feet.

David chose not to answer the question, and I walked out the door.

CHAPTER THIRTY

Penelope Hill studied her makeup in the rearview mirror of her car. As with her previous visits to the Royal Meridian, she was dressed up in casual chic clothing so as to look the part of a well-heeled guest. In her encounters with hotel security, she must have passed muster, because she'd never been stopped and asked for her name and room number.

She pulled into the public parking lot at Haskell's Beach. That spared her the scrutiny and price tag associated with valet parking. Because there are no private beaches in California, hotel guests have to share the coastline with the hoi polloi.

Staking out a spot on the sand, Penelope began doing a series of stretches and breathing exercises. The warmup wasn't only to loosen her muscles; Penelope also monitored the beach. A middle-aged couple out for a stroll caught her attention.

"Beautiful day, eh?" the man said.

"For sure," the woman said.

Their accents identified them as Canadians.

"'Oot and aboot,' are you?" Penelope asked with a laugh. "I love hearing Canadian accents."

The couple stopped walking. "We say it's people from the States who have the accent," the man said.

"Totally," Penelope said, in exaggerated surfer speech. "My good friend Jeannie is a Canadian snowbird, and usually stays at our place in the Bay Area every January or February."

"Where does she come from, eh?" the woman asked.

"Toronto."

"That's a lot colder than where we live in Vancouver," the man said.

"I love Vancouver," Penelope said. "It's so cosmopolitan, and yet the area has so much natural beauty."

"We're just outside of Vancouver in Kerrisdale Park, and we love it," the woman said.

"I can imagine," Penelope said. "By the way, I'm Laura."

"I'm Nicole and this is my husband, Michael," she said.

"It's nice to see a couple out walking together," Penelope said. "I couldn't get my husband to join me. Mr. Lazy Bones said he just wanted to relax in our hotel room."

"Nothing wrong with that," Michael said.

"I told Mikey he needs to work off his Molson muscle," Nicole said.

Michael patted his stomach.

Twenty minutes later, Penelope walked up the pathway to the hotel with her new friends. Security never gave her a second look.

Before taking leave of Michael and Nicole, Penelope learned the couple's last name and room number, and promised she would try to get "Mr. Lazy Bones" to join them for drinks later.

Penelope's precautions were probably excessive, but by now they had become a habit to prevent her from standing out.

During her previous visits, she had always entered and exited the hotel by different routes. There were surveillance cameras throughout the grounds, but Penelope had begun to walk around the property with a practiced insouciance.

Her destination wasn't where hotel guests typically ventured, but she made it appear as though she was out for a power walk. It was essential to confirm Abel Lynch was on the property, and the best way to do so was to locate his car in the employee car park. As she approached the lot, Penelope began raising and lowering her knees. If anyone in security was watching her movements, they'd assume she was just another exercise fanatic.

She kept an eye open for Lynch's five-year-old white Chevy Equinox. Within minutes, she had found the SUV. Even though no one was around, Penelope performed as if being watched, and made it appear as if she'd dropped an errant earbud and it had rolled under the SUV. Getting down on her knees, Penelope began patting the ground as if in search of something. While reaching around she was able to surreptitiously attach a GPS tracker to the underside of the Equinox. Then, getting to her feet triumphantly, she looked happily at the earbud she'd palmed in her hand.

In California, it's illegal to place an unauthorized GPS tracker on a car. Penelope knew that, and also knew it would be the first of several illegal activities planned for the day.

Once she reached Lompoc, Penelope checked the GPS tracker. Lynch's vehicle hadn't moved. She looked at her watch, and saw it was a quarter to one. Lynch's shift usually ran to 3:30, and it was a forty-five-minute drive from Goleta to Lompoc. That should allow her plenty of time to finish what she came to do, and leave long before Lynch's shift was over.

It's that detective's fault, she thought. He was the reason she'd have to place herself in a potentially dangerous situation. Why couldn't he have left well enough alone? Still, if things worked out today, maybe she'd secure the proof needed to show Lynch's guilt. That would force the detective to act, and get Lynch the death penalty sentence he deserved.

Not that they didn't already have proof enough, but the detective seemed to think it was necessary to fill in every blank in Lynch's timeline over the last quarter of a century. Hadn't Dr. Landers identified Lynch from an old picture as being the man who left her for dead? And wasn't the timing of Lynch's attack also damning? He had done the crime and then shipped out. And that didn't even take into account the false identity of Stu Burns, which he'd offered as an alias to the two hitchhiking teens, never imagining it would lead back to him. When he'd departed the crime scene, Lynch had thought both girls were dead.

It was one thing to be cautious, but another to turn a blind eye to the evidence. Lake's gumming up the works so late in the planning had thrown everything into flux, but maybe there was a silver lining to his interfering. She liked the idea of a dying man doing the hit, and not Dr. Landers. That is, if he followed through.

It was strange to think of Dr. Landers and the cop as a couple, though. Could the two of them really be in love? How was that even possible? One moment the two of them had been fighting like cats and dogs, and then the next they were suddenly in love.

Penelope felt like the third wheel. She missed being Dr. Landers's sole confidante. Where did she stand, now that she was no longer a patient, or even a good friend? The cop had usurped her role. He was now the one calling the shots. It was time to try and give him what he wanted. Incontrovertible evidence. If she succeeded in that, the detective would have to put up or shut up, and Dr. Landers would see him for what he really was.

She circled the block in her car. Nothing looked amiss. There were no police cruisers to be seen, and no unusual activity. Despite that, Penelope could feel her uneasiness grow. Most of her previous visits to Lompoc had been in the evening; she felt more exposed in the daylight.

Get over it, she thought. *And get on with it.*

Penelope grabbed a root beer from a convenience store. Drinking a soda made it look as if she had some purpose for being in her car. She drove to a lookout spot with a vantage point to Lynch's apartment building. In between taking sips from the can, she studied her surroundings, and occasionally looked at her phone. The GPS tracker showed Lynch's car was still in Goleta.

The foot traffic at Lynch's complex was light, but every few minutes someone went in, or came out. It wouldn't be hard for her to catch the door before it shut. That's what she'd done on previous visits, which had allowed her to study Lynch's second-floor apartment, as well as the grounds.

No time like the present, she thought.

She parked two blocks away from the apartment, and then lingered in the vicinity of the security gate while pretending to be talking on her phone. Her timing was good; a minute into her feigned conversation with "Aunt Lilian," she was able to catch the door before it closed, and slipped inside.

Penelope walked along a concrete path that took her to the

pool. A mother and her two young girls were playing at the children's pool. Penelope smiled and waved at them, and then lay down on a chaise lounge. She was wearing a hat, large sunglasses that covered most of her face, and had brought along the prop of a paperback book. While pretending to read, Penelope monitored the complex. There was no sign of a manager, and very few residents were visible.

Over the course of fifteen minutes, Penelope only saw one man leave an apartment, and she assumed he was a plumber due to the two toolboxes he was carrying. At the other end of the complex, a gardener who had his back mostly turned to her was working on an irrigation line.

Most of Penelope's scrutiny was reserved for Lynch's apartment, and those units on either side of it. She didn't see movements in any of them. From previous visits, Penelope knew there were security cameras around the complex, but most were positioned in the parking lot.

The mother and her two children gathered up their towels and exited the pool area. As they passed by, the mother said, "Now you can have some peace and quiet to read."

"They were angels," Penelope said.

The smallest girl said, "That lady says I'm an angel, Mommy."

Five more minutes, Penelope decided. She raised her book again, not looking at what was on the page, but over it, at Lynch's apartment. During her last surveillance, she'd secretly made a video recording of his unit. His front door had a Kwikset pin and tumbler lock. She'd spent hours working out the best way to bypass the lock, and in her oversized purse she had a lock-bumping key, a rebound ring, a tension wrench, and a small bump hammer. After experimenting on a similar lock at her apartment, it now usually took her less than ten seconds to gain entry. All she had to do was put a key in the tumbler then tap the hammer to get the pins in a row. If everything worked out, Penelope would gain entry without damaging the lock. She didn't want Lynch to know he'd had a visitor.

Penelope took a deep breath. The coast was clear. Once again, she checked the GPS app on her phone and saw Lynch's vehicle hadn't moved. It was time to proceed.

Her heart was in her throat as she slipped in the bump key she'd prepped with a rebound ring. After positioning the tension wrench, she tapped the key multiple times with the small mallet. Anyone in hearing range would think someone was lightly knocking on a door.

Open sesame, Penelope prayed, reaching for the knob. It turned, and she silently stepped inside, closing the door behind her. Before continuing into the apartment, she listened for any sounds. The silence reassured her enough to start breathing again, but it was still scary as hell being in the apartment of a murderer.

Penelope turned on her phone's video to record everything she was seeing, and moved forward. *Walking on pins and needles*, she thought. Never before had that expression felt so real. She silently entered the sole bedroom. Even though Penelope had been sure Lynch was at work, it was still a relief to find the room unoccupied. At first glance, the bedroom appeared stark and empty, with a queen bed, a chest of drawers, and little else.

Along one side of the room were mirrored sliding wardrobe doors with gold trim. Her reflection came into focus as Penelope approached them, and she saw how pale and drawn she looked. The night before, she'd barely slept in anticipation of the day's events. If she were to get arrested for breaking and entering, her private investigator's license would be revoked forever, but what scared her even more was the idea of Lynch walking in on her.

He's forty miles away, Penelope told herself... tried to convince herself. She reached for one of the closet's sliding doors and slid it open. *Bingo!* There was a large filing cabinet inside. And what was even better was that it was unlocked, sparing her from having to try to break in.

She put on latex gloves and pulled open the top drawer. Lynch's neatness surprised her. She had expected to find a hodgepodge of records and papers, but instead found hanging file folders that were neatly labeled. Penelope began flipping through them. The drawer was mostly filled with paperwork related to finances, including his tax returns from the last seven years, pension statements, and a variety of forms from the US Navy and the Veterans Administration.

Drawer number two contained folders with receipts, manuals, insurance statements, car financing, and sundry contracts.

Penelope checked the time and studied the GPS tracker app again. According to it, the Chevy Equinox was still in Goleta, but she found herself looking over her shoulder anyway. No one was lurking nearby, but she still felt uneasy. It almost felt like she was being watched.

"Third time's a charm," she whispered, opening the third drawer.

As she flipped through the hanging folders, Penelope began to despair at not finding personal items such as old pictures or letters. It was possible Lynch had parked his belongings in some storage locker. *Focus*, she said to herself. She wasn't even halfway through the cabinet's contents. There were still plenty of possibilities to find hidden treasure.

She started looking through a folder labeled *Detailing*, and saw Lynch had once operated a part-time car detailing business. It appeared he'd shut it down a few years ago.

Penelope continued going through the hanging folders. There were no dates attached to the labels, but there seemed to be a chronological order to them. The further she delved, the older the folders were.

A label caught her eye, and Penelope removed the file folder and looked inside. At first glance, she thought it was empty. Then she saw it contained a plastic bag. When she lifted it out, Penelope gasped.

Inside the bag were two old ticket stubs.

"My God," she said, her hands trembling.

It wasn't so much ticket stubs that Penelope was holding, as much as she believed it was Abel Lynch's execution warrant.

CHAPTER THIRTY-ONE

Abel Lynch checked the chits on the order rail. The restaurant's point-of-sale system was designed with a pantry printer and a hot-line printer. Today he was working as pantry cook, which meant he had charge over soups, salads, appetizers, and sandwiches. The restaurant was moderately busy, but none of the cooks were in the weeds.

The expediter made eye contact with him. Gina had a no-nonsense attitude and ran a tight kitchen. She was younger than most of her coworkers, but made it clear who was in charge.

"One gazpacho and one vichyssoise," she said.

"Heard," Lynch said.

"And one Cobb salad and one chicken Caesar salad."

"Heard that."

The chit printed out, and Lynch placed it on the board above the food window. He opened the lowboy and removed the salad ingredients from the undercounter refrigerator. The most time-consuming part of his job was the morning prep work. That's when he made the cold soups and cut up the ingredients for salads and sandwiches.

For a moment, Lynch paused in his preparations. His cell

phone was vibrating. As much as he wanted to look at it, he didn't want to court trouble. Employees weren't supposed to use their phones unless they were on break. In a minute or two, he'd sneak a peek once Gina wasn't observing him.

As his phone continued to shake, Lynch cursed under his breath. The vibrating was only supposed to occur if the hidden cameras in his apartment were picking up movement. It was probably nothing. There had been false alarms before. One windy day, falling palm fronds had activated the camera's motion detectors; another time the power had gone off in his apartment complex and set off warnings on his phone that sounded like DEFCON 1. And still another time, failing batteries had set the system off. It had to be another technical glitch.

But he still wanted to look at his goddamn phone to be sure.

He finished with the salads, and then ladled the soup into bowls. For garnish, he added some microgreens.

"Order up," he called.

Being the expo, Gina was in charge of quality control. She facilitated the timing for the hot and cold dishes, coordinating the delivery of the plates with the food runners and/or servers.

Gina came over to his station and eyeballed his dishes. She took a bar towel and wiped at a speck that only she could see. None of the master chefs Lynch had served under had been as picky as Gina.

"Soups and salads to table twelve," she told a food runner.

The food was put on a serving tray and disappeared into the restaurant. Lynch watched as Gina moved down the line and clarified a new order with a line cook.

"That au jus is an SOS," she said.

In kitchen lingo, that meant sauce on the side.

"Heard," the cook said.

As Gina continued down the line examining the hot plates,

Lynch reached for his cell phone, and cupped it in his hand to keep it out of view. Then he tapped on the security app, which gave a real-time view of what was going on in his apartment.

Shit. He bit down hard on his lower lip, drawing a little salty blood. This was no false alarm. There was a woman in his apartment rifling through his filing cabinet.

It was a fucking real SOS, he thought, not the kitchen kind.

There were two spy cameras in his bedroom. Both the smoke detector and electrical outlet had micro-cameras in them. The smoke detector allowed him a view from above, while the electrical outlet took in the length of the room. The spy equipment operated with wireless wifi, sending streaming footage.

He sure as hell didn't like seeing an intruder going through his papers. The woman was too methodical and focused to be some goddamn meth head trying to score some money for a fix. No, he wasn't that lucky.

Lynch couldn't call the police. Couldn't do a damn thing but watch.

There was something familiar about the intruder. With his thumb and index finger, he enlarged the screen so he could better see her face. The longer he stared, the surer he was that he'd seen her before. But where? And when? It hadn't been too long ago. Her hair was different now. And she was wearing less makeup.

Suddenly, he got this sense that he was being watched. Lynch knew to trust his lizard brain. It had saved his ass time and again. In the service, he'd always had this knack of knowing when an officer was around. Without looking up, without offering any giveaways, Lynch slipped the phone out of sight. People had forgotten how to listen to their lizard brain. Not Lynch. He knew its purpose was to provide the four F's of survival: feeding, fleeing, fighting, and fucking.

A few seconds passed before he casually looked up and saw a none-the-wiser Gina turning her attention elsewhere.

Lynch considered his options. Should he tell Gina he was feeling sick? He doubted it would do any good. The bitch rifling through his things would be long gone by the time he got home.

He thought about calling the apartment manager, but knew all he'd do was call the police. *No cops,* he thought. He couldn't have them nosing around.

His cognitive brain said there was nothing he could really do. Luckily, his lizard brain offered him a memory, and a way to fight. He suddenly knew who his intruder was, or at least knew the name she went by.

Gotcha.

Gina called to him. "We need a garlic aioli BLT on ciabatta bread, and a pan bagnat on a sourdough roll."

"Heard that," he said.

Lynch grabbed his eight-inch chef's knife and cut open the roll.

CHAPTER THIRTY-TWO

Chloe had invited me over for dinner at her place, and we were both enjoying the end of our workweek.

"TGIF," I said, pouring wine into two glasses.

"TGIF," Chloe agreed.

I placed her glass on the counter where she was preparing our dinner, and watched her put the finishing touches on an Indian dish that was new to me.

"That smells great," I said.

"I like to freshen up the dal by adding spices to the lentils, along with tomatoes, coconut milk, and Greek yogurt. The final touch is a squeeze of lime juice."

"When did you become such an accomplished cook?"

"I wish I could say I was. The truth is, I usually get by with pasta and salad."

"Frozen pizza is my usual entrée at Chez Lake," I said.

"You'll find a few of those in my freezer as well."

I took a sip of the California chardonnay I'd just poured.

"Good?" Chloe asked.

"Very," I said. "I probably should have waited for you."

"I'm glad you didn't."

"What can I do to help?"

"Not a thing," she said.

I took another sip of wine and said, "Today at work, I did a phoner with the *U-T* reporter. She mentioned that tomorrow the two of you will be meeting at your office."

Chloe nodded while continuing to stir. "Normally, I don't go into work on a Saturday, but I thought that would be a good day to meet up because I won't have to worry about ensuring the privacy of my clients."

"Why'd you agree to talk to her in the first place?"

"She contacted me not long after I made the decision to go after Abel Lynch. I thought doing the interview might provide me with cover if Lynch got linked to the attack after his death."

I had suspected something of the sort, and found myself nodding.

"All the reporter's going to hear tomorrow is that I've gotten on with my life, and have moved past any desire for revenge. And yes, I know how cold-blooded that sounds."

"It might not exactly be warm and fuzzy, but it was smart to try and set up a preemptive character alibi for yourself," I said. "In fact, you might have missed your calling as a criminal mastermind."

"If I'm ever deliberating a career change, I'll keep that in mind," she said.

"For what it's worth, if I was the detective investigating Lynch's homicide, you'd never have ended up on my suspect list."

"Why?"

"You're smart, charming, and have a sterling reputation. I would have assumed you were incapable of murder."

"Does my being in a wheelchair also rule me out?"

"Pretty much," I said.

"As much as I detest ableism, I suppose I was counting on that."

"Ableism?"

"It's when individuals discriminate against non-able-bodied people. Often, they do it subconsciously."

"You've convinced me. Next time, the disabled person becomes my prime suspect."

"I'm glad to have done my part for equal rights."

"You might not want to mention ableism to the reporter. Better to give her the 'every cloud has a silver lining,' and how you were able to find your true calling through the adversity you experienced."

"On the whole, that's true," Chloe said. "But there's a part of me that hates the idea I didn't choose my career, as much as have it violently forced upon me. I wonder what my life would have been like if Abel Lynch hadn't slithered into it."

"Do you think you would have been a psychologist?"

"I doubt it. Back in high school, I was toying with the idea of being a graphic designer, or an architect. Those were probably just pipe dreams, but I'll never know, just like I'll never know if I would have had the family and white picket fence I once imagined."

"Still, it must give you satisfaction that your career has helped a lot of people."

"It does, but that was never enough for me. I know time's supposed to heal all wounds, but that never really occurred. Jung was right when he said, 'What you resist persists.' Lynch crippled me as much mentally as he did physically, and brought out demons I didn't even know I had."

"You and your demons are going to have to be patient until I'm satisfied Lynch is guilty."

"They've waited a long time, and can wait a little longer.

But I'm still having trouble with you stepping in as my proxy for revenge. I should be the one exacting justice."

"Not a chance," I said. "The way I see it, acting out of revenge isn't forgivable, but acting out of love is."

Tears ran down her cheeks, and a few dropped into the dal.

"Let's eat before I make even more of a mess," she said.

I used a piece of naan to scoop the scant remains of the stew-like dish from my almost-empty bowl.

"My compliments to the chef," I said.

"There's still some dal left," she said. "Maybe I can talk you into taking it home with you."

"I wonder if Lenore could eat lentils," I said.

"I imagine they'd be okay as long they were cooked and served without any spices."

"I know she loves her grubs and slugs," I said.

"Who doesn't?" Chloe said.

When I finally stopped laughing, I told Chloe about the bottle cap, washer, and pink glass bead that had been left on the path, and how I believed Lenore had intended them as gifts.

"I collected what she'd left me and put them in a bowl on the mantel," I said. "Whenever I look at them, they make me smile."

"Like you're doing now," Chloe said, stretching out her hand and lightly touching my face.

My smile got a little larger.

"I admire her incredible will to live, and I know it sounds anthropomorphic, but I think she appreciates my leaving her food."

"When am I going to meet Lenore?" Chloe asked.

"Soon, I hope, but sometimes she's shy about letting herself be seen. Not heard, though. Thank God."

That got Chloe's attention. "What am I missing?"

I told her about the raven's mimicry skills, and how her impersonations might have saved my life. When I finished, Chloe was shaking her head in disbelief.

"Let me get this straight," she said. "Lenore's coughing made the gunman stop to look around, and then her barking drove him away?"

"That's pretty much it."

"Are you pulling my stump?"

I shook my head. "It's the honest to God truth."

"Wow," she said. "I'm feeling this sense of awe. And I'm also a bit upset. Why am I only hearing this story now?"

"With everything going on, it actually slipped my mind."

"And why was someone shooting at you?"

"I don't know yet, but I suspect it had something to do with the chain-gang homicides. It was probably a warning shot, but until I know better, I'm being cautious. That's one of the reasons I haven't invited you over to my house."

"One of them?"

"It's been a long time since I've entertained, so cleaning my house hasn't been a priority. Before you come over, I want to bring in a cleaning service to make everything look presentable. There's also the matter of replacing the window that was shot out with something other than a plywood board. And I thought I should hold off obligating you to come over so early in our relationship."

"Obligating me?"

"You have a full life that awaits you. I don't."

"You're who I want to spend time with," she said. "I'm here willingly, and happily, and with my eyes wide open."

I sighed in relief. "Thank you for that gift," I whispered.

"Let's go make love," Chloe said. "I'd rather do that here, than at your place."

"Because of the shooting?"

"No," she said. "I'd hate to think what Lenore might start mimicking next."

Chloe's moans built, and then her body suddenly clenched and tensed as she climaxed.

Afterward, she took a few deep breaths and said, "I can't move."

"Good."

"I don't want to move."

"Good."

"Thank you for being my nepenthe."

Hearing the word nepenthe was enough to awaken me from my post-coital fog. "I know that word," I said. "Poe used it in *The Raven*."

In her relaxed state, it took Chloe a moment to register what I was saying. "What word?"

"Nepenthe. When Lenore showed up, I reacquainted myself with the poem."

"Poe used the word nepenthe in *The Raven*?"

"He did. But you're the first person I've ever heard use the word in a conversation."

"Blame my long convalescence as a teen," Chloe said. "I went through a phase where I devoured Greek mythology, and nepenthe was a word that always seemed to be turning up. In the *Odyssey*, Helen was given nepenthe to forget her sorrows. Because of what I was going through at the time, the idea of nepenthe and oblivion appealed to me."

"And now?"

She ran her hand down my cheek and said, "Tonight's kind of oblivion was perfect. But now you've got me thinking there's a synchronicity at work that would explain the interconnectedness between nepenthe, and your Lenore, and Poe's Lenore."

"You'll need to break that down for me to understand what you're saying. I'm a curious cop, not an academic."

"The Swiss psychiatrist Carl Gustav Jung came up with the notion of synchronicity. As he saw it, synchronicity was a series of meaningful coincidences."

"That sounds like a contradiction in terms."

"In his idea of synchronicity, there's an unseen connection between things. For example, earlier you were talking about your Lenore, and then later I used the word nepenthe, which led you to remember Poe's writing about his Lenore and nepenthe. I imagine Jung would have seen connective threads in all of that. It's also likely he would have attributed the manner in which the two of us came together as being due to synchronicity."

"And here I thought it was just my animal magnetism."

"In that, I'll go with you over Jung," she said.

"I'd probably just attribute everything to coincidental timing," I said. "But I should confess to you that today I brought up the topic of love with David. I wanted his take on my falling in love at the same time I was dying."

"And what did he say?"

"*Mazel tov.*"

She started laughing. "That's perfect."

"I also told my best friend, Tommy, that I was finally serious about a woman. Unfortunately, I was constrained in what I could say and had to tell him some half-truths."

"Why?"

"Tommy and I worked on the same homicide team for ten

years. When I was given your case, we talked shop, and I told him what I was investigating. Because he grew up in the area, he remembered what happened to you when you were a girl. With the Abel Lynch situation being what it is, I didn't want to tell him anything more than necessary."

"I'm sorry you have to keep secrets from your friend."

"Don't be. It's not like I tell him everything anyway. He doesn't even know I'm sick."

"He's your best friend and you haven't told him?"

"I'm not quite ready yet. I thought it best that only we three conspirators know."

"Penelope called me from the road this morning," Chloe said. "She was traveling north to try and gather more information about Lynch."

"That makes me uneasy."

"Why?"

"If Lynch is the murderer, he's managed to keep his secret for twenty-five years. It's possible he's just been lucky all that time, but I kind of doubt it. Most criminals slip up. Often, they commit the same kind of crime, and that's how they're finally caught. That hasn't been the case with him."

"A leopard can't change its spots," Chloe said. "I'm sure Lynch has hurt other women through the years."

"I think that's likely as well, but he's avoided getting caught. Law enforcement catches bad guys because over time they slip up. Not Lynch. It's been my experience that wary criminals are the toughest to bring in. They have an almost animal alertness, and sense when even the smallest thing feels out of place. Penelope better be cautious."

Chloe's cell phone began ringing, putting an end to our pillow talk. Before answering, she looked to see who was calling.

"Synchronicity, or coincidental timing?" she asked. "It's Penelope."

Chloe picked up. As the two women conversed, I studied Chloe's expression. She looked immersed in whatever the PI was telling her.

After hearing her out, Chloe said, "Drive safely, then. We'll be waiting for you."

Chloe clicked off and turned to me. "Penelope's been fighting bad traffic, but said she should be here in half an hour. She told me there's important news that can't wait." In an excited whisper, Chloe added, "She found something. I could hear it in her voice."

I returned Chloe's smile, even though my gut clenched.

CHAPTER THIRTY-THREE

Even though we'd been expecting Penelope's arrival, at the sound of knocking, both Chloe and I started.

"I'll get it," I said.

The peephole had been installed at Chloe's eye level. As I bent down to look through it, I could see Penelope impatiently shifting from one leg to the other.

When I opened the door, she hurried past me and found Chloe in the living room.

"We've got the son of a bitch!" Penelope yelled, and then drew Chloe in for a hug.

"What?" Chloe said. "Tell me!"

Penelope began pacing around the room. "I don't want to sit," she said. "It was bumper to bumper for most of the drive home. But it was so worth it.

"When I set out this morning, I was prepared to break some rules. There was no way I could let Lynch get away with murder. I had to do whatever was necessary to prove his guilt."

That wasn't what I wanted to hear.

She said, "My first stop was in Goleta, where I made sure

Lynch was working. To monitor his whereabouts, I put a GPS tracker on his car."

"That's illegal," I said under my breath.

"It was also necessary. I wanted to be sure of Lynch's whereabouts before breaking into his apartment."

I said, "Shouldn't you have told us you were planning that?"

"I wanted both of you to have plausible deniability in the event things didn't go as hoped."

"That might yet happen," I said. "What if someone saw you, or there's CCTV footage with your image on it?"

"Before breaking in, I surveilled Lynch's apartment complex and made sure there was no sign of activity from his unit, or his neighbors. As for the building's surveillance cameras, most are positioned around the entrances to the building, and the parking lot."

"Which means there's footage of you."

"I was wearing a hat and oversized sunglasses."

"You promised me you'd never put yourself in that kind of danger," Chloe said.

"I did my best to minimize the risks," Penelope said. "And it's not as if I was acting on the spur of the moment. I had already spent considerable time in Goleta and Lompoc studying Lynch's workplace and apartment. If I hadn't taken a chance, who knows how long this investigation would have remained in a holding pattern? And we wouldn't have gotten our hands on this."

She opened her purse and pulled out an evidence bag. The writing on the plastic obscured whatever was inside it.

"This came out of a five-drawer filing cabinet inside Lynch's bedroom closet. Each drawer was filled with labeled hanging folders, and contained such items as warranties, tax forms, VA records, and rental agreements. Lynch was very methodical with his paperwork.

"There was also death and taxes."

She let those words hang in the air before continuing.

"In the second drawer, Lynch had tax returns from the past five years. And in the recesses of the third drawer, I came upon this."

Penelope held up her cell phone, and showed us a picture of a folder labeled Hg 80.

"When I came upon this, I didn't know what the label meant, and had no idea of its contents," Penelope said.

"Hg 80," Chloe said, sounding puzzled.

There was something familiar about the notation, but it took me a moment to make a connection.

"Is that a symbol from the periodic table?" I asked.

Penelope nodded.

"Mercury," Chloe whispered.

Project Mercury, usually just referred to as Mercury, was the name of the band Chloe and Dana had seen on the night they were attacked.

"Mercury is a heavy metal, which is why the band chose that name," Chloe said. "But the notion of Mercury was used as a motif in a lot of their songs. They got off on the mythology of Mercury being the messenger of the gods, and how he guided souls to the underworld. They sprinkled lots of alchemical references in their music, like how mercury was the foundation for the transmutation of the soul."

In her raspy words, you could hear the strain on her constricted vocal cords. I wondered if it was as painful for Chloe to speak as it was for us to have to listen.

"When Mercury came to San Diego, they were promoting their latest album, *Underworld*," she said. "A lot of the staging and special effects were part of their 'Tour of the Underworld.'"

The room grew silent. Chloe had been on the cusp of womanhood when she'd gone to that concert. She and Dana had been looking forward to their night of adventure. Mercury's tour of the underworld was supposed to be a fantasy. But it hadn't turned out that way for Dana. For either of them.

"Do you remember where you and Dana were seated?" Penelope asked.

"They were terrace seats," Chloe said. "Not the greatest location, but we didn't care. We just wanted to be part of the scene. Besides, the sports arena was notorious for its terrible acoustics. No matter where you sat, the sound was bad."

The poor acoustics notwithstanding, the concert had been a near sellout, with 14,000 people in attendance.

Penelope asked, "Do you happen to recall the row you were in, or the seat numbers?"

Chloe shook her head. "What I remember most is that my ticket cost thirty dollars. That was a lot of babysitting money."

"They were seated in row three," I said. "Dana had seat six; you were in seat seven."

"How do you know that?" Chloe asked.

"It was in the case file. The information was never made public because you told the lead detective that you'd kept a ticket stub as a keepsake. When no ticket stubs were recovered at the crime scene, or found on your person or Dana's, SDPD thought the killer might have taken them as trophies."

"All this time, I assumed the ticket was just lost," Chloe said.

"It wasn't," Penelope said. "And neither was Dana's. Your ticket stubs were inside an old business envelope placed in the Hg 80 hanging folder."

"Where they should have been left," I said. "You do know that because you obtained this evidence illegally, these ticket stubs are inadmissible in court?"

Even though I'd tried to speak in a measured tone, I couldn't hide my anger.

"Anything you found in Lynch's apartment linking him to

the crime would be considered Fruit of the poisonous tree," I said. "We now have no case."

"You wanted evidence putting Lynch at the crime scene," Penelope said. "Here it is. It wasn't the DA I was trying to satisfy. It was you. Now we'll see if you fish or cut bait."

"What if Lynch notices the absence of the tickets?" I asked.

"I think that's unlikely," she said.

"Really?" I asked. "You see how worn the stubs are?"

"That's because they're old."

"Or, is it because Lynch regularly examines them? Holds them? Incorporates them into his sick fantasies?"

"Enough," Chloe said.

Penelope and I turned to a pale and trembling Chloe. While we'd been arguing, she had been suffering.

"I'm sorry," both of us said, offering up the same apology at the same moment.

"Let me see that bag," Chloe said, extending her hand.

"Are you sure?" I asked.

She didn't respond, didn't lower her hand, and Penelope handed it to her. As Chloe studied the tickets, her complexion turned chalk white.

"How about I get you some tea?" I asked.

She either didn't hear me, or ignored me. Her attention was still on the tickets.

"Dana's ticket is discolored," she said.

Don't make the connection, I prayed. But she did.

"It soaked up some of her blood, didn't it?"

"It looks that way," I said.

She shrank into her wheelchair, and Penelope retrieved the bag from Chloe's lifeless fingers.

"Why didn't he get rid of the evidence?" Chloe asked.

"He probably couldn't bear to part with them," I said. "For some murderers, keeping trophies of their kills is a way for them to preserve the memory of what they did. They're a trigger to his sick fantasies. That's probably why he kept them nearby; it allowed for convenient access."

"I see," Chloe said.

She tried to sound calm, but her body began to violently shake.

"Excuse me for a minute," she said.

"Can I..."

She shook her head and wheeled off, taking refuge in the hallway bathroom. Through the closed door came the sounds of her retching.

I turned to Penelope and hissed, "Are you satisfied?"

"Don't blame the fucking messenger," she whispered. "You wanted proof. You *demanded* proof. Well, you got it."

"What I got is you backing me into a corner. If Lynch regularly uses these tickets for his strolls down memory lane, he might already know they're missing. It's possible he's planning on disappearing, or he's already fled."

"That would be convenient for you, wouldn't it?"

"I was prepared to do what I said I would, but in my own way. That meant being methodical, and planning accordingly. Now, if I wait, Lynch could ghost us. Or, it's possible he could come after you."

"He doesn't know who I am," Penelope said.

"Keep telling yourself that. You don't think you left a trail to follow? Think again."

We heard the bathroom door open, and both of us shut up. When Chloe rejoined us, she said, "I'm sorry I overreacted. For some reason, everything seemed to hit me all at once."

Penelope and I both made supportive noises.

"It must be that I'm tired," Chloe said. "I know I could use a good night's sleep."

"Then, I'll leave you to it," Penelope said, getting to her feet.

The two women made their way to the door and said their goodbyes.

When Chloe rejoined me in the living room, she said, "This wasn't how I envisioned our evening together. I'm surprised I reacted as violently as I did. Seeing those tickets brought back the trauma, and the terrified teenage girl."

I leaned down and hugged her. "Everything will be all right."

"I almost believe you."

"What can I do to help?"

"You can go home and get some sleep. I know you're tired. My plan for tonight is to take a sleeping pill and conk out. Tomorrow I've got that interview with the reporter, which will eat up a good part of my day."

"How about we spend the day together on Sunday? Ocean view brunch, an outing to Balboa Park, maybe catch a movie?"

"That sounds like a great plan."

"It's a date," I said.

CHAPTER THIRTY-FOUR

I was awakened in the morning by my ringing phone. The display read "Unknown Caller." When it's spam or scam, my phone typically screens the call. I decided to pick up.

"Wyatt?" A woman's voice.

"Speaking."

"This is Penelope. I'm calling you from a burner phone."

It made sense that she wasn't using her personal phone to contact me, but hearing the worried tone in her voice caused me to sit upright.

"What's wrong?"

"It might not be anything," she said. "But what you said last night got me concerned, so this morning I checked the *Navy Gravy* website to monitor any activity. Since yesterday, Abel Lynch has logged on to the site two times."

"That doesn't sound like a coincidence. What times did he log on?"

"Last night he went to the site just before six and stayed there for around half an hour. Then, at 8:15, he went to the site a second time and spent forty minutes there."

"Before yesterday, when was the last time Lynch visited the site?"

"It's been almost five weeks," she said.

"Something prompted his interest," I said. "Or, more likely, someone. My guess is that Lynch has surveillance cameras in his apartment, and got footage of you. That was enough for him to connect you with that cookbook author you were pretending to be. I'm betting your false identity has been blown."

"I put a firewall between me and my Sarah Williams persona."

"And you met in person with former naval culinary specialists, and even did cooking demonstrations with them. There's no way you could have covered all your tracks during those visits."

"I went to great efforts to not be found out." Penelope sounded as if she was trying to convince herself more than she was me.

"Don't be naive. You're a PI. You know personal privacy is more illusion than not. When you wrote and asked to meet with him, who's to say he didn't start looking into your background at that time? For weeks now, he might have known you were the notorious Penny Hughes. And yesterday, he would have learned just how big a threat you are."

"If he wants to come after me, I'll be waiting for him."

"We need to be concerned not only about you, but Chloe. If Lynch figured out that you're a PI, he'd want to know who you're working for. From there, I don't think it would be a stretch for him to link you with Chloe."

"You're making a lot of assumptions," she said.

"I'm pretty sure you've already done the same."

"What do you suggest I do?" she asked.

"Give me fifteen minutes to think about it, and call me back on your burner phone."

When Penelope called back, she said, "I'm feeling worse and worse about all this."

"That's two of us. Still, I don't think we should alarm Chloe, especially after what she went through last night. She's got that *U-T* reporter coming to her office at eleven. Just to be safe, is there any way you can surveil her workplace while that interview is taking place?"

"I'll make that happen," Penelope promised.

"Good," I said. "Now we need to talk about Abel Lynch."

My mother had the kind of faith I don't have. Whenever she was beset by her own insecurities, she prayed. And when she was torn by indecision, she prayed for guidance. I couldn't quite bring myself to do that. Given what I was intending to do, that would be more than a little hypocritical. But that didn't stop me from having a conversation with the universe.

"How about a sign?" I asked. "Anything to show me I'm doing the right thing?"

The universe remained stubbornly silent, and I couldn't wait on its answer.

I was wearing a hairnet and had on latex gloves when I went to my library, which consists of three mismatched bookcases I'd picked up at garage sales. Most of the books are well-thumbed paperbacks, the majority of which are nonfiction and mostly nature related. There are lots of identification guides for plants, trees, and wildlife, as well as such nature classics as Thoreau's *Walden*, Abbey's *Desert Solitaire*, Leopold's *A Sand County Almanac*, and Macdonald's *H is for Hawk*. My hand paused over one of my fiction favorites, Farley Mowat's *Never Cry*

Wolf, but I had no time to linger. On the top shelf, above my mostly pantheistic library, was an oversized book. Anyone seeing the tome would likely have assumed it didn't fit on any of the shelves. They also would have assumed what they were seeing was the family Bible. On tiptoes, I carefully brought it down.

Despite the cover identifying the book as the King James version of the Holy Bible, it was neither holy nor a Bible. Inside a hollowed-out compartment was a compact nine-millimeter Ruger EC05. The handgun weighed a little more than a pound, and was perfect for concealed carry.

I'd had the gun for two years. Tommy had gifted it to me when we'd gone rogue on the chain-gang investigation. We both had "just in case" throwaway guns. Tommy had commandeered our weapons from an arms dealer he'd arrested who had a huge cache of firearms in his trunk.

Two of those guns had never been turned in to evidence.

Despite being a cop, I'm not a fan of guns, as too many times I've seen how they shatter lives. I consider the gun I carry on the job a necessary evil. Today, it was possible my just-in-case gun was finally going to be used.

I set the dining room table not with plates and utensils, but tools and solvents. After removing the Ruger's magazine, I began disassembling it. I used a spray cleaner and an old toothbrush to clean the guts of the gun. For the finish work, I dabbed away at dirt and gunk with Q-Tips. Then I worked the bore cleaning brush on the barrel, making sure the metal was clear of any impediments. Using a rag, I did a final touch-up and then applied some oil.

Cleaning a gun wasn't anything new to me, but today it felt that way.

I reassembled the Ruger, filling the seven-round magazine with new bullets. Normally, I don't place a bullet in the chamber, but today I put one in the pipe. When the time came, all I'd need to do was pull the trigger.

"That's all," I tried telling myself.

The sudden tug in my gut, and trembling in my fingers, exposed my lie.

I placed the Ruger into an opaque plastic bag to minimize the potential of it picking up fibers or any trace evidence.

God hadn't called. The governor hadn't called. An execution awaited.

A one-word text with the message *mail* told me the package had arrived. Penelope had delivered a plastic evidence bag, as well as my own burner phone, through which we'd communicate.

I decided to call Chloe before traveling north. It wouldn't do to have her call my phone on this day, but neither did I want her to know what I was planning. After the deed was done, we'd talk.

She picked up on the second ring and said, "I was just about to call you."

"Anything up?"

"I just wanted to hear your voice."

"That's what prompted this call," I said. "And I also thought I should warn you that I'll need to be incommunicado for the rest of the day."

"Why's that?"

"Work," I said. "I'll be on a stakeout this afternoon into the evening, and we're prohibited from taking personal calls."

Would the lie fly?

"In that case, I hope you get your bad guy," she said.

I was evidently a better liar than Chloe, which didn't make

me feel good. "Any idea on where you want to go for brunch tomorrow?"

"There are a couple spots in Coronado that I like," she said. "Do you want me to make reservations?"

I pretended to be upbeat. "That would be great."

"Ten-ish?"

"Works for me."

"How late do you think your stakeout will go?" she asked.

"Fingers crossed, not too late," I said. "But just in case, I better wish you a goodnight right now. Sleep tight, don't let the bedbugs bite."

Chloe laughed. "That was what my father used to say when I was a little girl."

"Hard to beat a classic."

"Challenge accepted," she said. "I'll pull out the bard card. *Goodnight, goodnight! Parting is such sweet sorrow, that I shall say goodnight till it be morrow.*"

"Not fair," I said.

"All is fair in love and war."

"What are the words to that Mr. Sandman song?" I asked, stalling while trying to come up with something better.

"No hints from me," she said.

"It's on the tip of my tongue," I said. But it wasn't.

"Accept defeat?" she asked.

Another rhyme came to me. It almost felt heaven sent. I didn't know the source of the words. Maybe I'd planted them in my memory in the hope that one day I'd have a partner to speak them to.

"Love you yesterday, love you still, always have, always will."

"How'd you come up with that?"

"No idea. Really."

"I can't top that," she said. "I don't want to top that. I just want to be that person."

"You are."

———

There was one final thing to do before leaving. I put together a meal for Lenore and took it out to her. Today, the raven had decided to come out of hiding, and was basking on a branch in the morning sun.

"Morning, Lenore," I called out.

Her black eyes tracked me as I approached. It had been days since I'd seen Lenore, and the passage of time hadn't been kind to her. Her coat had lost much of its glossy sheen, and her bad wing looked as if it was hanging lower. Birds lose their musculature when they can't fly. It was also possible an infection had set in. I snapped a few pictures and hoped a vet could prescribe me something to put in her food.

"I'll dig some grubs for you tomorrow," I promised. "And get you peanut M&Ms. And more ripe bananas."

There would be no more green bananas for either of us.

Lenore shifted a little in her perch.

"On today's menu is dry oatmeal, raisins, peanuts, and a little banana. Good stuff."

I hoped she'd be hungrier than I was. It had been all I could do to choke down half a piece of toast. I wedged her food bowls into the crooks of some low-lying branches. Lenore couldn't see what I was doing, but could hear. She was smart, and would know that breakfast had been served.

Stepping back from my cherry tree, I spoke once more to the raven. "Enjoy your time in the sun, Lenore. Don't give up."

Words meant as much for me as her.

Normally, I enjoy the drive from San Diego to California's Central Coast, especially when I put Los Angeles in the rearview mirror, but today the coastal views were lost to me. I was too busy looking inward.

The plan Penelope and Chloe had come up with for assassinating Lynch had too many variables in it, too many things that could go wrong. Simpler usually worked better. I was more comfortable in the role of detective than that of a hit man. The best way for me to come at Lynch would be as a cop. I'd go to Lynch's apartment in the early evening, knock on his door, and ask if he wouldn't mind answering some questions on a case I was working.

My hope was that he'd invite me inside. Otherwise, I'd have to get in by hook or by crook. I'd start out easy, before sweating him on the Dana Silva homicide. At that point, he'd probably ask for a lawyer. That's when I'd have to make a decision which way to go. I'd either use my service revolver and end his life—as a cop—or shoot him up close with the Ruger. Either way, the next step would be to stage the crime scene.

If I painted it like he was resisting arrest, I'd tell police he was reaching for a weapon. Postmortem, I'd make sure his fingerprints and fibers were on the Ruger and bullets. After that, I'd go to the filing cabinet in the bedroom and replace the ticket stubs and envelope Penelope had taken from the Hg 80 Mercury file. Before calling the police, I'd go through Lynch's apartment and remove the hidden surveillance cameras I suspected were there. After smashing them into pieces, they'd be flushed down the toilet.

That scenario meant selling the investigators on the shooting being a justifiable homicide. I'd need to show that I acted out of necessity—that it was kill or be killed. My badge would lend credence to that story, especially when combined with the Silva/Landers cold case I was working. I'd say Lynch had become increasingly agitated during my questioning. When corroborating evidence like the ticket stubs turned up, that might be enough for them to not look any further. It's always hard to care about a scumbag.

The riskier way would be for me to make it look like suicide. I would have to get close to the right side of his head and shoot him point-blank. Doing so would spare me from a grilling by a bunch of cops, but I'd have to contend with blood splatter, noise from gunfire, ballistics putting me at the crime scene, and being seen coming or going.

Better to shoot him as a cop, I decided. Even if some detective doubted my story, what was the worst that could happen to me? If I was arrested, I'd be long dead before there was a trial. And Chloe would be safe. That's what really mattered, or at least that's what I wanted to believe. If anyone deserved to die, it was Lynch. I'd be meting out overdue justice.

Intellectually, I could justify my actions, but viscerally it wasn't so easy. It was a good thing my stomach was empty, because it kept doing flip-flops. You can't look at committing a murder through rose-colored glasses. But the way I saw it, there really wasn't any choice but to act. Lynch could already be targeting Penelope, and Chloe wouldn't be far behind. I no longer even had the fallback position of arresting him. Penelope's break-in was Lynch's golden ticket. If a lawyer found out about it, he'd skate, and I couldn't let that happen.

Today, I would murder Abel Lynch.

A car cut into my lane, and I braked hard. The near miss awoke me from my torpor. To my surprise, it was a sunny afternoon. I looked to road signs to get my bearings and saw I was only ten miles from Santa Barbara. On impulse, I exited on to San Ysidro Road, which would take me to downtown

Montecito. I'd never been there; it was home to the rich and famous. But today I wasn't going to hobnob with the gentry. At the first opportunity, I pulled to the side of the road and staggered out of my car. Bending over, I mostly dry heaved.

My face was hot and sweaty. Throwing up made me feel as if I'd violated some Montecito rule. You aren't supposed to get sick in paradise, nor did it seem like the right place to plot a murder.

I got back in my car and drank some water. Lompoc was an hour's drive away. There was no turning back now.

CHAPTER THIRTY-FIVE

The closer I got to Lompoc, the more I felt weighted down by the gravity of the situation. Einstein believed massive objects caused a disruption in the space–time continuum. To someone like me, his theory of relativity didn't mean much, but I always appreciated his simpler explanation. He said, "When you sit with a nice girl for two hours, you think it's only a minute, but when you sit on a hot stove for a minute, you think it's two hours. That's relativity."

It felt as if I were sitting on that hot stove, but unlike Einstein, I didn't have a good equation like $E=MC^2$ to explain murder. I wasn't even sure I had a good explanation.

Lynch is guilty. That's what I kept telling myself. But how many prosecutors have placed the innocent on death row? Loose ends are part of every case. I was used to collecting evidence, making an arrest, and handing off my case to the DA. Whatever the outcome of that case, I had to abide by the decision. When it came to Lynch, I didn't have the buffer of a judge and jury. The blood on my hands would be mine alone.

Time-out, I wanted to call. Was that a possible subset in Einstein's equation? Could I insert it into mine?

I heard a text tone and reached for my burner phone. *On the move,* was the message. Penelope and her GPS tracker told me Lynch was now driving home from his workplace. If I didn't make any more stops, I'd arrive in Lompoc in about half an hour. The sun wouldn't set for another two hours, though, and I didn't want to act until it was dark. That meant I needed to hole up somewhere.

Go scout out his apartment? Or wait in some quiet spot until it was time? Wait, I decided. The closer I got to Lompoc, the more anxious I felt. My hands began to shake, and my breathing was rapid and shallow. After exiting on to the Pacific Coast Highway, a sign welcomed me to Lompoc, home of the Vandenberg Space Force base. I turned on West Ocean Avenue but soon encountered heavy traffic. Because it was a Saturday, I blamed the weekend for the logjam, but then I saw cars parked on both sides of the road. Something was going on, even though there was no obvious cause. Canopies were set up, and people were standing outside their vehicles.

From the side of the road, a car signaled to merge into the flow of traffic. I slowed down, let it in, and then on impulse pulled into the spot it had vacated. Safety in numbers; I wouldn't stand out.

I parked behind a Rivian SUV, which had an open tailgate. An extension cord plugged into the SUV's electrical outlet was acting as a mini generator to several electrical devices set up along its third-row bench seat. A telescope, with a computer interface to a laptop, was positioned near the SUV. Based on the bumper stickers festooned on the vehicle, the telescope suddenly made sense. There were decals of *Falcon 1* and *Falcon 9* rockets, and bumper stickers that read OCCUPY MARS, LAUNCH AMERICA, CREW DRAGON, and CAPSULE SPACEX.

The driver's door to the Rivian opened, and a heavyset man who looked to be in his late sixties emerged. His T-shirt showed the spiral galaxy of the Milky Way. An arrow pointed to a microscopic object and offered the cosmos geography lesson of *You Are Here*. The man's Space Force cap, a rocket parsing the two words with a scarlet contrail, further revealed his passion. As he walked toward the back of his SUV, the man took notice of me and waved. I waved back, which encouraged his approach.

"I guess our erstwhile neighbors gave up," he said. "You probably heard the launch is delayed."

I nodded as if I knew that.

"At least the mission wasn't totally scrubbed. Of course, the operative words are 'at this time.'"

"Fingers crossed," I said.

"If they send the bird up between twenty hundred and twenty-one hundred, like they're saying, we ought to be witness to a beautiful contrail."

"Let's hope for that," I said.

"Name's Kent," he said.

For a moment, I considered offering up a fake name, but decided there was no need. In fact, the imminent space launch offered me the perfect reason for being in Lompoc.

"Wyatt," I said, extending my hand out the window.

After we shook, Kent said, "The wife sent me out here to make her a margarita. Can I fix one for you, Wyatt?"

"I appreciate the offer, but I better pass."

"If you change your mind, just whistle," he said. "I'm about to set up camp chairs for me and Marcia. You're welcome to join us, if you'd like."

"I don't want to put you out," I said.

"You wouldn't. We come to these launches equipped for an army. Marcia would love it if I wasn't the only one chowing down. She's on a mission to limit my caloric intake."

"How's it working?"

Kent patted his gut. "Not too well, I'd say."

Like Kent, Marcia was wearing clothing identifying her interest in the heavens. Her T-shirt read I NEED MY SPACE. Above the lettering was the NASA logo displayed in the midst of a circular orbit among the stars.

Seeing the couple in their space outfits made me think of Chloe. If the two of us had met when we were younger, would we one day have worn clothing like Kent and Marcia? Maybe I should get us some San Diego Zoo outfits for Christmas—that is, if Christmas didn't come too late for me. If we wanted to dress like an old married couple showing our shared passions, it would be better for me not to delay.

In the ten minutes since I'd sat with Kent and Marcia, I'd learned they were both retired. Kent had been an engineer, and Marcia a librarian. They had three grown children and a one-year-old grandson named Aidan. Like many couples that had grown old together, they knew all the same stories and liked to finish each other's sentences. It was comfortable listening to their good-natured bickering, and gave me a reprieve from ruminating.

As Kent returned with a new plate of food, Marcia asked him, "Is that your third helping?"

"Second," Kent said. "Are you having memory issues, or too many margaritas?"

Marcia turned to me and said, "It's easier when I just pretend he's right."

Kent looked at me, lifted an index finger to his lips, and made a shushing sound.

"That's Kent's idea of a librarian joke," Marcia said. "Just as it has been for the last forty-four years."

"Once a classic, always a classic," Kent said. "You need to believe in your *shelf*."

That got a groan out of me, and smiles from them.

"We're polar opposites," Kent said. "But also, peas in a pod."

Marcia asked, "Can I get you another plate of food, Wyatt?"

"No, thank you," I said. "I'm still working on what I have."

Despite telling her I wasn't hungry, Marcia had brought me a paper plate filled with chicken salad, pita chips, deviled eggs, and melon balls.

"You been to many other launches?" Kent asked.

I shook my head. "This is my first."

"Maybe you'll catch the bug," he said. "We saw our first launch almost twenty years ago. Since then, we've been traveling vagabonds and seen launches from California to Florida. No two are ever alike."

I raised my head and looked at the sky. The sun hadn't yet set, and the stars were still in hiding.

"We haven't asked you about your work, Wyatt," Marcia said.

Witnesses, on this night of all nights, would be a good thing. "I'm a detective with the San Diego Police Department."

Kent raised up his hands, as if surrendering. "Whatever Marcia claims I've done, I'm innocent."

She said, "You have the right to remain silent, Kent, and we hope you do just that."

Kent turned to me and asked, "Isn't drinking in public against the law?"

Marcia said, "I'd think the greater crime would be the dispensing of alcohol in a public space."

"Relax," I said. "I won't be writing either of you up."

"How do you like being an LEO, Wyatt?" She turned to Kent and said, "And I'm not talking astrology."

"Law enforcement officer," I explained.

"I love mysteries, and watching crime shows on TV," Marcia said.

"She screams bloody murder if a spider invades our house, but happily immerses herself in the goriest of shows," Kent said.

"What kind of police work do you do, Wyatt?" Marcia asked.

"I'm with the Cold Case Team," I said.

"You work unsolved murders?"

"Sometimes," I said. "But we're assigned a variety of cases, from missing persons to unidentified victims to unresolved sexual assault cases."

"Is the work as fascinating as it sounds?" she asked.

"It can be," I said. "Cold case investigators usually have the luxury of being able to commit time to a case. I like being able to dig deep."

"What case are you working on now?" Kent asked.

"I'm afraid I can't talk about an active investigation."

That wasn't exactly true, but tonight wouldn't be a good time to discuss the Silva homicide.

A puzzled-looking Kent asked, "But you're working an old case, right?"

"I am, but since it's a homicide, there's no statute of limitations attached to the case."

"You must have a lot of patience," Marcia said.

"What makes you think that?"

"It's tough enough to deal with things in the present. I imagine it's even more work dealing in the past."

"You're right about that," I said. "But cold case investigators know the race is not always to the swift. In fact, my team refers to itself as the *frozen chosen*."

Marcia smiled at our cold case pun.

"You lucked out, Marcia," Kent said. "With Wyatt as a neighbor, you've got your very own cop show."

"Are you married, Wyatt?" Marcia asked.

"Never have been," I said. "But there is a special woman in my life now."

"It's a shame she couldn't be here," Marcia said.

"She had another commitment, but I have no doubt she'll be jealous when I tell her about the gourmet food you served me."

"Please tell her that Kent and I would love it if the two of you could meet up with us for a future launch," Marcia said.

"I'll pass that on to her," I said. "When's the next launch here?"

"Four weeks," Kent said. "In a typical year, between twenty and thirty rockets get sent up from Vandenberg."

"That's more than I would have expected."

"They're sent up on a southward route," Marcia said. "You actually could have seen tonight's flight without leaving San Diego."

"I wanted to be close to the action," I said. "And if I'd stayed home, I wouldn't have gotten this wonderful feast."

Marcia said, "You hear that, Kent?"

"I'm not deaf, although sometimes I can imagine its advantages," he said.

Their verbal sparring was a game they both enjoyed. A smiling Marcia asked, "How about some brownies, Wyatt?"

The revised launch of the *Falcon 9* rocket was scheduled to go up just after sundown. My plan had been to leave before liftoff, but I kept putting off that moment. Seeing a rocket launch seemed like something that belonged on my bucket list. It was also a way of delaying what I didn't want to do.

Murder could wait, or that's what I told myself.

"T-minus ten minutes," Kent said, rubbing his hands.

"We're lucky. Not much of a marine layer tonight. We should get a good show."

"Don't jinx it." Marcia turned to me and added, "Not long ago we attended a launch that was scrubbed with only twenty-three seconds to go."

"Who's doing the jinxing now?" Kent said.

He went back to studying the screen of his laptop, and looking at a livestream of the *Falcon 9* rocket on the launchpad. The timeline was counting down, with just nine minutes and change to go. According to the display, engine chill was occurring.

"Winds are under ten miles an hour," Kent said. "Everything's looking good."

A new image appeared on the laptop's screen, a sort of bull's eye with an X marking the spot in the center.

"What's that?" I asked.

"That's the autonomous spaceport drone ship, or ASD, positioned out at sea. We're looking at the landing pad the booster rocket will set down upon after separation."

"The ASD is pretty much a modified barge," Marcia said.

"It's more than that, really," Kent said. "There are station-keeping thrusters on board that allow the ASD to be remotely controlled and maintain its position at sea."

Marcia said, "What I like most about this particular ASD is its name."

She turned to her husband. In a monotone, Kent said, "It's named *Of Course I Still Love You*."

"Be still my heart," Marcia said.

He shook his head and sighed.

"Kent likes to pretend he's a curmudgeon, but secretly he's a romantic," Marcia said. "He reminds me of this longtime library patron who always checked out a pile of romance novels he claimed were for a neighbor of his. We all pretended to go along with his story."

"I only read science fiction," Kent said.

"That's why he knows all about the ASDs," Marcia said. "The drone ships were named after some science fiction series."

"Iain M. Bank's *Culture* series," Kent said. "He was going to write a final novel in the series, but only had time to leave behind some notes after being diagnosed with an inoperable cancer. Gallbladder, I think."

The image of this author desperately scribbling out his final thoughts struck home harder than I would have expected. It felt like an omen, and I wondered if I would have to pass on my chain-gang homicides notes to someone else.

The image on the screen changed, showing the *Falcon 9* rocket and a countdown time of T-minus five minutes and twenty-four seconds.

Marcia and Kent stopped talking, and a hushed anticipation fell over those gathered around us.

When the countdown was T-minus one minute, my eyes went from the screen to a westerly spot in the sky where the *Falcon 9* would be traveling. When I looked back to the screen, the countdown was down to thirty seconds. Then twenty.

A thunderous growl was building, and a man-made earthquake began to shake the ground around us. Voices called out, as if to a deity: "Ten, nine, eight, seven, six, five..."

I turned my gaze to the sky.

"Four, three, two, one..."

The red glare of the rocket flared as it took leave of the earth.

CHAPTER THIRTY-SIX

While Kent was tracking the *Falcon 9* with his telescope, I told Marcia it was time for me to take my leave.

"So soon?"

"I wish I could stay, but I didn't travel to Lompoc just for the launch," I said. "I'm also working a case."

"At this hour?" Marcia said.

"You drop in at odd hours to catch people at home," I said. "I'd like to exchange contact information with you before I go, though."

Which would come in handy later that night when I provided it to detectives to establish my whereabouts, and my timeline for the evening. Marcia and Kent would be the perfect witnesses.

As Marcia and I exchanged information, Kent stayed busy with his scoping.

"Boys and their toys," Marcia said.

"Care for a last look at the heavens, Wyatt?" Kent asked.

"Thanks, but I'm afraid I have to turn my personal lens elsewhere."

From my car, I called Abel Lynch's cell phone. I wanted the time of the call to be on the record. I had to make all my actions appear plausible to those who would soon be investigating an officer-involved shooting.

Deep breath. Speak calmly. Make it sound as if I'm a cop with some routine questions. Don't spook him.

One ring.

Say that I just need five minutes of his time. Ask if it's all right to meet up at his place.

Two rings.

Tell him I thought it best to talk with him at home so as to not to bother him at his workplace.

Three rings.

Mention that since I was already in Lompoc for the launch, the timing was good for me.

Four rings.

Say I just needed to sign off on a few questions, and was trying to spare him the rigamarole of a formal interview.

Still no answer. I looked at the time. It was ten to nine. Could he already be riding his bicycle to the bar? Penelope said he usually didn't take off until after nine.

Five and then a sixth ring. And then a voice said, "Leave a message at the beep."

No pleasantries. No identification. Just a beep.

I decided to leave a message, but not so much for Lynch, as for those I expected would soon be investigating his death.

"Hello, Mr. Lynch, this is Detective Wyatt Lake of the San Diego Police Department. I'm in Lompoc tonight, and just finished watching the launch. I know it's late, but I'm hoping we can chat for just a few minutes about a case I've recently been assigned. I only have a few simple questions, and thought I'd save you the hassle of a formal interview. Please call me back as soon as possible."

I left him the number of my cell phone.

Go to his apartment? Or see if he was already drinking at the bar he frequented?

His place first, I decided. My armpits were already soaked. At our meetup, I'd have to wear my blazer to hide the state of my shirt.

I drove without even being aware of it, choreographing in my mind what I'd need to do. If things worked out and I was let into Lynch's apartment, I'd start in with a few innocuous questions and try to make him comfortable. I imagined we'd both be sitting. When the time was right, I'd reach for my service gun and shoot at his chest. Two rounds. After making sure Lynch was dead, I'd plant the Ruger. Should I leave the gun in his hand? No, that would be too much. Have it nearby.

The sound of a ringing phone awakened me from my grisly planning, and set my heart to pounding. *Lynch,* I thought.

But that wasn't the name on my vehicle's display. B. Davis of the Lompoc PD was on the line. How the hell had a local cop gotten my number, and why was he calling me? I tapped Accept, and took the call.

"This is Lake," I said.

"This is Detective Brian Davis of the Lompoc Police Department," the voice said. "Your name and telephone number came up on a phone in our possession, and I'm calling to find out the purpose of your call."

Davis sounded eager. Why? And what was he doing with Lynch's phone? It didn't sound as if he'd heard my message, but had just seen my number on the display and called back. Which meant what? In the space of a moment, I considered the best way to respond to Davis's question. Play it straight, I decided.

Establish my own bona fides. And then begin asking my own questions.

"I'm Wyatt Lake, a detective with the San Diego Police Department. I called Abel Lynch hoping he'd talk to me about a case I'm working."

"Are you acquainted with him?" he asked.

"Not personally," I said. "His name came up in a case I'm investigating."

"A case in San Diego?"

"That's right. But I'm actually in Lompoc now. That's why I wanted to talk to Lynch tonight."

Detective Davis said, "Isn't it late to be contacting him?"

"I didn't want to bother him at work, and decided to watch tonight's rocket launch before reaching out to him. My hope was that he would agree to sit down to an impromptu interview. What about you? What's your interest in Lynch?"

Davis hesitated a moment before answering, and then said, "It appears Mr. Lynch shot himself."

"He's dead?"

"Yes."

My sudden sense of relief was so overwhelming, I couldn't speak.

Davis said, "Detective?"

"Sorry," I said. "I wasn't expecting that, but maybe I should have. Where and when did the suicide occur?"

"In his apartment, earlier this evening."

"And that's where you are now?"

"Correct."

"Then I'll see you in fifteen minutes," I said. "I have some important information you'll need to hear."

CHAPTER THIRTY-SEVEN

All day it had felt as if I was the one who had a date with the executioner, but now I'd been spared. Lynch was dead, but not by my hand. Thank God.

Weak with relief, it was all I could do to hold on to the steering wheel. I was okay with being a tarnished knight, but had struggled with the prospect of being a murderer. Now it almost felt as if I'd been given another chance at life, like Scrooge on Christmas Day. I took some deep breaths and tried to find my equilibrium. Later, I could celebrate my good fortune, but now there were matters needing my attention.

The GPS guided me to Lynch's address, where I found a red-and-blue light show being put on by two police cruisers parked in front of the apartment complex. A uniformed officer was standing as gatekeeper in front of the building, checking identification and allowing entrance only to residents.

As I made my approach to the officer, I showed my badge wallet and said, "I'm Detective Lake. Detective Davis is expecting me."

The officer took his time studying my badge before offering a nod and stepping aside to let me pass by. There was no need to ask which way to go—even behind closed curtains I could see the flashes of a crime scene unit's camera.

I took the stairs to the second floor. Just beyond the landing, another uniformed officer was working bouncer duty in an area cordoned off with crime scene tape. Curious residents were gathered outside their apartments, whispering about what was going on. I edged around the onlookers, approached the crime scene tape, and lifted up the nylon barricade while extending my badge wallet for the officer to see.

"Thank you, sir," she said. "What can I do for you?"

"I'm here to see Detective Davis."

"Please wait here, sir, and I'll flag him down."

The officer walked over to the door and opened it, but was careful not to step inside. She began waving her hand, and eventually must have gotten the detective's attention. I saw her mouth something and then close the door behind her.

When the officer returned to where I was waiting, she said, "He'll be just a minute."

I thanked her. That minute passed, and another. The officer decided to engage in small talk while we waited.

"Did you see the launch tonight?" she asked.

"Saw it, heard it, and felt it," I said.

"Sometimes the launches are late at night," she said. "A few times I've been fast asleep and have been awakened by a shaking apartment. Usually, I think we're having an earthquake. And that doesn't even take into account the sonic booms."

"Those must get the blood pumping."

"They sure do," she said.

I looked at my phone for the time.

"I'm sure the detective will be right out," she said. "In Lompoc, we don't get too many calls like this."

"I wish I could say the same thing about San Diego. I guess trouble followed me here."

Our conversation was cut short when the door swung open, and a man wearing a hairnet, gloves, and booties emerged. From our phone conversation, I had mentally envisioned Davis as a young detective, and that's what he was. He looked to be about thirty, and appeared to have spent a lot of those years in a weight room.

"Brian Davis," he said.

That was apparently enough in the way of pleasantries.

"Wyatt Lake."

"On the phone you said there was information about the deceased that I needed to hear."

"I imagine you ran Abel Lynch's name through the system?"

"Clean record," he said. "No wants, no warrants."

"That's true enough, but it doesn't give you the full picture. Lynch is a person of interest in an old homicide case I'm working. It's my belief that twenty-five years ago he murdered a fifteen-year-old female named Dana Silva, and also attempted to murder Chloe Landers, the victim's best friend. Landers survived the assault with grievous bodily injuries."

"What makes you think he's your guy?" Davis asked.

"We obtained an old picture of Lynch taken only a few months before the Silva homicide. Based on that picture, Landers identified him as the man who attacked her. Since then, I've been gathering other corroborating evidence."

"Was he aware you were onto him?" Davis asked.

"It's possible," I said, looking and sounding as if I'd screwed up. "I might have tipped my hand while trying to gather more evidence. I suspect he smelled something fishy and realized the net was closing around him."

"And you think this was his way of not having to face the music?"

"That's my belief."

"Are you available to write up a statement describing your investigation of Lynch?" he asked.

"Whatever you need," I said. "I can do it tonight if that will make your life easier."

Especially if it would allow me access to the crime scene.

My willingness to co-operate, and not step on Davis's booties, made him relax.

"We think Lynch committed suicide," he said. "But we're still treating the crime scene as a potential homicide."

"I don't suppose he made things easy on you and left a note?"

"No note," Davis said.

That wasn't surprising. Only about one in four suicides leaves a note.

"But he actually did call 911 before he offed himself," Davis said. "In the recording, he sounds liquored up. And inside there's evidence he was drinking prior to his grand finale."

"Any chance I can hear his 911 call?" I asked.

The detective looked around, must have decided the bystanders were out of hearing range, and pulled out his cell phone.

"Dispatch forwarded his call to me," he said, and hit play.

On the recording there was a cough, then a raspy voice with a slight slur said, "I give up. I'm cashing in my chips. By the time you send someone here, I'll be dead. Tell the cops the door will be open."

There was a click, and the voice of the dispatcher said, "Sir? Sir?" Then the call ended.

"And was the door left open?" I asked.

"The officer who was dispatched found it ajar."

"Thoughtful of Lynch."

"Tell me that after you see the mess he left behind. I guess that was his FU to the world."

"Or to me," I said. "He knew I was coming after him. I'm kicking myself now for not stopping by earlier this evening. My not bringing him in feels anticlimactic."

"Take the W and be glad," Davis said. "By checking out, he saved you from being tied up for the next year with paperwork and court appearances."

"Yeah," I said, sounding unsure. "But putting cuffs on him sure would have felt nice."

As much as I wanted Davis to invite me into his case, I couldn't crash his party. This was *his* crime scene. I might be a fellow cop, but I was an outsider. There had to be a way to get in. Luckily for me, Davis decided I could be of use.

"How long will you be staying in Lompoc?" Davis asked.

"For however long you need me," I said.

"I better get you into some scrubs, then," he said.

Two members of the Santa Barbara County Sheriff's Crime Lab were working inside the apartment. The crime techs must have drawn their own conclusions that Lynch had killed himself, which explained their unhurried movements. If Lynch's death was being worked as a homicide, the scene would have been more frenzied, with a room full of crime scene specialists, and detectives hovering over them.

Davis and I stayed out of the way of the techs, standing on the periphery of the living room. The detective was right about Lynch leaving behind a mess, but I'd worked scenes far grislier. Most suicides in the US use a gun. Lynch had died of a head wound in his temple, shooting himself while sitting in his easy chair. A partially filled tumbler with amber liquid was sitting atop a coaster on a coffee table, and a small handgun lay on the carpet about two feet from the chair where he'd been seated.

Davis saw where my eyes were focused, and said, "Smith & Wesson MP Shield nine-millimeter. It's California compliant and contained seven rounds, with one in the pipe. The casing from the fired round ended five feet to the right of where he was sitting."

"Is the gun registered?"

Davis nodded. "Lynch was the legal owner."

I turned around, getting a view of the galley kitchen. On the counter was a half-empty 1.75-liter bottle of Jameson Whiskey. Next to it were three opened cans of Schweppes ginger ale, along with two halves of a squeezed lime. I went and examined the cans. Two were empty, and one was half full. I lifted the can with ginger ale inside and swirled it slightly. There was still some carbonation.

"Looks to me like he needed some liquid courage before pulling the trigger," Davis said.

"Lynch was a regular at an Irish bar in town," I said.

"Guess that explains his Irish goodbye," Davis said.

"Anyone hear the gun fire?"

"We've got an officer who's been canvassing apartments. So far, he's got nothing. It's possible the shot was fired around the time of tonight's rocket launch, which could have masked the sound."

"Maybe Lynch did a countdown to his own blastoff," I said. "Have you searched his bedroom?"

"I haven't gotten that far yet," he said.

"Before I close the book on Lynch, it would be nice if I could find more evidence linking him to my homicide," I said.

"Let's take a look," Davis said.

As Davis began his initial search of the room, I surreptitiously looked around for the most likely spots for surveillance cameras. The barrenness of the bedroom limited the possibilities of where the spy cameras could be positioned. There were no picture frames, phone chargers, or table clocks—items frequently employed to camouflage cameras. A smoke detector on the ceiling caught my eye, as did an electrical outlet without anything plugged into it.

I came up behind Davis as he opened the sliding glass door to the closet, and revealed the filing cabinet. He opened the top drawer, and we saw all the labeled hanging folders.

"Organized," he said.

"Very," I agreed. "He's a retired Navy cook, so I imagine being organized was a way of life for him after spending so much time at sea working in cramped quarters."

Davis nodded, and used his cell phone to take some pictures.

I said, "How about we divide and conquer? You start with the top two drawers, and I'll take the next two down."

"Works for me," he said. "There's a lot here to sort through, but let's take it slow and steady. If you find anything interesting, I'll want to document it in pictures."

"Understood," I said. "Is it okay with you if I take my drawers and place them on the bed? That will make it easier for me to look through them, and we won't be in each other's way."

"No problem," he said.

I removed the drawers, and we both began searching through the folders, occasionally making sporadic conversation.

"This guy sure was methodical," Davis said. "My system for keeping receipts and paperwork is to throw everything in a drawer, and only sort through it when tax season arrives. Last year, I tossed everything from my drawer into a bag and then dumped the whole thing on my accountant's desk. He wasn't too impressed with my filing system. But if I hadn't done it my way, I wouldn't have been able to write off the dog food receipts as security expenses."

"That's a legitimate deduction?" I asked.

"Let's hope so. Or hope that I don't get audited."

I continued with my methodical search. As tempting as it was to leapfrog through the folders and locate the folder labeled Hg 80, I resisted. The more I looked, though, the more nervous I got. What if Lynch had destroyed the folder after seeing what Penelope had removed from it?

Luckily, Mercury wasn't in retrograde, and Hg 80 finally turned up.

I removed the folder and placed it on the bedspread. Then I pretended to stretch, and pulled an envelope from the inside pocket of my sports coat. When I determined that Davis's back was turned to me, I placed the envelope inside the Hg 80 folder.

"I think I found something here," I said.

Davis turned his head, and I showed him the old envelope. Then I carefully removed the two ticket stubs inside of it.

"These stubs are from a Mercury concert held at the San Diego Sports Arena some twenty-five years ago. Dana Silva and Chloe Landers went to that concert. Afterward, they set out to hitchhike home. The driver who picked them up subsequently attacked them, leaving both for dead. When Chloe Landers was interviewed after the assault, she told the detective that she and Dana had retained their ticket stubs as mementos. Because neither stub was found among their possessions, SDPD kept that information under wraps. The hope was that their assailant kept the ticket stubs as trophies. Apparently, he did."

Davis came over to me and eyeballed the tickets. Then he extended his fist, and the two of us bumped. This was no longer just a suicide he was working. The detective was closing the book on a notorious wanted murderer.

"Let me take some pictures, and then we'll put these into an evidence bag," he said, intent on establishing the chain of custody.

He took his time processing the finds, and then turned his attention to the label on the hanging folder.

"What's Hg 80?" he asked.

"No clue," I said, wanting him to put the equation together himself.

"Someone's initials?"

"Maybe," I said. "But why would Lynch capitalize the *H*, and write the *g* as lower case?"

Davis scratched his chin. "It sounds like some kind of code," he said. "Hg 80."

"In all the other folders, the label matched up with the contents inside."

"What could two ticket stubs have to do with Hg 80?"

As much as I wanted to offer Davis a clue, I just shrugged my shoulders.

"Wait a second," he said, shaking his index finger as if trying to hammer something down. "Mercury concert, right?" He didn't try to hide the triumphant note in his voice. "I'm thinking Hg 80 has to be the chemical equation for Mercury."

It was time to push him over the finish line. "You mean, like from the periodic table?"

He nodded, and then posed the question to his phone. What he read made him smile.

Davis read: "'On the periodic table, Mercury has the symbol Hg, and its atomic number is 80.'"

"I'll be damned," I said.

CHAPTER THIRTY-EIGHT

I finished my write-up at just before two in the morning, and then printed out a copy.

"Some pleasure reading for you," I said, handing it to Davis. "If you need any clarifications or revisions, you got my number."

Davis covered up a yawn with his hand. We were both on our fourth cup of coffee. It wasn't helping.

"Have you given any more thought to taking up the department's offer to put you up for the night?" he asked.

"I'll pass," I said. "If I leave now, I should make it home before sunset."

"I'll make excuses for you at tomorrow's press conference."

"Missing out on that sounds like reason enough for me to leave now."

"Between us, you're making the right choice," Davis said. "I'll be the window dressing, while the chief does all the talking."

"Around the time I got my first hash mark, a detective warned me to never get between the brass and the cameras. It's time for me to get the hell out of Dodge."

"Thanks for everything," Davis said, extending his hand.

We shook, and I said, "Stay safe," the standard cop goodbye.

Because of the late hour, the 101 was virtually free of traffic. I pushed down on the accelerator, settling on a cruising speed of eighty-five MPH. It's almost unheard of for a law enforcement officer to give another a speeding ticket, but like any scofflaw, I remained on alert for any sign of CHP.

As much as I wanted to talk to Chloe, it was too late to call her. I thought about turning on the radio, but wasn't yet ready to unwind. The solitary drive finally gave me time to reflect on my crazy day, and even crazier night. I swiveled my head back and forth and heard the cracking in my neck. It would take the ride home, and then some, for me to decompress.

Covering up Penelope's visit to Lynch's apartment had been my final intrigue of the night. During a declared "bathroom break," I had gone down to the parking lot, found Lynch's car, and removed the GPS tracker. And when Davis had absented himself to go talk with the techs, I had searched for the suspected surveillance cameras in the master bedroom. Years ago, Tommy had taught me how to use my cell phone to pick up the infrared light of hidden cameras. When I checked the smoke detector and wall socket, I didn't detect any infrared light, which prompted me to do my looking the old-fashioned way. Using my Swiss Army knife, I popped out the outlet and smoke detector. Each had only two wires—one for power, and the other for the video outlet plug—which meant their casings were designed to camouflage the cameras that should have been inside, but weren't. What Lynch had done with the cameras was unclear, since they never turned up during our search of his apartment.

That indicated he'd gotten rid of them.

But if his plan for the evening was to kill himself, why would he care about any potentially incriminating evidence? The more I considered that, the more it nagged at me. When I'd first learned Lynch had committed suicide, it felt as if I'd been given a great gift. All night, I'd been blinded by relief. But now, the blinders were coming off.

The spy cameras had been set up to transmit through wifi. That meant there should have been an app on Lynch's phone for receiving the images. But Detective Davis had told me that he'd found little of interest on the phone. He was too good of a cop to overlook such an app. Did that mean it had been removed?

I began shivering and turned the heater to max. It didn't help. The more I tried to tamp down my doubts, the louder they called out. I know suicides aren't necessarily tidy, or logical. Sometimes they're inexplicable. In high school, my English teacher assigned the class a poem about some wealthy, handsome man who seemingly had everything, but for some reason chose to put a bullet through his head. What was his name?

My teacher had offered up his own rhyme about the man in the poem, referring to him as "Richard Cory, in all his deceptive glory." The reference, the notion of deceptive glory, had always stayed with me.

Lynch didn't have the advantages of Richard Cory. He'd been in the crosshairs of a murder investigation. There were reasons for him to kill himself. So why the hell couldn't I just accept that?

Abel Lynch had worked all day, and then he'd come home and started drinking. People under the influence make a lot of bad choices. Was it so hard to believe that Lynch decided it would be easier just to kill himself? It was probably a spur of the moment decision. That would explain why he spent his last day working. He hadn't consciously planned on killing himself, but had time to dwell on how his world was falling apart.

A drunken Lynch had called 911 and told the dispatcher

he'd had enough. Then he'd casually mentioned that the door would be left open for the cops. That was out of character. Would a man staring into the abyss care if his door had to be kicked open?

No.

During one of my sessions with David, he'd told me I didn't have to be crippled by the circumstances of my death sentence. He'd cited Socrates, and how he'd bathed himself before drinking hemlock so as to spare the cleaning women the task of having to wash him when he was dead. Maybe a philosopher could be that phlegmatic, but not me. And not Lynch, I was sure.

The man had stayed off of law enforcement radar for twenty-five years. In that time, it stood to reason he would have learned the ins and outs of the criminal justice system, including the need for a clear chain of evidence, as well as the ramifications from the fruit of the poisonous tree. Instead of running scared in light of what Penelope had uncovered, Lynch would likely have considered her presence in his apartment a godsend. Because of her illegal breaking and entering, and passing evidence my way, the ticket stubs would have been deemed inadmissible in a criminal trial. Based on that alone, the DA might not have brought charges against him.

The more I considered the matter, the more agitated I felt. *It's just nerves,* I tried to tell myself, too many hours going through the wringer. But my soft-soaping didn't help. Something wasn't right.

With all my ruminating, I hadn't noticed the passage of miles. I was already about halfway home, with the turnoff to Interstate 5 only ten miles away. At my current rate of speed, I'd be home in roughly 100 minutes.

I chewed hard on my lip, drawing the salty tang of blood, and recalled the blood splatter in Lynch's apartment. There was something there, but it wouldn't show itself. I worked the image like a word stuck on the tip of my tongue, trying to coax it out, trying not to be stymied by its stubborn reluctance to reveal itself. But there was nothing about the suicide scene that looked wrong, or out of place.

Maybe that was it. The suicide scene had a déjà vu feel. When I'd resolved to murder Lynch, I had choreographed in my mind what needed to be done. Eventually, I'd decided not to make his death look like a suicide. But if I *had* staged Lynch's death, it would have looked very much like the scene I encountered in his apartment.

I checked the rearview mirror. There was nothing behind me, but it didn't feel that way. The Interstate 5 turnoff grew nearer. When I exited the 101, my speedometer clocked in at 88 miles per hour. What was I rushing to? Just a feeling, maybe. Or was it something more?

Lynch had worked all day. After coming home, he'd started drinking and killed himself. There was nothing implausible about that. There was only one glass on the scene, and nothing to indicate anyone had been with Lynch. But what if someone *had* stopped by to see Lynch, brought the bottle of booze, and served him up a few heavy pours?

It was only speculation, but my right foot pushed a little harder on the accelerator, sending the digital gauge to ninety.

There had been no time for me to do an extensive background check on Lynch. Much of what I knew had been provided by Penelope. But what questions hadn't she asked? She had focused on Lynch's ex-wives, but there had been little about the circumstances of his childhood. Were his parents still alive? Did he have siblings?

Lynch's suicide had occurred around the time of the space launch. The noise, or the sonic boom, could have masked any gunfire. What if someone had known where he stored his gun, and been aware of the surveillance cameras?

Penelope's investigation had never determined what brought Lynch to Lompoc. It wasn't as if his job was in town. To get to his workplace, he drove forty-five miles. Long commute. Nothing I knew linked him to the area. Lynch had traveled all around the world. Why Lompoc?

I clicked on my phone and asked it, "What are the biggest employers in Lompoc?"

An electronic voice told me the city's three largest employers. One name stood out.

"Tell me about Lompoc Prison," I asked.

Lompoc Penitentiary was a low-security federal prison that housed male inmates. The facility had a residential drug abuse program.

The man who'd murdered Dana Silva and hacked off Chloe's legs had been smoking PCP, but Lynch had never failed a drug test administered by the Navy. After being honorably discharged, Lynch had chosen to settle in Lompoc. That's the kind of thing you do when you want to be near family.

I picked up my burner phone, and hit Penelope Hill's preprogrammed number. She answered on the third ring. "Yes?" she said cautiously.

"Lynch is dead. Lompoc PD believes he killed himself, but they were influenced by what I told them."

"What are you saying?"

"I had nothing to do with Lynch's death."

"He offed himself? Isn't that great news?"

"Probably. But some things have surfaced that have me feeling uneasy, even scared."

"What do you want me to do?"

"I'm about eighty miles from downtown San Diego. I'd like

you to call Chloe and ask if you can come over to her place. I'm probably overreacting, but better safe than sorry."

"Consider it done. Do you have the security code for her garage gate? That's always easier than going through the front-desk attendant."

I remembered the five-digit pin-pad code from my previous two visits, but to be safe, offered the numbers.

"You got it," she said.

CHAPTER THIRTY-NINE

As he drove through Hillcrest, he considered the best way to murder the Snoop. She and her employer had brought all this on, but there was a part of him that almost felt grateful.

Maybe he'd whisper his thanks while killing her.

His freedom was tantalizingly close. It was no time to get sloppy, or careless. Since he could remember, others had imposed restraints on him. Eddie had been the first. Not dad, not father; he'd always just been Eddie. His mother, Layla, had gone along with whatever Eddie said or did. She'd never raised any objections when Eddie had brutally beaten him. In fact, Layla had egged Eddie on, exaggerating what he'd said or done, knowing the consequences. May she rot in hell forever.

Beating him had always gotten the blood flowing in old mater and pater. It was foreplay to them. He was a sacrificial victim to their twisted love life, where his pain only added to their pleasure.

But soon, he would finally be free.

It had been a long night, but the adrenaline was still pumping through him. After tying up a few loose ends, he could get on with his life.

After taking out the Snoop, and stashing her body, he'd go after the Cripple. Their reunion, so many years in coming, would be epic.

Cracker had gotten him the intel on both the Snoop and the Cripple. He'd met Cracker in Lompoc. They both had the same parole officer. He'd been able to plead down to a misdemeanor for selling drugs, which was a blessing. If he'd been charged with a felony, his DNA would have been put into the system. All these years he'd been so careful, until that slipup. But doing his parole in Lompoc had proved to have its advantages. That's where he'd become friends with Cracker, who'd been busted for computer crimes.

Once more, he drove the car around the block. Hillcrest was a densely populated area in downtown San Diego with an outsized gay population. He didn't have any extra hate for fudge-packers or carpet-munchers, but did worry about all those potential eyes on his prize. Like all predators, he saw the world differently than the sheep.

The Snoop lived in a second-floor apartment. It wouldn't be easy to break in unobserved, and he doubted she'd be a pushover. According to Cracker, she'd tried to cut off her ex-husband's nuts, but had beaten the charges. It was something to keep in mind, though. He'd shoot the bitch before she got anywhere near his cojones.

In addition to getting him her address, Cracker had supplied the make, model, and license of the vehicle she was driving. The Snoop didn't have an office, but ran her business from her apartment. Curiosity had killed the cat. And it would kill the Snoop.

He parked on the street. Even at this hour, there was some scattered activity in the area. He looked at his phone. Five minutes before four. In another hour or two, the world would be coming to life.

He threw the backpack that held his tools over his shoulder and walked to the sliding security gate that opened up into the back parking lot of the apartment building. On either side of the security gate were six-foot concrete pillars. Above the entryway were CCTV cameras, but he doubted anyone was actively monitoring them. Usually, the cameras were just a deterrent. Using the shoulder straps from his backpack, he looped them around a light fixture and scaled up the concrete pillar. In seconds, he belayed himself up and over, swinging down to the other side.

The white Ford Escape he was looking for was the kind of generic vehicle you'd expect a private investigator to have. The tenants' vehicles were housed under carports, and it didn't take him long to find the SUV. Her vehicle didn't have an alarm. You'd think she would have known better. From his bag of tricks, he removed a Phillips screwdriver and a magnesium telescopic pole. The pole was supposed to be a self-defense weapon, but he'd found a better use for it. He put the screwdriver in the SUV's doorjamb, using it as a wedge for him to insert his ninja pole. Then, he angled the pole's tip downward and pushed the vehicle's unlock button.

In like sin.

From inside the SUV, he relocked the doors. As he expected, both its rear windows were tinted, something that came in handy during surveillances. That would make him all but invisible to anyone looking inside.

There were no merit badges for murder, but like a good Boy Scout, he'd come prepared. At the moment, he was leaning toward using the garrote on the Snoop, but he hadn't ruled out using the hammer. Face or claw? Something to decide before ending her life. He'd also brought a handgun, along with an empty two-liter soda bottle. The plastic bottle was a poor man's silencer. There were lots of good choices for taking the Snoop out. One way or another, she'd soon be dead.

He expected the Snoop was one of those up and at 'em types. She'd certainly been the busy bee of late. His hope was that she'd go for an early-morning drive. That would suit his purposes just fine.

A short time later, he heard footsteps approaching the car. He assumed one of the apartment dwellers was up early, but then the SUV's doors unlocked, and its interior lights came on. Even though he was hunkered down in the back seat, he was afraid the Snoop might see him, or somehow sense his presence, but she was oblivious to the threat.

He heard the click of her seat belt, and the engine starting. The SUV began backing out. Too late for the garotte, he decided. If he tried throttling her now, she'd start doing the funky chicken, and he couldn't chance a car crash. That would bring out all her neighbors. Besides, her early outing had him curious. It was still pitch dark outside. What had gotten her out of bed so early, and where was she going?

As she drove, he tried to catch sight of street signs and buildings. San Diego had changed in his time away, but it became apparent they were headed downtown. Could she be on her way to see the Cripple? According to Cracker's information, the Cripple owned a condo in a six-story downtown building. The Snoop could have been monitoring police activity in Lompoc. Maybe she'd learned that the big bad wolf was dead. That would be news the Cripple and the Snoop would want to celebrate. The champagne was probably already on ice. If so, by the time they arrived, the bubbly would be properly chilled.

And maybe, just maybe, he might soon be pouring a glass of his own.

Anticipation. Like the lyrics to that old song, it was keeping him waiting. The Snoop hadn't needed GPS. She was familiar with where they were headed, and it looked more and more as if their destination was the Cripple's place. If so, that was a huge stroke of luck for him. No, more than that. It felt like fate. Kismet. Because the Cripple lived in a security building, he had thought it would be necessary to ambush her outside of her workplace. He hadn't liked the idea of such an impersonal meetup. Now, the two of them might actually have a chance to chat. To catch up on old times.

All things considered, the timing of all this couldn't have been better. Abel had served his purpose. His being in Lompoc while he was on parole had made things go smoothly with the law. Just last week his parole status discharge had come through, but he couldn't leave town. Abel was already concerned about the Snoop's interest in him. Something didn't feel right about it, he said. Cracker had sure confirmed that.

Abel had always had him under his thumb. In a weak moment, he'd confessed, and been dumb enough to stash some items with him. When Abel settled in Lompoc, he'd made a point of telling him the apartment was set up with a security system that would transmit images of anyone breaking in. He'd also said he was the owner of a registered firearm.

But it was the Snoop who'd broken in, not him. And what she'd taken had freaked Abel out. There was no reasoning with him. Abel had said they needed to meet, and it was time for him to confess to the authorities.

He'd had no choice but to do what was necessary.

Huddled in the back seat, he continued to catch glimpses of downtown San Diego. They stopped at a red light, and he heard the Snoop impatiently tapping her fingers on the steering wheel. The light changed, and the SUV took off quickly. It wasn't quite a jackrabbit start, but close. They drove for a block, and then she made a slight left turn and lowered her window. He listened as she tapped a code into a pin-pad reader, and then heard a security gate open.

As the SUV pulled down into a subterranean garage, he silently reached for the garotte. But then he hesitated, still unsure if the time was right. Certainly, it would be a convenient killing spot, and the SUV would be a good place to stash her body. But what then? How was he going to get to the Cripple? If he was hoping for a two-for-one, he needed to see how things played out.

The Snoop shrugged off her seat belt, stepped out of the SUV, and slammed the door shut. A moment later, the door locked, and he listened to her footsteps walking away.

Like a turtle, he cautiously raised his head up, staring out through the opening in her headrest. She was walking toward a red exit sign. With unblinking eyes, he took in the garage. There was no one around. *Soon,* he thought. *Soon.*

She was going for the elevator, he realized. He extended an arm over the seat and pushed the door unlock button. To his ears, the lock release of the four doors resonated throughout the interior of the vehicle, but the Snoop didn't look back. Her preoccupation served his purposes. She punched the elevator's "Up" button and waited.

They were separated by around twenty-five yards. If necessary, he could be on top of her in seconds. But that wasn't his play, not today. He knew that the Cripple's condo was on the fourth floor. With the Snoop's help, he might just get invited inside.

From his backpack, he pulled out the hammer and silently opened his door. The elevator was still en route to the landing, descending at a leisurely pace. That it was slow was a good thing.

The elevator finally arrived. He watched as its double doors opened, and the Snoop went inside. Now, in classic bad-guy fashion, he had a chance to head her off at the pass.

He waited while the elevator doors closed. *Time to fly,* he thought, and sprinted toward the red exit sign that marked where the stairwell was. He'd always been fast. Hammer in hand, he pumped his arms, holding it like a runner would a baton. But he had no intention of handing it off to the Snoop in the usual way.

Taking two stairs at a time, he passed by the first-, second-, and third-floor landings. Bell lap. He sprinted up the last set of stairs to the fourth floor. There, he opened the door and looked down the hallway.

The Snoop wasn't to be seen, but he could hear the whirring of the elevator's conveyance system. Then a ding sounded, and the elevator doors began to open. He melted into the shadows and heard the Snoop's footsteps. *Wait,* he cautioned himself. *Wait.*

He didn't know the schematics of the Cripple's building, or how far her unit was from the elevator. Silently, he crept out of his hiding spot. The Snoop passed by one of the units without slowing. As much as he wanted to close the space between them, he resisted the temptation. Act in haste, repent in leisure. It was a life lesson he'd learned to heed.

The Snoop came to a stop. How far away was she? Somewhere around eighty-five, ninety feet. He seemed to remember the distance between the bases on a baseball diamond was ninety feet. Fast runners could cover that distance in around four seconds.

He watched the Snoop reach out to press what he assumed was a buzzer. How long would it take for the Cripple to get to the door? *At least a dozen seconds,* he thought. And then she'd probably look out a peephole before opening up.

It was time to begin the final countdown.

Silently, he counted. Twelve Mississippi, eleven Mississippi, ten Mississippi.

On your mark.

Nine Mississippi, eight Mississippi, seven Mississippi.

Get set.

Six Mississippi, five Mississippi...

Go.

The carpeted hallway masked the sounds of his charge. At first, the Snoop continued looking straight ahead. He'd covered about a third of the distance separating them when the Snoop began turning her head. *Too late,* he thought. By then, he was more than halfway home.

She didn't run. Instead, she began waving at the door and shouting, "No! No! No!"

At the last instant, she pivoted toward him. He came at her with the hammer, and she raised her arms to fend him off. His body crashed into the Snoop, knocking her sideways. Then he swung the hammer, catching the side of her head and dropping her to the ground.

Just as the door opened.

At the sight of the bleeding body on her entryway, the Cripple's mouth opened in shock. And that was even before she saw him.

Her scream caught in her throat; the sound choked off by his grip. He tightened it so she couldn't even gasp.

"If you and your friend want to live, you'll need to do exactly what I say. Capisce?"

He released his grip just enough for her to bob her head up and down.

"I am now going to loosen my grip," he said. "If you don't want your skull shattered into pieces, don't scream."

He ran the head of the bloody hammer along her cheek, and she shuddered at its cold touch. Then he released his grip, and she gasped for air.

"Miss me?" he asked.

CHAPTER FORTY

Breathe, Chloe thought. *Don't shut down. Don't freeze. For this moment, don't let your emotions overwhelm your thinking.*

But her demons did not want to be suppressed. Long hidden PTSD came to the fore. The monster was no longer in her dreams, or her past. He was in her present and presence.

Denial wasn't going to help. Accept it. Deal with it. *This is happening to me. And to my friend.*

Chloe watched him drag Penelope inside like she was a bag of trash. She was bleeding heavily from her wound, and her breathing was shallow. Chloe feared the worst. Her friend looked as if she might be dying, but that didn't stop him from tying her up with some cell phone cords he grabbed from the kitchen.

If Penelope was to survive, it would be up to her.

"How is she?"

"Still breathing."

"She needs medical attention."

"Shut up or I'll gag you. Understood?"

She nodded.

He moved out of sight to the kitchen, and came back with a

broom. Chloe half-expected him to strike her, but instead he pushed the broom through the spokes of her wheelchair.

"It wouldn't do to have you run off from our party, would it? I'm ready for a drink. What about you?"

"No," she said, unable to keep the distaste from her face. But then Chloe added, "Actually, I'd like a glass of water."

"Let me do your bidding then. But is it water you really want, or the glass to throw at me?"

Laughter trailed in the air as he returned to the kitchen. Next time her ploy needed to be less transparent. He was used to ruses and tricks; it was part and parcel for him. She had to be just as deceptive, and even more deadly.

"No champagne chilling?" he called out, sounding disappointed. "I guess I'll have to make do."

He returned with a wineglass in one hand and a paper cup of water in the other, which he placed in the wheelchair's holder. She said nothing, and made no move to drink. He took a seat in a nearby easy chair, and after sipping from his glass, offered up a satisfied "Ahh."

"It's been a long day," he said. "My brother, or half-brother, to be accurate, died today. By now, the police will have concluded he committed suicide. But you already knew about his death, didn't you?"

She said nothing.

"You and your hired help were ready to celebrate that news. The look on your face when you first saw me was pure gold. I'm actually surprised you didn't shit yourself. News flash in case you're having trouble making sense of all this. Abel and I always had a striking resemblance to one another."

"Were the two of you close?" she asked.

"Has our session officially begun?" he asked. "Should I be lying down on the sofa?"

"If that would make you comfortable."

"You're putting on a good front, Doc, but you don't fool me. Inside, you're dying. You're feeling pure panic. This is your worst nightmare come to life, and you'd be screaming your head off if you weren't so afraid of how I might respond and take care of our long-unfinished business."

When she didn't respond, he asked, "Cat got your tongue? The last time we talked, you and your friend had a lot to say. I've often thought back to our time together. What about you?"

"I don't respond to threats, veiled or otherwise."

"We're different that way, Doc. That's why your hired help over there is dying. And that's why you're up shit creek without a paddle. You came after me. Or maybe I should say, you came after my half-brother and *thought* it was me."

"I'm sure the police won't make that same mistake."

"I wouldn't bet on that. I'm the bastard no one knows about. Or ever cared about. Abel and I had the same father, but he was the only one who got his last name. My sperm father never married my mother.

"Abel was ten months older than me. His mother had the good sense to divorce our bio daddy while she was still pregnant. A few years later she remarried, and my brother won the lottery. He got spoiled by his mother and father. We only lived a few miles apart, but we had very different upbringings."

"Did you spend much time with your brother while growing up?"

"Is this supposed to be a shrink session where I gain insights into my behavior, and repent what I did? Ain't gonna happen, Doc."

"I asked you a question. Whether you choose to answer is up to you."

"Abel and I knew about each other, but any contact between us wasn't exactly encouraged. When we were teens, we began seeing more of one another when our father went to prison, and my mother took up with another man."

"Did you enjoy the time you spent with your brother?"

"Not really. Abel didn't have my same interests in booze, drugs, and porn."

"Were you jealous of your brother?"

"Why would I be? I used him. Abel was always an easy mark. He fell for my sob stories, and was always good for a few bucks. He even lied for me a few times when I needed an alibi."

"Did he know what you did to Dana and me? Was he aware you were a murderer?"

"He knew my version of what happened, although I'm pretty sure he suspected there was more to the story than what I told him. The only reason I admitted anything to him was I thought I'd need him to lie for me. It was his car I was driving that night. I had taken a bus out to NTC because we were supposed to go to a strip club together, but then he begged off and said he had a lot of stuff to do before being deployed. So, he gave me the keys to his car, and I was all on my own on the night you two ladies came into my life. When I heard you might survive, I went to Abel and said the two of you tried to roll me after we'd all done drugs together. I said I'd acted in self-defense, but he wasn't convinced. In fact, I had to talk him out of calling the cops. Some brother. When I needed him, he wasn't there. Not only that, he blackmailed me."

"By doing what?"

"He said if I refused to turn myself in to the police, I'd have to give him evidence that put me at the crime scene. That's how he got my trophies, or at least some of them. He promised to stash them away someplace safe. After that, our paths didn't cross for many years."

"But he ended up settling in Lompoc because of you?"

"He knew I was stuck there doing parole. But it was his choice to move there."

"'Am I my brother's keeper?'" she said.

"Abel wasn't a saint. We had the same father, after all. All his marriages failed. But he was able to keep things bottled up, things I preferred to let loose on occasion. That's probably why he joined the Navy. He wanted structure and discipline to keep him on the straight and narrow."

"To keep him from being like you?"

"Is this where I'm supposed to start crying, and repenting for all my sins?"

"We both know how insincere that would be. Do you know one of the things that compelled me to look for you? I was afraid you were still out there targeting other women. In good conscience, I couldn't ignore that."

"I guess I'm not the only liar in this room," he said. "You came after me because you wanted revenge."

"Yes, I wanted that as well."

"Sucks to be you," he said. "By siccing your Snoop on me, I'm finally free to come out from the shadows. Big brother isn't around to control me anymore. He thought he was safe, protected. But I knew about his gun, and the security systems he had in place. He had warned me if I ever tried breaking into his apartment, he'd sic the cops on me. Your Snoop actually did me a huge favor. By breaking in, she set everything in motion. Abel thought the jig was up. When I went to see him earlier tonight, he thought I was going to be turning myself in. Ultimately, we agreed to disagree."

His smile made her flinch.

"One more crime scene to stage," he said. "I was thinking of making what happened here look like a lover's quarrel. Care to brainstorm it with me?"

CHAPTER FORTY-ONE

Fifteen minutes away from downtown San Diego. That time frame didn't feel reassuring.

Penelope had said I'd hear from her after she and Chloe were settled. She still hadn't called.

It's nothing, I told myself. The two of them are probably having a cup of coffee and talking about Abel Lynch's death. They don't have any idea how worried I am.

Being as concerned as I was about someone else was new to me. I'd never really had anyone to worry over before, but now that I did, it felt both comforting and terrifying. Love had given me a new lease on life. And death.

Still, feeling the need for reassurance, I spoke to my Bluetooth connection: "Call Chloe Landers on her mobile phone."

I listened as her phone began ringing. The longer the call went unanswered, the wetter my palms got. When Chloe's message began to play, I hung up.

No need to overreact, I told myself. All my life, my thoughts had been dominated by the left side of my brain. The right side, the artistic side, had rarely been in the driver's seat, and was alien to my usual way of thinking. But ever since love had entered the equation, my brain had been hijacked.

My internal war of the roses propelled me to drive even faster. As I passed by Pacific Beach, I took in Mission Bay to the west. A vermillion hue in the sky portended the dawn, and maybe a little more.

Red sky in morn, sailor be warned.

The nautical threat kept whispering in my head, and as I sped by Old Town, I felt compelled to make another call, this time to Penelope. Once more, I waited out unanswered rings. Again, I left no message.

———

The bogeyman was supposed to be dead, thought Chloe. So how was it that he was sitting in her living room? Smiling at her. Talking to her.

The terror she'd felt when first seeing him had passed. She believed, or wanted to believe, that Nietzsche was right in thinking that which does not kill us makes us stronger. In her role as a therapist, Chloe tried to empower her clients. She liked to tell them there were two acronyms for FEAR, and that they could either Forget Everything And Run, or they could Face Everything And Rise.

It was time to rise.

"All this time I had hoped you were long dead," she said.

"Sorry to disappoint you."

His smile was smug, confident. She remembered he'd given her much the same look just before attacking her. The memory caused her fists to clench in anger. *It won't happen like that this time,* she thought, making a promise to herself.

Their stare down was interrupted by the muffled sounds of

a ringing phone coming from where Penelope's battered body was stretched out.

"Who the hell's calling?" he asked.

"How should I know?" she said.

"Because, while I was securing you and your friend, I heard the sound of a ringing phone coming from inside one of your bedrooms. At the time, I assumed it was work related. But why would you and your hired help be getting calls this early? I'm thinking that's more than a coincidence."

As he walked over to Penelope, Chloe considered what she could do to delay him. Say nothing, she decided. The ghoul was already suspicious. Wyatt was calling. She knew it. Hang up, she prayed. Don't leave a message. He began rummaging around for her phone, but it went silent just as he found it.

Now, Chloe thought, while his back is turned to me. She shifted to the edge of her seat, and then silently withdrew the broom handle from the spokes of her wheelchair. After pulling it free, she lifted the broom up and laid it across her lap. She couldn't fly off, but maybe she could still use the broom for witch-work. With the brake removed, she began to wheel away.

"Who the hell is Wyatt Lake?" he asked, staring at the screen of Penelope's phone.

When Chloe didn't answer, he turned around, and saw her opening the patio door.

"Where the hell do you think you're going!" he yelled.

Chloe wheeled through the door and heard him running after her. She tried slamming the door shut, but he blocked it with his shoulder. As he stepped out to the balcony, Chloe backed away from him.

He said, "Inside! Now. I'm not asking again."

Chloe continued backing up, until she was blocked by a large planter. Facing him, she made no move to comply with his demand.

"I guess you want it rough," he said, his voice low and threatening. "I like it rough. But you already know that, don't you?"

She said nothing, waiting him out. *He just sees me as a cripple in a wheelchair*, Chloe thought, *a victim in wait*.

"It'll be like old times," he said. "I've often thought back to our last encounter. What about you?"

She silently watched his every move. He took a step toward her, and then another.

"Boo!" he shouted, flailing his arms.

If he was hoping for a fright response, he didn't get it. Chloe raised the broom at the ready, but he wasn't deterred. As he came at her, she feigned a thrust of the broom handle to his chest, but then slashed at his face, catching him just below his cheekbone.

As he staggered back, she hissed, "First blood."

He raised his hand to his face in surprise. The gash was bleeding heavily. "You'll pay for that, bitch," he said, and came at her again.

Once more, she tried fending him off, but this time he was more watchful and got his hands on the broom. Grunts and gasps accompanied their tug-of-war. Then, Chloe suddenly released her grip, causing him to fall backward. Before he could get to his feet, she grabbed a small clay pot and hurled it at him. He covered up his head, but the pot still struck him, shattering into shards.

"Fucking cunt!" he yelled, getting to his feet.

"Help!" Chloe screamed. "Help!"

He ran at her. As he lunged for her throat, she struck his nose with the heel of her hand. Bone and cartilage crunched under the blow. He howled and staggered backward, blood spurting everywhere.

Chloe's year of training in wheelchair self-defense now felt like time well spent.

While he wiped the blood from his face, Chloe wheeled to a spot that gave her more space to maneuver.

He said, "When we're done dancing, bitch, expect no mercy. How's that sound to you?"

"Sounds like a good reason to fight like hell," she said.

He came at her, using feints and lunges to drive her back. The fourth-floor balcony became their combat ring. As he closed in on her, there were ever fewer places for her to maneuver.

"Nowhere to hide, is there?" he said, kicking at the armrest of her wheelchair and sending her back.

Then he followed up with a roundhouse kick, snapping her head back.

"It's good to have a leg up on the competition," he said.

"Help!" Chloe screamed, clinging to her chair. "Help!"

This time, he wasn't lured in by her cries.

"Better hold on tight," he said. "It's about to be a bumpy ride for you."

His kick sent her wheelchair skidding to the side, and he came at her from behind. As he tried to wrap an arm around her neck, she raised her arms up and put her chin down, thwarting his stranglehold. He grabbed at her, and she was able to bite deep into his flesh.

"Fucking cunt!" he gasped, trying to pull away his arm, but her teeth were locked in.

With his other hand, he delivered multiple blows to the side of her head, but her teeth only bit down all the harder. He panicked, and tried yanking his arm up to free it, pulling Chloe halfway out of her chair. She only fell back after tearing away a hunk of his flesh. Writhing and cursing, he took a step backward.

As Chloe stared him down, she made a hawking sound, spitting his flesh back at him. Then she bared a mouthful of feral red teeth.

Blood flowed from the gash in his arm, and tears ran down his face. In a strangled voice, he kept repeating, "Fuck, fuck, fuck, fuck."

Finally, he went silent and looked around the balcony. After a moment's deliberation, he took a few steps over to a tiered plant stand that lodged an assortment of small cacti.

"Ready to play dodgeball?" he asked.

He grabbed one of the ceramic pots and hurled the cactus. In rapid succession, more spiky projectiles rained down on her. Chloe tried covering up, but the potted cacti tore open her flesh.

I'm going to die by a thousand cuts, she thought.

Snatch, clean, and jerk. That's how weight lifters did it in competitions. He bent down low, preparing to lift one of her whiskey barrel planters.

Chloe read his intent. The planter and its contents probably weighed close to a hundred pounds. He was going to get close enough to drop it on her, and then watch her suffocate.

He gripped, beginning his snatch, then lifted the planter up to his waist. That's when Chloe wheeled at him.

Ramming speed, she thought.

As she charged, he hesitated for a moment and then dropped the planter. The wheelchair crashed into his legs and staggered him, but he was still able to throw himself at her. As he pressed down with the weight of his body, she tried holding him off, but her arms began to shake, and she finally collapsed under his weight.

He started squeezing her neck, choking off her airway, choking away her life. And there was nothing she could do.

Darkness. She was in the valley of the shadow of death. Two faces flitted in and out of her last vestiges of consciousness.

Dana stared at her with disappointed eyes. *I'm sorry,* Chloe tried to say, but she didn't have the breath. All these years she'd been feeling guilty about her best friend's death. Even now, she wished she could have done more for her.

And then it was Wyatt, coming to visit for a last time. Her love. It was a word, an emotion, she had never expected to experience. If only they'd had more time together.

CHAPTER FORTY-TWO

The front door wasn't latched shut. I pushed on it, but it didn't open very far before being blocked by something. Through the gap, I saw the obstruction: an unmoving body. Penelope. Around her was a pool of blood.

Another push, and the door opened wide enough for me to squeeze inside. I bent down and felt for Penelope's pulse. She was still alive.

Near her body were bloody shoeprints. I followed the tracks to where the balcony door was open. Movement caught my eye. Someone was out there. I drew my gun and ran forward. Much of the deck was in shadows, the only illumination coming from a solitary light in the living room.

I stepped out to the balcony, assumed the shooter's stance, and yelled, "Police! Hands up! Now!"

A man with his back to me slowly straightened. As he turned to face me, I saw what his body, and the darkness, had obscured. An unmoving Chloe sat in her wheelchair. There was blood on her face, and her clothes.

"Move away from the woman and lie flat on the ground," I said.

He made as if to step away from Chloe. I should have been watching him, but my eyes were on Chloe, desperately searching for any signs of life. He used that opportunity to throw himself down and come up behind her.

"Stop or I'll shoot!"

It was a threat offered too late. Chloe was now between the man and me. I watched as his hand snaked out, and he grabbed something. Then he was pressing a jagged shard into her neck.

"Come any closer and I'll cut her throat," the man said.

"Take it easy," I said, moving a step back.

"I'll take it easy when you drop your gun."

"Not going to happen," I said.

He raised his elbow, pushing the shard deeper into Chloe's neck. "Then she dies."

My heart pounding, I kept the gun pointed at him. "How do I know she's alive?"

"She's still kicking," he said, and slapped her.

Her chokes and gasps reassured me. Frightened me. It sounded like a diver coming up for a long-overdue lungful of air. And then there were more breaths and groans, enough for me to lower my gun.

"Toss your piece over here," he said.

"I can't do that."

"You want to see her bleed out?"

Chloe continued to make gagging sounds. Her eyes were blinking involuntarily, and her body was twitching. I prayed that all I was seeing was her life functions beginning to reawaken.

"If you try harming her, I'll empty my gun into you. I don't want to have to do that. How about we figure out a way for everyone to get out of here alive."

His head slowly emerged from the shadows, coming out

from behind the wheelchair. I found myself looking at the doppelgänger of the dead man I'd seen in Lompoc.

"How's this for a win–win?" he said. "You stay here, and let the two of us go. Once we're downstairs, she goes free."

Chloe's breathing still sounded strained and raspy, but she was looking more aware of her surroundings. Her eyes had stopped their erratic blinking, and they appeared fixed on me.

"I can't let her leave with you," I said. "She needs immediate medical attention."

Chloe's gurgling and wheezing noises made a case for her being in respiratory distress, but what she was signaling me told a different story. Only *I* could see her clenched fists. Chloe was ready to fight.

"If you want her to stay with you, lose your gun."

"I can't give it to you."

"I said lose the gun, not hand it over. Just toss it down to the street."

I began shaking my head, but then noticed Chloe showing me two thumbs up. She wanted me to agree to the impossible.

"Your choice," he said. "Her life's in your hands."

Chloe continued making it sound as if she was struggling to breathe. Her head rocked backward. What was she trying to say?

Getting rid of my gun went against my training, and my instincts. You don't give up your firearm, even when someone you love has a weapon held to her throat.

"She's not sounding very good," I said. "Let me call the paramedics."

"No paramedics," he said. "And no more stalling."

Chloe encouraged me with a raised thumb. She was all-in. I had this sense she was telling me not to worry. She had this.

Another jerk of her head, accompanied by her Darth Vader sounds of respiratory distress. Was it a real spasm, or an act?

Chloe read my concern, and answered my question by signaling all was A-okay.

Even if it didn't feel okay, not to me.

"Let her go, and I'll toss the gun."

"That's not how it's going to work," he said. "The three of us will do a little do-si-do, and change up positions. You'll walk over to the railing, while we make our way toward the door. When you drop your gun, she'll go free."

He was lying. We all knew that. But Chloe was still telling me everything would be all right.

I wanted to believe her, but was afraid to.

He read my uncertainty and doubts, and jabbed the shard into Chloe's neck. Her gasp was real, but she wasn't the one who was wavering. Her upraised thumb held steady, and gave me the courage to act.

"Move," he said.

"All right."

"Stay in the light, and go all the way forward to the railing. While you're doing that, we'll make our way to the door."

I nodded, and took a tentative step forward, and then another. Chloe continued to struggle for breath, making it sound as if it was all she could do to take in air. From behind, he wheeled the chair, keeping Chloe between us, not giving me an open shot. As I walked to the railing, they made it to the door.

"Raise the gun above your head," he said.

I held it up.

"Now toss it."

Still sounding like a barking seal, Chloe signaled her encouragement. His head came out over her shoulder, watching my every move. *Lover's leap,* I thought, taking a deep breath. With the gun's grip in my thumb and forefinger, I let it drop.

"Adios," he said, a word spoken not to me, but Chloe.

He angled the shard, ready to cut her throat, but Chloe had

anticipated that. She moved her head and hand simultaneously, delivering a backward blow to his upper chest, while grabbing his weapon hand and locking it down to her body.

Already off-balance, he tried to steady himself. As I ran toward them, Chloe threw her head back, slamming his face. Then she twisted in her seat and clawed at his eyes. He raised up a protective hand, not taking into account where his weapon was positioned.

Next to his exposed throat.

Chloe slammed the shard home. It penetrated the soft spot of his throat just under his jaw.

I reached her side and shielded her as best I could from the spraying blood. Together, we moved away.

Neither one of us looked back.

CHAPTER FORTY-THREE

Chloe hadn't supplied any specifics to our meetup spot, other than its general location. She spotted me from a distance, and we came together and kissed in front of the Fischer's lovebird display.

"We're not going to be one of those PDA type of couples, are we?" I asked.

"We are," she said.

We weren't alone in our public display of affection. The lovebirds were also busy spooning, or, in avian talk, they were billing with one another.

This was Chloe's first public outing since being attacked. She'd spent three days in hospital, one day fewer than Penelope. I was the only member of our conspiracy to have come out physically unscathed, which was somewhat ironic for someone who was dying.

To cover up the beating she'd suffered, Chloe was wearing lots of clothing: a hat, sunglasses, and heavy makeup. She also had on her blue morpho racing gloves.

"How are you feeling?" I asked.

"I'm getting there," she said. "The bruising has gone from

black and purple to yellow and green, but I can't say the new color combo is much of an improvement."

"You look great."

"Thank God love is blind," she said.

Another kiss.

"We're making the lovebirds jealous," I said.

"Good. How's Lenore?"

"She's hanging in there."

"And you?"

"The same," I said.

"How was today's session with David?"

"It was good," I said. "We discussed the poem *Resume* by Dorothy Parker."

"I'm afraid I'm not very familiar with her work, and don't know that poem. What's it about?"

"Suicide, or I should say, the pitfalls associated with the ways in which to kill yourself."

"That sounds rather grisly."

"It's not a Hallmark card, but the poem is this darkly humorous cautionary tale. David said the poet had more than a passing familiarity with the topic, having attempted suicide on multiple occasions. But the last line in the poem is the most telling, and resonated with me: 'You might as well live.'"

"I like the sound of that, at least."

"Beats the alternative, as they say."

"Is the department still considering suspending you for surrendering your gun?" she asked.

I had been assigned desk duty while under departmental review. "I've heard through the grapevine that I'm just going to be written up, which amounts to a slap on the wrist."

She drew my hand toward her and kissed my wrist.

I said, "If I'd known what you were planning on your balcony, I would have kept my gun."

"Cain would have killed me if you had," she said. "I knew he was never going to willingly let me go, and that our battle had to finally end one way or another. When you dropped your gun, I knew all his attention would be focused on you, and that was going to be my chance."

"You took an awful risk."

"Know thy enemy," she said. "I did. If I hadn't acted, he would have cut my throat, and then used my wheelchair to try and bulldoze you."

"You sound sure of that."

"I am. My continued existence would have been an affront he couldn't tolerate. And you were a threat."

"Your plan was incredibly dangerous."

"It was premeditated," she said, and then whispered, "Does that make me a murderer?"

"It makes you a survivor."

She looked comforted by my words. By my half-lie.

"The detectives working the case think you're a hero," I said.

"I'd be happy to disabuse them of that notion."

"Cain, that is Donald Heaney, got what he deserved. The investigative team thinks so, and I think so. End of story."

To Chloe and me, Heaney would probably always be thought of as Cain. That name just seemed to fit. And like the Biblical Cain, our Cain had killed his brother Abel.

"I wish it was that simple," Chloe said. "I wish it was the end of the story. But it's not. The day before Cain came to kill me, I had this epiphany that I desperately wanted to share with you. In fact, the only reason I didn't was because you'd told me you would be incommunicado."

She had thought I was on a stakeout; a story I'd concocted on the day I'd traveled north to go and commit a murder.

"I'm sorry," I said.

"Don't be," Chloe said. "I understand why you did that. But I still want you to know what I would have told you on that day. I realized I no longer needed to feed the wrong wolf inside me. Our love liberated me, allowing me to let go of the past. Revenge was no longer my reason for living. And there was no way I was going to jeopardize what we have for the sake of vengeance. That's what I was going to tell you. That's what I would have told you. I wanted you to hear that just because you're sick, you're not disposable, and in fact, what you're going through only makes me want to cherish our time together all the more."

That's why she'd had us meet up at the lovebirds. It was a perfect spot to speak from the heart. I tried to tell her what she meant to me, but my throat tightened with emotion, and I couldn't even get a whisper out. But Chloe saw my smile, and my nodding head, and wet eyes. She knew the state of my heart.

The lovebirds began smooching again. As their billing continued, my voice came back.

"I think we should keep up with the competition," I said.

"I think you're right."

We came together for a kiss.

CHAPTER FORTY-FOUR

They'd prepped my body. In one arm was a catheter, and in the other, there was an IV bag dripping something into me. But what I was aware of more than anything else was the hand holding tight to mine. My body felt cold, save for that hand.

"Do you need anything?" Chloe asked.

"A new body?"

"I like the one you already have. It just needs some modifications."

I had agreed to participate in a clinical trial. For Chloe. For us. It was a longshot. I knew that. We knew that. But maybe it would buy us time. That's all we were hoping for.

Because I don't have a science background, coming to terms with the details of my clinical trial had been quite an education. Luckily, Chloe had been there to interpret for me. To advocate for me. In laymen's terms, they were hoping to regulate cell proliferation and invasion in my growth factor receptors to the nucleus and other organelles. Or something like that. It was easier to just refer to the clinical trial as what it was: a Hail Mary pass.

"I feel like I've already donated my body to science," I said.

"Too late," Chloe said. "I've got dibs on your body. Not to mention designs."

I squeezed her hand. She squeezed back.

"The Twelve visited me last night in a dream," I said. "But it wasn't their usual haunting. In fact, there was a thirteenth juror. Daniel Hernández was with them."

Chloe knew about Hernández, and had been at my side on other nights when the original Twelve had visited. It felt liberating not having any secrets from her.

"Tell me about your thirteenth juror."

"He was a silent observer," I said. "But this time I had the sense that the jury wasn't there to judge me. It almost felt as if they were only there to encourage me. I came away from their visit with this feeling that they wanted me to keep going."

"If that's their verdict, I'm in complete accord with your jury."

"Do you ever dream about Dana?"

"Sometimes," Chloe said. "But now that I've mostly come to terms with my survivor's guilt, I feel like the two of us are finally good."

"Maybe there's hope for both of us."

Hope. That operative word. We squeezed each other's hand.

A patient transporter walked up to us. Smiling, he asked, "Ready to roll?"

"Ready," I said. But the word was spoken prematurely. I found it hard to loosen my grip on Chloe's hand, to my tether to this world.

Her wheelchair was higher than my gurney, so Chloe leaned down to kiss me. "I'll be here waiting for you," she whispered.

"Promise?"

"Cross my heart."

That was more than good enough for me.

"Be back as soon as I can."

"Can't wait."

Words that made me smile, and hope, even as I was rolled away.